Praise

THE BOOK SPY

"The walled-off feeling of loneliness in a crowd pervades the pages of Hlad's piercing historical thriller. Based on a fascinating and little-known true story of World War II.... Hlad's immersive portrayal of wartime Lisbon and its inhabitants, of the loneliness caused by the terror that anybody at any time could be an informant, plus his captivating thriller/romance tale make this a must-read, especially for fans of Kate Quinn's *The Rose Code*."
—*firstCLUE* (Starred Review)

CHURCHILL'S SECRET MESSENGER

"Hlad does a nice job of intertwining the romance and action stories, treating both realistically and largely without melodrama. The early parts of the novel, detailing Rose's work in the below-ground War Rooms and her encounters with Churchill, prove every bit as compelling as the behind-the-lines drama. Good reading for both World War II and romance fans." —*Booklist*

THE LONG FLIGHT HOME

"Hlad's debut snares readers with its fresh angle on the blitz of WWII, focusing on the homing pigeons used by the British, and the people who trained and cared for them.... Descriptions of the horrors of war and the excitement of battle are engaging, and the unusual element of the carrier pigeons lends an intriguing twist. This story will speak not only to romance readers and World War II buffs but also to animal advocates and anyone who enjoys discovering quirky details that are hidden in history."
—*Publishers Weekly*

Books by Alan Hlad

THE LONG FLIGHT HOME

CHURCHILL'S SECRET MESSENGER

A LIGHT BEYOND THE TRENCHES

THE BOOK SPY

FLEEING FRANCE

A SECRET IN TUSCANY

Published by Kensington Publishing Corp.

A SECRET IN TUSCANY

ALAN HLAD

John Scognamiglio Books
Kensington Publishing Corp.
kensingtonbooks.com

JOHN SCOGNAMIGLIO BOOKS are published by
Kensington Publishing Corp.
900 Third Avenue
New York, NY 10022

Copyright © 2025 by Alan Hlad

This book is a work of fiction. Names, characters, businesses, organizations, places, events, and incidents either are the product of the author's imagination or are used fictitiously. Any resemblance to actual persons, living or dead, events, or locales is entirely coincidental.

To the extent that the image or images on the cover of this book depict a person or persons, such person or persons are merely models, and are not intended to portray any character or characters featured in the book.

All rights reserved. No part of this book may be reproduced in any form or by any means without the prior written consent of the Publisher, excepting brief quotes used in reviews.

Without limiting the author's and publisher's exclusive rights, any unauthorized use of this publication to train generative artificial intelligence (AI) technologies is expressly prohibited.

All Kensington titles, imprints, and distributed lines are available at special quantity discounts for bulk purchases for sales promotion, premiums, fundraising, and educational or institutional use.

Special book excerpts or customized printings can also be created to fit specific needs. For details, write or phone the office of the Kensington Sales Manager: Kensington Publishing Corp., 900 Third Avenue, New York, NY 10022. Attn. Sales Department. Phone: 1-800-221-2647.

The JS and John Scognamiglio Books logo is a trademark of Kensington Publishing Corp.

ISBN: 978-1-4967-4558-3

ISBN: 978-1-4967-4559-0 (ebook)

First Kensington Trade Paperback Edition: November 2025

10 9 8 7 6 5 4 3 2 1

Printed in the United States of America

The authorized representative in the EU for product safety and compliance is eucomply OU, Parnu mnt 139b-14, Apt 123
Tallinn, Berlin 11317, hello@eucompliancepartner.com

For the women and men of the OSS and Italian Resistance

Chapter 1

Brooklyn, New York—June 11, 2003

On the day of the discovery that would change her life, Gianna Farro, an eighty-three-year-old widow and retired art teacher, was painting pictures with her grandchildren in the kitchen of her rowhouse. She retrieved a box of metal tubes from a closet and squeezed globs of blue, red, yellow, black, and white tempera paint onto two plastic palettes—one each for Bella, age seven, and Enzo, age five. While Gianna covered a table with sheets of newspaper, her grandchildren rummaged through a mason jar of brushes, their bristles stiff with paint residue.

Gianna—a spry gray-haired woman wearing rimless glasses and a casual teal linen dress—plucked long-sleeved, paint-spattered aprons from a basket and turned to her grandchildren. "Let's put these on," she said, with the Italian accent she had never lost.

Enzo—a boy with a small barrel chest and plump cheeks—drooped his shoulders. "Do I have to wear a bib?"

"It's not a bib," Gianna said. "It's an artist's smock, and it'll keep your clothes clean."

Bella—a thin, wiry girl with curly chestnut hair and a gap where she'd lost a baby tooth—fiddled with a paintbrush. "Nonna, the teachers at school don't make us wear a smock, and it's hard to paint with long sleeves."

"Please, Nonna," Enzo said. "I promise not to get paint on me."

It was her daughter Jenn's idea for the children to wear Gianna's old aprons while doing artwork. Unlike Jenn—who, even as a child, had an aversion to getting her clothes dirty—Enzo and Bella didn't mind getting messy. And neither did Gianna.

The paint is washable, Gianna thought, tossing the smocks into the basket. "All right. We'll be careful."

The children hugged her around the waist and got into their seats.

Gianna put a record, Antonio Vivaldi's *Four Seasons*, on a vintage console stereo in the living room and joined Bella and Enzo. Using a color wheel, she guided the children in producing shades of purple, orange, and green paint. She put down sheets of white sulphite paper and, with the sound of violins mimicking birdsong in spring, she joined the children in painting pictures. While Bella liked to create images of green cats and rainbows, Enzo—whether working with paint, chalk, or clay—was fond of making bugs.

The time with her grandchildren was the best part of her life. Gianna relished learning about their lives and encouraging their curiosity, and she loved teaching them to read, bake, and make crafts. Although she was a part-time instructor at a center for creative individuals with developmental disabilities, much of her time was spent helping her only child Jenn to care for her two children. She was a bit old to have young grandchildren. She'd given birth to Jenn later in life, and her daughter had adopted Bella and Enzo after many years of infertility and miscarriage. Several times a week, Gianna either went to Jenn's apartment in Manhattan or the grandchildren were dropped off at her home.

Gianna, a first-generation Italian immigrant from Tuscany, had lived in her rowhouse in Park Slope, a tree-lined neighborhood in western Brooklyn, for nearly a half century. After the passing of her husband, Carlo, who had died from stomach cancer several years earlier, she remained in her home, much to Jenn's disappointment. "Maybe you should consider moving to a retirement community," Jenn had said, helping Gianna clean out Carlo's closet. Although she respected her daughter's opinion, it was her life. And most of her life, at least to this point, had been dedicated to being a wife, mother, and teacher.

She'd decluttered the house by having a tag sale and hired a handyman to remove old wallpaper, refinish hardwood floors, and paint the rooms white. Rather than rehang old decorations, she moved paintings that she'd made as a young aspiring artist from the attic and displayed them on the walls. And although Jenn didn't like her childhood residence being transformed into an art gallery, Gianna's grandchildren had grown quite fond of hanging their paper drawings next to their *nonna*'s artwork.

"Nonna," Enzo said, turning his paper. "How do you like it?"

Gianna looked at his painting and smiled. "I love it. It's a beautiful spider."

Enzo rubbed his nose. "It's supposed to be a ladybug."

"*Mamma mia!* My lenses need to be cleaned." Gianna adjusted her glasses and leaned in. "Oh, now I see it. It's splendid."

Bella peeked at her brother's artwork. "It has too many legs. It looks like a spider."

Enzo put down his paintbrush and furrowed his brows.

Gianna scooched her chair next to him. "Want me to show you a trick to make a ladybug?"

He nodded.

Gianna held Enzo's thumb, dipped it in red paint, and pressed it to his paper. She lifted his hand to reveal a thumbprint. "Use some black paint to make a head, six legs, and dots on the shell."

He dipped his paintbrush and drew a ladybug with a plethora of polka dots.

"Bravo!" Gianna said, clapping her hands.

Enzo grinned.

"Can I try, too?" Bella asked.

"Of course," Gianna said. "What color are you going to use?"

"Aren't ladybugs red?"

"Most are, but you're the artist, and you get to decide which color it will be."

Bella's eyes brightened. She dipped her thumb in green paint and pressed it to her paper.

For the next hour, the trio made thumbprint ladybugs while talking about their plans for the summer, which included going to the Prospect Park Zoo, Coney Island, and the American Museum of Natural History. Eventually, when the papers were covered with bugs, they set down their brushes and admired their work.

"Your pants," Bella said, pointing at smears of red paint on Enzo's khaki pants.

He looked up at Gianna. "Sorry, Nonna."

"It's all right." Gianna ruffled his hair, and her eyes gravitated to green splatters on Bella's white shirt. "You got some on you, too."

Bella lowered her chin. "Oops."

"It's okay," Gianna said. "Let's leave our paintings to dry, clean up, and get a snack."

Enzo smiled and followed his sister and Gianna to the washroom, where they cleaned the brushes and palettes, and scrubbed paint from their hands.

They snacked on prosciutto and mozzarella sandwiches and homemade lemonade in the dining room. For the remainder of the afternoon, they planted flower seeds in small garden pots, made sugar cookies with colorful sprinkles, and played a board game called Trouble.

A knock came at the door.

The children got up from their seats in the living room and waited by the door while their grandmother checked the peephole.

"It's your mom." Gianna opened the door and looked at her daughter. "Hi Jenn."

"Hi." Jenn put down a leather briefcase and hugged her children.

"You're early," Gianna said.

"I have a work event tonight, remember?"

"It must have slipped my mind," Gianna said, noticing her daughter's designer navy dress, pearl necklace with matching earrings, and coiffured brown hair. Jenn, an accomplished corporate attorney—as well as a divorced single mother raising two children—always seemed to be rushing off somewhere.

"Can we stay with Nonna?" Bella asked.

Jenn shook her head. "I've arranged for a sitter."

"They could spend the night with me," Gianna offered.

"Please," Enzo said, pressing his hands together.

"Another time." Jenn looked at the stains on the children's clothing, turned to Gianna, and frowned. "Mom, why didn't you use aprons?"

Gianna shifted her weight. "I will next time. The paint is washable."

Enzo lowered his chin and placed his hands over red streaks on his pants.

Jenn glanced at her watch. "We need to go."

"But you haven't seen our artwork," Bella said.

Jenn picked up her briefcase. "I will when we come back. We need to leave."

The children reluctantly nodded and gave their grandmother a hug.

Gianna gave them a big squeeze and felt them slip away.

"See you on Friday," Jenn said. "Would you like me to give you a call so you won't forget?"

"No need," Gianna said. "I'll remember."

She watched her walk away with Bella and Enzo en route to the subway station. She adored Jenn, and she believed that her daughter was fond of her. But they were, quite simply, two women with different personalities. As the trio disappeared down the street, she thought of Enzo and Bella's designer clothing, likely purchased by their mother at Saks or Bloomingdales, spattered with paint. She closed the door and chuckled.

She made a cup of jasmine tea and placed an Ornella Vanoni

record on the stereo, hoping that the Italian singer's angelic voice would deaden the loneliness that always accompanied the departure of her grandchildren. She put the children's artwork on a shelf in the laundry room, and as she was removing the protective newspaper from the table, her eyes locked on a partially paint-smudged headline and froze.

TUSCAN METAL DETECTORIST DISCOVERS ENCRYPTED MESSAGE HIDDEN IN WORLD WAR II BULLET!

Gianna, staring with wide eyes, adjusted her glasses and read the article.

1944. While Allied forces were fighting to liberate Florence from Hitler's army, an unknown soldier encrypted a secret communication and placed it inside an empty bullet casing. The hidden message has gone undiscovered for nearly six decades, until Aldo Ajello, an amateur metal detectorist, found the object in a remote area of Tuscany.

"I was searching a hillside with my metal detector," Ajello said to reporters. "I received a strong signal near the base of an old cypress tree and began to dig. At first, I thought it was an empty ammunition shell. But after I cleaned away the soil, I saw that the bullet was inverted into its case."

Mr. Ajello pried open the bullet and discovered an encrypted note. Copies of the message have been sent to cryptologists in Rome, London, and Washington, D.C., and most of the experts think that the message was encrypted with a British or American field cipher. To date, the code remains undeciphered.

Images of German soldiers, raiding a Tuscan village, flashed in Gianna's brain. A chill ran down her spine. She turned over the page of the newspaper to reveal a photograph of the coded message, and her breath stalled in her lungs.

```
VQ
ZPRWX        TSPAJ        MCDWQ
BNIOR        LHTVS        NPGEW
XOKDS        VNTRE        WPHYZ
372QV/TN
```

"*Oh, mio Dio*," Gianna whispered. Her hands trembled as she stared at the code that she had last seen many years ago. She recognized the handwriting of Tazio, an American operative who perished in the war—and a man who remained in her heart regardless of the passage of time. And given the communication's last two letters, she had no doubt that the message was intended for her.

This can't be real! Gianna slumped into a chair and tears welled up in her eyes. Horrid memories of German occupation swirled in her head, resurrecting the pain of the past. She'd never spoken to Jenn, or her late husband, for that matter, about her life during the war. The tragedy that she'd experienced in Tuscany, and her role in the conflict, were matters that she had planned to take to her grave. *How does one talk about unspeakable things?*

The music stopped and the needle scratched, over and over, on the record.

Gianna's mind toiled, contemplating what she needed to do. She weighed the pros and cons and, after careful consideration, she made her decision. She wiped tears from her cheeks, rose from her seat, and turned off the stereo. Before she changed her mind, she thumbed through a telephone book, called a travel agency, and booked the next available flight to Rome, Italy. She went to her bedroom and packed a suitcase, all the while struggling to find the words to explain things to her daughter and grandchildren.

Chapter 2

Strada in Chianti, Italy— September 19, 1943

Gianna Conti—a slender twenty-three-year-old Catholic woman with a dimpled chin and wavy hair the color of coffee—entered the door to a long stone cellar that was embedded into the hillside of her family's vineyard. An earthy, dried-fruit aroma of aged wine filled her nose. She adjusted her grip on a basket that held a jar of olives, a hunk of cheese, a canteen of water, and a loaf of bread. Her eyes gradually adjusted to the dim space, and she made her way past rows of stacked oak wine barrels to the end of the tunnel, where her father, Beppe, was speaking with a young Jewish couple in well-worn clothing.

"*Buongiorno*," Gianna said, approaching them.

Beppe—a middle-aged man with salt-and-pepper hair and a stubble beard—turned and adjusted his grip on his wooden walking cane. "Any sign of soldiers?"

"No—the road and countryside are clear."

"*Va bene*," Beppe said, sounding relieved.

Gianna approached the couple, a man named Davide and his wife, Sara, who'd arrived two days earlier. "I brought you food and water."

"*Grazie*," Davide said.

Gianna handed the basket to Sara. "It's not much. I'll get more food when I go to Firenze to secure your travel papers."

"Bless you," Sara said.

"Tonight," Beppe said, "my son Matteo will arrive from the north and lead you on the first leg of your journey to Switzerland. A few weeks from now—you'll be free."

Tears pooled in Sara's eyes, and her husband placed an arm around her shoulder.

A feeling of hope swelled inside Gianna.

Under the Italian Racial Laws—established in 1938 by Benito Mussolini's Fascist government—Jews were banned from positions in government, banking, and education. Soon after, they were stripped of their assets, restricted from travel, and confined to internal exile. Also, sexual relations and marriages between Italians and Jews were forbidden.

Gianna and her family despised fascism and racial laws. And when war erupted in Europe, she resigned from her studies at the University of Florence to help her father, a widowed winemaker, run the family vineyard, while her brother, Matteo—who had refused to enlist in the army—joined the Italian Resistance. Gianna, like her brother, was determined to fight Italy's authoritarian regime, and she convinced her father to help an Italian and Jewish resistance group called DELASEM (Delegation for the Assistance of Jewish Emigrants). The organization, which was supported by international Jewish institutions and members of the Catholic church, provided aid to Jewish refugees. Also, it helped many of the refugees to flee Italy and reach sanctuary in neutral countries. The Conti family was a small but crucial cog in the wheel of DELASEM's Florence network. Gianna and Beppe provided food and shelter on their vineyard, and Matteo served as an escape line guide to help refugees reach Beppe's only sibling, Uberto, a priest who lived in Switzerland.

Initially, DELASEM was viewed as a legal organization by the Kingdom of Italy, and the Fascist government did not always enforce the Racial Laws. But this past July, things began to change when the Allies invaded Sicily. The Grand Council of Fascism—with the support of King Victor Emmanuel III—overthrew and arrested Benito Mussolini, the Italian dictator and prime minister. And at the beginning of September, when the Allies invaded southern mainland Italy, the country dropped out of the war and signed an armistice with the Allies. Hitler had retaliated by ordering German troops to seize control of the northern half of Italy, forcibly disarm Italy's armed forces, and free Mussolini from prison to establish a Nazi German puppet state. DELASEM was declared to be an illegal organization, and its members were forced to go underground. And now, the German occupiers were free to execute their own plans to persecute Jews—and those who protected them.

"After you eat and stretch your legs," Beppe said, "it's best that you stay hidden. Gianna or I will give you breaks when we are sure that the area is clear of German soldiers."

Sara and Davide nodded.

Gianna felt horrible for them, and her eyes shifted to a wall of wine barrels. Behind it was a hidden chamber that had been constructed by Beppe. The room was accessed by removing a bottom barrel's chime hoop and head cover, and then crawling through the empty barrel to the hidden space, big enough to hold three or four refugees. In addition to this chamber, she and her father had created another secret hiding place in the attic of their farmhouse.

"Do you need any more blankets?"

"No," Davide said. "We have more than enough to keep us warm."

"How about more books and candles?" Gianna asked.

"We have plenty," Sara said.

Gianna and Beppe remained with them while they ate, and they stood lookout while the couple scurried away to the nearby outhouse. Afterward, Davide and Sara hunkered into their hiding spot, and Gianna and Beppe secured the barrel's head cover and left the wine cellar.

Outside, the morning sun illuminated the Tuscan sky with hues of yellow and orange. The rolling hills of the Conti vineyard were lined with rows of plump, dew-covered Sangiovese grapes that were nearly ready to be harvested. In addition to grapes, scores of olive trees covered the landscape. The vineyard was far too much work for Beppe and Gianna, and for the past several years they had enlisted part-time help from farmers, mostly old men and women, during the pruning and harvest seasons. The remote property, with no other residents in sight, provided Gianna and her father the privacy that they needed for harboring refugees. But with the swelling number of Wehrmacht troops occupying Florence and surrounding areas, it was merely a matter of time, Gianna believed, before German soldiers took notice of their vineyard.

Gianna walked with Beppe, limping as he used his cane, to their two-story stone farmhouse with a weathered terra-cotta tile roof. They entered the front door to a living room with an old green-upholstered sofa and a matching chair, which were placed on opposite sides of a fireplace, its stone marred with soot. Timber beams spanned the ceiling, and the place was quite rustic and drab, except for the walls, which were decorated with several bright-colored oil paintings created by either Gianna or her late mother, Luisa.

Beppe entered the kitchen and slumped into a seat at the table.

"How's the leg?" Gianna asked, scooching a wooden chair next to him.

Beppe grimaced as he propped his right leg on the chair. "It's fine. A little rest, and I'll get to work."

During the Great War, Beppe was an infantry soldier who served on the Italian Front, and he was shot in his right leg while fighting German and Austro-Hungarian forces. Despite chronic pain and needing to use the aid of a cane, he never complained, nor did he let his lack of mobility get in the way of tending to the vineyard and, more important, hiding refuge seekers.

"I'll warm the *caffè*," Gianna said, approaching a wood-burning cast-iron stove.

"No need," he said. "I'll drink it cold."

She retrieved a tarnished aluminum moka pot from the stovetop, poured an espressolike coffee substitute—made from ground roasted barley—into a cup and gave it to him.

"*Grazie.*" He took a sip. "It's good."

"You and I both know it tastes like tar."

Beppe smiled. "Have some with me."

"No thanks. I need to get on the road to Firenze." She glanced out the window to rolling hills, and a memory of German Panzer tanks, rumbling southward, flashed in her head. Her shoulder muscles tensed. "Do you think the Allies are strong enough to break through the German lines?"

"I do."

She shifted her weight. "But countless divisions of Hitler's troops have flooded into Italy. His army appears invincible."

Beppe looked into his daughter's eyes. "It might take a year or more, but I have faith that the Americans and British will battle their way up the boot of Italy and liberate the kingdom."

Gianna clasped her arms.

"Someday," he said, "Italy will be free from fascists, and Jews will no longer need to hide."

Gianna thought of Sara and Davide, and the many other refugees that they'd hidden on the vineyard. "I hope so."

"And when the war is over," Beppe said, "you'll resume your studies at the university and create a beautiful future."

"Right now, that's the last thing on my mind."

"Understandable," Beppe said. "But you must hold onto your dreams."

Gianna nodded, appreciative of her father's efforts to raise her spirit.

Beppe looked at a framed black-and-white photograph that hung on the wall: his late wife, Luisa, wearing a wedding dress and holding a bouquet of flowers. "I wish your *mamma* was here to see what you and Matteo are doing. She'd be so proud to see her children protecting people in terrible times."

Gianna clasped her necklace, which held her mother's wedding band engraved with the words *Amore Mio* (My Love) and matched the one on her father's finger. "She'd be proud of you, too, Papà."

He rubbed his eyes and nodded.

Gianna's mother had died from influenza when Gianna was fourteen years old. She was a gifted grape grower and an amateur artist, and the love of her father's life. Despite the passing of years, her father's heartache remained raw.

Gianna placed a hand on her father's shoulder. "I should go."

"Take extra wine with you. It might be helpful if you're stopped by the Germans."

"I will."

Beppe rose from his chair and hugged her. "Catch the moment."

She squeezed him.

Catch the moment, Gianna thought. It was her father's phrase of affirmation, spoken seldom, but when she needed it most. He had always been supportive of her aspirations, instilling a sense of confidence that she could accomplish anything through persistence and optimism. And he always encouraged her to make the most of a situation, no matter how bleak things appeared to be.

"Be attentive," he said.

"I will."

Gianna left the house, retrieved bottles of wine from the cellar, and wrapped them in old newspapers. She loaded the wine, along with jars of olives and bottles of olive oil, into the front and rear wicker baskets of her bicycle, and hiking up her gray wool skirt, straddled the seat and pedaled away.

For several kilometers, she rode her bicycle over a dirt road that wound through rural hills that were filled with umbrella pines and tall, thin cypress trees. She passed a few farmhouses and vineyards but saw no people other than an elderly woman named Ida who was walking away from a chicken coop with a wire basket of eggs. At the base of a hill, she reached a paved road and turned north toward Florence.

The rumble of an oncoming vehicle engine grew louder and deeper. She pedaled faster, sending a burn through her thighs and calves. As the bicycle crested a hill, a dark gray transport truck—emblazoned with an iron cross and filled with German soldiers—came into view. A chill ran down her spine and her foot slipped from the pedal. She regained her footing and gripped the handlebars as the truck passed her, blasting her body with wind and forcing her bicycle to the berm of the road. Whistles and jeers arose from the soldiers. She ignored their calls, steered onto the roadway, and continued her journey.

An hour later, after passing several German transport and supply vehicles, the skyline of the medieval city came into view. She saw the Florence cathedral and its immense, Gothic-style red dome. *Catch the moment*: Beppe's words echoed in her head. A wave of determination rose up inside her. Gianna coasted down a hill and traveled along the Arno River, which glistened with sunlight, and then crossed the Ponte Vecchio, a medieval stone arch bridge.

She weaved through the narrow streets of Florence, which were cluttered with pedestrians, most of whom were stoic-faced women and old men. A swastika flag hung from the side of the Palazzo Vecchio, the town hall of Florence, and the laughter of German soldiers emanated from a nearby café. As she traveled through the city, she passed three Waffen-SS officers, wearing field-gray uniforms, who were exiting a hotel that appeared to have been requisitioned by the Wehrmacht. In the past weeks, the number of German military personnel in Florence had swelled. Italian soldiers were nonexistent. They'd been disarmed, taken prisoner, and deported by German forces.

She went to a basement apartment of an elderly couple and bartered her goods—save two bottles of wine—for zucchinis, a half loaf of brown bread, a small dry salami, and a hunk of pecorino cheese. Heavy rationing made it difficult to acquire many items, such as meat, grain, and butter, and Italians often turned to the black market for better food. Afterward, she traveled to a narrow street, far too small for motorized vehicles. She got off her bicycle and pushed it—all the while scanning her surroundings for onlookers—to a small weathered door of a stone building. When she was certain the area was clear of people, she clasped a tarnished brass ring mounted on the door and knocked.

She fidgeted with the ring on her necklace. Seconds passed and a metal mesh peephole, reminiscent of a confession booth window, slid open.

"Are you alone?" a familiar male voice asked.

Gianna glanced down the passageway. "*Sì*."

A lock clicked, the door swung open, and Gianna pushed her bicycle inside. The door abruptly shut behind her and a bolt was slid into place. She turned and was greeted by Nathan Cassuto, a doctor and rabbi in his mid-thirties with a clean-shaven face, round-rimmed glasses, and neatly trimmed brown hair that was parted on the side.

"Any chance you were followed?" Nathan asked.

"It's possible, but I don't think so."

He slipped his hands into his pockets. "How are Davide and Sara?"

"Okay," she said. "They'll be leaving with my brother tonight."

"Lilla is working on their travel documents," Nathan said.

She turned to the sound of approaching footsteps in the hallway.

Don Leto Casini, a tall Catholic priest in his early forties who was wearing a black suit with a clerical collar, approached Gianna. "*Ciao*."

"*Buongiorno*, Don Casini."

"How is Beppe?" the priest asked.

"He's well."

"Please send him my regards, and inform him that we have three refuge seekers that we want to move out of the city. Do you think that you and Beppe could accommodate them?"

"Of course."

The priest smiled.

"*Grazie*," Nathan said. "We'll be in contact when we are able to move them."

Gianna left her bicycle with the rabbi and priest, both of whom were leaders of the DELASEM network in Florence. As she traveled down the hallway, she felt a deep admiration for Nathan and Casini. *Under the oppression of Fascist rule, leaders of different faiths have united to protect Jews from persecution.* She buried her thought and ascended a narrow stone stairway to a third-floor room. The odor of glue and chemicals filled the air. The window shutters were closed, and a lantern cast amber light over the space and a young woman, who was seated at a long table covered in writing supplies.

"*Ciao*," Gianna said.

Lilla, a Jewish woman in her late twenties with fair skin and beautiful long black hair, rose from her seat and hugged her. "It's good to see you."

"You too," Gianna said, releasing her.

"I won't be finished with Davide's and Sara's papers for several hours. I'm sorry. I've been inundated with work. Do you want to come back later?"

"I'll wait." Gianna sat in a spare wooden chair at the table, which had on it a typewriter, bottles of ink and chemicals, wax, glue, carved wood stamps, real and replica passports and birth certificates, and an array of paper. "It'll give us a chance to visit, and for me to watch the best forger in Firenze at work."

Lilla smiled.

Gianna was a student at the university when she first met Lilla, who'd been terminated from her job as a clerk at the Florentine State Archives because of the Racial Laws. They'd become close friends, and it was Lilla who had recruited Gianna to join DELASEM. Most members of DELASEM provided financial aid or safehouses for Jewish refugees, but Lilla created and altered passports, birth certificates, and travel papers.

While growing up in Rome, Lilla worked at her family's dry-cleaning business, where she learned a special technique, using lactic acid to remove permanent blue ink. Now, she was employing this skill to erase the identification of "Jew" that was ink-stamped on government documents. And with much trial and error, Lilla had become a master falsifier, with the ability to erase and match ink, fabricate documents, and use dentistry tools to sculpt rubber blocks to mimic seals.

"You do incredible work," Gianna said, observing Lilla apply a liquid chemical to a blue ink stamp.

"With practice," Lilla said, "you could do this. I've seen your paintings."

"That's kind of you to say," Gianna said. "But I'm a novice painter who is accustomed to applying thick, sweeping layers of paint to canvas. Your attention to detail is extraordinary. I could never achieve your level of precision."

Lilla slid a piece of paper and a fine nib fountain pen to Gianna, and she pointed to a birth certificate. "Try to replicate the typewriter letters."

Gianna carefully wrote a few letters and frowned.

Lilla nudged her friend's arm. "You're right—it's best that you stick to painting pictures."

Gianna chuckled.

"I'll give you an old fountain pen to practice with."

"*Va bene*," Gianna said.

For three and a half hours, Gianna remained with Lilla while she worked on the birth certificates and passports for Sara and Davide. When the documents were finished, they were set aside to dry.

Lilla stretched her back and rubbed her hands.

"The papers appear authentic," Gianna said.

"I hope so," Lilla said. "They'll need to look real for them to pass German security checks."

Gianna's mind drifted to Lilla's parents, who'd fled the country after having their home and dry-cleaning business stripped from them. "Have you considered fleeing to Switzerland to join your family?"

Lilla shook her head. "My work is needed here. There are many Jews to make invisible."

"It's dangerous for you to remain in Firenze. German soldiers are everywhere. You should stay with me and Beppe."

"That's a generous offer that I must decline."

"But things will only get worse with German occupation."

"Perhaps," Lilla said. "But I cannot leave my work. How else will refugees obtain papers to protect themselves?"

For several minutes, Gianna tried to convince Lilla to be open to leaving Florence, but her friend politely refused. She sighed and folded her arms.

"I appreciate you looking out for me," Lilla said, getting up from her chair. "I intend to stay for as long as possible, and I hope you understand."

Gianna stood. "I do, but I don't like it."

Lilla glanced at the documents. "The ink is dry."

Gianna hugged her. "Stay safe."

"You too."

Gianna released her friend and retrieved the documents. She traveled down the stairs, all the while hoping that with time, she could eventually convince Lilla to change her mind. Near the entrance, she found Rabbi Nathan and Don Casini standing by her partially disassembled bicycle.

"We heard you coming down the stairs," Nathan said, picking up a wrench from a tool box.

"Are you ready to go?" Casini asked.

Gianna nodded and she wondered, although briefly, if the men had overheard her conversation with Lilla. She handed the documents to Casini, who carefully rolled and inserted them into the hollow tube frame of her bicycle. Once the items were inserted, Nathan reassembled the pieces.

"You're all set," Nathan said, setting aside his tools. "How does it look?"

"Perfect."

"I'm grateful for what you and your father are doing for us," Nathan said, his voice somber.

Gianna took hold of her bicycle. "We're honored to help."

Nathan placed his ear to the door and peeked through the peephole. "It's clear."

Casini looked at Gianna. "May God protect you from danger."

"You too," she said.

Nathan opened the door, Gianna rolled her bicycle into the alleyway, and the door closed behind her. She got onto her seat and rode away.

She worked her way through the streets of Florence and twice had to backtrack to avoid German checkpoints. Eventually, she reached the Ponte Vecchio and a wave of relief washed over her as she crossed the river. The sun was low on the horizon, and her leg muscles ached with fatigue as she pedaled over rolling hills. Eight kilometers from home, the chain on her bicycle broke. She veered to the side of the road and examined the chain, which looked as if it could be repaired with the proper tools. Having no other choice, she pushed her bicycle. And when she detected the sound of an approaching vehicle, she lugged it off the road and hid in the underbrush to avoid potential encounters with Wehrmacht troops.

Gianna, hungry and tired, reached the Conti vineyard after nightfall. She pushed her bicycle to the front door, and her eyes were drawn to candlelight that flickered from a gap in the window shutters. Muffled voices drifted from inside the house. *Matteo's home*, she thought, setting aside her bicycle. Gianna, feeling excited to see her brother, went inside to the kitchen and froze.

A stocky, bearded, middle-aged partisan leader named Carmine Florentino, who was a friend and comrade to Matteo, adjusted a rifle that was slung over his shoulder.

Beppe—with red, puffy eyes and mussed hair—grabbed his cane and got up from a seat at the table.

Gianna swallowed. "What's wrong?"

A tear fell down Beppe's cheek. "Matteo is dead."

Gianna stepped back. "No—he can't be!"

Carmine's jaw quivered. "Matteo and I were returning from Marliana, where we placed a Jewish family in a safehouse. We encountered a German scout unit. Matteo was shot and killed."

A surge of nausea rose from Gianna's stomach. Her legs buckled and she fell to her knees.

Beppe wrapped his arms around his daughter, trembling and sobbing. Together, they wept until no more tears could be shed.

Chapter 3

Tuscany, Italy—September 24, 1943

Ten thousand feet above the Tyrrhenian Sea, Tazio Napoli, an operative of the Office of Strategic Services (OSS), the wartime intelligence agency of the United States, tightened his seatbelt as turbulence jolted the B-17 Flying Fortress. Instead of carrying a payload of explosives, the four-engine heavy bomber was packed with airdrop containers filled with supplies and weaponry. Two waist gunners, wearing electrical heated suits and positioned at open windows on opposite sides of the fuselage, scanned the night sky for enemy planes. The thrum of propellers filled Tazio's ears, and a mix of patriotism and anxiousness stirred inside him. An hour before, he and his fellow OSS agent Frank Russo had boarded the aircraft at Massicault Airfield in Tunisia. But he and Frank would not be returning to the base with the aircrew. They, along with their equipment, were going to be parachuted into German-occupied Italy.

The plane shuddered, and Tazio felt the loss of gravity as the aircraft lost altitude and gradually leveled off.

Frank, who was seated next to Tazio on a metal bench, gripped his safety strap and furrowed his brow.

"The pilot will find us smooth air currents before we jump," Tazio said, hoping to allay his friend's unease.

"It's not the turbulence that bothers me," Frank said. "I wish Major Tompkins hadn't ordered me to turn in my St. Christopher medallion. I hate not having it with me."

Tazio felt bad for him. Frank—a jovial, stocky young man from New Jersey with a zeal for telling funny stories—had worn the medallion, a gift from his mother, as a pendant around his neck. But before leaving the airfield, they were required to relinquish all personal belongings. Even their military uniforms were replaced with clothing—worn under their jumpsuits—that was fabricated by OSS tailors to include Italian clothier tags. Buttons, a few of which contained a hidden compass, were stamped with Italian markings. The brands of American zippers, on the metal pull, had been carefully ground off with a dentist's drill. The OSS, Tazio believed, had gone to great lengths to ensure that their past lives were erased and they appeared authentically Italian.

"I'm sorry about your medal." Tazio patted Frank's shoulder. "After we settle in, how about we find you a real Italian-made one?"

The lines on Frank's face softened. "That would be swell."

Tazio—an athletic, brown-eyed twenty-four-year-old Californian and son of Jewish Italian immigrants—was recruited earlier in the year for the OSS. He was a US Army first lieutenant who was expecting to be deployed to either Europe or the South Pacific. But everything changed when his name, as well as several other men with Italian surnames, was called during a morning lineup. He was led to a room where he was questioned by a silver-haired army colonel about his family, education, and political affiliations. And when the colonel learned that Tazio was fluent in Italian, he'd said with a deep Southern accent, "Son, how'd you like a chance to fight to free your family's homeland?" Tazio eagerly accepted and, after several rounds of interviews and a physical and psychological examination, he was reassigned to the OSS's Italian Operational Group.

He'd expected to be sent someplace in Georgia for paratrooper training, like Camp Toccoa or Fort Benning. Instead, he'd undergone his OSS training at the Congressional Country Club in Bethesda, Maryland—a little over ten miles away from the White House. The club's four hundred acres of grounds, which included a beautiful clubhouse and manicured fairways, had been commandeered by the OSS to conduct training for parachuting, hand-to-hand combat, survival, espionage, and sabotage. The country club grounds, which had once hosted golfers, politicians, and affluent guests, was transformed into a demolition zone. Many of the trees had fallen, and the fairways were marred by explosives and lined with trenches and barbed wire. With weeks of grueling instruction, the OSS recruits were taught the skills to be a commando, and Tazio excelled at advanced weapons training and the use of plastic explosives. He had graduated near the top of his class, but he'd never experienced real combat.

Tazio was deployed to North Africa, and after Allied forces landed on the west coast of Italy at Salerno, he was selected to be on a two-person squad with Frank—whom he'd befriended in training—to be parachuted into the remote Tuscan hills. Their mission was to organize and arm the Italian Resistance and prepare for when the Allies eventually fought their way northward through the German military lines. Tazio was ardent to serve his country, yet deep inside him he had conflicted emotions about fighting in his parents' homeland. *I might have to combat fellow Italians, or maybe a distant relative,* Tazio had thought, lying awake in his bunk. *But I also might be liberating them, too.*

The B-17 struck a pocket of turbulence, shaking the aircraft.

"Jeez," Frank said, looking at a waist gunner. "Did they forget to install the shock absorbers on this jalopy?"

The gunner grinned, revealing a gold tooth. "This is nothing. You should have been on board a few weeks ago. We got stuck in a storm over the Mediterranean and half the crew got sick." He motioned to the other waist gunner. "Iron-stomach Donny here spewed his lunch."

"It was the mincemeat and stewed prunes that got the best of me," Donny said, his eyes fixated on the night sky.

The plane juddered and bounced, compelling the gunners to put on safety belts that were fastened to the floor of the airplane.

Frank took a deep breath and exhaled, puffing his cheeks.

"We'll be on the ground soon," Tazio said.

Frank nodded.

Tazio leaned his back against the fuselage, and he admired how the men used humor to cope with stress. And for the moment, the banter took Tazio's mind off the fact that the OSS was airdropping them from an aircraft that was not designed for paratroopers.

A young crewman with a freckled face named Woody emerged from the cockpit. He worked his way through the fuselage, like a sailor maneuvering across the bow of a bobbing ship, and he slipped between the waist gunners and approached Tazio and Frank. "We're nearing the coast and will soon be over the drop site. The pilot is going to slow the aircraft and lower its altitude to under eight hundred feet. Once he spots the torch lights from the Resistance, he'll give the signal to drop you and your equipment."

"Okay." Trepidation swirled within Tazio, despite having rehearsed the jump procedures multiple times.

Woody retrieved helmets and helped Tazio and Frank with securing the straps under their chins. "Time to take your places."

Tension spread through Tazio's shoulder muscles. He unbuckled his seatbelt and followed Frank and Woody to the edge of the bomb bay doors. The plane descended and he felt his stomach rise into his chest. *Here we go.*

Using metal clasps, Woody attached their parachute cords to a static line that was rigged to a wire on the fuselage. Behind Tazio, he attached the dropping containers to the same line. As the plane leveled off, he turned to the men and said, "It's showtime, boys."

The bomb bay doors gradually opened. Air blasted Tazio's body, and the roar of aircraft engines pounded his eardrums. *It'll be like training. All I need to do is jump and the parachute will automatically open.* He glanced down through the open doors to a dark forest, and he turned his attention to a light, mounted on the side of the fuselage, and waited for it to turn green.

"Get closer to the edge," Woody said, his voice almost drowned by roaring engines.

Frank and Tazio shuffled forward.

The light turned green, and Tazio's breath stalled in his lungs.

"Go!" Woody shouted.

Frank stepped forward, dropped through the bomb bay doors, and vanished into the night.

Tazio, his adrenaline flowing, sprang forward.

"Wait!" Woody grabbed Tazio's harness. "It's tangled!"

Tazio's body teetered on the edge of the opening and he grabbed a rail on the fuselage to keep from falling. His heart pounded as wind blasted his jumpsuit.

Woody unhooked Tazio's harness from the static line, adjusted his parachute pack, and refastened the cord to the static line. "Okay!"

"Are you sure?"

"Yes!"

Tazio let go of the rail and placed his hands over the reserve parachute, near his stomach, in the event he needed to use it.

"Give 'em hell!"

Tazio gathered his courage, stepped forward, and dropped through the bomb bay doors. His body plummeted through the night sky. Wind whistled through the gaps in his helmet. His mind raced, hoping that Woody had fixed the problem with his parachute. Seconds passed, and as he prepared to pull his reserve chute, he felt a tug and the sensation of being pulled up by his shoulders and thighs. The wind went quiet, and he peered upward at an open parachute canopy. *Thank goodness.*

He scanned the partly cloud-covered sky that was illuminated by a crescent moon. Above him were the equipment canisters attached to descending parachutes. An orange light flickered in the distance, and his eyes were drawn to Frank's canopy deflating on a hill, approximately a mile away. *The time it took to fix my gear created a gap between us. It will take time to reach him and the partisans, and the Germans will likely be alerted by the sound of aircraft engines.* He peered down and realized how badly he'd missed the landing area when he saw what looked to be towering pines rushing toward him. He pulled hard on the parachute cords, attempting to veer away from the trees, but it was too late. His boots struck the top of a pine. He crashed through several branches, scraping his arms and legs, and came to a jarring stop.

His legs dangled in the air, approximately ten feet from the ground. The harness pulled hard against his armpits and thighs, and the cords to his deflated parachute were tangled in the tree. He unbuckled his harness and fell to the forest floor, stinging the joints in his ankles. As he got to his feet, the equipment containers dropped through nearby trees, snapping their branches. He removed his helmet and the jumpsuit that covered his Italian civilian clothes.

At one of the containers, he released the latches and opened the lid to reveal a trove of rifles, service pistols, submachine guns, ammunition, and plastic explosives. He removed a Colt Model 1903 Pocket Hammerless, a semiautomatic pistol, and slipped it in his jacket pocket. From another container, he removed a canvas rucksack that held a radio, maps, a lunch-box-size field cipher, and paper-based encryption systems—all of which were too critical to the mission to abandon while trying to locate Frank and the partisans.

One by one, he lugged the containers into the underbrush and retrieved the parachutes, except the one that was tangled high in a tree. He bundled the parachutes and placed them, as well as his jumpsuit, next to the containers and covered the stash with foliage. He paused and listened. Wind whistled through branches. Crickets chirped. An owl hooted from an adjacent hill. He examined his trouser fly button—which was a secret compass that consisted of two bowl-shaped buttons, both black in color with four holes—but it was too dark to read without the aid of a flashlight. *It'll be difficult to hold a straight line without a compass, but it's better to take a crooked route than risk disclosing my location.*

Tazio put on the rucksack, which weighed approximately fifty pounds, and headed in the direction where he'd seen the light. Within minutes of hiking, the straps of the rucksack dug into his shoulders, and his legs and back muscles stung with fatigue. He struggled to find his footing on the uneven terrain that was littered with rocks and broken branches. Also, the dense forest blocked out most of the moonlight, which made it difficult to see. Thorn bushes pricked at his clothes and exposed skin. He pushed forward, shielding his face with his arms, and as he emerged from the thicket, his boot caught on an exposed tree root and he tumbled to the ground. The full weight of the rucksack slammed into his back, sending a sharp pang through his spine. He worked his way to his feet, buried his pain, and continued his slog.

At the summit of a hill, he stopped to rest and wiped sweat from his brow. A speck of orange light flickered through the trees, spawning a rush of adrenaline. *I can make it. It's not much farther.* He adjusted his direction and plodded toward the beacon.

He labored his way for several minutes and, as he neared the edge of a clearing, a smell of burned wood and petrol penetrated his nose. And he froze at the sound of guttural voices.

"*Schnell!*"

Hairs rose on the back of Tazio's neck. He carefully put down his rucksack and slipped his pistol from his jacket. On his belly, he crawled forward and peeked through bushes.

Forty yards away, a squad of German soldiers got out of the back of a transport truck near a parked Kübelwagen, its doors emblazoned with an iron cross. A cottage, twenty yards away from the vehicles, was engulfed in flames, and there were no partisans in sight.

Damn it. Tazio tightened his grip on the pistol. *It wasn't the torch light of partisans that was spotted by the pilot. It was the Germans setting fire to a cottage.*

On the opposite side of the clearing, Frank—with his hands raised and still wearing his jumpsuit—emerged from the forest with two German soldiers pointing submachine guns at his back.

Oh, God. A wave of dread washed over Tazio. He raised his

weapon but stopped short of firing, given that he was greatly outnumbered and inadequately armed. *I'm so sorry, Frank.*

The two soldiers tied Frank's hands behind his back and forced him into the Kübelwagen. The engine roared to life, and the vehicle disappeared down a dirt road.

A German officer wearing a visor cap appeared from the opposite side of the burning cottage. He slipped a pistol from a holster and pointed to the forest. *"Dieser Weg! Schnell!"*

Ten German soldiers joined their officer and fanned out over the perimeter of the clearing. With their weapons raised, they made their way toward the edge of the trees where Tazio was hidden in bushes.

His heart pounded. Every fiber in his body wanted to flee, but he held his ground and hoped that the soldiers, their faces illuminated with firelight from the flaming cottage, would have difficulty seeing in the forest until their eyes adjusted to the darkness. He pressed his chin to the ground and held his breath. Within seconds, they passed by him, no more than fifteen feet away.

The sound of footsteps gradually faded and disappeared. Tazio rose from his hiding spot, gathered his rucksack, and crept away in the opposite direction from the soldiers. A sense of loneliness and despair filled his core. He silently prayed for his friend, and he hoped that he'd find the Italian Resistance before the enemy found him.

Chapter 4

New York City—June 12, 2003

Gianna rolled her suitcase, a blue carry-on Samsonite hardshell that she had seldom used over the past several years, through a congested concourse of the John F. Kennedy International Airport. Crowd noise filled the air as she made her way around a throng of luggage-toting travelers to a row of payphones. She glanced at a wall clock that read 4:40 PM and picked up a receiver, inserted a quarter from her purse, and pressed the numbers to the law firm where her daughter worked.

She'd barely slept. Throughout the night, her mind was plagued with memories of the war and the irreversible consequences of her decades-old mistakes. She purposely delayed calling Jenn to avoid having to face the ghosts of her past, and to eliminate the chance of her daughter rushing over to her house to try to talk her out of taking the trip. *She'll be shocked and upset about me leaving,* she thought, struggling to hear the ringing over the chatter of people. *Someday, I'll find a way to make things right between us.*

"Levine, Cooper, and Stone," a female receptionist said.

Gianna pressed the receiver to her ear. "Jenn Farro, please."

"I'm sorry. She's in a meeting with a client. May I take a message?"

"No." Gianna glanced at a dozen or so people who were congregated at a gate for the flight to Rome. "Please interrupt her."

"I'm afraid she cannot be—"

"I'm her mother," Gianna said, "and it's important that I speak with her."

The woman paused and said, "Hold, please."

Gianna listened to elevator music, a cheesy-sounding bossa nova that reminded her of an electric piano organ with programmed melodies. She wiggled her toes inside her shoes in an attempt to dispel her apprehension.

"Mom," Jenn's voice said, picking up the line. "Are you okay?"

"I'm fine."

"You had me worried," Jenn said. "You never call me at work unless it's an emergency."

"I need to talk to you about something."

"I have an out-of-state client waiting for me in a conference room. Could I call you back when I'm finished?"

"Now is best." Gianna fiddled with the phone cord. "It won't take long."

"It's awfully noisy. Are you in a subway station?"

"No," Gianna said. "I'm at JFK."

"Why are you at the airport?"

Gianna's heart rate quickened. "I'm taking a trip, and I'll be unable to watch Bella and Enzo for a while. I'm sorry about the short notice, and for pulling you out of a meeting."

"I'm confused," Jenn said. "Where are you going?"

"Florence."

"Italy?"

"Yes," Gianna said. "My flight is about to board."

"What the hell, Mom!" Jenn said, her voice filled with alarm. "Who is going with you?"

"No one. I'm going alone."

"Hold on—this makes no sense," Jenn said. "What's going on?"

"I need to go back to Tuscany."

"But Mom," Jenn said, "there is no family left for you there. You never talk about Italy—except for discussing music and food with the kids—and you haven't been back there since you moved to the United States."

"That's true—"

"Good afternoon, passengers," a male voice said over the intercom. "This is the pre-boarding announcement for flight four twenty-eight to Rome. We are now inviting those passengers with small children, and any passengers requiring special assistance, to begin boarding."

"They're starting to get on the plane," Gianna said. "I need to go."

"Wait!" Jenn said. "What's happening—are you sick and not telling me?"

"No, it's nothing like that."

"Then what is so important that you need to make a spur-of-the-moment trip to the old country?"

A knot formed in Gianna's stomach. "Yesterday, I found an article in the newspaper about an encrypted wartime message that was discovered in Tuscany. I want to meet with the person who found it."

"For God's sake," Jenn said. "If you're interested in connecting with this person, did you stop to think that it might be easier for you to write a letter or make a phone call?"

"No." Gianna shifted her weight. "The message was intended for me."

"Oh, Mom," Jenn said, sounding skeptical. "What makes you think that this has something to do with you?"

Tension spread through her shoulders. "There are events in my past—that happened in the war—that I've never spoken about to you or your father. I hate harboring secrets, but some things are too terrible to talk about and not meant for one's child to hear."

Jenn paused, as if she were stunned by her mother's words. "You're freaking me out."

"I'm sorry to upset you." Gianna glanced at an elderly couple entering the jet bridge for her flight. "I need to go. It's the only way I'll find out what the message says."

"Hold on—I can help you deal with this from here."

"I wish that were possible," Gianna said. "I need to leave, and it's something I must do on my own. I hope you understand."

"But Mom!" Jenn said, raising her voice. "It's not safe for you to fly off to Italy by yourself. You're eighty-three years old, and you don't even own a cell phone."

"If I had a cell phone, would it work in Italy?"

"Probably not. You'd likely need a new SIM card, but that's not the point. Whatever you read in the paper has shaken you, and you're not thinking clearly. Stay put and I'll come and get you."

"My decision is made," Gianna said. "I'm going."

"But—where are you planning to stay?"

"Probably a hotel in Florence. I didn't get a chance to make a reservation."

"Oh, God," Jenn muttered. "How long will you be there?"

"I'm not sure—maybe a week or two." Gianna switched the receiver to her opposite ear. "I'll leave a message for you at your office to let you know the name of my hotel. Send my love to Bella and Enzo."

"Please, Mom! Don't go!"

Tears welled up in Gianna's eyes. "Goodbye, Jenn."

"Wait—"

Gianna hung up the receiver and wiped her eyes. She gathered her luggage and got in line at the gate, where she gradually made her way forward to show her boarding pass and passport to a ticket agent. Her legs felt heavy as she followed a line of passengers down the jet bridge and into the plane. She was greeted by a young female flight attendant, wearing a navy-color uniform with a red scarf, who led her to a window seat and placed her suitcase in an overhead bin.

The plane departed from the gate and taxied to a runway. She felt bad for leaving things the way she did with Jenn, and she longed to see her grandchildren, Bella and Enzo, despite not yet missing a day of caring for them. She peered through the window at the airport's control tower and an angst grew inside her. *There is no turning back now.*

Jet engines roared and the plane surged forward, pressing Gianna's back to her seat. She squeezed her hands together as the plane accelerated down the runway and rose into the air. Minutes later, the aircraft reached cruising altitude and she retrieved a pen, small pad of paper, and the newspaper article from her purse that was stashed under the seat in front of her. She placed the items on her tray table and informed the flight attendant that she would pass on her meal. While most of the passengers ate their food and watched movies on in-flight entertainment screens, she studied the encrypted message. And for much of the trip, she sipped weak lukewarm tea and scribbled on her notepad, all the while racking her brain to remember fragments of her past to crack the code.

Chapter 5

Strada in Chianti—September 25, 1943

Gianna entered her bedroom, reached under her mattress, and removed an envelope with her name written in a familiar shade of blue ink. The message had been hand-delivered by Don Casini when he'd visited, days earlier, to pay his condolences on the death of Matteo. Although she'd read the letter several times, seeing her friend's words dulled her heartache. She removed the paper from the envelope and unfolded it to reveal Lilla's exquisite handwriting, created with a fine nib fountain pen.

> *Gianna,*
> *I wish I could be with you. I'm deeply saddened by the loss of Matteo, and I'm holding you close in my heart and hoping that you find comfort during this difficult time. I feel like I know your brother from your stories, especially ones where he encouraged you to follow your dreams of painting.*

A memory of Matteo, gifting her a paint kit, echoed in her mind. "Keep practicing," he'd said, patting her shoulder. "Someday, your work will be decorating the walls of the Uffizi." Gianna smiled. *He always made me feel good about myself.*

> *Matteo was a good and generous person, and I believe, with all my heart, that he would be immensely proud of you for aiding people in need of protection. His sacrifice will not be in vain. Many families will never forget his courage to protect them from persecution and the threats of war. His spirit will live on through the lives he saved.*

Gianna blinked her eyes, fending off tears. She squeezed the paper between her fingers and continued reading.

> *Rabbino Nathan asked me to pass along his condolences and that he regrets not being able to properly pay his respects. You and your papà remain in my prayers, and I hope that your memories of Matteo will provide you with peace.*
> *With much love,*
> *Lilla*

Gianna wiped her eyes. She knew that she should dispose of the letter, given that it could be used as evidence, if discovered by the Blackshirts or Gestapo, that she was complicit in aiding Jews. But she refused to burn the message that eased her pain, and she carefully folded the letter and hid it under her mattress.

There could be no church funeral for Matteo. The partisan leader named Carmine had used a pack mule to bring Matteo's body home from a rugged mountainous area near Marliana. They arranged for a local priest, who was a trusted friend of Don Casini, to have Matteo discreetly buried in a cemetery with an unmarked grave, adjacent to the plot where Gianna's mother was laid to rest. They had never disclosed Matteo's role as a partisan to any of the residents of Strada in Chianti, and they feared that a church funeral might bring undue attention to their family and jeopardize their operation to hide Jews. As far as the rural residents of Strada in Chianti knew, Matteo had fled to Switzerland to avoid service in the army. Most Italians despised the German occupation, but there were many Tuscans who remained Mussolini loyalists or Nazi sympathizers. Informants were everywhere, and no one could be trusted. It broke Gianna's heart to deprive her brother of a proper funeral and burial. To honor him, she inconspicuously placed a bouquet of wildflowers—along with a cluster of grapes from the vineyard—on his burial mound and vowed to someday give him a proper headstone.

The front door opened, and the sound of Beppe's footsteps and cane grew in the hallway.

Gianna, her eyes red and watery, took deep breaths to gather her composure. She smoothed her skirt and left her bedroom.

Beppe's eyes met hers, and his shoulders drooped.

He knows.

Beppe shuffled to her and gave her a hug. "I cried today, too."

She squeezed him. "I feel broken."

"So do I." He released her and placed a hand to her cheek. "I wish there was something I could say or do to make the hurt go away."

"Me too," she said. "How are you holding up?"

"Same." He lowered his hand and shifted his weight on his cane. "Our new guests will be arriving soon."

She nodded. "I'll place more supplies in the shelter."

Sara and Davide had left earlier in the week with Carmine and another partisan to lead them on the first leg of their journey to Switzerland. Although Gianna was happy to see them embark on their quest for freedom, it was heartbreaking for her to see them leave without Matteo as their guide.

"How about I make you something to eat?" Beppe asked.

"I'm not hungry."

"You need your strength, and so do I. Take a few minutes to prepare the shelter for our guests, and I'll make us a meal."

"All right," she said.

Gianna gathered wool blankets, a basket of food, canteens of water, and placed them in the wine cellar's hiding space. She returned to the house and found Beppe in the kitchen. On the table were plates of sliced bread, a saucer of olive oil, and cups of steaming coffee.

"*Grazie*," Gianna said, sitting across the table from him.

"*Prego.*" Beppe crossed himself and said grace, giving thanks for the food and asking for the safety of refugees and partisans, and a swift end to the war. He placed his hands on his lap. "*Buon appetito.*"

Gianna took a sip of the roasted barley coffee, hot and bitter. She winced and lowered her cup.

"Have it with bread," he said. "It'll hide the harshness of the burned barley."

Gianna soaked a bit of bread in olive oil and chewed. Normally, she savored the rich, fruity flavor of their homemade olive oil, but it—as well as any of the food that she'd eaten in days—tasted bland and unpalatable. Her mind drifted to her brother, and tension spread through her body. "After the war, I want to give Matteo a proper funeral and gravestone."

"We will." Beppe took a small sip of coffee, set aside his cup, and peered out the window. His bottom lip quivered. "God, he loved this vineyard. He always dreamed of carrying on our family's wine and olive business."

"He did." Gianna clasped her cup, and she wondered how long it took for broken hearts to mend. *A month—a year—a lifetime?*

"I can't stop wondering if there is anything I could have done to protect him."

Me too, she thought. "It's not your fault."

He gave a subtle nod and looked at Gianna. "There's something I would like to discuss with you."

"*Va bene.*"

He picked at a groove in the rustic wooden table. "I want you to go with the next group to Switzerland."

She straightened her back. "No."

"It'll be safer for you to live with your uncle Uberto until the war is over."

"You need my help to hide refugees, and the resistance network is relying on me to smuggle travel papers."

"I'll find a way to manage things on my own."

She shook her head. "You can't do it alone. People need *us* to protect them."

He leaned forward. "I'd never forgive myself if something happened to you."

"How can I leave when there are so many Jews who are at risk of being arrested and deported to concentration camps?"

Beppe shifted in his seat.

"Their lives are at stake," she said. "Do you think Mamma or Matteo would abandon people in need?"

"Of course not," he said, "but things have gotten far too dangerous with German occupation."

She looked into his eyes, filled with anguish. "If you hadn't injured your leg in the Great War, would you have become a partisan fighter like Matteo?"

Beppe shifted in his seat. "That has nothing to do with why you need to go to Switzerland."

"It has everything to do with it," Gianna said. "Tell me the truth—what would you have done?"

He glanced at the framed photograph of his late wife on the wall. "I would have taken up arms and joined the partisans."

"That's my point. I can't turn my back to what is happening to our homeland and innocent people. If anything, I need to do more to fight—not less."

A clopping of hooves came from a dirt lane leading to the vineyard.

"They're here." Beppe retrieved his cane. "We'll discuss this later."

"There is nothing left to talk about—I'm staying."

"You've got your *mamma*'s spirit and my stubbornness." Beppe rose from his chair. "But I've made my decision. You will leave with the next group of refugees." He turned and left the house.

Gianna got up from the table, walked outside, and followed Beppe to the wine cellar.

An elderly hunchbacked man named Piero, a member of the

DELASEM resistance network, steered a horse-drawn wagon to the entrance of the wine cellar. He tugged on the reins to a skinny old plow horse with a tangled mane, and the wagon slowed to a stop.

Gianna raised her hand. "*Buongiorno.*"

"*Ciao.*" Piero stepped down from the wagon, approached Gianna and Beppe, and slipped a felt beret from his bald, age-spotted head. "I heard about Matteo. I'm sorry."

"*Grazie*," Beppe said.

Gianna nodded.

Piero shuffled to the rear of the wagon that was filled with straw. He lowered a rear gate and removed a wide horizontal board, revealing a false bottom to the wagon. He extended his hand and helped a young woman, who appeared to be pregnant, and a preschool-age boy from the hidden compartment.

"This is Aria Cavalieri and her son, Eliseo," Piero said. "They're from Siena."

"Welcome." Gianna gestured to her father. "This is Beppe and I'm Gianna. You'll be safe here."

"I'm grateful for your help." The woman, wearing a gray weathered dress, kneeled and held her son.

The boy nestled his head against his mother's shoulder and whimpered, "I want Papà."

"It'll be all right," the woman said. "They're here to help us."

While the woman consoled her child, Gianna approached Piero and Beppe and lowered her voice. "Don Casini told me that there would be three."

"Her husband was arrested by the Gestapo," Piero said. "He was apprehended when he left a safehouse in search of food."

"*Oh, Dio,*" Gianna breathed.

Beppe lowered his chin.

Piero reached into his jacket pocket, removed two passports and folded papers, and gave them to Beppe. "These are their identification documents."

Beppe flipped through the papers. "They're not updated."

"Correct," Piero said. "You'll need to get them to the network in Firenze to be fixed."

"Could you deliver the documents for us?" Beppe asked.

"No—I'm sorry," the old man said. "I must return to Siena to smuggle two more people to another safehouse."

Beppe frowned and slipped the documents into his pocket.

Gianna glanced at the woman and her child, and she wondered, although briefly, how many Italian families were hiding Jews from the Germans.

Piero bid farewell to Aria and Eliseo, and he climbed onto his wagon. He tugged the reins, the horse plodded ahead, and the wagon gradually disappeared down the lane.

Gianna approached the woman. "I'm sorry about your husband. I'll keep him in my thoughts."

Aria released her son but continued to hold his hand. "*Grazie.*"

Gianna and Beppe led the woman and her child inside the wine cellar. They traveled to a row of wine barrels at the end of the tunnel, and Beppe removed a bottom barrel's chime hoop and head cover to reveal the secret chamber.

"It's best that you stay hidden as much as possible," Beppe said. "The Germans are traveling on the roads, and they could show up here at any moment. Gianna or I will be back when we are sure that the area is safe."

The woman, her eyes surrounded in dark circles, wrapped an arm around her son's shoulders.

"Once your identification papers are fixed," Beppe said, "a partisan will arrive to escort you and your son to the north. You'll travel from safehouse to safehouse, until you cross the border. In Switzerland, my brother Uberto will help you get settled."

"Bless you," the woman said.

"There is food, water, candles, books, and blankets in the shelter." Gianna stepped forward and kneeled to the boy, who was peeking around the waist of his mother. "How old are you, Eliseo?"

He shyly held up five fingers.

"Seven?" Gianna asked.

The boy shook his head. "Five."

"Oh, you're five." Gianna smiled. "There are children's books in the shelter. And there is a toy, a tin carousel that my brother and I played with when we were about your age. I hope you like it."

Eliseo's eyes brightened. "I once rode a big carousel." He looked up at his mother. "It had painted wooden horses that went up and down. Remember?"

"I do," Aria said.

Gianna stood and looked at the woman. "How far along are you?"

Aria placed a hand on her belly. "Six months."

Gianna smiled. "Your baby will be born Swiss."

Tears welled up in the woman's eyes.

Beppe instructed Aria and her child to crawl through the bottom barrel to access the shelter. Once they were inside and lit a candle, he placed the cover over the barrel and sealed it with a chime hoop.

Gianna felt horrible for the child and the woman, who—in addition to having to endure the capture of her husband—was fighting to get her son and unborn child to freedom. She left the wine cellar with Beppe and walked toward the house.

"It's going to be a difficult journey for them," Gianna said, breaking the silence.

"It will," he said.

"Give me their papers and I'll go to Firenze."

He stopped. "I don't want you to leave."

"We have no choice," she said, facing him. "You can't ride a bicycle with your leg."

Beppe ran a hand through his hair. "I shouldn't have sold our horse and wagon."

"It was the right thing to do. We needed the money for refugees." Gianna held out her palm. "The sooner I get the papers to Lilla, the sooner Aria and Eliseo will be able to leave for the next leg of their journey."

Beppe reluctantly removed the documents from his pocket. "All right. But when they leave, you will go with them."

Gianna, deciding it was not the time to debate with her father, took the papers. She followed him, limping with his cane, to her bicycle—its chain repaired and propped against the side of their house. She gathered a toolbox and they partially disassembled the bicycle. The passports and papers were carefully rolled and inserted into the tube of the frame. Once the bicycle was reassembled, Gianna gathered her purse and placed two bottles of wine, wrapped in newspaper, into the front basket.

"I don't want things to ever be bad between us," Beppe said.

"Impossible." She looked into his eyes, weary and filled with sadness. "Catch the moment."

The lines on his face softened. "Catch the moment," he repeated, as if grateful to hear his own words of affirmation.

She got onto her bicycle and rode away.

The late afternoon sun beat down on her body as she pedaled to Florence. Despite the unseasonably warm temperature, as well as the growing ache in her calf and thigh muscles, her mind remained on her brother—and Beppe. *He's hurting and fears for my safety*, she thought, turning onto the main road. *It's not the natural order of things—no parent should have to bury their child.* She fought back her sorrow and pedaled faster.

On the journey, she passed three German military trucks that were traveling in the opposite direction with armament and troops. The sight of the soldiers evoked a deep detestation for Nazis and Fascists, and she silently pledged to fight them with every fiber of her being.

An hour after leaving the vineyard, Florence came into view. Going down the steep hill toward the Arno, she gave her legs a short-lived reprieve from pedaling, then resumed on the flat road running parallel to the river. She veered onto the Ponte Vecchio and weaved her way through pedestrians, a mix of women, children, and elderly men. As she left the bridge, her eyes widened at the sight of a roadblock with two Wehrmacht soldiers who were stopping people to inspect their identification. Her foot slipped from the pedal, scraping her ankle. She ignored a twinge in her leg, regained her foothold, and scanned her surroundings for a detour but the area was closed off with barricades.

A thick-necked soldier with a barrel chest locked eyes on Gianna and motioned for her to get in line behind a group of pedestrians.

Her skin turned cold. With no other choice, she got off her bicycle and pushed it to the end of the line.

"*Documenti!*" a second soldier called out in Italian with a thick German accent.

At the front of the line, a bearded man wearing a crumpled brown fedora removed identification from his wallet and gave it to one of the soldiers.

The German eyed the document, returned it to the man, and waved him through the checkpoint.

The line crept forward, and a dense crowd of people, who'd crossed the bridge, filed in behind Gianna. She felt trapped, like a sheep herded into a pen.

The Wehrmacht had randomly stopped Italian citizens on the street, often to demonstrate to the masses that they were in charge. But the number of locations and frequency of checkpoints had swelled, and it was clear, to Gianna, that the Germans were imposing a systematic method to screen the people of Florence. *They're searching for Jews*, she thought, inching her bicycle forward. Her shoulder muscles tensed.

An old woman, who had a rounded back and tufts of gray hair sticking out from under a scarf, reached the front of the line and shuffled to a soldier. With crooked arthritic fingers, she fumbled to open her purse and rummaged inside.

"*Schnell!*" the soldier shouted.

The woman flinched. The purse fell from her hands and its contents spilled over the ground. She grimaced as she struggled to bend over to pick up her things.

Gianna peeked around the crowd and furrowed her brows.

The soldier nudged the woman's foot with his boot. *"Beeilt, euch!"*

The woman, frail and trembling, gingerly lowered herself to her hands and knees.

Gianna clenched her jaw. As if by reflex, she put down her bicycle, cut through the line, and approached the woman.

The second soldier, a lanky man whose uniform sagged on his thin frame, grabbed his rifle that was slung over his shoulder. *"Halt!"*

Gianna raised her palms. "I'll help her give you what you need," she said, hoping the soldiers could understand her Italian. She kneeled beside the woman, her wrinkled face etched with fright.

Eyes of the Florentines fell upon them.

Gianna's heart raced.

The lanky soldier glanced at his comrade, who crossed his arms and nodded.

Gianna placed strewn items into the purse and helped the woman to her feet.

"Grazie," the woman whispered, accepting her purse. She removed her identification and held it to the soldier, breaking his stare on Gianna.

The larger of the two men examined the paper and motioned for the woman to proceed.

Gianna walked toward her place in line. Her anxiety gradually waned as she threaded her way through the crowd. But upon reaching her bicycle she froze.

"During the commotion, a boy took some of your things and ran that way," a silver-haired man said, pointing to a crowd of people near the Ponte Vecchio. "I tried to stop him, but he was too fast. I'm sorry."

Gianna picked up her bicycle, its basket missing one of the bottles of wine and her purse that contained her identification. A knot twisted in her stomach.

"Documenti!" a soldier called over the crowd.

Goose bumps cropped up on her arms.

The line moved forward.

Her legs felt weak. *They'll never let me through without identification papers, especially after what I did.* With little choice, she nonchalantly left her place in line and pushed her bicycle toward the bridge.

"*Halt!*"

Her body went rigid. A clack of boot steps came from behind her, and she turned to see the broad-chested soldier walking toward her with a hand on a holstered pistol. *It's over.*

A siren sounded.

The German tilted his head and stopped.

Another siren wailed, then another.

The line of people looked up at the sky. Wehrmacht soldiers emerged from a hotel on the other side of the checkpoint and sprinted down the street. Florentines scattered over the area as the sirens intensified to an ear-piercing roar.

"Air raid!" a man's voice shouted.

"*Fritz,*" the lanky soldier called to his comrade, "*wir müssen hier weg!*"

The broad-chested soldier glared at Gianna and turned away. He and his partner abandoned their post and ran down the street to join a group of soldiers who were climbing into a truck.

A choice burned inside Gianna. Instead of crossing the bridge to leave the city, she fled toward the Resistance hideout in the center of Florence. She tried to ride her bicycle, but the streets and sidewalks were clogged with hundreds of residents who were pouring out of apartment buildings in search of underground bunkers. German antiaircraft guns, stationed around the city, began to fire. White puffs of smoke dotted the sky. Her heart pounded against her rib cage as she pushed her bicycle through the throng.

The mass of people jostled their way through the narrow streets, nearly knocking Gianna from her feet. She pushed her way forward, all the while determined to reach Lilla. Several streets away from her destination, screams erupted from the crowd, compelling Gianna to raise her eyes to the sky. Over a dozen American bombers with white star insignias soared high above Florence, contested only by inaccurate German antiaircraft fire. Bombs dropped from the bellies of the planes and whistled to the ground.

Fear flooded Gianna's veins. She pressed through the multitude of people, and she prayed that there would be enough bunkers in Florence for everyone.

Chapter 6

Florence—September 25, 1943

Gianna's heart rate surged from the rumble of bombs detonating over the city. The ground quaked beneath her feet as she pushed her bicycle through the dense, fast-moving crowd. A middle-aged man—who was carrying a small white dog with a cottonlike coat—slammed into her shoulder. She lost her balance, fell on top of her bicycle, and a paper-wrapped bottle of wine ejected from the bicycle's basket and smashed over the cobblestones. Panicked screams filled the air. People's shoes crunched over the broken glass, and the heel of a man's boot stepped onto the back of Gianna's hand, sending a flare of pain through her fingers.

Explosions and antiaircraft fire reverberated through the streets. Smoke plumes rose into the sky, and a squadron of American bombers soared high overhead. Shouts and screams pierced the air.

Gianna scrambled to her feet, gathered her bicycle, and joined the surge of people running in the street. The air turned thick with an acrid smell of burned wood and expelled explosive, which irritated her throat and induced coughs. She worked her way forward and veered onto a narrow alleyway, leaving the smoke and the masses of people behind, except for a woman who was running away with a wailing toddler clutched to her chest. Gianna gulped air into her lungs and rapped on the small weathered door of the DELASEM hideout.

A cascade of explosions erupted no more than a hundred meters away, breaking windows and showering shards of glass over the passageway.

Gianna crouched and covered her head with her hands.

The door opened, and Rabbi Nathan pulled Gianna and her bicycle inside.

She slumped against a stone wall.

He shut the door and bolted the lock. "Are you all right?"

"*Sì*," she said, picking glass from her hair.

"We need to get underground," he said. "Leave the bicycle and follow me."

Nathan led her through a hallway and down a steep, stone stairway to a basement that was dimly illuminated by candles. The windowless space was void of furnishings, save a few wooden crates and a pile of burlap sacks, and the air was damp and laced with a sour, moldlike odor. Several members of DELASEM, whom Gianna recognized from her trips to smuggle papers for Jews in hiding, were hunkered in the far corner of the basement.

"Gianna!" a familiar woman's voice called out.

Tears welled up in Gianna's eyes as Lilla sprang forward and hugged her.

"Thank goodness you're okay," Lilla said.

"You too," Gianna said.

Rabbi Nathan joined the group in the corner, and Gianna and Lilla sat on the floor in the center of the basement. The sound of antiaircraft guns, firing from several streets away, resonated through the subterranean bunker.

Lilla looked up at the low, timber-beam ceiling. "Do you know what is happening?"

Gianna wiped her eyes. "American bombers raided the city."

"Is it bad?"

"*Sì*," Gianna said, "but I didn't see where the bombs exploded. The route I traveled was overcome with crowds and smoke."

"Why would the Allies strike areas with innocent civilians?" Lilla asked.

She felt sick to her stomach. "I don't know."

In the early years of the war, Florence—compared to other Italian cities—was given favorable treatment by both the Germans and Allies. The city was a center of the Renaissance, and it contained some of the world's finest architecture and artwork. For the past few years, Florentines heard the roar of Allied planes, which carried on their flight paths to other cities. "They're going to Milan," Beppe had often said to Gianna, "where Mussolini's arms factories are located." But things changed with the Italian surrender and German occupation. The drums of war began to beat louder and in closer proximity, and rumors of the Uffizi hiding its artwork in the countryside grew rampant amongst Florentines. Gianna prayed that Florence and her family vineyard would be spared the wrath of war, but deep down she believed that things would get much worse before Italy was liberated.

"I'm so sorry about Matteo," Lilla said.

"*Grazie*," Gianna said.

"I wish I could have been there for you."

"You were." Gianna patted her friend's arm. "I got your letter—your words meant a lot to me."

"I'm pleased to hear that."

"I smuggled two sets of papers for you to work on," Gianna said, changing the conversation. "They're hidden inside my bicycle. Also, could you make a set of papers for me?"

She raised her brows. "Of course—what happened?"

Gianna told her about the German checkpoint, and how her purse with her identification documents was stolen while she was helping an elderly woman.

"I appreciate you creating forged papers for me. It will take months to receive replacement documents from the government."

Gianna rubbed her forehead "It was foolish of me to leave my bicycle and purse unattended. If the bicycle had been stolen, I would have lost the papers of two refugees."

"It's all right," Lilla said. "With time and the right materials, there's nothing I can't fabricate."

Tension eased from Gianna's shoulders. "True."

"Once I create the papers," Lilla said, "I'll ask Don Casini to deliver them to your vineyard. There's no reason for you to take the risk of bicycling to Florence to get them. And in the meantime, I want you to stay off the roads and as far away as possible from German checkpoints."

She nodded.

The rumble of explosions faded away and was replaced by the howl of police, ambulance, and fire brigade sirens. The entrance door to the building opened and shut. Footsteps came from the stairs and Don Casini, dressed in a black suit with a clerical collar, entered the basement. Rabbi Nathan greeted him, and members of the DELASEM network gathered around the priest.

"Bombs hit areas near the stadium and Costanzo Ciano Square," Don Casini said, his voice somber. "Also, I was told by a man on the street that the Mannelli Tower was heavily damaged."

An image of the small tower, located on the southeast corner of the Ponte Vecchio, flashed in Gianna's mind. She hoped that the Florentines, who were gathered near the bridge at the time of the air raid, had managed to find an underground shelter.

Don Casini wiped sweat from his brow. "Given the location of most of the strikes, the planes might have been trying to destroy the railways at Campo di Marte."

Rabbi Nathan adjusted his round-rimmed glasses. "Are there any civilian casualties?"

"*Sì.*" Lines deepened on the priest's face. "Injuries and loss of life might be extensive."

Gianna's heart sank. A muted roar of an ambulance siren filtered through the basement, and she looked at the priest. "We must do something to help."

Don Casini nodded. "When the all-clear signal is sounded, I'm going outside to see what I can do to aid with the aftermath."

"I'll come with you," Nathan said.

The priest placed a hand on the rabbi's shoulder. "The Germans are hunting for you. Your work is critical to our mission, and we can't take the risk of you being arrested. It's best that all Jews remain underground."

Nathan rubbed his jaw and nodded.

A long drone of a siren howled, giving the all-clear signal, and members of the DELASEM network left the basement. Don Casini, along with two Catholic men in the group, departed the building, and Gianna and the Jewish members of the group remained inside.

Gianna approached Rabbi Nathan. "I'm going to leave to see what I can do to help. I have two sets of identification papers hidden in my bicycle. Do you mind taking it apart and giving the papers to Lilla?"

"Not at all," Nathan said. "The bicycle will be ready for you when you return." He glanced at the door. "I wish I could be out there."

Gianna looked into the rabbi's eyes, surrounded with dark circles and filled with dismay. "You're saving lives. Because of your planning and leadership, many people will be shielded from being arrested and deported to concentration camps."

"We couldn't do this without your and Beppe's help." The tension on Nathan's face softened. "*Shalom aleichem.*"

"What does that mean?" Gianna asked.

"Peace to you."

"*Shalom aleichem* to you, too."

The rabbi smiled. He gathered Gianna's bicycle, wheeled it down the hallway, and disappeared into a storage room.

"You should stay," Lilla said, approaching Gianna. "You don't have identification."

"The Germans will likely be distracted from the attack, and I doubt that they'll be placing much effort on civilian checkpoints while fire brigades are racing over the city. Even if I'm stopped and detained, they'll eventually release me when they are satisfied that I'm not—" Gianna swallowed.

"A Jew," Lilla said, finishing her friend's words.

A thorn of guilt pricked at Gianna's conscience. "I hate that I can go outside while you must hide."

"It's all right," Lilla said.

"No, it's not," Gianna said. "When I come back for my bicycle, I want you to go with me to the vineyard. You'll be safe there—away from the German checkpoints and Allied bombing raids."

"I can't leave," Lilla said. "My work is in Firenze. The people who are smuggling ink, chemicals, glue, and paper to me are all located in the city. It's too risky to travel back and forth from your vineyard for supplies."

"I've been giving this some thought," Gianna said. "I think you should fabricate papers to be my cousin from Switzerland. If the Germans question you, your cover story could be that you are helping me and Beppe take care of the vineyard."

"That is a kind offer," Lilla said. "But I must stay in Firenze until the city is liberated."

"Things are getting worse," Gianna pleaded. "The German checkpoints are expanding, and American bombers have targeted the city."

"I'm staying," Lilla said.

"Where will you hide?"

"Here for much of the time," Lilla said. "But Nathan is arranging for the Jewish members of DELASEM to sleep in safehouses. He wants us to be constantly on the move, changing location every few nights."

An ambulance siren howled from a few streets away.

"I need to go," Gianna said.

Lilla went to the door and peeked through the peephole. "It's clear. Are you ready?"

"*Sì.*"

Lilla unbolted the lock and opened the door.

Gianna stepped into the alley, void of people yet filled with distant shouts and the blare of fire brigade horns. The door closed behind her and a key jostled inside a lock. She turned and her eyes widened at the sight of Lilla, standing in the alleyway.

"What are you doing?" Gianna asked.

Lilla inserted the key into her skirt pocket. "I'm coming with you."

"No—it's too dangerous."

"People need help and—like you said—the Germans will be occupied with the aftermath of the attack."

"But—"

Lilla turned and ran down the alley.

Gianna's adrenaline started to flow. She sprinted after her friend and caught up with her at the end of the alleyway, where they turned onto a street filled with chaos. Hundreds of people, who'd taken shelter during the raid, emerged from dwellings and underground bunkers. Shrieks and shouts pierced the air, tainted with a pungent smell of discharged explosives.

"That way!" Lilla shouted, pointing to plumes of smoke rising above the city.

They made their way through the crowd and veered onto a narrow, cobblestone street that was packed with people, some of whom were elderly men with shovels and digging bars. They followed the men and worked their way forward. Two streets before reaching Costanzo Ciano Square, the street and sidewalks were blocked by a mountainous mound of building debris.

"Mamma!" an adolescent boy cried, kneeling at a pile of bricks.

Florentines—composed of firefighters, a police officer, gray haired men, and several women—searched through the rubble of what appeared to be an apartment building, given the remnants of a sofa and a white-enameled wood stove that protruded from the wreckage.

"*Oh, mio Dio,*" Gianna breathed.

The boy, tears streaming down his dirt-covered face, tossed aside bricks. "Mamma!"

Gianna hiked up her skirt, climbed onto the debris field, and joined the search crew. Lilla clambered onto the mound and, together, they labored to move away remains. Bricks. Stones. Broken lumber. Chunks of plaster. Destroyed furniture.

Jagged splinters pierced Gianna's hands, and her arms and back flared with pain. Dense dust infiltrated her lungs, spawning rounds of horrid coughs. She fought away her fatigue and dug through the debris, all the while hoping to recover survivors.

A police whistle shrilled through the air.

Hairs raised on the back of Gianna's neck, and she put down a broken board.

The soot-covered police officer, who was standing on a mound of debris, waved his arms.

The volunteers, including Gianna and Lilla, climbed over the wreckage to the policeman. People pulled away broken bricks, a crushed bed frame, and a mattress. A moment later, two firefighters removed a motionless woman, her clothes, skin, and hair covered in ash, from the rubble. They carried the woman, her limbs limp, and placed her at the base of the wreckage. One of the firemen placed his ear to the woman's chest and shook his head.

"Mamma!" The teenage boy shot forward, fell onto his knees, and clasped his mother's lifeless hand.

Tears welled up in Gianna's eyes. Then she put aside her heartache, and she and Lilla resumed lugging away debris. For several hours, they helped to remove wreckage from the destroyed building. At nightfall, the rescue workers were ordered by a solitary German soldier, who was patrolling a nearby street, to refrain from using flashlights or oil lamps. It infuriated Gianna that the Germans were mandating the blackout rules while the workers raced against time to save lives. Also, she resented that the German military had not deployed their troops to aid in the rescue effort of Florentines. She and Lilla worked through much of the night, and clergymen and nuns arrived on the site to aid in the rescue effort. In all, eight inhabitants of the apartment complex were recovered—seven dead and a severely wounded woman who was placed in an ambulance and rushed away to a hospital.

Gianna, her mind and body ravaged, sat down on a pile of bricks. For hours, she'd fought to remain strong and resilient while witnessing death and horrific injuries. But now that her work was finished, the floodgates that had held back her emotions allowed them to spill over. Her body trembled, and tears welled up in her eyes.

Lilla sat beside her.

"All those innocent people," Gianna said, her voice raw. "Hundreds may have been killed in the attack."

Lilla's bottom lip quivered. "It's unfathomable."

"It's not supposed to happen this way," Gianna said. "Wars are supposed to be fought on battlefields—not in cities." She wiped her eyes and glanced at an elderly man who was being consoled by a nun. Her stomach felt nauseous.

Lilla placed a hand on her friend's arm.

Gianna blinked tears from her eyes. "No matter what happens, I'll never give up."

"Nor will I."

Gianna and Lilla sat on their pile of bricks in silence until the rescue workers left the site. To avoid the main streets that might be patrolled by German soldiers, they took a long detour around the city. They passed by dozens of destroyed buildings, a few of which were still undergoing rescue efforts by firefighters. At Campo di Marte, the railway lines were unscathed. And on the opposite side of the tracks near the stadium, several structures were in various states of ruin.

"The Americans hit everything but the railroad lines that carry German supplies," Lilla said, her voice faint.

Gianna nodded and continued her slog.

For the remainder of their journey, they encountered no German patrols or checkpoints. The city was silent, except for the occasional sound of ambulances or police sirens, and they reached the entrance to the DELASEM hideaway a few hours before dawn.

Lilla retrieved the key from her skirt pocket, undid the lock, and ushered Gianna inside. She shut the door and lit a candle that illuminated the entryway with amber light.

Gianna looked at her bicycle that was propped against the wall. "Rabbino Nathan might be upset about you leaving."

"Perhaps," Lilla said. "Maybe you should get some sleep before you go."

Gianna shook her head. "Beppe will be worried about me, and it's better to travel before the bulk of the German military is awake."

"Wait a moment." Lilla retrieved a piece of paper and pencil and handed it to Gianna. "Write down your place and date of birth, and anything else you can recall from your identification papers."

Gianna placed the paper against the wall, scribbled the information, and gave it to Lilla. "Before you create my papers, finish with the ones for the people who are staying with me and Beppe."

"I'll finish them together," Lilla said. "Remember—don't come here to get them. Don Casini or another Catholic in our network will arrange to deliver them to you."

"*Va bene*," Gianna said.

She hugged Lilla goodbye and retrieved her bicycle. After peeking through the peephole, she left the building and pedaled down the alleyway. Alone, her mind drifted to the death and destruction bestowed upon Florentines. Images of corpses and maimed bodies flashed in her head. She squeezed the handlebars and prayed for it all to end.

She rode out of the city by using an alternative bridge that crossed the Arno River, and she veered onto a less traveled unpaved road that led toward Strada in Chianti. The countryside was dark and silent, except for the chirp of crickets and an occasional bark of a dog. With her energy depleted, she struggled to pedal her bicycle over a deserted road that was littered with ruts and holes. She hated taking a longer route, but the backroad would likely limit her chances of an encounter with the Wehrmacht.

Several kilometers from the vineyard, she stood from her bicycle seat and pedaled up a steep incline. Her thigh muscles were exhausted, but she yearned to confide in Beppe and continued her push toward home. At the summit, she sat and coasted down the hill. She relaxed her legs and the bicycle picked up speed. Wind ruffled her hair and brushed over her face, and a bead of sweat rolled into her left eye, stinging it. She squinted, which made it worse. Using a sleeve, she rubbed her eyes and wiped her brows. As her vision cleared, the silhouette of a man emerged from behind a nearby tree and stepped into the road.

A chill shot down her spine. She slammed her foot back on a pedal to apply the brake, but it was too late. The rear wheel locked up, and her bicycle skidded out of control toward the person who was blocking her path.

Chapter 7

Near Strada in Chianti— September 26, 1943

Tazio, standing in the middle of a moonlit dirt road, waved his arms to get the attention of what looked like a woman racing toward him on a bicycle. But her head was lowered, like a Tour de France cyclist fighting wind resistance, and she showed no indication of slowing down. *She doesn't see me*, he thought as the woman barreled toward him. He considered shouting to get her attention, but decided it was best not to take a chance of alerting any nearby residents or the enemy. The bicyclist closed in and, as he stepped aside, a sound of tires skidding over gravel broke the still night air.

He darted to the berm, but the bicycle swerved toward him. The front tire slammed into his right leg, flaring pain through his knee, and he tumbled with the bicyclist into a thicket. He raised his head to the silhouette of the woman, tangled in her bicycle.

"Are you hurt?" Tazio asked in Italian.

"*Uffa!*" The woman pushed her bicycle off her legs and stood. "You could have killed me! What the hell is wrong with you?"

"I'm sorry." Tazio got to his feet, sending a twinge through his knee. He adjusted his weight and raised his palms. "I mean you no harm. I was trying to alert you to a German patrol. Down the road, there are two Wehrmacht soldiers in a parked Kübelwagen."

"I can take care of myself," she said, brushing leaf litter from her skirt.

"Are you sure you're all right?"

"I'm fine," she said.

He limped forward and picked up her bicycle.

"Did you injure yourself?"

"Just a bruise," he said, favoring his leg. "You're out past curfew."

The woman grabbed the handlebars and pulled away her bicycle. "So are you."

"If you're willing to disobey curfew restrictions, you're either a German collaborator or a resistance fighter."

"I'm neither," she said. "I had to work late in Firenze."

"Where do you work?"

"A wool factory."

He tilted his head. "It seems strange that your boss would require you to work late, and then permit you to leave during the German-imposed curfew. Why not work until morning, when there is no threat of getting in trouble?"

"It's none of your business." The woman looked at him. "What are *you* doing out at this hour?"

A choice churned inside him. He'd been hiding in the hills for over a day, ever since he parachuted into Tuscany and his companion was captured. He survived on wild berries, stream water, and a chocolate bar that was stashed in his jacket. He had no luck with locating the Resistance, his radio failed to work, the roads were constantly patrolled by Germans, and his parachute containers with armament and supplies had been recovered by the Wehrmacht. He had little left to lose by breaking his cover, and his gut told him that the woman was not a collaborator, but he decided to test her further.

Tazio looked at her. "Like you said, it's none of your business."

"It is when you make me crash my bicycle and nearly get me killed."

"I'm sorry about that. It was an accident." He shifted his weight away from his sore leg. "You're welcome to leave. When you reach the Wehrmacht soldiers, maybe you could ask them to give you a ride in their Kübelwagen to where you need to be."

"I'm in no hurry." She leaned on her handlebars. "You're young and able-bodied, except for that bruise you got by jumping in front of my bicycle. So, which is it—are you a deserter from the Italian Army, a spy for the Germans, or a member of the Resistance?"

"I'm none of those," he said. "I'm a farm laborer."

"I don't believe it. Your dialect is not from here."

He rubbed his knee. "I'm from Napoli."

"*Cazzata*," she said. "You don't speak with an Italian tongue. Where were you born?"

Damn it. She's sharp. Tazio considered continuing with a cover story, at least until he knew for certain that the woman could be trusted, but he sensed that she would never help him unless he came clean about his identity. He drew a deep breath and said, "My parents are from Napoli, but I was born in California—the United States."

The woman stepped back.

"I'm an American agent. I was parachuted into Tuscany to aid the Italian Resistance."

"*Mamma mia!*" She placed a hand to her cheek. "You came alone?"

"No. I arrived with another agent, but he was captured by the Germans."

"I'm sorry," she said.

"*Grazie.*" He thought of Frank, who was likely undergoing a brutal interrogation, and he hoped that his friend would find a way to survive the war. "We were parachuted into the wrong location. I've been searching for partisans but have been unable to locate them."

"So, you're lost."

"*Sì.*" A wave of vulnerability washed over him. "Is there any chance that you could point me in the right direction?"

She paused, as if she were pondering his request. "How do I know that you are not a German spy?"

"I can show you my wireless radio transceiver." He pointed to a tree. "My rucksack is over there."

"I know nothing about transceivers," she said. "Let me inspect your firearm."

"What for?"

"If you're an American agent, you'll be carrying an American-made weapon."

Jeepers! Who is this woman? With little choice, he slipped his Colt pistol from his jacket, removed its 8-round detachable box magazine, and handed her the unloaded weapon.

The woman examined the firearm. "It's too dark to see the markings, but it doesn't appear to be Italian or German." She gave it back to him.

He placed the magazine into his pistol and slipped it into his jacket.

"You're taking quite a risk by revealing all of this," she said. "I could be on my way home from an evening with a German soldier."

"True," he said. "But I don't think you're a collaborator."

"You're right—I despise the Nazis." She rubbed the back of her neck. "I could tell you where to find partisans, but it's a long journey on foot. You'll likely be captured before you find them."

"It's a chance I'm willing to take."

She glanced down the road. "How far is that German patrol?"

"Two kilometers," he said. "Maybe less."

"What's your name?"

"Tazio." He extended his arm.

"Gianna." She shook his hand. "I'll arrange for you to reach partisans, but first I need to go home. Follow me." She turned, pushed her bicycle out of the thicket, and crossed the road.

Tazio, disregarding the pain in his knee, retrieved his rucksack and followed Gianna into a grass-covered field. Without speaking, she led him to a babbling stream, where a narrow footpath ran along a tree-protected shoreline. Under the weight of his rucksack, his boots sank into the soft soil, and he struggled to see the path. But even more difficult, for Tazio, was keeping pace with Gianna, who skillfully pushed and lifted her bicycle over roots, rocks, and fallen limbs.

The murmur of the stream gradually dissipated as the waterway fed into a pond surrounded by cattails. They trekked up and down several hills, covered in shrubs and cypress trees. His knee throbbed, and the straps of his rucksack rubbed at his clothing and turned the skin on his shoulders raw. He wiped sweat from his forehead and clambered his way up the slope to reach Gianna, barely winded and standing beside her bicycle.

"How is your knee?" she asked.

"*Va bene*," he lied.

She pointed. "It's not much farther. We need to sneak through a farm, so we need to be quick and quiet."

He sucked in air and nodded.

They traveled down the hill, crept by a stone cottage, and entered a field that looked like it hadn't been plowed in years, given the copious amounts of weeds and brambles. To Tazio, the farm showed no sign of being inhabited. But he soon discovered that he was mistaken when a dog's bark pierced the air.

His adrenaline swelled and he sprang forward.

Gianna sprinted ahead with her bicycle.

The dog barked, closer and louder.

Tazio tried to run, but the fifty-pound weight of his rucksack, as well as the pain in his knee, hampered his pace. Growls and the patter of paws grew from behind him. He lowered his head and willed his legs to move faster, all the while expecting the canine to leap upon him. As he cut onto a dirt path, he felt a nip at his heel. Through the corner of his eye, he saw what appeared to be a small scruffy dog with large batlike ears.

The dog growled and snapped at his boot.

Tazio gripped the straps of his rucksack and lengthened his stride. But the dog chomped onto the hem of a pant leg and snarled while viciously shaking its doll-size head. He shot his leg forward, freeing himself from the dog's jaws.

The dog gave a few barks and trotted away.

Tazio glanced in the direction of the cottage, which remained dark and silent, and slogged his way forward.

Minutes later, he caught up with Gianna. On the horizon, a faint pink hue broke through the dark predawn sky. He followed her down a dirt lane to a sprawling vineyard with clusters of olive trees, their limbs filled with tweeting sparrows. The property was calm and isolated, which exuded an aura of safety. Fifty meters farther, they reached a stone house with windows covered by blackout curtains.

"This is my home," Gianna said, propping her bicycle against a wall of the dwelling.

Tazio removed his rucksack and rubbed his knee, swollen and riddled with ache.

She approached the entrance to the house and the door swung open. A cane-bearing man with salt-and-pepper hair and a stubble beard hobbled outside and embraced her.

"Thank God you're all right," the man said. "What happened?"

"I'll tell you everything inside." She released him and gestured with her hand. "This is Tazio—he claims to be an American."

The man's eyes widened.

Gianna looked at Tazio. "This is my father, Beppe."

He approached Beppe and shook his hand.

Beppe looked at Gianna. "Are you certain he can be trusted?"

Gianna shrugged. "We'll soon find out."

"*Va bene*," Beppe said. "Let's get in the house."

Tazio retrieved his rucksack and joined Gianna and Beppe in the living room. He sat on an old green upholstered sofa next to Gianna, while Beppe hunkered on a matching chair near the stone fireplace. The blackout drapes remained closed and the room was illuminated with the amber glow of an oil lamp, which gave Tazio a better look at the woman who was risking everything to help him.

Gianna was about his age, give or take a year, with a slender yet athletic frame, a dimpled chin, chestnut color eyes, and dark disheveled hair. Her cheeks were streaked with dirt, and her gray skirt and white blouse were covered in soot, giving her the appearance of a chimney sweep. But to Tazio, she looked strong, confident, and beautiful.

"Tell me what happened," Beppe said, setting aside his cane.

"American planes raided Firenze."

"*Mio Dio*," Beppe said. "Yesterday, I heard echoes of explosions."

"Me too," Tazio said. "Do you know the extent of the damage to the Germans?"

Gianna crossed her arms. "None."

Tazio furrowed his brow.

"The German-controlled railway lines were unscathed," she said. "The bombs struck civilian buildings, and hundreds of Florentines were killed in the attack. I spent the afternoon and most of the night helping rescue workers dig bodies out of the rubble."

Beppe lowered his head and crossed himself.

"Oh no." A knot formed in the pit of Tazio's stomach. "I'm so sorry."

"Your military is incompetent," Gianna said. "Your pilots parachute agents into areas far away from partisans, and their bombs miss their targets and slaughter innocent men, women, and children."

Tazio slumped his shoulders.

For several minutes, Gianna told him and Beppe about the raid and the devastation to the people of Florence. Tazio felt horrible for the victims, and for Gianna having to endure the gruesome task of excavating remains. He clenched his hands and vowed to himself to do everything he could to bring the war to an end.

Beppe wiped his eyes with a handkerchief from his pocket. He looked at Tazio and asked, "Tell me why you're here."

He leaned forward in his seat and revealed everything. His role as an OSS agent, his mission to aid the Italian Resistance until the

Allies liberated the country, the capture of his fellow agent, the loss of most of his supplies to the Wehrmacht, and his inability to locate partisans.

"I've been unable to contact my headquarters." Tazio pointed to his rucksack. "My radio isn't working properly. It might have been damaged when the parachute container hit the ground."

"You've fallen into a hornet's nest," Beppe said, rubbing his beard.

"I have."

"Where did you learn Italian?" Beppe asked.

He glanced at Gianna, who silently sat with her arms and legs crossed, and turned his attention to Beppe. "There are many Italian immigrants in Beaumont, California, and I grew up speaking Italian at home. My parents are from a small village near Napoli. They are Jewish immigrants who came to the United States after the Great War."

Gianna straightened her back. "Did the OSS provide you with Italian identification?"

"Yes."

"Show me," she said abruptly.

He reached into his jacket, removed identification, and gave it to her.

Gianna eyed the paper. "It's not perfect, but it'll suffice." She handed it back to him.

"It's unsafe for a Jew to be here," Beppe said.

Tazio nodded and put away his identification. "I appreciate you bringing me into your home, and any help with connecting with partisans. Do you know how I can reach them?"

Beppe looked at Gianna and gave a nod.

She turned to Tazio and smoothed her skirt. "My brother, Matteo, was a partisan. He was killed by the Germans."

"I'm sorry."

"*Grazie*," she said. "Matteo worked closely with a partisan leader named Carmine. His group is hiding in a remote area of the countryside."

"Carmine makes visits to our vineyard," Beppe added.

"Do you know when he'll be here?" Tazio asked.

Beppe shook his head. "It could be days, maybe weeks."

"I prefer not to wait," Tazio said. "Perhaps you can give me the location."

"It's a secluded area," Beppe said. "You'll never find it."

"I know where it is," Gianna said, looking at her father. "I was there once with Matteo. I could take him there."

"No," Beppe said. "It's too dangerous. We'll wait for Carmine to arrive."

"I appreciate your offer to guide me," Tazio said to Gianna, "but I'll either go alone or wait for Carmine to show up." He ran a hand through his hair. "Do you mind me asking why Carmine comes to your vineyard?"

Gianna looked at Beppe. "If he's staying, it's best that we tell him. He'll find out anyway when Carmine or one of his men arrives."

Beppe clasped his cane and nodded.

"Tell me what?" Tazio asked.

"We'll show you," Beppe said.

They rose from their seats, Gianna gathered a basket of food from the kitchen, and the trio left the house. Tazio, his mind racing, followed them to a large stone wine cellar that was dug into a hillside. A smell of oak and fermented wine filled his nose as he walked, limping on his right leg, to the back of the building.

Beppe approached a wall of stacked wine barrels. Using his cane, he gave three taps on a bottom barrel.

A muted rustling came from behind the barrel.

Beppe removed the barrel's chime hoop and head cover, and a woman and a young boy crawled out from a hidden shelter.

Tazio's eyes widened.

"*Buongiorno*," Beppe said, helping the woman to her feet.

"*Buongiorno*." The woman's eyes locked on Tazio, and she wrapped an arm around the boy, who was clinging to her side.

"It's all right," Gianna said. "This is Tazio. He is staying with us."

Tension eased from the woman's face. "*Salve.* I'm Aria, and this is my son, Eliseo."

"It's nice to meet you," Tazio said.

The boy peeked around his mother. "Are you Jewish, too?"

A wave of admiration for Gianna and Beppe washed over him. He looked into the boy's eyes and said, "I am."

Chapter 8

Strada in Chianti—September 26, 1943

Mixed emotions swirled inside Tazio as he left the wine cellar and walked with Gianna and Beppe toward the house. He was glad that Aria and Eliseo would be safe inside the hidden compartment of the wine cellar, but he felt sorry for them to be confined to a cramped, dark space.

"Aria and Eliseo will soon be leaving," Gianna said, as if she could sense Tazio's thoughts. "A partisan will guide them north, traveling from safehouse to safehouse, until they reach Switzerland. My friend, Lilla, in Firenze is fabricating new identification papers for them. They should be ready in a few days."

"I'm glad to hear that," Tazio said.

"I hate that they must stay out of sight," Beppe said. "But it's safer this way, until they get papers that conceal their true identity."

Along their walk, Gianna told him about the DELASEM network in Florence, her role as a courier to transport fake identification papers, and how she and Beppe used the vineyard as a safehouse. Prior to his mission, an OSS intelligence officer had briefed him about Nazi racial persecution, and the countless number of people—most of them Jewish—who were being systematically rounded up and murdered. But the intelligence officer, whose focus was preparing agents for guerilla warfare, provided only basic information about the Italian underground network that was fighting to save Jews. *Gianna and Beppe are fighting a different kind of war,* Tazio thought. *They're helping to save innocent lives, rather than battling to kill the enemy.*

At the house, Beppe turned to him and said, "Get your things and come upstairs."

Tazio gathered his rucksack and gingerly scaled the steps by using the banister to limit weight on his swollen knee. He met Beppe and Gianna at the landing, and he put down his load.

"I didn't get a chance to ask you about your leg," Beppe said. "What happened?"

He glanced at Gianna. "I made the mistake of—"

"I ran him over with my bicycle," she interrupted.

Beppe raised his brows.

"It was my fault," Tazio said, looking at Gianna. "I was on the road, and it was dark. I should have been more cautious trying to get your attention."

"True," she said. "But I was tired and not paying much attention."

"I'm sorry about the accident, but I'm glad it wasn't worse." Beppe tapped his cane on the floor. "I have a spare walking stick, if you need one."

"No, *grazie*," he said. "But I'll take you up on the offer if my knee gets worse."

Gianna turned and took a few steps down the hallway. She reached up, clasped a metal chain attached to a door in the ceiling, and pulled down a wooden retractable ladder.

"You'll sleep in a secret space in the attic," Beppe said. "I realize that you have forged papers, but we'll have a difficult time explaining—to a Blackshirt or German soldier—why a fighting-age man is on our vineyard."

"Of course," Tazio said.

"The attic space is much smaller than the compartment in the wine cellar," Beppe said. "It is only big enough to hide one person. But it can be sealed off by the person hiding inside, so you may roam the house if you're prepared to get out of sight at a moment's notice."

"I will."

"Gianna will show you to the attic," Beppe said. "Meet me in the kitchen after you stow away your things."

Tazio put on his rucksack and followed Gianna up the ladder and into a dark, windowless attic. She turned on a flashlight that had been placed on a crate, to reveal a rectangular room with a low-hanging, sharply pitched roof that required them to lower their heads. The space was cluttered with boxes, travel trunks, and wooden crates with empty dust-covered wine bottles. The warm, stagnant air smelled of ancient timber and musty clothing.

"It's over here." Gianna kneeled to the interior boards of the sloped roof and located a small and barely noticeable string that looked like a piece of fishing line. She tugged on the string, which loosened two of the lowest boards, and she slid them aside to reveal a small compartment.

"Clever," Tazio said.

"Beppe's doing," Gianna said. "He built it in less than a day. The most challenging part for him was scaling the ladder to the attic."

Tazio, borrowing the flashlight from Gianna, peeked inside the small interior space. "It should be big enough for me and my rucksack, if I scrunch my legs."

"It'll have to be. Try getting inside."

Tazio inserted his rucksack into the space and wriggled his way inside. He couldn't fully extend his legs, nor could he sit upright, but the hidden compartment was big enough to contain him. He crawled out and, for several minutes, he practiced opening the boards, squeezing into the space, and replacing the boards from inside his hiding spot.

"Batteries are nearly impossible to obtain," Gianna said. "I suggest that you refrain from using the flashlight, except to find the opening."

"I will."

Tazio, being careful not to bump his knee, crawled from the hole and replaced the boards. He flipped off the flashlight, placed it on a crate, and they left the attic.

Gianna, standing on her toes in the hallway, pushed the retractable ladder into the ceiling and yawned.

"You must be exhausted," he said.

"You too." She glanced at her filthy blouse. "I'm going to wash and get a few hours of sleep before getting started on chores. After you see Beppe, prop up your leg."

He nodded.

She turned away, traveled down the hallway, and disappeared into a room.

Tazio went downstairs, using the banister to ease weight from his bad leg, and found Beppe in the kitchen.

"Where's Gianna?" Beppe asked, placing a bowl of seasoned olives and gray bread on the table.

"She's going to wash and get some sleep."

"I'll leave a plate for her," Beppe said. "Have a seat."

He settled into a chair and stretched out his right leg, stiff and sore.

"When was the last time that you ate?"

"Two days ago," Tazio said. "Except for some wild berries, I did have a chocolate bar that I found stashed in my jacket."

"Then you'll be hungry, and the barley *caffè* and stale bread will be tolerable." He poured a steaming brew into cups, gave one to Tazio, and sat across the table from him.

Tazio picked up a piece of bread, dense and hard.

"Soak it or you'll break a tooth," Beppe said.

He dipped his bread into the brew and took a bite, filling his mouth with a bitter taste of burned barley. "It's good."

"I'm glad you like it."

Tazio plopped an olive into his mouth and chewed. The rich,

earthy taste of the olive reawakened his hunger and his stomach growled.

Beppe grinned and took a sip of coffee. "Tell me what is happening with the war. Our radios and newspapers provide nothing but Fascist and Nazi propaganda."

Tazio told him what he knew about the Allied invasions of Sicily and Italy, and the plans of the OSS to support the Italian Resistance.

"How long will it take for the Allies to reach Tuscany?"

"I don't know," Tazio said. "But our boys won't give up the fight until Italy is free. And the sooner I unite with partisans and get my radio to work, the sooner I'll be able to relay coordinates for the airdrop of armament."

Beppe leaned forward in his chair. "So, tell me—how did you get selected for a mission in German-occupied Italy?"

"My fluency in Italian got the attention of the OSS, and I jumped at the chance to help liberate my family's homeland."

"Did the OSS inform you about the risks of being here as a Jew?"

"They did." Tazio took a sip of coffee.

"It might not have been the smartest idea for you to parachute into German-occupied Italy, but I'm thankful that you're here." Beppe took a bite of bread. "What were you doing before the war?"

"I attended Whittier College and got a degree in chemistry." Tazio chewed an olive and deposited the pit on his plate. "And before I enlisted for service, I was working on my parents' farm."

"What do they grow?"

"Grapes."

Beppe's eyes brightened. "Do they make wine?"

"I wish," Tazio said. "Years ago, they made wine but were forced to stop production due to Prohibition. So, they turned to growing grapes and apples to sell."

Beppe frowned. "I can't imagine a good reason to outlaw wine."

"Me either," he said. "Someday, I hope to restore my family's winemaking business."

"Later," Beppe said, "you will taste our Chianti. It's the best in Tuscany."

"I look forward to it." Tazio glanced at a picture on the wall. "Is that your wife?"

Beppe nodded. "Luisa. She died from influenza when Gianna was a teenager."

"I'm sorry."

"*Grazie.*" Beppe gazed at his wife's photograph. "There isn't a day that goes by that I don't think about her, and how lucky I was to be married to her."

Tazio clasped his cup but made no effort to drink.

"Luisa was a wonderful wife and mother—she was kind, smart, and a gifted grape grower and artist." Beppe rubbed his temple, as if he were sifting through memories. "Every day, she made me laugh."

"Luisa sounds like an incredible woman," Tazio said. "I noticed oil paintings on the walls in the living room. Did she make them?"

"Some by her, and some by Gianna." Beppe nibbled a piece of bread. "Gianna has a lot of the same qualities as her mother."

"You must be proud of Gianna."

"More than words can describe." Beppe drew a deep breath. "She's all I have left in this world. I want her to go to Switzerland with Aria and Eliseo, but she is stubborn—like me—and refuses to go."

Tazio paused, taking in the man's words. "I barely know you and Gianna, but something tells me you both will do the right thing."

Beppe chewed an olive and nodded.

Tazio finished his meal and chatted with Beppe, who told him about the collapse of the Italian Army, Mussolini's recently established puppet government for Hitler, and the plague of Blackshirts and Nazi sympathizers. But most of all they talked about their families and hopes of a world without war and dictators. He felt at ease speaking with Beppe. To Tazio, the man felt more like a long-lost friend than a stranger.

Tazio helped him wash the dishes and, while Beppe went to the wine cellar to check on Aria and Eliseo, he located a candle and a box of matches and returned to the attic. Rather than prop up his leg to rest, he removed the radio and a minuscule tool kit from his rucksack. He wasn't a skilled repair person. His partner, Frank, had an electrical engineering degree and was, by far, the more technically adept member of their two-man mission. Under the glow of candlelight, Tazio painstakingly examined the crystal, transmitter, Morse key, wires, battery, headphone, vacuum tubes, coils, and fuses. He labored for hours, the candle gradually burned down to a nub, and the radio was still not working.

At nightfall, Tazio joined Gianna and Beppe in the kitchen. The blackout curtains were closed and Gianna, wearing clean clothing, prepared a sparse dinner of sauteed zucchini and slices of stale bread. Half the meal was placed in a small metal pail, which Beppe delivered to Aria and Eliseo in the wine cellar.

The trio spoke little during the dinner, given that none of them had slept much over the past twenty-four hours. After their meal, they retired to the living room, where Gianna placed a record— from a collection of keyboard sonatas by Domenico Scarlatti—on a wind-up gramophone. She dampened the volume by placing a scarf in the gramophone's horn, ensuring that they could be alerted to noise outside of the house, and sat on the sofa with Tazio. Minutes into the first piece, Beppe leaned back in his chair and drooped his eyelids.

"You should go to bed," Gianna said to him.

Beppe raked fingers through his hair. "*Va bene.*" Using his cane, he got to his feet and kissed Gianna on the top of her head.

Tazio rose from his seat. "*Buona notte.*"

Beppe patted Tazio's shoulder. "I forgot to give you a taste of our Chianti. I'm sorry."

"It's all right," Tazio said. "It gives me something to look forward to."

Beppe smiled and hobbled upstairs to his room.

Tazio sat on the sofa and turned to Gianna. "Did you get some rest this afternoon?"

"Not much."

"Please don't feel obligated to stay up for me," Tazio said. "I can retire to the attic."

"I don't think I can sleep. I keep thinking about the air raid in Firenze, and I was hoping the music would distract my mind." She drew a deep breath. "It's all so senseless. So many innocent lives were lost."

A knot formed in his stomach. "I feel horrible about what happened. I wish there was something I could do to change things."

She peered at the fireplace, which contained ashes and charred pieces of wood. "I hate what has become of our people, misled by the promises of dictators. Now, our kingdom is in the hands of the Nazis, our people are starving, and Jews must hide like moles to survive."

He turned toward her, but made no effort to speak.

"The war has come to Italian soil." She lowered her chin and picked at a loose thread on her skirt. "Sometimes, I feel like I could die in an instant from an Allied bomb or a German bullet."

She's been through years of hell, while I've endured a mere few days of war. "I can't begin to imagine what you've been through."

She chewed on her bottom lip.

"The pain that you and Beppe have experienced will someday end. The Allies are fighting their way north, and Italy will be free."

Gianna nodded. "My father enjoyed speaking with you this afternoon," she said, changing the subject.

"Me too."

"He said that he likes your spirit."

Tazio smiled. "Beppe seems like he'd be a great papà."

"The best."

He paused, listening to the muted piano sonata coming from the gramophone. "Beppe mentioned that he wants you to go to Switzerland."

"I'm not leaving Italy."

"May I ask why?"

"I refuse to abandon people who need help, and DELASEM and my friend Lilla are counting on me to courier fake identification papers. Many lives are at stake."

"I admire your bravery."

"It has little to do with courage," she said. "I feel vulnerable and scared every time I get on my bicycle and pedal over German-controlled roads. It has everything to do with fighting for freedom, and protecting people who are persecuted by the Nazis."

He nodded.

"If I venture from this vineyard, it will be to do more to aid the Resistance."

"Like what?"

"Become a partisan."

He straightened his back. "You want to fight?"

"I do," she said confidently.

"What about your role as a courier?"

"I will continue to deliver identification papers for the resistance network in Firenze, and I'll help Beppe provide a sanctuary for refugees." She turned to him and placed her fingers together. "I've been giving this some thought. I'm already smuggling forged documents—so why can't I smuggle food, weapons, and ammunition to partisans who are hiding in the hills?"

He rubbed his jaw.

"If the Allies are coming—as you said—the battle will eventually come through this vineyard." She looked into his eyes. "I plan to bear arms and fight."

"Like your brother."

"*Sì.*"

He placed his hands on his lap. "Why are you telling me all of this?"

"Because—I know where Carmine and his group of partisans are in hiding, and I plan to take you there."

He shifted his weight. "That might not be such a good idea."

"We can't afford to waste time," she said. "It could take weeks for a partisan to arrive here to guide Aria and Eliseo on their journey to Switzerland. Also, we need to get you to Carmine sooner so you can arrange to provide his fighters with armament. With each day that the war lingers, more lives will be lost."

"What about Beppe?"

"He'll continue to try to protect me, but it will not sway my decision."

He scratched his stubbled chin.

"Also, when you fix your radio and order supplies to be parachuted into the countryside, you might need someone like me to smuggle them."

"You're not going to give up on this, are you?"

"No."

The music stopped, and the needle scratched over the record.

Gianna rose from her seat, started the record over, and resumed her place on the sofa.

The muted melody filled Tazio's ears. He rubbed his sore knee, and desiring to talk about something other than the war, he gazed at the framed paintings that adorned the walls. "Beppe told me that you are an artist."

"I'm a novice painter."

"Which ones are yours?"

"Those are mine," she said, pointing to two paintings on a wall. "The others are my mother's work."

"Your paintings are quite different from Luisa's."

Gianna smiled, as if pleased to hear the name of her mom. "My mother was an impressionist style painter. She loved to create pieces of our vineyard, and she used small, thin brush strokes to accurately depict the light at sunset. Unlike my mother, I'm more of an avant-garde painter." She looked at him. "I like to break rules."

Tazio chuckled. "I've noticed." His eyes were drawn to an abstract painting composed of long, thick strokes in shades of yellow and gold. "What is the name of that piece?" he said, pointing.

"It's untitled."

He got up from his seat and walked, trying to hide the pain in his knee, to the painting. "It's beautiful. You should name it."

"*Grazie*, but I haven't given a name to any of my pieces."

"How does a painter create the title of an abstract painting?"

She tilted her head. "I guess it would be based on the feelings that the piece evokes."

He gazed at the piece—taking in the warm colors and broad brushstrokes—and turned to her. "May I suggest a title for you?"

"Of course."

"Hope."

A smile spread over her face. "I like it. Hope, it is."

For an hour, Tazio sat with Gianna and discussed family, and he learned more about Gianna's best friend Lilla and their work with DELASEM. The flame of the oil lamp gradually dimmed. They left the sofa, turned off the gramophone, and went upstairs.

At the landing, Tazio pulled down the retractable ladder to the attic, and he turned to Gianna, holding the lamp. "*Buona notte*."

"*Buona notte*," she said, softly. "Get some rest. When your leg feels better, we leave."

Tazio looked into her eyes, reflecting lamplight. "All right."

He carefully climbed, his knee gnawing with ache, into the attic and peered down at Gianna. She paused, staring upward, and raised the ladder to close the entrance. In the darkness, he located the flashlight and used it to access the hidden space. He wriggled into the small cavity, replaced the boards, and turned off the flashlight. The blackness and tight quarters of the space made him feel as if he were sealed inside a coffin. He took in deep breaths of stale air and tried to fall asleep. But he remained awake, his mind on the woman who would lead him to the partisans.

Chapter 9

Rome—June 13, 2003

Gianna, feeling jet-lagged and nervous, rolled her luggage into a crowded Rome train station. She got in the back of a long line that was composed of foreign tourists and Italian travelers, and gradually made her way forward to a service booth. Using euros that she'd acquired from a currency exchange at the airport, she purchased a high-speed train ticket to Florence. Rather than sit on a hard wooden bench and wait for her train, she went to a café at the entrance to the station.

"*Buongiorno*," Gianna said, greeting the barista, a young tattooed woman with bright blue hair. "*Cappuccino, per favore.*"

The woman prepared the drink in a white ceramic cup and placed it on the counter.

Gianna's eyes were drawn to the woman's forearm tattoo of a black monochrome paintbrush with splashes of purple, green, yellow, and orange colors. "I love your paintbrush."

The woman smiled. "*Grazie.* I'm working toward a degree in art."

"That is what I studied, but it was a long time ago." Gianna placed money from her purse on the counter. "I'm a retired art teacher."

"Where did you teach?"

"A grade school in New York."

"I would love to live there." The woman tilted her head. "For an American, your Italian is very good."

"I was born in Strada in Chianti." She picked up the cup. "I'm Gianna."

"It's nice to meet you," the woman said. "I'm Chiara. Are you visiting friends and family?"

They're all gone, Gianna thought. "No. I'm taking a trip to Firenze."

"You must be going to the Uffizi."

Gianna nodded, despite having no intention of setting foot inside an art gallery. "It was nice speaking with you, Chiara. Best of luck with your studies."

"*Grazie.* Enjoy your holiday."

Gianna turned and left the counter. She placed her cappuccino on a small table, pushed aside a dirty ashtray, and sat with her luggage at her side. Despite having passed on receiving her airline meals, she felt little urge to eat. The brief interlude of conversation had distracted her mind from the purpose of her quest. But now that she was alone, her thoughts drifted to her coded message, and the deadly repercussions of her misguided wartime actions that she'd kept hidden for nearly six decades. To pass the time, she sipped her cappuccino and watched people pass through the station.

She finished her drink, gathered her things, and used a public toilet. She walked through the station, filled with travelers, and located the departure terminal. The area had a towering roof that spanned over rows of railroad tracks and platforms, a few of which had parked trains. She adjusted her glasses on the bridge of her nose, peered at an electronic departure board, and her eyes locked on the illuminated words: FIRENZE—PLATFORM 3.

She rearranged the purse strap on her shoulder and rolled her luggage toward the platform that had a train with open doors. As she got closer, her eyes widened at the sight of carriages that were full with seated passengers and a few stragglers who were rushing to board the train. *Madonna mia! I've lost track of time! I'm going to miss it!*

Gianna tried to quicken her pace, but her eighty-three-year-old legs, stiff and achy from the hours of confinement in an airplane seat, struggled to lengthen their stride.

"Hold up!" she called out in Italian. "I'm coming!"

The last of the passengers entered carriages, leaving Gianna alone on the platform. But she pushed ahead, all the while determined not to miss her train.

"Wait!" she shouted.

A young, mustached man poked his head out of the entrance to a carriage. "Hurry!"

Gianna, her heart racing and out of breath, lugged her suitcase over the concrete platform. At the carriage, the man helped her inside and the electronic door closed behind them.

"That was close," the man said. "Are you okay?"

Gianna nodded and sucked in air.

He smiled. "You run like a gazelle."

Gianna chuckled and drew in deep inhales. "You're too kind. I appreciate you holding the door for me."

"*Prego.*"

The train jerked and pulled away from the platform. Gianna, attempting to maintain her balance, clasped a metal handle that was mounted near the door.

"Do you need help getting to a seat?" the man asked.

"You've done more than enough. I think I'll stand here for a moment and catch my breath."

"Are you sure?"

"*Sì, grazie.*"

The man made his way through the carriage and sat next to a woman who was holding a baby. He kissed the woman on the cheek and tickled the baby's chin with a finger.

A time of innocence and bliss, she thought, looking at the young family. She gripped the handle of her suitcase and yearned to see Bella and Enzo.

The train slowly rumbled over steel tracks and departed the station. Sunlight beamed through the carriage's windows, illuminating the passenger-filled compartment. Her breathing and heart rate gradually returned to normal. She opened her purse, removed her ticket, and read her seating assignment. With her ticket in hand, she rolled her suitcase down the aisle of the compartment—void of empty seats—and made her way to the next carriage, which was also completely full.

Gianna scanned the compartment for signs with rows and seat numbers, but she found none. *This must be the general seating area.* She looked for a train attendant, but saw no one wearing a uniform. So, she paused beside a plump middle-aged man who was seated next to the aisle and reading a newspaper.

"*Mi scusi, signore,*" Gianna said.

The man lowered his newspaper.

She held out her ticket. "Is there any chance that you might know where my seat is located?"

He glanced at her ticket and frowned. "You're on the wrong train."

Gianna's jaw dropped open. "The departure sign indicated that this train is going to Firenze."

"It is, but this is a slow train that has lots of stops." He pointed to markings on her ticket. "The fast train departs on platform five, and it leaves ten minutes after this one."

Her shoulders slumped. "*Mamma mia.*"

The carriage was blasted by a gust of wind, produced by a sleek modern train that was traveling toward the terminal.

"I think that was your train," the man said.

Gianna put away the ticket. "At least I'm going to Firenze. Do you know how long the trip will take?"

"Three hours and forty minutes," the man said. "Two hours longer than the fast train."

She sighed. "*Grazie.*"

The man raised his newspaper and continued reading.

Gianna, feeling witless and disappointed, rolled her suitcase through two more passenger-filled carriages. Eventually, she found a vacant aisle seat, which was made of hard rubbery plastic and located beside a toilet. She enlisted the aid of a man, who was seated on the opposite side of the aisle, to help her stow away her luggage in an overhead compartment.

I'm such a fool, Gianna thought, getting in her seat. *How could I have mistaken these old boxy-shaped carriages as belonging to a high-speed train? Maybe Jenn was right about me making this trip on my own.* She took a deep breath, opened her purse, and took out the newspaper article and her notepad. Setting aside her insecurities, she studied her notations and the encrypted message. *My faculties are fine—my brain is merely fogged with jet lag. I'll get some sleep in Firenze, and I'll find a way to crack the code.*

For much of the trip, the passengers endured stifling heat because the train had no air-conditioning, and Gianna regretted not packing snacks and a water bottle in her purse, because the slow train provided no food or beverage service. Along the journey, there were sixteen brief stops at train stations, including ones at popular tourist destinations of Orvieto, Chiusi, Terontola-Cortona, and Arezzo. As the train drew closer to Florence, her mind drifted to memories of the war—arrests, air raids, gunfire, death, and destruction. She tucked away her papers, closed her eyes, and tried to forget the past, if only for a little while. But her mind remained on her encrypted message, and a long dormant ache began to grow. Her broken heart, pieced together by time, had once again begun to crack. And accompanying the pang in her chest, a strange sense of indiscretion. Her thoughts were on Tazio, not Carlo.

She'd met Carlo Farro after the war—not long after completing her studies, moving to the United States, and accepting a position as an art teacher. Carlo, a manager of a local bank, had pursued her, despite her clear lack of interest in him. But he was persistent, polite, and, according to her teaching colleagues, a good suitor. After a year of declining his offers to join him for dinner, she finally accepted. *Tazio's gone*, she told herself as Carlo sat across from her, eating a bowl of pasta with meatballs.

She liked Carlo, despite his bland business attire and risk-averse nature. And who was she to be critiquing suitors? After all, she was sometimes referred to as the "vowel lady" by some of her students because of her Italian accent and the habit of adding a vowel sound—usually an *a*, *e*, or *o*—to the end of her spoken words. After a year of somewhat one-sided courtship, Carlo proposed, and she accepted. It could have been she didn't want to live her life alone, or perhaps the passing of time had impelled her to follow norms of social expectations—get married, have children, and leave one's mark in the world. But deep down, she'd simply come to accept that there was only one truly beloved in a person's life, and her Tazio was gone.

She'd had a good life. She had Jenn and her grandchildren Bella and Enzo, and she had no doubt that she'd made the right decision to get married. Over the years, Gianna had grown quite fond of Carlo. He was kind, gentle, fatherly, and always bringing her confections. *Sweets for a sweet*, he'd often say, giving her a box of chocolates. By all accounts, Carlo was a good and decent man. But she never again experienced those beautiful butterflies in her stomach, the ones that had migrated away in the war and never returned.

Three hours and forty minutes after leaving Rome, the train stopped at the Florence station. Passengers rose from their seats and made their way to exits. Gianna thanked the man for retrieving her suitcase from the overhead, and she made her way to the carriage door. Anxiety swelled inside her as she stepped onto the concrete platform of the train station, once used by the Germans to transport troops, armaments, and worst of all, Jews en route to concentration camps. She drew a deep breath and joined the flow of people leaving the arrival area.

Outside the train station, she hailed a taxi. The driver, a man in his thirties who was wearing a flat black cap, assisted her with getting into the rear seat, closed the door, and placed her luggage in the trunk.

"Where to?" the driver asked, taking his place behind the wheel.

"Take me to a hotel in the historic center. Someplace nice but not too expensive."

The driver peered through the rearview mirror and raised his brow. "No reservation?"

She placed her purse on her lap. "No."

"It's tourist season," he said. "It might be difficult to find a room."

"I'll take my chances," she said. "Pick a hotel close to the Piazza del Duomo. If there's no vacancy, I'll find another place on my own."

He adjusted his cap. "*Va bene.*"

The taxi pulled away from the curb and left the train station. She lowered the rear window, bringing in fresh air, and gazed over the narrow medieval streets as the taxi weaved through the city. Despite the passing of decades, Florence's magnificent Renaissance buildings with terracotta roofs looked much like they did before and during the war. However, the city's inhabitants appeared quite different to her. Florentines freely walked through the city, absent German checkpoints, and the sidewalks were cluttered with camera-toting tourists. The atmosphere of Florence was vibrant and cheerful, but for Gianna, returning home to Tuscany resurrected long suppressed feelings of loss and guilt. *So many perished in the war*, she thought, peering at an elderly woman who was laboring to climb stone steps to a church. *Why them and not me?*

Minutes later, the driver stopped at a curb and said, "I can't get any closer. It's pedestrian streets from here."

"This is fine." Gianna opened her purse and paid the driver.

He stuffed the money into his pocket, retrieved the suitcase from the trunk, and helped her out of the vehicle.

"*Grazie,*" Gianna said, taking hold of her suitcase.

The driver tipped his cap, got into his taxi, and drove away.

She peered up at the Florence cathedral, its massive masonry dome pointing to the sky. Her hands trembled and her legs felt weak. She gathered her strength, and as she made her way through the crowded Piazza del Duomo, the bells of Giotto's Campanile began to ring. Pigeons fluttered from a rooftop. She paused, listening to the majestic resonance of the bronze bells that she'd last heard as a young woman filled with hopes and dreams. Tears welled in her eyes.

Gianna remained in the *piazza* until the chimes subsided, and then she rolled her suitcase down a congested sidewalk. A few streets away, she reached a familiar hotel that had, during the war, been adorned with Nazi flags and billeted German officers. She buried her fear, opened the entrance door, and crossed the threshold.

Chapter 10

Florence—October 2, 1943

Shortly after daybreak, Gianna pedaled her bicycle onto the Ponte Santa Trinita, an ancient stone bridge that spanned the Arno. The air was silent and the water was still, reflecting orange sunlight and creating a mirrorlike image of the grand Renaissance buildings that bordered the river. She pedaled harder, stinging her thigh muscles, and silently prayed that she wouldn't encounter a German roadblock.

It had been a week since the air raid on Florence and the arrival of Tazio. She'd spent much of her days caring for Aria and Eliseo. She and Tazio, whose knee was feeling much better, had helped Beppe with repairing casks and preparing an iron crusher and grape press for the coming harvest. Their work was confined to the wine cellar, out of sight of potential unexpected arrivals, and Aria, Eliseo, and Tazio remained alert and ready to dash inside the secret chamber at the sound of someone outside. During lunch, Gianna chatted with Aria about her pregnancy, parenthood, and her upcoming journey to Switzerland, and Beppe and Tazio took turns reading a book to Eliseo, who sat quietly between them as he nibbled on bread and olives. Their daily routine, concealed from the world at war, gave them a small sense of peace. And Gianna relished her time with their temporary guests, knowing full well that once they departed, she might never see them again.

In the evenings, after Beppe had gone to bed, she sat with Tazio in the attic while he worked to fix his radio. Under the glow of candlelight, they talked as he painstakingly examined wires, tubes, and intricate components. Initially, their conversations were about the war, protection of Jews, and the Italian Resistance. But with each passing night, they gradually turned their talks to personal matters—her stories about her mother and Matteo, her passion for painting, her longing for real coffee beans and sugar, and his dreams of someday turning his family's farm into a vineyard, much like the one Beppe had created. She did most of the talking, given that his eyes were locked on his radio, but it felt good to be heard and understood. And she wished that she could have more time to get to know the man who was risking his life serving behind enemy lines.

Lilla had instructed her to stay away from Florence, and that Don Casini would deliver the forged papers—for her, Aria, and Eliseo—to the vineyard. But there had been no sign of the priest, nor were there any messages delivered to her or Beppe by other Catholic volunteers of DELASEM to inform of a delay. Also, none of Carmine's partisans had shown up on the farm.

"Something is wrong," she'd said to Beppe as they carried food and water to the wine cellar. "Don Casini should have arrived by now with their travel documents. I need to go to Firenze to check on things."

Beppe had urged her to be patient. But with much discussion, she convinced her father that it was best for her to go to Florence. Also, she'd persuaded her father that *she*—upon her return from the city—would take Tazio to Carmine in the remote hills, rather than wait for a member of his group to arrive at their farm. However, Gianna had not told Beppe that her identification papers were stolen on the day of the air raid on Florence. She hated keeping secrets from her father, but she knew he would never agree to her taking the risk of encountering a German checkpoint without identification.

After I get my papers and take Tazio to the partisans, she thought, steering her bicycle, *I'll tell him what happened.*

Gianna crossed the Ponte Santa Trinita and entered the city. To limit the risk of checkpoints, she took a less traveled route, avoiding areas of Florence that suffered damage in the air raid. The streets were void of pedestrians, except for two gray-haired men who were emptying trash cans into the back of a horse-drawn garbage wagon. A sulfuric smell, reminiscent of rotted cabbage, penetrated her nostrils. She turned on to an adjacent street, leaving the stench behind. But fifteen meters ahead, a door to a hotel opened and a German officer stepped onto the sidewalk.

Her skin turned cold but she continued to pedal her bicycle. *Stay calm*, she thought, gripping the handlebars. *Everything will be all right.*

The officer, a tall man in his thirties with light brown hair and polished jackboots, placed a cigarette to his lips and locked eyes on Gianna.

She forced a smile and confidently coasted near the officer. "*Guten Morgen.*"

The officer, appearing pleased to hear his native language, took a drag on his cigarette. "*Guten Morgen.*"

Gianna, her heart thudding against her rib cage, pedaled by the officer and turned on to a nearby street. She loosened her grip on her handlebars and sucked in air.

Minutes later, she reached the alleyway of the DELASEM underground and got off her bicycle. On shaky legs, she scanned the area and knocked on the door. Seconds passed and the lock clicked. The door opened, revealing Lilla, and she darted inside with her bicycle.

"You're not supposed to be here," Lilla said, bolting the door.

"I know, but it's been a week and Don Casini did not—" Gianna paused, getting a better look at friend. Her black hair was oily and disheveled, and dark circles surrounded her eyes, giving her the appearance of someone who hadn't slept in days.

"I know," Lilla said. "I look terrible."

"No—you're exhausted." Gianna placed a hand on Lilla's shoulder. "Is everything all right?"

"No." Lilla pushed strands of hair from her face. "Don Casini thinks he might be under surveillance by the Gestapo, and we're working nonstop to get Jews out of the city."

"*Oh, Dio.*" Gianna lowered her hand from Lilla's shoulder.

"Don Casini delayed delivering your papers because he was worried that he might lead the Gestapo to you and Beppe."

Gianna clasped her arms. "Is he here?"

"No," Lilla said. "He's working to aid refuge seekers from his church, but he remains in communication with Rabbi Nathan by leaving messages at a dead drop. He is being cautious to prevent drawing attention to our location."

Tension spread through Gianna's shoulders. "You need to leave."

"I will—after we provide more Jews in the city with forged papers, and get them into a rural safehouse."

"How many?"

"Several hundred," Lilla said. "We don't have an exact number, and many have refused to abandon their homes."

Gianna slumped her shoulders.

A door squeaked open and Rabbi Nathan, his clothes wrinkled and his face unshaven, emerged from a room and approached them. "*Buongiorno.* I thought I heard your voice, Gianna."

"*Buongiorno,*" Gianna said. "Lilla told me what was happening."

He rubbed sand from his eyes. "We have far too many Jews who are hiding in Firenze, and we're working to get them out. Is there any chance that you and Beppe can make room for more people?"

"Of course," she said. "We'll find a way to accommodate them."

"I thought you only have space to hide three," Lilla said, "and you still have Aria and Eliseo in your care."

"Actually," Gianna said, "we have three people who are sheltering at the vineyard."

Lilla furrowed her brows.

"Who is the third?" Nathan asked.

She told them about Tazio, an OSS agent who parachuted into Tuscany on a mission to aid the Italian Resistance and prepare for the Allied fight to liberate Italy. Also, she informed them of her plans to take Tazio to Carmine, rather than wait for one of his men to arrive at the vineyard.

Lilla's eyes welled with tears of happiness. "It's really happening—the Allies are coming to free us."

Gianna nodded.

Nathan ran a hand through his hair and smiled. "We just need to hold on a little while longer."

Gianna shifted her weight. "Work on plans to smuggle three more people to our vineyard. Tonight, I'll take Aria and Eliseo with me and Tazio on our journey to Carmine—it'll free up the space we need. Also, I'll ask Beppe to construct more hiding places in the wine cellar."

"Are you sure?" Nathan asked.

"I am."

"*Grazie*," he said. "Please pass along my gratitude to Beppe. I'll get my toolbox and take apart your bicycle."

"I'll get the papers." Lilla turned to Gianna. "Come with me."

Gianna followed Lilla up the stairs and into her workroom, its windows boarded shut and the air filled with a smell of glue and chemicals. The dull glow of a lantern illuminated the dank space that contained the long table with stacks of what appeared to be forged passports and identification papers.

Lilla retrieved a small stack of documents and gave them to Gianna. "Those are for you, Aria, and Eliseo."

Gianna sifted through the papers. "They are perfect. Mine looks better than the original."

"I'm glad you think so," Lilla said. "There is something else

I want to show you." She pulled a passport from her table and handed it to Gianna.

She opened the document and her eyes widened at the sight of a partially completed Swiss passport with a picture of Lilla. "*Madonna!*"

"Is your offer for me to pose as your cousin still good?"

"Of course," Gianna said.

Lilla smiled. "In a month or two—after we finish our work in Firenze—I'll come to your vineyard to stay until Italy is liberated, assuming it's all right with Beppe."

A wave of hope and happiness washed over Gianna. She wrapped her arms around her friend and squeezed her tight.

An hour after leaving Florence, Gianna arrived at the vineyard. She leaned her bicycle, its frame containing identification papers for Aria and Eliseo, against the front of the house and went inside. "*Papà!*"

"Up here!" Beppe called.

Gianna scaled the stairs to the landing and discovered that the retractable ladder to the attic was lowered. She climbed a few rungs and poked her head inside. Her eyes widened at the sight of Beppe, who was sitting on a crate next to Tazio and his radio. "*Mamma mia!* How did you get up here?"

"Tazio helped me," Beppe said, his cheeks flush with enthusiasm.

Tazio looked at Gianna. "Your father rapped on the side of the radio and I heard a flash of static over my headphones. It is still not working, but at least we know it might be fixable."

"*Stupendo!*" Gianna said.

"I'm a genius." Beppe nudged Tazio and grinned. "Italian ingenuity, my boy."

Tazio chuckled.

Beppe looked at Gianna. "We've been working for a short while. How about we meet you in the wine cellar in thirty minutes?"

"The radio work will have to wait," Gianna said. "I have news to tell you."

"Good, I hope," Beppe said.

She shook her head.

The joy drained from Beppe's face. With the aid of Tazio and Gianna, he labored his way down the retractable ladder and hobbled to the living room with his cane in hand.

"Tell me," Beppe said, slumping into his chair.

She sat next to Tazio on the sofa and, for the next several minutes, she told them about Don Casini's suspicion of being trailed by the Gestapo and Rabbi Nathan's request to hide more Jews at their vineyard.

"I told Nathan that we could accommodate more people," Gianna said, "and that I would ask you to build more hiding space in the wine cellar."

Beppe nodded. "I'll get started on the construction."

She leaned forward in her seat and clasped her hands. "I also told him to immediately send three more people."

"But it'll take time for me to build another hiding shelter," Beppe said. "And we don't know when a partisan will arrive to take Aria and Eliseo to the north."

Gianna swallowed. "I told Nathan that I would take them away with me and Tazio tonight."

Beppe rubbed his jaw. "It's already a dangerous trek for two people, especially with Tazio lugging a heavy pack with equipment. The journey to the partisans will be slower and more precarious with a pregnant woman and a five-year-old child. It will be safer and faster to travel in small numbers. When you and Tazio reach Carmine, request him to deploy one of his men to retrieve Aria and Eliseo."

"We can't wait any longer for a partisan to arrive to guide them away," Gianna said. "If the Gestapo is stalking Don Casini, it's because they think he is aiding Jews. Things are getting worse by the day in Firenze. We need to get as many refuge seekers out of the city as we can—as soon as we can."

Beppe shifted in his seat.

"We can do it," Tazio said. "We'll get them safely to Carmine."

Gianna glanced at Tazio.

"My leg is fine," Tazio said, placing a hand on his knee. "Even with the heavy weight of my rucksack, I can help Aria and Eliseo with their hike. Also, taking them with us will save time by not having to deploy one of Carmine's partisans to travel here."

"Please, Papà," Gianna said, lowering her voice. "Doing this might save lives."

Beppe paused, twisting his wedding band on his finger.

He's wondering what Mamma would think about this. Gianna, as if by reflex, clasped her mother's engraved wedding band on her neck chain.

Beppe drew a deep breath. "*Va bene.*"

Gianna's shoulder muscles eased.

Beppe clasped his cane and rose from his seat. "Does your bicycle contain their travel papers?"

"*Sì*," she said.

"I'll dismantle it and set aside the documents for your trip," Beppe said. "I will let Aria and Eliseo know the plans, and I'll prepare dinner—I want everyone to have a proper sit-down meal before they go."

"That would be lovely," Gianna said.

"Get some sleep. You have a long trek after the sun goes down." Beppe hobbled out of the living room and left the house.

Gianna followed Tazio up the stairs to the entrance to the attic. As he clasped the ladder, she approached him and said, "*Grazie.*"

"For what?"

"For supporting my idea to bring Aria and Eliseo."

"*Prego*, but even if I had remained silent, I think Beppe would have eventually agreed for you to bring them with us." He looked into her eyes. "He believes in you—and he trusts your judgment. He's also a father who wants to protect his daughter, and sometimes it takes a bit of time for one's heart to agree with one's brain."

"True." She placed her hand next to his on a rung of the ladder. "Either way, I appreciate what you did."

He nodded. "Get some rest."

"I will." She glanced at the attic. "We're going to be hiking all night. Don't work too long on your radio."

"I won't."

Gianna slipped her hand from the rung and watched him ascend into the attic, pull up the ladder, and disappear. She went to her room, where she closed the blackout curtains and slipped off her shoes and clothing, except for her undergarments. On her bed, she peered through the darkness, and thoughts of the journey weighed heavy on her conscience. *Their lives are in my hands. They're relying on me to guide them to the partisans, all the while avoiding Blackshirts and German soldiers.* Unable to sleep, she rehearsed the passage and alternative routes, over and over, in her head.

Chapter 11

Strada in Chianti—October 2, 1943

Shortly before sunset, Gianna sat down at the table with Tazio, Beppe, Aria, and Eliseo. In front of them were Gianna's mother's best plates and silverware, which Beppe had retrieved from a storage cabinet. In the center of the table was a platter with gray bread, olives, grapes, cheese, and a bottle of Chianti.

Beppe crossed himself, poured wine into his glass, and raised it. "To freedom. *Buon appetito.*"

They spoke little during their meal, especially Aria, who frequently glanced at the curtain-covered window, as if she were apprehensive about being away from the haven in the wine cellar. Despite Aria's discomfort, Gianna was glad that Beppe had insisted that everyone come together for dinner. It was unusual for her father to take the unnecessary risk of having their guests congregate in the kitchen, given that there wasn't enough hiding space in the house. But she could tell, by the smile on his face as he helped Eliseo with selecting the best olives, that it was important to him that everyone enjoy a final meal together.

They finished dinner, rose from the table, and gathered jackets and supplies. Gianna put on Beppe's canvas backpack, which contained her identification documents, food, and water, and Tazio slid on his rucksack, which contained his equipment.

"How's the leg?" Gianna asked.

Tazio bent his knees, testing the weight of his pack. "*Bene.*"

Aria put down a bag that was stuffed with blankets and kissed Beppe on both cheeks. "I'll never forget what you did for us."

Beppe nodded. "You and your children will have a beautiful life."

The woman placed a hand on her round pregnant belly, and tears welled up in her eyes.

Beppe turned to Eliseo, who was clinging to his mother's side. "I have a gift for you."

The boy perked up his head.

Beppe reached into his trouser pocket and removed an object that looked like a tarnished pocket watch until he opened the cover. "This compass kept me safe during the last war, and now it will do the same for you and your *mamma*. It has magnetic power to guide one in the right direction."

"How?" the boy asked.

Beppe showed him the needle that always pointed north, and then placed the compass in the boy's palm and cupped his hands over his. "Can you feel its magic?"

Eliseo's eyes brightened. "*Sì*. I can feel it."

Beppe smiled. "You're a brave boy, Eliseo."

"*Grazie*," the boy said.

Gianna blinked her eyes to fight back tears.

Beppe approached Tazio and shook his hand. "Good luck to you."

"You too," Tazio said. "I hope I can someday repay you and Gianna for your help."

"Your service to liberate Italy is more than enough." Beppe glanced at his daughter. "It's unfortunate that you'll miss our harvest—it's a glorious time of year. After the war, how about you return to our vineyard for a grape harvest?"

"It would be an honor," Tazio said.

Beppe turned to Gianna and held out his arms.

She leaned in and hugged him.

"Catch the moment," Beppe whispered.

Her eyes welled with tears. "Catch the moment," she said, repeating his affirmation.

Gianna released her father. She gathered her composure and gave brief instructions to her group, which focused on walking softly and keeping silent. She led them outside and, as they began to leave, she glanced over her shoulder to find Beppe standing in the doorway. A deep resolve stirred inside her. She gave a final wave goodbye and walked into the night.

The temperature was cool, and the evening sky was covered by thick clouds that masked the moon and stars. Rather than make their way down the dirt lane to the road, she led them in a northwest direction through the vineyard, which was filled with the chirp of autumn crickets. Aria and Eliseo walked hand in hand behind Gianna, and Tazio followed in the rear of the group. They traveled along rows of grapevines as their eyes gradually grew accustomed to the lack of light. The vineyard gave way to an orchard of ancient olive trees, their trunks split and hollow due to the passing of the years. A childhood memory of climbing the branches with Matteo flashed in her head. *God, I miss him.* She set aside her grief and led the group into a forest. Its air was laced with a spicy scent of umbrella pines.

Under normal circumstances, it was a three-hour bicycle ride to reach the base of the hills that led to Carmine's remote forest hideaway. Initially, she calculated that an alternative path on foot—which avoided villages and most of the roads—would take approximately ten hours. But that estimate did not include taking along a five-year-old-boy and a woman who was six months pregnant. And she had little doubt that the journey would take two nights, rather than one.

We'll need to be concealed during the day, she thought, weaving around a briar patch. She made mental notes of potential hiding places along the route, but her decision would depend on the distance they could travel under the cover of darkness.

Two hours into the trek, Aria's breathing turned heavy. She began to drag her feet, and she tripped and nearly fell over a tree root. Eliseo slipped away from his mother, ran to Gianna, and tugged on her jacket.

Gianna turned to find Tazio helping the woman to sit down on a moss-covered log. She approached her and whispered, "Are you having labor pain?"

"No." Aria took in deep inhales. "Out of breath."

"We'll rest a bit," Gianna said, feeling relieved. She took the woman's bag that contained wool blankets.

Tazio gestured for Gianna to add the bag to his rucksack.

"I got it," Gianna said quietly. "Your load is already heavy." She looped the straps of the bag over her shoulder and they silently waited for Aria to catch her breath.

Soon, they resumed their hike and made their way through the pines, which eventually opened to a dirt road that ran perpendicular to their path. Gianna stopped, scanned the area, and detected no lights or movement. She waited for the rest of the group to catch up to her, then motioned for them to cross the road.

Tazio helped Aria to step over a drainage ditch, while Gianna and Eliseo jumped over the narrow channel. They slogged forward and, as they reached the middle of the road, the ground vibrated beneath their feet.

Gianna's eyes widened.

"What's happening?" Aria breathed.

Gianna, her adrenaline peaking, peered through the darkness. A clacking of steel plates emanated from up the road.

"Tanks," Tazio said.

Aria gasped.

They scurried across the road, pushed through thorn bushes—pricking their skins and clothing—and crouched in a thicket.

Gianna, her heart racing, peeked through a gap in the underbrush, and her eyes locked on the silhouette of a German Panzer, identifiable by its long gun barrel. Within seconds, a convoy of tanks emerged from the darkness and clambered over the dirt road. She hoped that the tanks would pass them by and continue their route. But as the lead tank neared their location, it came to a halt with its engine running.

Oh, Dio! Gianna's skin turned cold.

Aria wrapped an arm around Eliseo, who tightly held Beppe's compass in his hands.

The steel hatch opened and a commander—wearing a radio headset over his cap—stood and waved his arms at the approaching tanks.

Tazio looked at Aria and Eliseo and held a finger to his lips, and the group silently hunkered low to the ground.

The tank commander removed his headset, raised himself out of the turret, and climbed down from the tank.

Petrol fumes, omitted from the Panzer's exhaust, penetrated Gianna's nostrils and she fought back the urge to cough. Every fiber in her body wanted to flee, but she held her ground.

The commander removed a flashlight from his jacket, walked in front of the tank, and shined a light over the road.

A soldier, wearing a side cap, rose up from inside the tank turret and pointed. "*Was ist das?*"

Fear flooded Gianna as the commander reached down and picked up a gray wool blanket. *Oh, no! It fell out of my bag!*

The commander held up the woolen material to his comrade. "*Wolldecke.*" He dropped the blanket, slipped a pistol from a leather holster, and—using his other hand—shined the flashlight over the perimeter.

A beam passed over the underbrush, flashing light near Gianna. She held her breath and silently prayed that he didn't see them.

The German scanned over woodland on both sides of the road and put away his weapon. He turned off the flashlight, climbed back into the turret, and gave a wave to the tanks behind him. Engines growled and the convoy of tanks clambered down the road.

Gianna and her group remained in the underbrush until the sound of the tanks disappeared. They crawled from the bushes and Gianna returned to the road. With trembling hands, she picked up the blanket—crushed and torn by steel tank treads—and placed it inside her bag.

They hiked for several hours, stopping twice to drink water and allow Aria to catch her breath. Kilometer by kilometer, Gianna guided them through forests and fields, and across streams, and she avoided routes that would take them through hamlets. The winding path greatly increased the distance that they needed to cover. But to Gianna, the only thing that mattered was to get them to the partisans without being detected.

An hour or so before sunrise, they entered an abandoned hazelnut grove, and a light rain began to sprinkle. The wind gusts grew, and then heavy rain marched through the trees, the drops striking the leaves sounding like a rolling crescendo on a snare drum.

Tazio, his back hunched from the weight of his rucksack, slogged his way next to Gianna. "It'll be daylight soon. Do you have someplace in mind to hunker down?"

Gianna, cold and tired, wiped rain from her face. Her mind toiled with options, most of them too far away to reach before dawn. She peered at the silhouette of a distant hill against the night sky, and an adolescent memory of exploring a cave flashed in her head. "There is an abandoned iron mine up there," she said, pointing.

"That's a long way off." Tazio glanced at Aria and Eliseo, their heads drooped and feet dragging. "Do you think we can make it there before sunup?"

"We'll have to." She adjusted her bag and backpack, and pushed ahead.

She led the group out of the deserted orchard and up a narrow trail, bordered by shrubs and pines. The temperature dropped, and heavy raindrops pelted their bodies, stinging their exposed skin and saturating their clothes. Aria and Eliseo labored to walk, and she and Tazio helped them to scale the steep slopes, covered in mud and loose scree. They trudged their way toward the summit, and the dark sky gradually turned to twilight.

Gianna paused at a large rock, scanned the hillside, and her eyes locked on a dense grouping of crooked pines. Her heart rate quickened. "I think I see it."

She led them to the trees, where they worked their way through wet branches to discover an ancient timber-frame opening in the hillside. They shuffled inside and ducked under a partially collapsed ceiling beam, to reach an area with a toppled minecart and a narrow set of rusted steel tracks that led underground.

Tazio slipped off his rucksack and helped Aria and Eliseo to remove their wet coats.

Gianna put down her bag and backpack. She retrieved the blankets, setting aside the top one that was soaked with rainwater, and wrapped them around Aria and Eliseo.

"You've given us all the blankets," Aria said, her teeth chattering. "Keep some for yourself."

"I'm not cold," Gianna lied.

Tazio wiped rain from his face and looked at the boy, bundled next to his mother. "Well done, Eliseo. I'm proud of you."

The boy held out his hand with Beppe's compass. "Signor Conti was right. It kept us safe."

Gianna smiled and dried the boy's hair with a corner of the blanket.

They each ate a hunk of bread and consumed water from a canteen, which they passed back and forth. Immediately after the meal, Aria and Eliseo curled together between blankets and fell asleep.

"I'll keep lookout," Tazio said to Gianna. "You should get some rest."

"I don't think I can sleep," she said. "I'll join you."

They went to the entrance of the mine, which was concealed by the pines. They removed their wet jackets and placed them over low-hanging branches to dry. The rain tapered off and a chorus of sparrows filled the morning air. They sat—shoulder to shoulder—on a thick layer of pine needles with their backs against a tree, and they gazed through the branches as the sun slowly rose on the horizon.

"You're an ace of a hiker," Tazio said, breaking the silence.

"*Grazie*, but I almost got us killed by dropping that blanket. That German tank commander stopped his convoy because he spotted it in the road."

"It was an accident, and it doesn't matter now. We're alive—and you got us to this shelter."

She nodded, despite a pang of regret in her gut.

He glanced at the timber beams that framed the entrance to the mine. "I'm glad that Aria and Eliseo have a dry place to rest. How did you know about this place?"

"I came here as a teenager with Matteo and some of his friends. He learned about it from speaking with a man, whose grandfather worked here as a miner before it closed." She peered up through the branches that blocked most of the sky. "Matteo's friends didn't want a girl to tag along with their group of boys, but he told them that he wouldn't reveal the location of the mine unless he brought his sister along for the trip. As far back as I can remember, he was always sticking up for me."

"It sounds like Matteo was a great brother," Tazio said.

"He was."

Tazio adjusted his back against the tree. "I didn't get a chance to talk with you about Lilla before we left. How is she?"

That's kind of you to ask about her. Gianna smoothed her damp skirt that clung to her legs. "She's tired, but her spirit remains strong. After more Jews are safely out of the city, she is going to create a fake identity for herself and come to the vineyard to stay with me and Beppe. It'll be safer for her to continue her work outside of Firenze."

"That's wonderful news," Tazio said. "I get the impression that you and Lilla make a good team."

"We do. She's like a sister to me. Someday, I'll introduce you to her."

"I'd like that."

She looked at him, his hair mussed and wet. "I appreciate your inquisitiveness, but I feel like I've told you a lot about me, and you've shared little about yourself."

He rubbed the back of his neck. "Okay. What would you like to know?"

"Tell me about your family."

He drew a deep breath. "My parents are from Napoli. My mother's name is Concetta, and my dad's name is Antonino."

"How'd they meet?"

"During the Great War, my mom was a nurse at a field hospital. She dressed a wound on my father's shoulder." He clasped a handful of pine needles and sprinkled them over the ground. "My dad said it was love at first sight."

She smiled. "What does your mom have to say about this?"

"She claims that it was the letters that he wrote her, after leaving the hospital, that won her heart."

She tucked strands of loose hair behind her ear. "That's sweet."

"Soon after the war ended, they married and emigrated to the United States to begin their life on an orchard. Years later, they had me."

"Any brothers or sisters?"

"I wish," he said. "I'm an only child. My mom had a difficult time conceiving, and she had several miscarriages before she had me."

"I'm sorry."

"*Grazie*," he said. "I think my parents would have loved to have more children."

"Do you have any family left in Napoli?"

He shook his head.

"Will you go back to California after the war?"

"*Sì*," he said. "Before I joined the service, I obtained a degree in chemistry from Whittier College. I've always had a fascination with oenology."

She scratched her head. "What is oenolo—"

"Oenology. It's the science and study of wine."

"In Tuscany, we call it the art of winemaking."

He smiled. "I like your term better. Someday, I'd like to make a go of turning my parents' orchard into a vineyard with a winery."

"Beppe would have loved for Matteo to someday run our vineyard. I bet your parents will be happy to have you carry on the family business."

"I hope so."

A wind blew through the trees and over her damp clothes. She shivered and clasped her arms.

He blew on his hands. "I think our jackets are too wet to keep us warm. Would it be all right if I put my arm around you?"

"*Va bene.*" She felt his arm wrap around her and she leaned against him. A wave of warmth and comfort washed over her.

"Better?"

"*Sì.*" She raised her eyes. "What would your Californian girlfriend think about you keeping a Tuscan woman warm?"

He blushed. "I don't have a girlfriend."

"Fiancée?"

He chuckled. "There is no one like that. I've dated a little in college, but nothing serious." He adjusted his arm around her shoulder. "Do you have anyone special?"

"No," she said. "Before the war, I was briefly seeing a man named Fedele when I began studies at the University of Firenze, but it didn't work out."

"What happened?"

"He ended our relationship when he learned that I wanted nothing to do with Mussolini and his Blackshirts. He told me it was blasphemous to speak badly about *Il Duce*, and that I was a fool for not supporting the regime." She drew a deep breath and exhaled. "A few months later, Fedele married a woman whose family was loyal to Mussolini, and he dropped out of his studies and joined the Italian Army."

"Gosh. Were you upset?"

"Not for long," she said. "We were quite different people. I joined DELASEM because I despise fascism and want to protect people from Italian and German racial laws. Someday, I want to be with a man who is willing to fight crimes against humanity and place the needs of a nation ahead of his own." She tilted her head and her eyes met his. "Does that sound like too much to ask?"

"Not at all," he said. "I like your moxie."

"What's that mean?"

"I admire your character and courage."

She smiled.

For an hour, they talked about their families, Gianna's passion for art, and his ardor for viticulture. For the first time since the war erupted, she felt at peace. Eventually, they grew tired and Gianna rested her head on his shoulder. Her body relaxed as she took in his warmth. *It feels good to be with you, but we both have our duties to fulfill.* She closed her eyes and tried to forget about their divergent paths. She gradually drifted to sleep, but hours later she was jolted awake by the sound of gunshots.

Chapter 12

Tuscany—October 3, 1943

Gunfire echoed over the hillside and roused Tazio from his slumber beneath a pine tree. He shot up, bumping his head on a branch, and helped Gianna to sit up.

"They're close," he said, crouched next to her.

"German?" she asked.

"Most likely."

Tazio grabbed his jacket and removed his pistol. Together, they crept to the edge of the pines and scanned the area from their high-ground vantage point. The morning sky was strewn with puffy, cottonlike clouds, and below them was a sparse forest whose foliage was composed of evergreens and oaks.

"Do you see anything?" Tazio whispered.

"No," she said.

A crack of gunfire exploded, and a flock of starlings flew from trees a few hundred meters away.

Tazio's eyes narrowed in on movement—two German soldiers, with shell-like helmets and raised rifles, dashing through the woodland. Approximately fifty meters ahead of them, a man was struggling to run away from them.

"There," Tazio said, pointing.

"*Oh, Dio*," Gianna breathed. "They're catching up to him."

Aria, her face etched with fright, emerged from the iron ore mine with Eliseo, who was holding Beppe's compass.

"Should we flee or hide?" Aria asked.

"Hide," Tazio said. "I'll let you know when it's safe to come out."

The woman wrapped an arm around her child, and they disappeared into the mine.

Tazio checked the ammunition in his pistol and looked at Gianna. "Go with them."

Her eyes widened. "You can't go down there."

The crack of gunfire resounded through the valley.

Tazio clasped her hand. "They are hunting him down like an animal. I must do something."

She squeezed his fingers. "It's too dangerous."

He peered down to the hollow, and the need to make a choice simmered inside him. Before he changed his mind, he slipped away from Gianna and scurried down the hillside.

His heartbeat thudded inside his chest as he quietly clambered down an embankment, all the while trying to estimate when and where he would intersect with the German soldiers. He slipped on loose stones and nearly fell, but he regained his balance and scrambled down the treed slope.

Gunshots fired, closer and louder.

Hairs rose on the back of his neck. The ground leveled off, and he stopped where he hoped would be the right location to head off the soldiers. He crouched behind an oak tree and silently took deep breaths.

"*Nein, er ist da drüben!*" a guttural voice shouted.

Tazio, his hand trembling, raised his pistol and peeked around the tree.

Gasps and snapping of branches grew.

Tazio, using both hands to steady his weapon, aimed toward the sound of approaching footsteps. His pulse pounded inside his eardrums.

A young man—who was no more than seventeen or eighteen

years of age and wearing civilian clothing and a backpack—broke through bushes and rounded a tree. His eyes locked on Tazio's pistol and fear flooded his eyes. He tried to change course, but he tripped on broken branches and tumbled to the ground. He got to his knees and held up his hands.

Tazio motioned with his weapon to a thicket, and he pressed his back against the tree, out of sight of the approaching Germans.

The young man, gasping for air, got to his feet and hid in the undergrowth.

Guns fired and bullets struck a nearby tree.

This is it. Tazio placed his finger on the trigger. *It's them or me.*

The footsteps of the soldiers grew.

Tazio fought back his urge to fire his weapon and run. A bead of cold sweat trickled down his back.

"*Schnell!*"

In one swift motion, Tazio stepped out from the tree, aimed, and fired.

Twenty meters away, the bullet struck the lead soldier's shoulder. He screamed in pain, dropped his rifle, and fell behind bushes.

The second soldier sprinted for cover. "Heinrich!"

Tazio fired two shots at the fleeing soldier and missed.

The unscathed German dived next to a large oak, ten meters away from his comrade. He raised his rifle and fired.

A bullet whizzed by Tazio's cheek. He dropped to his stomach and discharged rounds, forcing the uninjured German to hide behind the tree.

"*Hilfe!*" the injured soldier yawped. "*Mich hat's erwischt!*"

"*Festhalten!*" his comrade called.

Tazio scrambled behind the tree trunk. His mind raced, trying to recall how many bullets remained in the eight-round detachable box magazine of his pistol. *Two rounds left—maybe one.*

The German leaned out from his cover and fired.

The bullet struck the side of Tazio's tree, scattering bits of bark into his hair. He inched over and wished that he'd taken more ammunition from the parachute containers.

A crunching of dry leaves emanated from the bushes.

The injured one is crawling to his partner, Tazio thought. His emotions surged like electrified wire, and he sucked in air to steady his nerves. *They're not carrying grenades, otherwise I'd be dead by now.*

Gunshots rang out, battering Tazio's tree with bullets. He returned fire, then curled into a fetal position, trying to make his body smaller. The barrage of gunfire ceased, and the ringing in his ears was replaced by the sound of footsteps and rattling rifles.

Tazio, his adrenaline at maximum, rolled away from the tree and discovered the soldiers—one of them pressing a hand to his wounded shoulder and dragging his rifle—fleeing through the woodland. He raised his pistol but the Germans disappeared behind a cluster of pines. The crunching of boots gradually faded and disappeared. His finger eased from the trigger. He let out a huge breath, stood on shaky legs, and checked the magazine of his weapon to find it empty.

Tazio, feeling like he'd come within a whisker of death, wiped sweat from his brow. He gathered his composure, slipped his pistol between his belt and pants, and said, "They're gone. It's safe to come out."

The young man emerged from the thicket and cautiously approached Tazio. He was tall and skinny with a boyish face, except for the peach fuzz on his upper lip, and his well-worn trousers were two sizes too short for his long legs.

"*Grazie*," the young man said.

"I'm Tazio." He extended his arm.

"Sante." The man shook his hand. "Resistance?"

Tazio nodded. "Why were they trying to kill you?"

Sante clasped a strap to his backpack. "I stumbled across them while I was trying to deliver food and supplies to partisans who are hiding in the hills. I ran and they started shooting at me." He glanced in the direction that the soldiers had fled. "I think they are a scout unit."

"What's in your backpack?" Tazio asked.

"Bread, salami, a few kitchen knives, and three boxes of ammunition."

Tazio placed a hand on his pistol. "Do you have any thirty-two-caliber cartridges?"

"No, only shotgun shells for hunting pheasant."

Good God—they are fighting a war with cutlery and birdshot. Tazio ran a hand through his hair.

"Your voice is different," Sante said. "Are you from the north?"

Tazio shook his head. "The west—United States."

The young man's jaw dropped open.

The sound of footsteps came from the hillside, and Gianna emerged from the trees and ran to Tazio. "Are you all right?"

"I am." He felt the urge to hug her but harbored his emotions. "This is Sante," he said, gesturing to him.

She approached the young man. "I'm Gianna. Are you hurt?"

Sante shook his head.

Gianna turned to Tazio. "From the hillside, I was able to see the soldiers run away. It's not safe to travel in daylight, but I think we should leave. Another Wehrmacht patrol will likely be back to scour the area."

"I agree." Tazio looked at Sante. "There are two refugees, a mother and son, who are with us. We are on our way to find a partisan leader named Carmine. Do you know him?"

"I do," Sante said. "That is where I'm going. His camp is a two-hour hike through the forest."

Gianna furrowed her brow. "His base was much farther away. Did he move?"

"*Sì*, three days ago," Sante said. "The Germans infiltrated the area near his last camp, and he'll likely relocate his men again when he hears about my encounter with a German scout unit." He adjusted a strap on his back pack. "I'll take you to him."

Gianna looked at Tazio. "Good with you?"

Tazio nodded.

"I'll get Aria and Eliseo." She turned and ascended the hill.

Minutes later, Sante led the group through the forest. Unlike Gianna, who provided breaks for Aria and her son to rest, the young man paid little heed to his followers. He swiftly trekked ahead, allowing space to grow between him and the rest of the group. Initially, Tazio thought that the young man was anxious to get away from the area of the attack. But as time passed, Sante did not stop to allow them to catch up. The young man's lack of consideration for Aria and Eliseo frustrated Tazio, which was compounded by his inability to increase his pace with his load. And he relied on Gianna, on more than one occasion, to run ahead and request Sante to slow down.

With each step, the heavy weight of Tazio's rucksack jarred his back and legs, gradually aggravating his prior knee injury. Pain radiated from under his patella, but rather than be a burden to the group, he fought back his discomfort and slogged ahead.

They traveled through the forest for nearly two hours, then waded through a shallow stream, soaking their feet and legs. They squelched along its muddy edge and veered onto what appeared to be a deer or boar trail, given the plethora of hoofprints that ran up a steep wooded incline. As they ascended the trail, the vegetation turned thick, and a dense tree canopy blocked the sky. To Tazio, the place looked like an ancient woodland of old-growth trees that had never been logged. He clambered up the slope, sending a pang through his knee. He gritted his teeth and pressed ahead.

The sound of a shotgun racking broke the silent air.

Tazio and the group froze.

"Don't shoot!" the young man called out. "It's Sante!"

A gray-haired partisan, who was holding a double-barreled shotgun, emerged from behind a tree and scowled at Sante. "What are they doing here?"

"They've come to speak with Carmine." Sante pointed. "That one is American—he defended me from a German scout unit."

"I'm Tazio." He shifted his weight away from his aching knee. "I'm an intelligence agent deployed here to aid the Resistance."

The partisan glanced at the women and the boy. "What about them?"

Gianna stepped forward. "I'm Gianna from the Conti vineyard in Strada in Chianti. Aria and Eliseo are Jewish refugees."

The partisan eyed Gianna. "Are you Matteo's sister?"

"*Sì*."

The lines on the partisan's face softened. He lowered his weapon and signaled for them to climb ahead.

Tazio exhaled. He adjusted his rucksack, and he and the others continued their ascent.

At the top of the hill, they walked along a path of thigh-high weeds to reach what looked like an old hunting shack with a sagged roof that was covered with moss. Adjacent to the dwelling was a small shaded clearing with eight men—ranging from teenagers to old men—who were sitting in a circle on an assortment of large stones and logs.

The eyes of the partisans fell upon the approaching group, and a stocky, broad-shouldered man with a gray beard and mustache rose from his seat.

"Carmine," Sante said, shuffling ahead to the bearded man. "These people are here to see you. I know we are not supposed to bring outsiders, but the man is American, and he defended me from a German scout unit and—"

Carmine placed a hand on the young man's shoulder. "It's all right. I know this woman." He approached Gianna and kissed her on both cheeks.

Sante lowered his chin and slipped his hands into his pockets.

"It's dangerous to come here," Carmine said. "You should have waited for one of my men to come to the vineyard."

"We couldn't wait," Gianna said. She put down a bag of blankets and introduced him to Aria, Eliseo, and Tazio.

"So, you're an American," Carmine said, facing him.

"I am." Tazio removed his rucksack and shook his hand. "My partner and I were parachuted into Tuscany to aid the Resistance."

"Where is your partner?"

An image of Frank—forced by Wehrmacht soldiers into a Kübelwagen—flashed in Tazio's head. "Captured."

"I'm sorry." Carmine turned to Sante. "I'm going inside to speak with Tazio and Gianna. Introduce Aria and Eliseo to the men, and get them something to eat."

"But I need to tell you about the location of the German scout unit," Sante said.

"We'll talk later," Carmine said.

Sante, appearing disappointed, nodded and gave a wave to Aria and Eliseo to follow him.

Tazio gathered his rucksack and joined Carmine and Gianna inside the shack. The space was small and devoid of furnishing, save an unlit cast-iron stove that was surrounded by a handful of empty wine crates. It had one window, which was covered in dust and cobwebs, and a faint smell of charred wood and burned tobacco filled the air.

"Have a seat," Carmine said, gesturing to the wine crates.

Tazio set aside his pack and sat next to Gianna. He stretched his leg and winced.

"Did you reinjure your knee?" Gianna asked.

"No," Tazio said, not wanting to alarm her. "It's a little sore."

Carmine scooched a crate in front of them, and sat and clasped his hands. "Tell me why you're here."

"You first," Gianna said, looking at Tazio.

For several minutes, he told Carmine about the Allies fighting their way north from the southern tip of Italy, his role as an OSS agent, his mission to aid and organize the Resistance, the miscalculated parachute deployment that resulted in the capture of Frank and their supplies, and his broken wireless radio.

"When I'm able to get my radio to work," Tazio said, "I will send orders to air-drop armament."

Carmine scratched his beard. "Your army failed to parachute you into the right location. Why should I believe that they will be successful with getting weapons to us?"

"The Allies will not give up until the Kingdom of Italy is liberated from Hitler and his forces. The OSS will continue to send supplies at my request. If they miss the drop zone, I'll send another request." Tazio leaned forward. "You have my word—I will find a way to get us the supplies we need to fight."

Carmine removed a cigarette from his pocket and lit it. "To make sure we understand each other—these are my men, and they will only take orders from me."

"Of course," Tazio said. "But to be clear, I will be responsible for their training, and the planning and execution of sabotage missions."

"They have been trained by me," Carmine said, his voice defensive. He took a drag and blew smoke from his nose. "I served on the front line in the Great War, and so did several of my men. We know how to fight."

Tazio's shoulder muscles tensed. "With all due respect, you and your men will need training in modern warfare and weaponry."

Carmine flicked ash from his cigarette. "I've heard enough."

"Please, Carmine," Gianna said. "Hear him out."

Carmine paused, rolling his cigarette between his fingers. "*Va bene.*"

Tazio drew a deep breath. "The parachute containers will contain a multitude of weaponry, including machine guns, combat rifles, semiautomatic pistols, grenades, and plastic explosives. I will instruct you and your men on their use, and I will provide guerilla warfare training."

"Tell me about guerilla tactics," Carmine said.

"You and your men will become saboteurs. We will conduct missions to blow up railway lines used to transport German military supplies. We'll destroy armament depots, and we'll raid unsuspecting Wehrmacht convoys." He placed his fingers together and looked into Carmine's eyes. "Your men will no longer be relegated to small skirmishes. You'll be going on the offensive. We will wreak havoc on Hitler's military, choking the flow of military supplies to the battle lines in the south. And when the Allies break through to Tuscany, we will join them in the fight to liberate the country."

Carmine, his face stoic, looked at Gianna. "Do you trust him?"

"I do," she said.

Carmine dropped his cigarette butt on the floor and ground it with his boot. "*Va bene.*"

Thank goodness. Tazio silently let out a huge breath.

Carmine lit another cigarette and looked at Gianna. "I'm surprised to see you. Don Casini usually informs me, by leaving a message at a dead drop, when refugees need to be guided to Switzerland."

"You might not hear from him for a while," Gianna said. "I was told, by members of DELASEM, that Don Casini suspects that he's under surveillance by the Gestapo. He's keeping a low profile until things are safe."

"*Merda,*" Carmine muttered. He took a deep drag on his cigarette.

"We're moving more Jews from Firenze to our vineyard," she said. "We will not have enough room for them, so I needed to bring Aria and Eliseo to you."

Carmine nodded. "Tonight, I'll have one of the men take them to a safehouse—a convent that is a half night's journey by foot from here. They'll get a day or so of rest, and begin their journey to the border."

"*Grazie,*" Gianna said.

Tazio glanced out the window. In the clearing, Eliseo and Aria were sitting on the ground and eating bread. A strange mix of happiness and sadness flowed through him.

Carmine looked at Tazio. "One of my men—his name is Daniele—worked at a radio station before the war. Would it be all right if I ask him to inspect your radio?"

"By all means," Tazio said.

Carmine rose from his crate and turned to Gianna. "At nightfall, I'll have a partisan accompany you back to the vineyard."

"That will not be necessary," she said, remaining seated. "I'm not leaving, at least not yet."

Carmine furrowed his brow. "Why?"

"Because I want to be a partisan."

Tazio swallowed.

Carmine eased onto his seat. "You're doing your part, Gianna. You and Beppe are risking your lives to protect Jews."

"I will continue to hide refugees," she said, "but I want to do more to fight the Germans."

Conflicting emotions stirred inside Tazio. *She could be of great value to the OSS and the Resistance, but she'll be safer if she remains at the vineyard.*

"It's brave of you to want to honor Matteo by becoming a partisan." Carmine ran a hand through his hair. "I know that you are heartbroken—and I'm hurting, too. He was more than a friend to me. He was like a son."

Angst chewed at Tazio's core.

"He cared deeply for you, too, Carmine," she said. "But even if Matteo was alive, I would be having this conversation with you. You need my help."

"No, we don't," Carmine said, firmly.

"We do," Tazio said.

The air turned silent.

Gianna looked at Tazio.

"She's right," Tazio said. "We can use her as a courier—she'll be the eyes and ears of the Resistance."

Carmine shook his head.

"Unlike your men," Tazio said, "she can get through German checkpoints and travel the roads on her bicycle."

"We'll find a way to use my men," Carmine said.

"When was the last time any of your partisans walked the streets of Firenze?" Tazio asked.

Carmine shifted on his seat.

"She can smuggle supplies for us, and she can conduct reconnaissance on enemy targets—in broad daylight."

"I can do it," Gianna said.

Carmine looked at her. "This might get you killed."

"I know," she said, her voice soft. "But it's my life, and I choose to fight."

Carmine got up from his seat, went to the window, and peered outside. Curls of smoke rose from the cigarette pinched between his fingers. "*Va bene.*"

"*Grazie,*" Gianna said.

Carmine gave a subtle nod. "I'll inform the men about what we discussed, and I'll retrieve Daniele to take a look at the radio." He placed his cigarette into his mouth and left the shack.

Tazio got up and went to his rucksack, where he kneeled on his good knee. As he began to unpack his radio, Gianna approached him.

"I appreciate what you did for me," she said.

Tazio nodded.

She placed a hand on his shoulder.

His skin tingled, and a deep regret pricked at his conscience.

"I don't want you feeling responsible for this," Gianna said, as if she could sense his thoughts. "Even if Carmine had refused my request, I would not have given up on becoming a partisan."

He looked into her eyes. "I know. You don't strike me as the type of person who accepts rejection."

She smiled.

Tazio felt her hand slip away from his shoulder, and he watched her leave the shack and disappear as the door closed behind her. Alone, he felt the full weight of his actions come crashing down upon him. He had little, if any, doubt that she could be of value to the OSS and the Resistance, but selfishly he wanted to protect her. He had only known her a short while, and in that time, she had touched his heart. He removed the radio from his rucksack and began to set it up, all the while wondering if he had made a grave mistake.

Chapter 13

Tuscany—October 3, 1943

Tazio, his legs stiff from lack of circulation, rose from his seat in front of his radio and leaned his back against the wall of the shack. Near him, Daniele—a bespectacled man with a receding hairline and nimble fingers—examined its inner components.

Tazio rubbed his knee, sore and swollen. "I heard a flash of static over my headphones when Gianna's father thumped the side of the radio with his hand."

Daniele scratched the side of his head. "Then it's likely not a bad fuse."

"Do you think you can repair it?"

"*Sì.* I was a technician at the Unione Radiofonica Italiana before Mussolini took over the airwaves for his fascist propaganda." He raised his chin. "There's not a radio that I can't fix."

Tazio smiled.

The man, appearing eager to put his knowledge to work, lowered his glasses on the bridge of his nose, and resumed checking tubes, wires, and connections.

The door creaked open and Eliseo peeked his head inside the shack.

"Would you like to watch?" Tazio asked.

Eliseo nodded.

"Okay with you, Daniele?"

"*Sì*," the man said, his eyes fixated on the radio.

Tazio sat down on the floor, a few meters away from Daniele, and patted the space next to him.

The boy sat with his legs crossed and slipped his hands into his jacket pockets.

"Did you get some sleep?" Tazio asked.

The boy nodded. "What's he doing?"

"Fixing my radio."

"To listen to news and music?"

"No," Tazio said. "It's a special radio to communicate with people at my headquarters, far away from here."

Eliseo watched the man tinker with the radio, and he looked at Tazio. "How does it work?"

Tazio pointed to an external Morse key that was plugged into the radio with a rubber cable. "I will use that device to tap out a message to request supplies for the partisans who are fighting to free the country from the Germans."

Eliseo tilted his head. "How does a message fly through the air?"

"That is an excellent question." Tazio raised a finger toward the ceiling. "Radio waves. We can't see them, but they travel through the atmosphere."

"Like the power that moves the needle on Beppe's compass?"

"Something like that," Tazio said. "They both have invisible forces, but the compass works because the Earth is a huge magnet." He ruffled the boy's hair. "Someday, you'll learn all about it in school."

The boy smiled. He watched Daniele work on the radio and his joy faded. "I wish I had a magic radio."

"Like this one?" Tazio asked.

Eliseo shook his head. "One to talk with my *papà*."

Tazio swallowed.

Daniele paused, glancing at the boy.

"What would you tell him?" Tazio asked.

"That I miss him, and love him." His bottom lip quivered.

"I'm sure he knows how you feel." Tazio rubbed his eyes and placed a hand on Eliseo's shoulder. "You are a remarkable, brave boy. Your *papà* would be proud of you."

He wiped his nose with his sleeve. "Do you really think so?"

"I do," he said.

For thirty minutes, they silently watched Daniele work on the radio. The light, coming through the sole window of the shack, gradually faded. And, as the end of their time together drew near, a wave of melancholy washed over Tazio.

Footsteps emanated from outside and Gianna appeared in the doorway. "Eliseo, are you ready to go?"

The boy nodded and looked at Daniele. "*Grazie* for letting me watch."

"*Prego*," the man said. "Good luck to you."

Tazio helped Eliseo to his feet, and they followed Gianna outside where Carmine and a partisan who had a waistband of ammunition shells and a shotgun strapped over his shoulder were helping Aria to place blankets in her bag. Several of the men, who were hunkered on either rocks or logs, gathered around them.

The boy ran ahead and hugged his mother.

"You are in good hands," Carmine said to Aria. "Paride is one of my best men. He has traveled this leg of the escape route to Switzerland many times."

"*Grazie*," Aria said.

Gianna's eyes welled with tears. She approached Aria and kissed her on both cheeks. "Take good care of your baby."

"I will," Aria said, placing a hand on her round stomach. "I'll never forget you."

"Nor I." Gianna wiped her eyes and kneeled to Eliseo and hugged him.

"Do you want Beppe's compass back?" the boy asked.

Gianna shook her head. "He wanted you to have it. It's yours to keep."

"Will we see each other again?" Eliseo asked, his voice quavering.

Gianna placed a hand to his cheek. "We will. I believe that with all my heart."

Aria approached Tazio and kissed him on the cheeks. "*Lech l'shalom,*" she said, softly.

A calm smile spread over Tazio's face. "*Lech l'shalom.*"

Eliseo gave Tazio a squeeze around the waist and joined his mother. He removed Beppe's compass from his pocket, eyed the needle, and pointed. "Switzerland is that way, Mamma."

"It is," Aria said. She picked up her bag, placed an arm around her son, and they followed the partisan out of the camp.

Carmine approached Tazio. "Are you Jewish?"

"I am."

The eyes of the partisans fell upon Tazio.

Gianna placed a hand on his arm. "What were the words that you and Aria said to each other?"

"*Lech l'shalom.*"

"What does it mean?" she asked.

A swell of hope rose up inside him. "Go toward peace."

Darkness set in and Tazio and Gianna entered the shack. They placed a tarp over the shack's window to serve as a blackout curtain, and they lit candles to allow Daniele to continue tinkering with the radio. Carmine ordered his partisans—except for Sante and Daniele—to disperse from the camp and sleep in rural safehouses for the night. It was clear, to Tazio, that the partisan leader was being cautious about congregating too many of his men in one location.

Carmine, puffing on a cigarette, approached Tazio and Gianna. "We need to establish how and when we are going to communicate with Gianna."

A smell of burned tobacco penetrated Tazio's nose. "I agree."

Gianna nodded.

Carmine turned to Sante, who was seated on a crate near the unlit cast-iron stove. "Stand lookout."

The young man drooped his shoulders. "I kept watch the last time I was here. How about Daniele taking it?"

Daniele, who was using a pocket knife as a makeshift screwdriver, raised his head from the radio. "I'm busy."

"Go, Sante," Carmine said. "We need to get that radio working, and I have matters to discuss with Tazio and Gianna."

"*Va bene*," Sante said, his voice disappointed. He got up, retrieved a shotgun that was propped in the corner, and left the shack.

Daniele looked at Carmine. "That boy will not stop until he gets a seat at your table."

Carmine sat down on a crate. "He's eager to fight and wants his voice to be heard, like we did when we were his age."

Daniele ran a hand through his thin, receded hair. "True."

Tazio sat on a crate facing Gianna and Carmine. "All right. Let's establish a protocol for communication."

Gianna placed her hands on her lap. "I'm already delivering forged documents for the DELASEM network in Firenze. They are hidden inside the frame of my bicycle. I can do the same with the intelligence I collect on the Germans."

Carmine nodded.

"Smuggling intelligence inside your bicycle is not ideal for a dead drop," Tazio said. "You'll be on your own, and you won't have time to disassemble and reassemble your bicycle. Also, it will be cumbersome to lug or hide tools. You'll need to get in, deposit the message in the dead drop, and get out. The messages will be on small pieces of paper. I suggest hiding them someplace with easy access."

"Like where?" she asked.

Tazio rubbed his chin. "Inside the lining of your purse. Sealed in the hem of your skirt. Behind the mirror of a compact. Under the lining of a shoe. Rolled inside a hair ribbon. It's your call."

She nodded. "I'll think of something."

"Also," Tazio said, "the messages will need to be encrypted."

"Why?" Gianna asked.

"For security." A knot formed in Tazio's stomach. "And to protect you in the event that you are captured."

Gianna swallowed.

Carmine puffed on his cigarette.

"An encrypted message will prevent the Germans from reading the intelligence," Tazio said, "and it will give you a chance to lie, which might save you from a firing squad."

"*Va bene*," Gianna said. "How do I encrypt a message?"

Tazio retrieved his rucksack. He rummaged inside and removed a metal box, the size of a lunch pail, and lifted the cover to reveal what looked like a cross between a scrolling combination padlock and a ticker tape stock price telegraph. "This is a portable mechanical cipher machine. I'll be using this to encrypt radio transmissions to my headquarters. The problem is—I only have one of these machines. We would need two of them for us to communicate through a dead drop."

"Is there a way to copy the codes for her?" Carmine asked.

"No," Tazio said. "It's mechanical. At some point, once my radio is working, I will need to train you on how to use it, in the event I'm captured or killed."

Cigarette ash fell onto Carmine's lap, but he made no effort to brush it away.

Tazio set aside the portable cipher machine, removed two leatherbound notebooks from his rucksack, and handed one of them to Gianna.

"What's this?" she asked.

"A field cipher called a Slidex," Tazio said. "The codebooks were supposed to be used by me and Frank if we found ourselves working with separate partisan groups and needed to communicate messages through a dead drop."

"Is Frank the name of your partner who was captured?" Carmine asked.

Tazio nodded, hoping that his friend was alive. "This method of encryption is not as secure as the cipher machine, but it is easy to use."

He opened his Slidex notebook to reveal sheets of paper and vocabulary cards that contained tables with 17 rows and 12 columns. "For each vocabulary card, there are two-hundred-and-four cells available in which words or phrases are printed in black. Also, each cell contains a letter or number in red to make it possible to spell out words that are unlisted or to communicate numbers."

Gianna's eyes widened. "*Madonna mia*. It looks complicated."

"It does," Carmine said. "The codes we used for trench messages in the Great War were a hell of a lot simpler."

"It's not as bad as it looks." Tazio looked at Gianna. "With a few hours of practice, you'll be an ace at encrypting and deciphering messages."

Gianna drew a deep breath and exhaled.

Tazio put down his codebook. "Let's decide on the location of a dead drop. I was thinking that we could pick a spot along a road, at a rural safehouse, or in a village cemetery."

Gianna shook her head. "That would mean that you or Carmine would need to leave the safety of the countryside. There's no need for you to take the risk of exposing yourself to roads and areas that are traveled by the Germans."

Carmine took a drag on his cigarette and blew smoke through his nose. "She makes a good point."

Tazio looked at Gianna. "Do you have someplace in mind?"

"I do," she said. "How about the abandoned iron mine?"

"Too far," Tazio said. "It took us a day's journey to get there from the vineyard."

"Not on a bicycle," Gianna said. "I can get there in an hour to ninety minutes by using the main roads."

Tazio's shoulder muscles tensed. "We encountered a German scout unit below the mine."

"*Sì*, but the entrance is well hidden and hard to find." Gianna looked at Carmine. "Do you have a map?"

The man nodded, retrieved a weathered folded paper from a duffel bag, and gave it to her.

She unfolded the map and traced her finger along two routes that led to the iron mine—the first from the area of her vineyard, and the second from the city of Florence. "There is a road in close proximity to the mine. It's on the opposite side of the forest that we traveled to get there. I can be at the mine within minutes of leaving the road—and you and Carmine can get there by remaining in the protected cover of trees."

"I like it," Carmine said.

Tazio straightened his leg and rubbed the ache in his knee. "All right."

"*Bene*," Gianna said. "I'll bury each encrypted message under a flat stone, twenty paces into the mine from that toppled minecart. You do the same."

Tazio nodded.

They discussed venues where Gianna might acquire intelligence on armament depots, the quantity and movement of German troops, and train schedules for the transport of Axis supplies. Afterward, Tazio and Gianna gathered their codebooks, and they practiced encrypting and deciphering messages on pieces of paper. At first, the coded notes were simple, such as the name of a road or village. But with each additional message, Gianna increased the length and detail of the information by using key words and phrases to describe troop numbers, quantity and type of weaponry, and times of patrols and railway shipments. Hour by hour, they practiced encrypting and deciphering messages long into the night.

"Here," Gianna said, handing Tazio a message on a folded slip of paper.

Tazio unfolded the paper to reveal a series of codes.

WPJWX   NJPAC   RCDQW
RVTHS   HLTFN   PGYEW
AIPLK   JXBRT   ZGFWQ
187ZQ/GC

Tazio placed the paper next to his Slidex. Using the corresponding letters and phrases in the cells, he transcribed the message.

I leave at sunrise. Until our paths cross again, I will keep you in my thoughts.

"I will too," Tazio said, yearning for more time together. He slipped the note into his jacket pocket and looked into her eyes. "I think you got the hang of this."

She smiled.

Carmine, several meters away, ground out a cigarette on the floor and yawned. "I'll give Sante a break from lookout."

"All right." Daniele moved a lit candle, burned down to a nub, closer to the radio and examined a wire.

Tazio rose from his seat and patted Carmine's shoulder. "I'll take lookout. Get some rest."

"Are you sure?" he asked.

"*Sì*. If I have trouble remaining awake, I'll return for you to relieve me."

"*Grazie*." Carmine curled on the floor, propped his duffel bag under his head, and closed his eyes.

"I'll join you," Gianna said. "I can't sleep. My brain is buzzing with codes."

Tazio nodded.

Outside, they relieved Sante from his post. The young man, groggy from remaining up for most of the night, handed Tazio the shotgun and shuffled inside the shack.

Tazio checked the ammunition and engaged the weapon's safety switch, which had been left off, and he sat beside Gianna with their backs against a towering tree. The chirp of crickets and the smell of pine pervaded the cool night air.

"It's not too late to back out on smuggling intelligence to us," he said, his voice low.

"Never," she said.

"That's what I thought you would say." Tazio set the shotgun beside him and rubbed his neck. "We shouldn't talk on lookout, but I think we'll be okay if we remain alert and keep our voices low."

"*Va bene*," she whispered.

Tazio glanced at his luminous dial watch. "The sun will be up in an hour, and you have a long journey ahead of you. Are you sure you don't want to try to rest?"

"I'm sure," she said. "I'll sleep when I get home. Besides, my trip back to the vineyard will be much shorter than our journey here. While you were spending time with Eliseo, Carmine ordered one of his men to find and stash a bicycle for me in a roadside barn, about an hour's hike from here. I'll be home before noon."

"I'm glad." He leaned his head against the tree. *You haven't left and I already miss you.*

"I keep thinking about Aria and Eliseo," she said softly. "I'm always sad and worried when people leave the safety of our vineyard. I thought I might feel better having guided them partway on their escape, but I don't."

"They are going to be all right," he said. "Because of you and Beppe, they've been given a chance of freedom, and they're going to make it to Switzerland."

"*Grazie*," she said. "I needed to hear that."

"*Prego*, but I meant what I said." He looked at her, and a warmth flowed through him. "What are your plans after the war?" he whispered.

"I haven't given it much thought."

"You must have dreams," he said. "They make life worth living. What do you want your world to be like?"

She smoothed her skirt. "I'd love to have a life like my parents."

"Tell me more."

She touched her mother's wedding band on her necklace. "My parents adored each other, more than any couple I've ever met. They were always holding hands, hugging, kissing, and laughing. They were wonderful parents, who made every effort to give me and Matteo a good life."

"I would have loved to meet Luisa and Matteo."

"They would have liked you."

He smiled. "It sounds like you and your brother were close."

"Inseparable—we could have been twins."

"I always wanted siblings," Tazio said. "My mother had a rough childbirth. She was unable to have any more children after she delivered me."

"I'm sorry."

"No need to feel bad for me," Tazio said. "They spoiled me rotten."

"You don't look rotten to me," she said. "They obviously did something right with raising you. You're here, risking your life to help liberate your parents' homeland."

They spoke in soft whispers as predawn sparrows chirped from the trees. And the darkness that enveloped the forest gradually faded.

Tazio picked up a handful of pine needles and sprinkled them onto the ground. "Do you want to have children someday?"

"I do."

"How many?"

"One or two," she said. "How about you?"

"Loads of kids," he said.

She chuckled and lowered her voice. "Like ten?"

"No," he said, smiling. "One or two would be nice."

She scooched close to him, her arm touching his.

He gently clasped her hand.

She intertwined her fingers with his. "I hate that our time is coming to an end, at least for now."

"Me too," he said. "But someday the war will be over. Italy will be free from fascism. Jews will no longer need to hide. Food will be plentiful. You'll paint again, and you'll finish your studies at the university."

"And you'll go back to the United States," she breathed.

A jolt struck Tazio. The reality of their different paths felt like a wedge coming between them. He had a mission to accomplish, and so did she. Their families and homes were on separate continents. But Gianna had resurrected his hope and joy, and he wasn't about to let anything drive them apart—not even a war. "I don't want to leave," he breathed.

Gianna looked into his eyes.

"I want to be here—with you."

She leaned in.

Tazio wrapped his arms around Gianna, feeling her warmth, her chest rising and falling, and her soft hair brushing against his chin.

Gianna raised her head and placed her palm on his neck.

He felt her heart thumping against his chest. His pulse pounded faster as her lips approached his own.

The door to the shack swung open, and Carmine's voice broke the still air. "Tazio."

Their embrace faded. Gianna eased back, space falling between them.

Tazio's arms fell to his sides. He got up and helped Gianna to her feet. "Over here."

Gianna brushed pine needles from her skirt.

Footsteps approached and Carmine emerged from the shadows.

"What is it?" Tazio asked.

"Daniele has your radio working."

Tazio retrieved the shotgun, and he and Gianna followed Carmine to the shack. Inside, they found Daniele smoking a cigarette and Sante rubbing sleep from his eyes.

Tazio kneeled to his radio, its meter showing power. "You did it!"

"Of course!" Daniele raised his arms like an Olympic champion. "I am the great Daniele, repairer of all broken radios!"

Gianna grinned.

"It was an open circuit due to a broken wire," Daniele said. "It was difficult to locate, but an easy fix."

Tazio approached Daniele and patted him on the shoulder. "Well done."

Daniele beamed.

"Get your message to your headquarters," Carmine said. He turned to Gianna. "Gather your bag with your codebook, and I'll accompany you to where you'll pick up the bicycle."

Gianna looked into Tazio's eyes. "I'll be in touch through the dead drop."

He nodded. "Take care."

"You too."

Tazio, compelled by a sense of duty, sat in front of the wireless radio. Using his mechanical cipher machine, he prepared a message. Through the corner of his eye, he watched Gianna gather her things and leave with Carmine. He put on headphones and tapped out an encrypted Morse code message, all the while hoping that his words would reach headquarters—and that he'd see Gianna again.

Chapter 14

Florence—June 14, 2003

The electronic ring of a hotel room telephone roused Gianna from a restless sleep. Her brain was fogged with jet lag as she opened her eyes to a dark room with a sliver of light between blackout curtains. She pushed off the covers, as well as an extra pillow between her knees, and rolled over.

Another ring pierced the air.

Gianna extended her arm, jamming her hand against the bedside table. Pain flared through her fingers. *"Mamma mia!"*

The telephone rang again.

She sat up and slid a hand over the side table. *Where is the light?* A few inches farther, she located the base of a metal lamp and ran her hand upward until she located the switch. She turned it on, illuminating the room with fluorescent light, and squinted.

The phone rang.

She slipped on her glasses and, as her eyes adjusted to the brightness, she glanced at a clock radio with red digital numerals that read 9:37 AM. *I thought my wakeup call was for ten.* She struggled to think, her mind and body still operating on New York City time, six hours earlier than Florence.

Gianna picked up a plastic phone receiver and placed it to her ear. "*Pronto*," she said, her mouth dry.

"*Buongiorno*," a male voice said.

"*Buongiorno*. You're early with my wakeup call."

"My apologies, *signora*. You have a visitor in the lobby."

Gianna rubbed her mussed hair. "I'm not expecting anyone."

"She says that she is not expecting anyone," the man repeated in a muted tone, as if his hand was placed over the receiver.

"Tell her it's her daughter," a familiar but muffled voice said.

Gianna gasped. *Oh, shit! Jenn is here!*

"The woman says that she's your daughter," the man said.

"I heard," Gianna said, her heart racing.

"Would you like to come to the lobby to greet her," the man said, "or shall I send her to your room?"

Gianna stood up, accidentally tugged the handset cord, and the phone base toppled from the table. "Oh, Madonna!"

"*Signora*, are you still there?"

"*Scusa*," she said, the phone base dangling from the cord. "Please send her to my room."

"I will," the man said. "*Buona giornata*."

Gianna, shocked and confused, put the phone on the table and hung up the receiver. She had called Jenn's law firm soon after arriving in Florence to leave the name and number of her hotel. However, she'd purposely left the information with the main receptionist to avoid having to talk with her daughter.

She scurried to her suitcase and searched for something to put on in place of her pink cotton nightgown. *How did she get here so fast?* Gianna pushed aside underwear and grabbed an olive-green sundress.

A knock came from the door.

Hairs raised on the back of her neck, and she dropped the dress back into her suitcase. *She's going to be mad as hell.* She braced herself for an argument, went to the door, and opened it.

Their eyes met, and Jenn leaped forward and wrapped her arms around her mother.

Moved by her daughter's embrace, Gianna's eyes welled with tears. After all, Jenn wasn't a hugger. Even as a child, she had disliked being held, let alone touched.

"Are you okay?" Jenn asked, squeezing her.

"Yes. What are you doing here?"

"Jesus, Mom! You scared the hell out of me!" Jenn stepped back and smoothed her wrinkled navy dress. "I came to make sure you're all right."

"I am." Gianna wiped her eyes. "You look like you came straight from work?"

"I did," she said, her voice perturbed. "I had to arrange for another attorney to cover my cases for me, and I had to obtain permission from the head of the firm to take a leave of absence—despite that I've used up all my vacation time for the year—to fly off to Italy to track down my runaway mother."

Gianna clasped her elbows. "I hope you're not in trouble."

Jenn, ignoring her mother's comment, grabbed a carry-on suitcase and purse from the hallway, placed them in the room, and shut the door.

"Where are Bella and Enzo?" Gianna asked.

"They're staying with Theresa."

Gianna scratched her head. "Theresa?"

"My friend who is a kindergarten teacher. She's tall with curly black hair and has a daughter the same age as Bella. Remember?"

"Oh, yes," Gianna said, recalling the woman whom she'd met once or twice at her granddaughter's birthday parties.

"Theresa has summers off and agreed to watch them for me."

"Why couldn't their father take care of them?"

Jenn frowned. "Bill claims that he has a work trip that can't be rescheduled."

Gianna felt horrible for her daughter, and even worse for her grandchildren. Jenn's ex-husband had rarely, if ever, been supportive of Jenn's career, and he didn't always follow through with his duties of raising Bella and Enzo. He often missed the children's events, such as Enzo's peewee league soccer games and Bella's dance recitals, and once or twice a month he used the excuse of unexpected work travel to cancel or change his coparenting schedule.

Gianna slumped her shoulders. "I'm sorry."

Jenn nodded.

"How did you get here so quickly?"

"I booked a flight after your call from the airport, and I got the name of your hotel when I landed and checked my office voicemail for messages."

"I didn't mean to cause trouble," Gianna said. "I hope you're not too angry with me."

Jenn placed her hands on her hips. "I'm beyond pissed—and scared—but too damn exhausted to show it."

Gianna lowered her eyes. "You didn't need to come to Firenze."

"I need to know what is going on," Jenn said, "and I'm not leaving here until you tell me everything."

A decision stirred inside Gianna. She'd kept her secrets hidden inside her for over half a century, and she'd planned to take them to her grave. But now that Jenn was here—in Florence—she knew, deep down, that there was no way she could make things right between them without revealing the truth.

Gianna opened the curtains, filling the room with sunlight. "Have you eaten?"

Jenn furrowed her brow. "No, and I'm not hungry. I want to know why—"

"Let me get dressed," Gianna interrupted. "We'll go to a café."

"Mom, we need to talk."

"We will, over coffee." She went to her suitcase, removed a dress, and turned to her daughter. "You likely didn't sleep on the flight, and I have jet lag. There is much that I need to tell you, and I think we both could use a little caffeine."

Chapter 15

Florence—November 26, 1943

Gianna entered the living room and approached her vibrant gold-colored abstract painting that Tazio had given the title of *Hope*. A memory of his arms wrapped around her emerged in her brain, conjuring a deep yearning inside her. She carefully removed the art piece from a hook on the wall and placed it facedown on the floor. Using a knife from the kitchen, she removed a thin-board backing to reveal its hidden contents—her Slidex codebook, a handful of deciphered messages from Tazio, and a couple of handwritten letters from Lilla.

She removed Tazio's recently decoded message, sat on the sofa, and read it for the third time.

Gianna,
I'm grateful for your messages. You are making a difference in our world. You're protecting lives and helping us to forge a path toward freedom. Now, more than ever, I believe in you.

She smiled and glanced at the space next to her on the sofa, where they once sat together.

> *Give my regards to Beppe, and that I look forward to someday returning to your family's vineyard for a grape harvest. Your notes give me strength. I hear your voice when I read the words.*
>
>   *Tazio*

A wave of optimism flowed through Gianna as she folded the note and placed it inside the painting. She retrieved the codebook, a pencil and paper, and—recalling her recent surveillance of the Florence railway station—she began to encrypt a message.

Over the past month and a half, Gianna had monitored the transport of German troops and supplies. Much of her time was spent riding her bicycle near railway lines, along routes used by Wehrmacht transport trucks, and through streets near the German headquarters in Florence. She'd pedaled her bicycle—its basket filled with bottles of wine and olive oil—all the while making mental notes on the enemy. Locations of troops. Armament warehouses. Dates and times of German supply train arrivals. Hotels that billeted soldiers. Routes used by Wehrmacht convoys. Cafés where soldiers congregated. And Panzer tank tallies. Little attention was paid to the young Tuscan woman who was traveling with farm goods stowed in her bicycle basket. She had few close encounters with the enemy, with the exception of German checkpoints to examine her papers and occasional catcalls from soldiers.

Each evening, Gianna arrived home physically exhausted but with her mind buzzing with intelligence. Rather than rest, she went straight away to encrypt a message for Tazio. She delivered intelligence, at a minimum of every forty-eight hours, to the dead drop in the abandoned iron mine. Each of the messages included an encrypted personal note to Tazio, and they were buried under a flat rock the size of a dinner plate, twenty paces away from the toppled minecart. Soon after her first visit to the dead drop, she received her first coded message from Tazio that was hidden inside a German-made ammunition cartridge, the length of Gianna's index finger. She'd assumed that he wanted to keep the message dry or to confuse the enemy, so she used this method for her future dead drops. After deciphering Tazio's messages, she burned the communications that contained surveillance requests or information about the Resistance, but she kept the ones that pertained to matters of the heart.

Gianna's partisan role had not been limited to delivering secret messages: she'd transported several small shipments of weapons, buried under dried flowers in her bicycle basket. Tazio had used his radio to give coordinates, deep in the Tuscan countryside, for an Allied parachute drop of weaponry. Due to the size of the airdrop, Tazio and Carmine's partisans stashed much of the munitions in an abandoned barn. Soon after that, at the dead drop, Gianna received a message that requested her to deliver some of the weapons—a mix of pistols, ammunition, and boxes of plastic explosive—to a partisan safehouse. She'd expected to see Tazio during one of her deliveries or while she was making a dead drop, but the two never met. Their interaction was limited to encrypted communications, and she hoped that their paths would soon cross.

In addition to delivering weapons and intelligence for partisans, she continued to smuggle forged identification papers, fabricated by Lilla, from the DELASEM hideout in Florence. Gianna acted as the key cog in the communication wheel between Carmine's partisans and leaders of the Jewish aid network—Lilla, Rabbi Nathan, and Don Casini. She coordinated the secret transport of Jews—hidden beneath a false bottom of a horse drawn wagon—to her family's vineyard and, once each of the refugees had acquired fake papers, she delivered a message to the dead drop to request a partisan to guide them on their escape to Switzerland. Her actions had expedited the number of Jews who could be given aid. Since the departure of Aria and Eliseo, Gianna and Beppe had harbored over a dozen Jewish refugees, all of whom were provided with fake identities and left the vineyard on their journey to freedom.

Gianna cared deeply for each of the people who found sanctuary at their vineyard, but none had touched her heart more than Aria and Eliseo. Each night she silently prayed that they had made it safely across the Swiss border, and that Aria would give birth to a healthy baby. And she liked to imagine—usually while pedaling her bicycle through German-patrolled streets—that Eliseo gained solace by carrying Beppe's compass, as if it were a magical talisman that protected and guided its keeper to safety.

Footsteps approached in the hallway and Beppe, using his cane, entered the living room. "Would you like something to eat before you leave?"

"No, *grazie*." Gianna finished her encrypted message and stashed it under a hidden compartment of her purse.

Beppe hobbled to her. "You need to eat to keep up your strength."

Gianna hated to admit it, but the bicycling between the vineyard, Florence, and the remote dead drop had taken a toll on her body. She'd lost weight and had to take in the waistband of her skirt. The many kilometers of pedaling on her bicycle seat had rubbed sores, the size of lemons, on her thighs which required countless applications of a homemade salve of olive oil and beeswax. Also, she was plagued by dehydration and leg cramps.

"*Va bene*," Gianna said. "But I need to leave in fifteen minutes."

"I'll meet you in the kitchen." He turned and hobbled away.

Gianna placed her codebook inside the picture frame, and she fixed the backing by tapping metal tabs back into place with the butt of her knife. She lifted the painting and, after struggling to slip the wire over the hook, fastened it to the wall.

She went to the kitchen, put away the knife, and sat with Beppe at the table with a plate of olives, bread, shriveled grapes, and a piece of slightly moldy cheese.

Beppe slid her a cup of barley coffee. "It's left over from yesterday. I can warm it up if you like."

"No need." She took a sip, filling her mouth with a bitter taste of burned barley.

"I prepared Matteo's room for Lilla."

"*Grazie*." A mix of anticipation and relief stirred inside Gianna. She plucked an olive from the plate and chewed it.

"Do you know when she will arrive?"

"Tomorrow, most likely. I'll find out when I go to Firenze, after I deliver a message to Tazio." She set aside the olive pit, and her mind drifted to a Jewish couple who left last night with one of Carmine's partisans. "I'll also let the network know that we can accommodate more visitors."

"*Bene*. It's a shame to leave our hiding space vacant."

She nodded.

Beppe nibbled a piece of cheese. "How is Tazio?"

"All right." She chewed a piece of bread, dry and bland.

"I can tell that you miss him."

"Is it that obvious?"

He placed a finger to his temple. "I'm your *papà*—it's my job to see and know everything about my daughter."

She chuckled.

He smoothed his beard. "You've grown quite fond of him."

She clasped her mother's wedding band on her necklace. "I have."

He reached across the table and held her hand. "This war will not last forever. You'll see him again."

She squeezed his fingers and nodded.

He released her hand and leaned back in his chair.

Her mind drifted to her recent message. "Speaking of Tazio, he mentioned in his last communication that he's looking forward to returning to the vineyard for a harvest."

Beppe smiled. He glanced out the window and his levity faded. "We sure could have used his help this year."

Gianna nodded.

Beppe was unable to harvest much of the vineyard because of the lack of farm laborers. This was compounded by the fact that there were few people whom Beppe and Gianna could trust, considering they were harboring Jews. Now, much of the Conti vineyard's vines were covered with old shriveled grapes that would eventually rot.

"I doubt that we'll be able to find anyone to harvest our olives,"

Beppe said. "They'll go to waste, like the grapes. It sickens me to think that people are starving and much of our crop will end up as food for worms."

A pang of guilt needled Gianna's conscience. "I wish I could have done more to help with the harvest."

"Nonsense. Our work to save Jews and your role with the partisans are far more important." Beppe fiddled with his wedding band and gazed at the framed photograph of his late wife on the wall. He blinked his eyes, as if he were fending off tears. "I hate that you are placing yourself in danger. I'm scared every time you leave our home, but I know that you are doing the right thing by taking the fight to the enemy. I'm so proud of you."

A warmth welled up inside Gianna. "I'm merely doing what you always said to do."

He wiped his eyes. "And what would that be?"

She rose from her seat and hugged him. "Catch the moment."

Beppe squeezed her tight.

Gianna finished her meal with her father, packed up her bicycle with several bottles of wine and olive oil, and left the vineyard. Several kilometers into her trip, her legs—weary from lack of rest—began to ache, and the abrasions on her inner thighs started to sting. She ignored her pain and pedaled en route to the dead drop, all the while making mental tallies of the number and type of German military vehicles.

An hour after leaving her home, Gianna veered to the berm of a dirt road and coasted to a stop. She scanned the area to make certain there were no onlookers and hid her bicycle in waist-high weeds. She trudged through a forest, her legs feeling like lead, and fifteen minutes later she arrived at the entrance to the mine. Light dwindled and the temperature dropped as she made her way into the tunnel. She located the flat stone, lifted it, and discovered an ammunition cartridge with its bullet inverted into the casing. She removed the bullet, plucked out a tightly folded piece of paper, unraveled it, and eyed the encrypted codes with Tazio's handwriting. Her heartbeat quickened. She placed the paper under the hidden compartment of her purse, put her intelligence into the cartridge, capped it off with the bullet, and buried it under the rock. She dusted dirt from her skirt and left the mine with renewed energy and optimism.

On the journey to Florence, she was passed by dozens of German transport trucks carrying either troops or military supplies. To Gianna, it looked as if Hitler's military was relocating much of their forces to their defensive line, rumored to be four hundred kilometers south of Florence. *If the Germans are moving this much armament, the Allies might be making progress with breaking through the line.* Wind from a passing truck blasted her bicycle. Bottles rattled in her basket. She gripped her handlebars and pedaled faster, sending a burn through her thigh muscles.

Upon entering the city of Florence, she encountered a pedestrian checkpoint with a sole German soldier, no more than eighteen or nineteen years of age, checking identification papers. She got off her bicycle and walked to the back of a small line, composed of two women and an elderly man who was carrying a shoeshine box. The line crept forward. Tension spread through her shoulders.

Reaching the soldier, she leaned her bicycle on its kickstand, removed her identification from her purse, and handed it to him. He eyed the paper, gave it back to her, and examined the bottles in her basket.

As she began to put away her papers, the German pointed to her purse. "*Handtasche.*"

She calmly handed him the purse.

The soldier turned the purse upside down, dumping its contents onto the ground.

Her breath stalled in her lungs, and she prayed that the false bottom of the purse would remain secure.

Using the tip of his boot, the soldier nudged the items—a coin pouch, a tin of salve, and a piece of bread and cheese that was loosely wrapped in a napkin. He picked up the tin, opened it, and smelled the beeswax salve.

"*Unguento*," Gianna said.

The soldier dropped the tin, along with the purse, to the ground and motioned for her to leave.

She kneeled and gathered her things. *Thank goodness.* She placed her purse into the bicycle basket and rode off. But within meters of leaving the checkpoint it became clear, to Gianna, that something was amiss. Many storefronts and windows were shuttered, and there were few Florentines on the streets. And a distinct whine of German motorcycles blaring through alleyways caused hairs to raise on the back of her neck.

Nearing an intersection her eyes locked on a brick apartment house where a Kübelwagen, its doors emblazoned with an iron cross, was parked on the street. Cries erupted from the entrance to the building, and her feet slipped from the pedals. Within seconds, German soldiers with rifles forced a family—a man, woman, and a grammar-school-age girl—into the back of the Kübelwagen. Wails rose from inside the building.

No! She struggled to control her bicycle and gouged her ankle against the pedal. Pain shot through her leg. She regained her footing, veered around the corner, and discovered two more soldiers who were dragging an unconscious man—his nose badly broken and his face covered in blood—from a ground-floor apartment. Anger flooded her veins as she helplessly watched the soldiers carry the man away. *Oh, God! Why are they doing this?* But deep down, she knew the answer.

Gianna, her heart pounding against her rib cage, sped over uneven cobblestones. Bottles of wine fell out of her basket and smashed over the ground. A few streets away, more arrests were being made by German soldiers who were accompanied by baton-wielding Blackshirts. She forced her legs, their muscles flaring with fatigue, to pedal faster, all the while determined to reach Lilla and the members of DELASEM to warn them of the mass arrests.

The alley to the network's hideout was bare. No soldiers. No pedestrians. *Please, let them be all right*, she prayed, squeezing her handlebars. She pedaled ahead and, as she began to brake, the entrance to the hideout came into view and a wave of dread washed over her.

The door was shattered and lay in pieces on the ground. And two German SS officers—wearing all black uniforms with a silver skull and crossbones emblem on their caps—stood in the entryway.

Fear flooded her veins. *Oh, God! Not Lilla!*

An officer placed a cigarette to his lips, glanced at Gianna, and slipped a lighter from his pocket.

She hid her emotions and calmly pedaled ahead.

The officer turned his attention to his comrade, who was scribbling inside a pocket-size leather notebook.

Through the corner of her eye, she caught a glimpse of the open doorway, its frame riddled with bullet holes, and no sign of members of the network. *Maybe they fled before the Germans arrived.*

Gianna, her body ravaged with heartbreak, bicycled down the alley and turned onto a side street. Tears flooded her eyes. She fought back her pain and sorrow as she fled the area of the raids, all the while praying that she'd find a way to save Lilla and the others before it was too late.

Chapter 16

Florence—November 26, 1943

Gianna furiously pedaled her bicycle to San Pietro a Varlungo, an ancient Roman Catholic church that was located outside the former walls of medieval Florence. She got off her bicycle and leaned it against a stone well. The courtyard was empty and silent, except for the distant barking of a dog. On shaky legs, she made her way to the entrance of the church, its bell tower topped with an iron cross that pointed to the sky, and rapped on the pair of pitted wooden doors with Gothic-style hinges. She sucked in deep breaths, bringing air into her lungs. Footsteps grew from inside and the door opened to reveal a young bespectacled nun with a tuft of brown hair sticking out from under her headpiece.

"May I help you?" the nun asked.

"My name is Gianna Conti," she said, her voice raw. "I'm looking for Don Leto Casini."

The nun peeked outside the door, glanced in both directions, and said, "Come in. I'll get your bicycle."

Gianna shuffled inside.

The nun rolled the bicycle into the vestibule, bolted the door shut, and led Gianna to the sanctuary of the church that had a barrel-vaulted ceiling with a fresco that depicted the baptism of Christ. The space was void of clergy and parishioners, and the air contained a faint smell of incense. She gestured for Gianna to sit in a pew, and she retrieved a clay pitcher from a table and handed it to her.

Gianna gulped water, cool with a metallic, bitter taste. She wiped her mouth with her sleeve. "*Grazie.*"

"*Prego,*" the nun said. "Wait here."

She nodded and drank more water, soothing a dry burn in her throat.

The nun disappeared down a corridor. A moment later, a short elderly nun with deep vertical jowl lines, reminiscent of a marionette, entered the sanctuary.

"I'm Sister Rosetta," the woman said.

She rose from her seat and a knot formed in her stomach. "I'm Gianna Conti."

"I know who you are. Don Casini informed me about you and your father Beppe."

"I'd like to speak with him," she said, hesitant to confide in a person she did not know. "Something terrible has happened."

"I'm aware of the raid on the DELASEM sanctum."

Gianna swallowed.

Sister Rosetta's eyes filled with sadness, and she placed a hand to a small wooden cross, hanging from a cord around her neck. "The committee members, including Don Casini, were arrested by the Nazis."

Gianna felt like she was punched in the gut. *No! This can't be happening!* She drew a jagged breath. "Do you know anything about Lilla Milano or Rabbino Nathan Cassuto?"

"Both arrested."

Gianna, devastated and heartbroken, sat in the pew and wept.

The nun knelt beside her. "Last night, the Germans began conducting raids to round up Jews. This morning, Don Casini joined members of DELASEM for an emergency meeting to try to evacuate Jews who remained hidden in Firenze. The Germans infiltrated the network and raided their shelter. Everyone was apprehended, except for a man named Antonio Rossi, who escaped by climbing to the roof and jumping onto another building. He came here after the attack, and we arranged to smuggle him to a safehouse outside of the city."

Gianna wiped her eyes. "Where did the Germans take them?"

"We think they were sent to Villa Triste for interrogation."

Her skin turned cold. A memory of bicycling past the building that housed the Sicherheitsdienst (SD)—the intelligence service of the SS—flashed in her mind. Since the start of the German occupation of Florence, rumors about the SD's brutal interrogation techniques, including torture and abuse, had grown rampant.

"We must try to help them," Gianna said.

"If we go there to plead for their release, we'll be arrested, too." The nun sat beside Gianna. "There is nothing we can do, except pray for those who have been captured. But we can—and will—continue to hide Jews from the Germans."

Gianna's brain told her that the nun was right. If the Germans were willing to apprehend a Catholic priest, they likely would not hesitate to detain a nun or a Catholic woman who protested for the release of people who aided Jews. But deep down, her heart refused to give up on trying to save Lilla, Don Casini, Rabbi Nathan, and the rest of the resistance network.

She rose from the pew and looked at the nun. "I need to go."

"Stay here," Sister Rosetta said. "It will be safer to leave after the German raids have ceased. Also, you look exhausted and in no condition to travel."

She shook her head. "I'll rest when my friends are free."

The nun stood and clasped Gianna's hands. "May God support you in danger."

"And you."

Gianna left the church and retrieved her bicycle. She got onto the seat and, as she pedaled away, her mind raced with options. *I need to warn Beppe and Tazio about what has happened. But any chance of helping Lilla and the others will rest upon gaining intelligence on the Germans.* Before she could change her mind, she steered her bicycle along the Arno and headed north toward the Nazi lion's den—Villa Triste.

Twenty minutes after leaving the church, she pedaled along Via Bolognese, a long hilly road that led to the SD headquarters. To increase her surveillance time in the area, she got off her bicycle and pushed it up the hill. As she neared the summit, Villa Triste—a five-story brick building that was surrounded by a stone wall—came into view. Several black automobiles, including one with swastika flags on its fenders, were parked along a sidewalk. And four German soldiers with submachine guns were posted as sentries—two at the iron gate to the property, and two at the front entrance.

Gianna's pulse rate quickened. She gathered her courage, pushed the bicycle onto the sidewalk, and walked along the front wall of Villa Triste. Through the corners of her eyes, she looked at the windows of the building, most of which were covered with shutters or curtains. There was no movement and the place was quiet, except for the faint sound of classical music—Ludwig van Beethoven's Symphony no. 9—that emanated from a closed cellar window. Her brain flashed with an image of a German interrogator, playing a record on a gramophone to drown out screams from torture. A chill shot down her spine. She set aside her thought, leaned her bicycle against the property's stone wall and pretended to tie a shoelace.

One of the German sentries left his post at the gate and approached Gianna.

Her skin prickled at the sound of boots clacking on the pavement, but she continued scanning the windows of the upper floor.

"*Geht weiter!*" the soldier shouted. He motioned to move along with his submachine gun.

Gianna nodded. She quickly tied a double knot in her shoe lace, retrieved her bicycle, and continued her walk along the wall. As she passed the soldier, she put on a fake smile and said, "*Scusa.*"

The German, his face stoic, returned to his post.

Gianna left Villa Triste feeling defeated that she gained little insight from her surveillance, other than identifying that the SD headquarters was heavily guarded. She gripped the handlebars, silently prayed that Lilla and members of DELASEM would survive their imprisonment, and traveled to the train station.

German transport trucks were parked along the entrance, and armed Wehrmacht soldiers were ordering captured Jews—a mix of women, men, and children—to get out of the vehicles. A crowd of Florentines, a few of whom wearing dark clothing reminiscent of Mussolini's Blackshirts, watched the soldiers corral approximately a hundred people, their faces filled with fear, in front of the station.

"*Schnell!*" a soldier shouted, pointing his rifle.

A woman clutched a swaddled infant to her chest and shuffled forward.

"We must do something to stop this," Gianna said, standing amongst the onlookers.

An old man with a bulbous nose looked at Gianna and held a finger in front of his lips. "*Silenzio*," he hissed. "If you protest, you'll be shot or sent with them to a concentration camp."

Gianna helplessly watched the Germans round up scores of Jews. *They must have been planning the raids for months to capture so many so quickly.* A wave of nausea rushed through her.

The soldiers forced the arrested people to line up in a single file and walk, one by one, through the entrance of the station, where a soldier counted them and recorded tallies on a clipboard.

Once the detainees were inside, the crowd of Florentines began to disperse. Instead of leaving, Gianna pedaled her bicycle up the street and crossed the railroad tracks. She located a spot with a clear but distant view of the interior of the station, put down her bicycle, and peeked through a patch of thorn bushes.

Soldiers, who were holding leashes to German shepherds, walked along the platform and separated Jews into several large groups. Cries erupted from people who were forced apart from family members. A Wehrmacht officer blew a whistle, and soldiers opened the doors to empty rail cattle cars. The masses of people, compelled by the fear of being shot, shuffled forward.

Tears flooded Gianna's eyes.

People were packed, shoulder to shoulder, in the cattle cars and the doors were closed.

A train whistle pierced the air.

Gianna flinched.

The locomotive jerked forward, and the train crept down the track. It gathered speed and chugged past Gianna. Eyes of imprisoned Jews peered through gaps in boards. A surge of sorrow flowed through her, and she wished that she could have done something to save them all. As the train faded from sight, she wiped away tears and vowed to continue to do everything in her power to fight back against the Nazi regime. With little choice but to leave Florence, she got on her bicycle and pedaled away.

Gianna arrived home after sunset. The house was dark, except for a glint of lamplight escaping through a crack in the blackout curtains. She put down her bicycle and trudged to the front door. Her fatigue and muscle pain made lifting her feet a struggle. She entered and found Beppe sitting in his chair in the living room. They locked eyes, and her bottom lip trembled.

Beppe grabbed his cane and stood. "What's wrong?"

"The Germans arrested hundreds of Jews in Firenze." Her vision blurred with tears. "DELASEM was infiltrated, and every member—except for one—was captured."

"*Oh, mio Dio.*" He swallowed. "Lilla?"

"Taken," she cried.

He dropped his cane and wrapped his arms around her. Together, they sat on the sofa and wept.

Gianna dried her eyes with her sleeve, and she told her father everything about the mass arrest of Jews who were hiding in the city, the German SS officers who were standing in front of the broken doors to the DELASEM hideout, her conversation with Sister Rosetta, and her surveillance at Villa Triste and the train station.

"The Germans locked them in railcars and shipped them away, like cattle," Gianna said.

"*Bastardi,*" Beppe said, shaking his head in disgust. "Hitler and

Mussolini's puppet state are fighting two wars—one against the Allies and another, a campaign of annihilation."

Gianna rubbed her thighs, riddled with ache. "We must try to free Lilla, Don Casini, Rabbino Nathan, and the others. If we do nothing, they'll be shot or sent to a German concentration camp."

"I wish there was more that we could do. We'll be arrested, or worse, if we make an appeal to the Germans to release them."

"I'm not talking about pleading to the Germans," Gianna said.

Beppe swallowed. "What are you trying to say?"

She looked at him. The lines on his face appeared deeper, as if the strains of the war had accelerated the aging process. "We make a plan with the partisans to free them."

Beppe shook his head. "It is impossible for anyone to break into the SD headquarters without being killed. Partisans armed with hunting rifles will be no match for the German soldiers."

"But Tazio has arranged for parachute drops of Allied weaponry. Carmine's men now have some modern armament, including plastic explosives."

"*Sì*, but most of his partisans are old men who haven't been in combat since the Great War. For the past twenty years, the only action they've seen is hunting for quail or wild boar. Even if the partisans have new rifles, they're no match for youthful, well-trained Wehrmacht soldiers."

Gianna looked into his eyes. "What would you do if I was arrested?"

He shifted in his seat. "That's not what this—"

"Please tell me, Papà. What would you do if I was held captive in Villa Triste?"

A deep determination filled his eyes. "I would do everything I could do to save you, even at the risk of losing my life."

"That's how I feel about Lilla and members of DELASEM. They're like family to me—to us."

"I feel the same way," he said. "But I still think we should wait this out. The Allies will eventually break through the German lines in the south and liberate Firenze."

"There has been little, if any, news about Allied advances. It might be a year before they arrive. We don't have time to wait. The captured DELASEM members might have less than a week before they are either shot or sent away to a concentration camp."

Beppe paused, running a hand over his beard.

Gianna rose from her seat, sending a twinge through her calf muscles. She went to her painting that hid her codebook and removed it from the wall.

"What are you doing?"

"I need to encrypt a message for Tazio. I'll inform him about what has happened, and he and Carmine can decide if there is anything they can do to try to free them." She placed the painting face down on the sofa beside Beppe.

"*Va bene*," he said.

She retrieved a knife from the kitchen, opened the backing of the painting, and removed the codebook.

"There is another matter we need to discuss," Beppe said.

She looked at him.

"The members of DELASEM will likely undergo torture to reveal names and location of people providing safehouses for Jews. Someone might give them our names, and we need to consider leaving since staying here means to risk arrest."

Horrid images of an abusive interrogation flashed through Gianna's brain. She pushed away her thoughts and asked, "Do you want to leave?"

"No. This is my home and our family's vineyard—I'll never abandon it. But you should hide with Tazio and the partisans, at least for a while."

"I know Lilla, Don Casini, and Rabbino Nathan. They'll never give in to the enemy, no matter how bad things get for them."

"But there are more network members under arrest. If one person cracks under interrogation, the Germans will come for us."

A fiery resolve burned inside her. "I'm staying, and I will continue to fight."

Chapter 17

Tuscany—November 27, 1943

Shortly before sunrise, Tazio was awoken by birdsong outside the ruins of an ancient stone villa. A few meters away, Carmine lay asleep on the earthen floor with his head propped on a duffel bag. Near a collapsed wall was a metal container—filled with American M1 Garand semiautomatic rifles and ammunition—that he and Carmine had collected, hours earlier, after it was parachute-dropped from the belly of an Allied plane.

Tazio stretched his arms and got to his feet. Being careful not to disturb Carmine, he clambered over the rubble of the fallen wall and sat next to a cluster of cypress trees that overlooked a remote area of the Tuscan hills. The air was crisp, with an earthy scent of decayed leaves, and the horizon of the dark blue sky was giving way to shades of red, orange, and yellow. He blew warm air on his fingers and removed a stash of deciphered messages from Gianna. His eyes adjusted to the twilight and, as he looked at the first note, the sweet timbre of her voice whispered inside his head.

I miss you, and I wish you were by my side.

Tazio ran a finger over the paper, then retrieved another message.

Liberation will come and we will see each other again.

I wish I could be with you, hold you in my arms, and never let you go, Tazio thought. But how could he reveal his true feelings? After all, the chances of him surviving his mission in German-occupied Tuscany were bleak at best. He couldn't imagine causing her any further sorrow, considering that she'd already lost her brother to the war. As much as he wanted to open his heart to her, the most he could do was journal his emotions on a piece of paper that he stowed inside his codebook.

For the past month and a half, he had communicated with Gianna through the dead drop. He admired her commitment and courage. To Tazio, she had an inner strength and resilience like no other person he had ever met. She'd become invaluable to his mission, but he hated placing her in danger.

After joining the partisans, Tazio arranged for two Allied parachute drops of armament, including the one that he and Carmine had just retrieved from a nearby hilltop. His aim was to build a small arsenal for Carmine's group, but the men were nowhere near ready to do combat with the enemy, given their lack of physical fitness and training. Half of the men had difficulty running, a handful of them had poor eyesight despite wearing corrective lenses, and one man was hard of hearing and carried a tin ear trumpet. The few young partisans in the group lacked any type of military training, and the older men who'd fought in the muddy trenches of the Great War needed to learn modern combat techniques. But regardless of their age and experience, the partisans shared a common commitment to liberate Italy from the Nazis.

In addition to acquiring arms and gathering intelligence, Tazio spent a great deal of effort on the primary goal of his mission—preparing partisans for action when the Allied invasion eventually reached Tuscany. He instructed Carmine and his men on the use of Allied weapons, in particular M1 rifles, Colt semiautomatic pistols, and grenades. A challenge for their training was that they could not discharge ammunition without the risk of alerting German scouts to their location. So, all practice was done without firing a round or pulling a pin from a grenade. And as for plastic explosives, his teaching of its use was limited to Carmine and the young, eager-to-take-responsibility partisan, Sante.

For Tazio, demonstrating the use of weaponry was the easy part of his mission. The far more complicated piece was transforming ordinary men into skilled saboteurs. For weeks, he tutored them on OSS tactics and techniques to destroy and disrupt German occupied infrastructure, such as supply depots, bridges, rail lines, and electrical transmission lines. Also, he trained them on methods to ambush unsuspecting enemy supply convoys and ways to avoid detection.

Six days ago, a group of the men—composed of Tazio, Carmine, Sante, and two other partisans—conducted a raid on a German fuel supply depot between Pistoia and Florence. The attack was based on Gianna's intelligence, which had informed them that the area was poorly guarded by the Wehrmacht. She was right—only two German soldiers manned the refueling spot, and they fled at the sound of exploding grenades. The raid was a success, given that they destroyed a few dozen barrels of petrol and recovered crates of German semiautomatic rifles and ammunition that were stashed in a truck with a broken axle. Tazio and his crew of saboteurs returned to their hideout in the forest, and they informed the other men of their success. That night, they gathered in a hunting shack and celebrated their victory with bottles of grappa passed around. Long into the night, the partisans told jokes and stories. And for the first time in months, they were joyful.

Throughout Tazio's time with the partisans, he remained in contact with Allied headquarters through his radio. He'd asked the OSS to deploy another agent to replace his former partner, Frank, who was now a prisoner of war, but the OSS declined his request because the stronghold of German military lines—south of Rome—had stalled the advances of Allied troops. He was informed that the OSS, for the time being, would be concentrating agent deployments closer to the front lines, and he was given the choice to either stay put and carry out his mission alone, or join forces with a small team of OSS agents who were located north of Rome. Tazio, without hesitation, opted to stay. In his short time with Carmine and his partisans, he'd grown to trust and believe in the men. He had confidence that Allied soldiers would eventually break through the German lines, and he would have the Tuscan partisans ready for combat. And perhaps even more, he had no intention of abandoning his work with Gianna.

The sound of footsteps emanated from the ruins of the villa.

Tazio perked up his head and turned.

Carmine, wearing a weathered wool coat with a rifle slung over his shoulder, stepped over a pile of bricks. "*Buongiorno*," he said, sitting beside Tazio.

"*Buongiorno*." Tazio slipped the notes into his jacket pocket.

"What were you reading?"

"Intelligence from Gianna."

Carmine raised his brows. "Are you sure it wasn't something else?"

"I'm not sure if I understand."

"For a skilled saboteur, you're an amateur liar," Carmine said.

Tazio shifted his weight. "How so?"

"Each time you go to the dead drop, you receive two messages from Gianna. After you decipher them, you destroy the evidence except for a piece of paper that you tuck away in your pocket. Why?"

He fiddled with his watch. "We exchange personal messages."

Carmine raised his hands toward the sky. "Tazio has been struck by a thunderbolt."

His face turned warm. "We're simply writing notes to keep in touch."

Carmine grinned. "Do you expect me to believe that?"

"No."

Carmine slipped his rifle from his shoulder and placed it on the ground. "Gianna's brother Matteo would have liked you, despite being an *americano*."

Tazio chuckled. "*Grazie.*"

He patted Tazio on the shoulder. "If Matteo were alive, I think he would approve of you proposing to his sister."

"That's nice of you to say, but Gianna and I haven't known each other very long."

"Time has little to do with it," Carmine said. "Do you care for her?"

"*Sì.*"

"Have you told her how you feel?"

"Well, not exactly."

"If I were you," Carmine said, "I would tell her. She might grow tired of waiting for you to reveal your intentions and find someone else."

Tazio's shoulder muscles tensed. "We have a war to fight."

"Doesn't matter."

Tazio crossed his arms. "What makes you an expert on relationships?"

"I'm not, but I'm older and wiser than you." Carmine gazed at the sun rising on the horizon. "And I was once married."

"Oh," Tazio said. "Why haven't you spoken of this?"

Carmine rubbed the back of his neck. "It was ages ago."

Carmine, who had lived alone on a farm before the war, refrained from discussing his family and personal life. At times, some of the partisans referred to Carmine as a "lone wolf" because of his solitary nature. Despite Carmine's independence, Tazio had befriended him through their shared pursuit in the liberation of Italy. And through their fight as partisans, the pair had grown to trust each other with their lives.

"What was your wife's name?" Tazio asked.

"Catarina," he said softly.

"Will you tell me about her?"

"*Va bene.*" Carmine peered up and smoothed his beard, as if he was searching through his memories. "We met after I returned from the Great War. I was working as an attendant on the railway in Bologna, where my family is from. The train that day was going to Firenze, and I was walking through the carriages to check the tickets of the passengers. In the last seat of the last carriage, I met Catarina, who would turn out to be the most sweet, beautiful, and caring person I ever met."

Tazio wrapped his arms around his knees.

"Our eyes met as she handed me her ticket, and I could barely breathe with my heart pounding inside my chest. Somehow, I managed to talk with her, mostly about her trip to see her family in a Tuscan village called Comeana. And I knew—before the train arrived in Firenze—she was the person I wanted to spend my life with."

Tazio smiled.

"We courted for a month, with me traveling back and forth between the Bologna and Firenze train stations. I proposed, and she accepted. She preferred to live in Comeana, near her family, but we decided to move there once we saved enough money for us to buy a small farm. We married at the church where she was baptized and moved into a cottage on an orchard in Bologna that was owned by my uncle. In addition to my job on the railroad, Catarina worked as a seamstress, and we both labored to pick fruit in my uncle's orchard in exchange for free rent. Within a year of our wedding day, she gave birth to a son who we named Valerio. We had three joy-filled years raising our son while working to save enough money to fund our dream of owning our own farm."

Tazio looked at him, gazing at the sky, and a knot formed in his stomach.

"Eventually, we found a house with a plot of land that we could afford. The week before we moved, I was asked by my railroad boss to work an extra shift, and I eagerly agreed because we needed the money. While I was away at work, my uncle needed someone to transport a harvest of figs, so it was Catarina—instead of me—who took the horse-drawn wagon to the market."

Tazio gripped his knees.

"She'd brought Valerio with her—*Dio*, that boy loved to ride in the wagon. I can still hear his laughter in my head." His jaw quivered as he drew in a deep breath. "I was told by the *polizia* that the backfire of an automobile engine startled the horse. It veered the wagon into oncoming traffic. The horse survived, mostly unscathed, but Catarina and Valerio were killed."

Oh, dear God. A chill drifted down Tazio's spine. "I'm so sorry."

Carmine rubbed his eyes and nodded. "After their funerals, I moved to the farm where we had planned to live. They've been gone for two decades, and I still can't help thinking—they'd be alive today if we moved away sooner, or if I didn't work that extra shift."

"It's not your fault," Tazio said. "Sometimes horrible things happen to good people. There is nothing you could have done."

"Perhaps." He turned to Tazio. "I'm telling you this so you don't have any regrets. If you care about someone, don't wait to do something about it. Life is fragile—and the world you want to create could be taken away at any moment."

Tazio intertwined his fingers as he absorbed Carmine's words. "*Grazie* for telling me about Catarina and Valerio. I can tell that you loved them very much."

Carmine nodded and pulled his coat tightly around his chest.

Tazio felt horrible for him. He silently promised to take his friend's advice, yet the severity of the situation weighed heavy on his mind. *I took an oath to fight against tyranny. How can Gianna and I build a future together when the war has created a mountain between us?* He shook away his thoughts and resolved to find a way to figure things out.

"Enough about the past," Carmine said. He retrieved his rifle and stood. "The sun is coming up, and we need to get the airdrop of weapons to a secure place."

Tazio got to his feet. "We also need to address another problem."

"What's that?"

"We need more partisans."

"True," Carmine said.

Their group was composed of twenty-three partisans, most of

whom were hiding among hunting camps in the hills, far from roads traveled by the Germans. Since Tazio began his mission, they had enlisted five fighters, including Gianna.

"With our recent airdrop of armament," Tazio said, "we have enough weapons to equip our partisans. But we'll be receiving more shipments, and we must muster more fighters before the battle comes to Tuscany."

Carmine rested the butt of his rifle on his boot. "Informants are everywhere. There are few able-bodied men who can be trusted."

"Then we enlist women."

Carmine tilted his head. "Like Gianna?"

"*Sì*," he said. "Many women are hiding Jews, throughout Italy and on the escape line to Switzerland. They're already risking their lives, so why not provide them with weapons and the choice to fight?"

"I agree," Carmine said. "But most of the men will think you've gone mad."

"I don't care what they think," Tazio said. "To liberate Italy, we'll need the help of every Tuscan who opposes Fascism to—"

The snap of a branch broke the stillness.

Tazio, his adrenaline on high, slipped his pistol from his jacket.

Carmine crouched and raised his rifle.

Tazio pointed his weapon toward the tree line below them, where the sound of approaching footsteps grew.

"It's Sante," a voice called out.

Tazio exhaled and eased his finger off the trigger.

Sante, carrying a hunting rifle, emerged from the trees and scampered up the hill.

"I almost shot you," Carmine said, his voice angry. "What the hell are you doing here?"

"I've come with news." Sante leaned on his weapon and gulped air. "Daniele's niece informed him that the Germans are conducting large-scale arrests of Jews."

"Oh, God," Tazio said. "Where?"

"Firenze," Sante said. "Raids are happening all over the city."

Tazio clenched his jaw.

"*Bastardi.*" Carmine looked at Sante. "Do you know if any of the arrested people have connections to our partisans?"

Sante shrugged.

"I need to get to the dead drop," Tazio said.

"I'll come with you." Carmine stepped to Sante. "There is a container with weapons in the villa. Gather some of the men and move it to camp."

"But I came all the way here to alert you," Sante said. "How about I go with you to the dead drop, and the three of us transport the weapons on our return to camp? It might be quicker that way."

"No," Carmine said, firmly. "Go."

"*Va bene.*" Sante wiped sweat from his face and scuttled down the hillside.

Tazio retrieved a weathered canvas backpack from the villa and left with Carmine. As they trekked through the forest, his mind flashed with images of German soldiers seizing innocent civilians. Anger boiled inside him. He quickened his pace and prayed for those who were arrested—and for Gianna to be far away from the Nazi raids.

Chapter 18

Tuscany—November 27, 1943

Tazio, his pulse surging, entered the abandoned iron mine with Carmine. Sunlight dwindled and the air turned stagnant as they traveled through the tunnel. Weeks earlier, Tazio gave Carmine a copy of his Slidex codebook and showed him the dead drop to ensure that he and his partisans could carry on communication with Gianna in the event he was killed or captured. He knew it was an unnecessary risk for them to be here together, given that they were the only ones with the codes and knowledge of the dead drop's precise location, but the news of the mass arrests of Jews had shaken him. And he was determined to make certain that Gianna was safe and to see if she had delivered information on the German raids.

Carmine removed a metal cigarette lighter from his pocket and lit it, casting a glow over the craggy subterranean passage.

Tazio located the dead drop and got on his knees, sending a twinge through his old injury. He disregarded the pain, lifted the rock, and discovered the ammunition cartridge with its bullet inverted into the casing. He removed the bullet and pulled out not one, but three tightly folded pieces of paper.

Thank God—she's been to the dead drop, Tazio thought. He got to his feet and looked at Carmine, the flame of the cigarette lighter reflecting in his eyes. "Gianna left messages. Let's go outside."

Carmine nodded.

They went to the entrance of the mine, shielded by pine trees. While Carmine scanned the area for possible signs of the enemy, Tazio sat down and removed his codebook and a pencil from the backpack. On most visits to the mine, he carried a prewritten encrypted message, so he usually left his codebook and writing supplies stashed away with his radio at a hunting shack. He brought the items with him to save time with communicating details of the airdrop to Gianna. And now, he was grateful that his decision to carry his codebook would allow him to decipher her words without having to return to camp.

Tazio unraveled the pieces of paper and eyed the encrypted codes with Gianna's handwriting. He deciphered the first two messages—one which contained intelligence on the schedule of German supply trains, and the other was a personal message.

I think about you all the time.

Me too, Tazio thought. *I miss you more than you will ever know.* He set aside the paper and picked up the third message, which was longer and contained more codes. And, as he deciphered the note onto paper, a wave of dread washed over him.

The enemy began mass arrests of Jews in Firenze. Hundreds captured and deported by train. DELASEM infiltrated. Lilla Milano, Rabbino Nathan Cassuto, Don Leto Casini, and all but one member of the network were arrested and interrogated at SD headquarters located at Villa Triste. Requesting partisan help to rescue them. Intelligence on the building, location of prisoners, and number of guards will be forthcoming.

Tazio felt sick to his stomach. "It's worse than I thought."

Carmine's shoulders drooped.

He handed him the deciphered message.

Carmine read the note and lines formed on his face. "*Cazzo*. How could this have happened?"

"It only takes one infiltrator to bring down the network and reveal the locations of Jews hiding in the city." A deep sadness swelled inside Tazio. "All those poor innocent people."

Carmine nodded and raked fingers through his hair. "I know the names of the members in Gianna's message, and I consider Don Casini a friend. We worked together with partisans to guide Jews to the escape line. And I always thought that his role as a priest might somehow protect him from the Germans." He shook his head in disgust and handed the message back to Tazio.

"What do you think we should do?" Tazio asked.

Carmine slipped his hands into the pockets of his coat. "Nothing."

"I disagree." Tazio tucked away the message in his jacket and got to his feet. "We need to do something."

"The arrested Jews are gone; the trains that took them away have probably already reached a German concentration camp. The DELASEM members will be mercilessly interrogated, and then they will either be shot or sent to a death camp. There is no hope for them. The only thing we can do is prepare for if, or when, the Germans gain information from DELASEM members who crack under torture."

"Like the names of you and your men," Tazio said.

He nodded. "And Gianna and Beppe."

Dread swelled in Tazio's chest. He pushed back his emotions and confidently looked at Carmine. "I will work on a plan to free the prisoners, with or without your help."

"*Porca miseria*," Carmine said, raising his hands. "They are being held at the SD headquarters. It will be a suicide mission."

"We can't give up on them," Tazio said.

Carmine shook his head. "Even if we deployed a team of partisans who were armed with submachine guns and grenades, they would never get past the German checkpoints in Firenze, let alone the front gate of Villa Triste."

"Gianna can plant pistols and plastic explosives inside the city," he said. "And if she can pinpoint the location and number of guards, as well as provide a diagram of Villa Triste, we might be able to get close enough to detonate explosives and breach a wall of the building."

"Prisoners might be killed in the blast."

"True," Tazio said. "But they'll be dead anyway if they are headed to a firing squad or death camp. A rescue attempt will at least give them a chance to escape and live."

Carmine removed a cigarette from his pocket and lit it. His hand trembled as he took a deep drag. "All right," he said, exhaling smoke. "But I want to see Gianna's intelligence on Villa Triste before I commit any of my men to a mission."

"*Va bene*," Tazio said. "Are you carrying your Beretta pistol?"

"*Sì*."

"Give it to me."

Carmine wrinkled his forehead. "Why?"

"I want to leave a weapon for Gianna—she might need it if one of the prisoners reveals her name and the Germans come looking for her."

"Why not give her your Colt pistol?"

"If she is apprehended by the Germans, it is best that she has an Italian weapon. It will give her a chance to lie about how she got it. Being in possession of an American-made pistol, or one of the German weapons we acquired, would be more difficult to explain."

Carmine nodded. He removed a compact pistol from his coat pocket and gave it to him.

Tazio checked the weapon's magazine and found it to be full. "Do you have any extra cartridges?"

"No."

Tazio retrieved his codebook and encrypted a message to

Gianna, which he rolled up and placed inside the empty ammunition cartridge with a bullet inverted into the casing. He traveled back into the mine, where he used a pocket knife to dig a deeper hole for the dead drop. He deposited the sealed message and weapon, covered the hole with the rock, and paused, placing the knife into his jacket. His heart prodded him to remain at the mine. *If I stay long enough, I'll eventually see her.* But his mind told him otherwise. *Time is running out for the people being interrogated, and we need to plan a mission.* Driven by a sense of duty, he reluctantly left the dead drop. He joined Carmine on the trek back to camp and, along the way, he made mental notes on schemes to rescue the prisoners and ways to protect Gianna.

Chapter 19

Florence—June 14, 2003

Gianna and her daughter Jenn left the hotel and walked, passing by sunscreen-covered tourists with fanny packs and bottles of water, to a café near the Duomo. They sat at an outside table with an umbrella, which shaded them from the intense Tuscan sun. Few words were spoken until a server brought them their order—a cappuccino for Gianna, and an Americano with soy milk for Jenn.

Jenn sipped her drink and fiddled with a pearl earring. "Would you tell me if you were sick?" she asked, breaking the silence between them.

She always rubs her lobes when she's anxious. "Absolutely," Gianna said, hoping to reassure her daughter. "I'm not terminally ill, and I'm not suffering from dementia or any other geriatric condition."

"Then why run away?"

Gianna crossed her ankles, bumping the table and spilling milk foam from her cappuccino. "Sorry."

"You never talked to me about your family or life before coming to the United States," Jenn said. "You only told me that your time in Italy was difficult and you didn't want to relive those memories, which I've always respected."

Gianna placed a paper napkin onto her spilled cappuccino.

"Out of the blue," Jenn said, raising her voice, "you call me from the airport to tell me that you read a newspaper article about a secret war message that you believe was intended for you, and that you're flying off to Florence."

A middle-aged couple, both of whom were holding zoom lens cameras, glanced at them from a nearby table.

Jenn leaned forward. "Mom, put yourself in my shoes. It's not far-fetched for me to presume the worst."

"You must think I'm crazy," Gianna said.

"I don't. But you haven't been truthful with me."

Her daughter's words stung her. "You're right. I haven't been honest with you."

Jenn lowered her chin.

"I wish that there was something I could do to change the past. It was never my intention to mislead or hurt you." She paused, running a finger over the rim of her cup. "My experiences in the war were too painful to talk about, so I compartmentalized my past. But I'm getting old, and I'm tired of keeping secrets."

"I'm here for you," Jenn said. "Please, you can tell me anything."

Gianna's chest felt tight, like it was being compressed in a vise. She drew a deep breath, gathering her courage, and said, "I fought as a partisan during the war."

Jenn's jaw slacked.

"I also acted as a courier, delivering intelligence and weapons, for the Italian Resistance, and my father and I hid Jews from the Germans on our family's vineyard."

"Oh, my God," Jenn said, her eyes wide. "I can't begin to imagine what you went through."

Gianna nodded. "I'll tell you what happened in the war, but I need your patience with revealing my story. Most of my life has been spent trying to forget the ghosts of my past. It will take time for me to tell—and to show—you everything."

"Okay." Jenn, her hand shaking, took a sip from her cup and looked into her mother's eyes. "I'm here for you. Your secrets are safe with me, and you no longer need to endure the burdens of your past alone."

"*Grazie.*" Gianna blinked her eyes, fighting back tears. "I will tell you about my Italian family and the fight to liberate the country from fascism. But for now, I want to start with what brought me back to Italy." She removed the newspaper clipping from her purse and handed it to her daughter.

Jenn read the article and placed it on the table. "Incredible," she said, straightening her spine. "Are you certain that this encrypted message was intended for you?"

"I am. I recognize the codes, and the handwriting of the person who sent it." A knot formed in her stomach. "It's from an American agent named Tazio who was deployed to German occupied Tuscany to aid the Resistance. He didn't survive the war."

"I'm so sorry," Jenn said. She glanced at the article's photograph. "Do you know what the message might say?"

"No," Gianna said. "But I think the communication might contain more than intelligence."

"What do you mean?"

"A personal message." Gianna looked at her daughter. "Tazio was before I met your father."

She glanced at the newspaper clipping, then gazed at her mother.

Gianna noticed how much Jenn looked like her father—cleft chin, aquiline nose, and large deep-set eyes. Seeing the resemblance and realizing what she was about to say caused a lump to form in her throat. She swallowed and, for the next hour, she told her about the partisans and the Italian and Jewish resistance organization called DELASEM. And how, during the German occupation of Italy, she sheltered Jews and smuggled intelligence to an American OSS agent named Tazio.

"My God, Mom." Jenn slumped in her chair.

Gianna expected her daughter to be upset. Confused. Perhaps even betrayed by the fact that her mother once had feelings for another man. But Jenn surprised her.

"Were you in love with him?" Jenn asked, picking at a scratch in the table top.

Gianna clasped her cup between her hands and nodded.

Jenn looked at the article. "I wish you could read the message. With the metal detectorist's discovery published in major newspapers around the globe, it'll attract the attention of lots of cryptologists. Maybe someone will crack that code."

"Perhaps," Gianna said. "But there were only two copies of the codebooks—mine was destroyed in the war, and the other was lost when Tazio perished."

"Did you come here to see the message for yourself?"

"Yes, and part of me holds hope that being here will help me to remember some of the codes to read his words." She took a sip of her cappuccino, lukewarm and bland. "I have much to tell you but my brain is overwhelmed. Do you think you could stay a few days in Florence?"

"Of course."

Gianna smiled and placed her hand on the newspaper article. "You've always been clever at crosswords. Maybe you could help me solve this puzzle."

"I'll try," Jenn said. "How about we track down that metal detectorist and pay him a visit?"

"All right." Gianna slipped the newspaper article into her purse and rose from her seat. "First, I want to show you something. Follow me."

Jenn stood and walked with her mother down a cobblestone sidewalk. "Where are we going?"

"To where it all began."

Chapter 20

Strada in Chianti—December 1, 1943

Gianna, partially dressed in undergarments, opened a bedside drawer and retrieved her Beretta M1934, a compact semi-automatic pistol, that Tazio had left for her at the dead drop. She paused, feeling the weapon's weight in her hand, and an image of Lilla—locked in a prison cell—flashed in her head. Angst grew inside her.

"We're going to get you out," Gianna whispered to herself.

She set aside her thoughts and inserted the pistol into a makeshift holster that she had created by sewing together straps of her girdle. She adjusted the Beretta, its cold steel pressed against the inner thigh of her right leg, and she practiced pulling the pistol out of her girdle, again and again.

She went to her drawer and removed two blocks of plastic explosive—each weighing two-thirds of a kilo and sealed in a rubber-coated fabric—that she'd smuggled home from the iron mine. She carefully molded one of the blocks, malleable like clay, to the back of her thigh and affixed it to her leg by wrapping it multiple times with cloth tape. She taped the other block of explosive to her opposite leg, and jumped up and down to test her work. One of the blocks shifted, sliding down to the back of her knee, so she carefully removed the tape and started over from scratch.

Once she was satisfied that her firearm and explosives would remain in place, she put on a gray calf-length wool skirt, white long-sleeve blouse, well-worn shoes, and a beige linen trench coat. She retrieved her purse, left her bedroom, and descended the stairs, the holstered pistol rubbing against her thigh. In the living room, she found Beppe sitting in his chair. A few feet away from him was her propped-up bicycle and a wooden grape crate.

"Can you see that I'm concealing things under my clothing?" Gianna raised her arms and turned around in a circle.

"No." Beppe clasped his cane and rose from his seat. "Let me see you without the coat."

She put down her purse, slipped off her coat, and slowly spun around.

"You look normal," he said. "Where are the explosives?"

"Taped to the back of my legs," she said, feeling a bit guilty that she hadn't told him about the Beretta. *He'd worry even more if he knew that I've been carrying a loaded pistol for days.*

"Do you have the fuses and detonators?" he asked.

"Inside the hidden compartment of my purse."

"Matches?"

"In my purse."

"*Va bene*," Beppe said, his voice apprehensive. He held the handlebars of her bicycle. "Try getting on."

Gianna straddled the seat. While Beppe balanced the bicycle, she put her feet on the pedals and checked the space between the seat and hidden explosives with her hands.

"Are you sure that the blocks are secure and will not rub against the seat?" he asked.

"*Sì*." She got off her bicycle and leaned it on its kickstand. "Where did you hide the remaining explosives?"

Beppe reached into the crate, removed two green warty gourds, and carefully handed one of them to her.

"Clever." She examined the gourd that, when combined as a pair, contained approximately three kilos of plastic explosive.

"I hollowed them out and filled each of them with a block of explosive. The plug is on the bottom of each gourd and is held in place with pins. I considered stuffing the explosive into the frame of your bicycle, but it would have required cutting off the rubberized fabric. Also, the explosive would be difficult to remove if it was crammed inside a tube."

"You did well, Papà," she said. "The cuts you made for the plugs are nearly impossible to see."

"They look ordinary," Beppe said, "but they're heavy. If the gourds were to be examined at a checkpoint, the person handling them would know that something is amiss."

"I'm taking a long detour to avoid checkpoints," Gianna said, hoping to alleviate her father's fear. "No one will touch them." She gently placed each of the gourds into the front basket of her bicycle.

Beppe went to the crate and transferred bottles of wine and jars of seasoned olives to the bicycle basket. "For camouflage, and your bartering cover story."

"Perfect." She picked up her purse and added it to the basket.

He helped her to put on her coat. "I hate that you are doing this. As your father, I feel like I should be safeguarding you rather than putting you in danger."

"I know you do, but the partisans need me to plant the explosives. And if the tables were turned, DELASEM members would do everything they could to save us." She looked into Beppe's eyes, filled with worry. "They're protecting us. Not one of them has revealed our names during their interrogation, otherwise we would have been arrested by now."

Beppe nodded. "I can't begin to imagine what they're going through."

"Neither can I." She stepped forward and hugged him. "I'm going to be all right."

"You will," he said.

* * *

Gianna slipped away and wheeled her bicycle out of the house. The early morning sun was blocked by gray clouds, and the air was cool and damp. She got onto her seat, gave a wave to her father, who was standing in the doorway, and pedaled down the lane.

"Catch the moment!" Beppe shouted.

A deep inner courage rose up inside her. She raised a hand into the air and called back, "Catch the moment!"

Gianna coasted down the lane, its uneven dirt and gravel surface jostling her body and rattling bottles of wine. Her heart rate quickened, and she squeezed the handlebars. *It will not blow up without my lighting the fuse to a detonator*, she thought, reassuring herself. But as a precaution, she maneuvered around holes and ruts. At the main road, she turned toward Florence and pedaled ahead, leaving the safety of the vineyard behind.

Over the past few days, Gianna had conducted surveillance of the SD headquarters at Villa Triste. She'd acquired details of the building's exterior and the placement of guards by riding her bicycle through the area at different times of the day. There was no way to tell for certain where the DELASEM prisoners were being held or interrogated, but she suspected it might be in the basement, given the faint sound of classical music that continuously resounded from a closed and bar covered cellar window. Due to a German-imposed curfew, she was unable to inspect the area at night. However, she did identify a location where the partisans could launch an attack—a section of the property's exterior wall with an overgrown hawthorn tree that blocked the view of sentries.

She'd delivered the intelligence to the dead drop. The following day, she returned to the mine and discovered blocks of plastic explosive, detonators with fuses, and a reply from Tazio. She stashed the note and explosives in her coat pockets and bicycled to the vineyard, taking detours on less-traveled roads, and deciphered his message.

> *A partisan fireteam will conduct a mission within seventy-two hours to free prisoners. Need your help to plant explosives in Firenze. Confirm precise location of supply drop.*
> *You are in my thoughts. Godspeed.*

The news renewed Gianna's hope that the prisoners might be saved. But she also felt culpable for endangering partisans, especially Tazio, whom she suspected would lead the raid on Villa Triste. She resolved to set aside her personal feelings, pray for their safety, and embark on finding a place in Florence to hide the explosives.

Gianna had few options to stash supplies within the city, given the German raids on safehouses and the collapse of the DELASEM network. So, she traveled to the church of San Pietro a Varlungo and met with Sister Rosetta. Initially, the nun was hesitant to collude to store explosives because of her devout Catholic beliefs. But she desperately wanted to free Don Casini and network members from the Germans, and Gianna reassured her that the mission was designed to save the lives of people, rather than kill soldiers, and that she would not commit a sin by aiding partisans. Sister Rosetta agreed to help and created a hiding spot inside a large bronze tabernacle behind the altar. After leaving the church, Gianna delivered a message to Tazio to inform him about the supply drop location, and then she raced home to work with Beppe on a plan for her to smuggle the explosives into the city.

Gianna, her legs taped with explosive, pedaled en route to the church of San Pietro a Varlungo. The tires of her bicycle rumbled over a badly neglected road, pocked with potholes. Bottles clanged inside the basket and one of the gourds tipped on its side. She scanned the countryside to make certain there were no onlookers. Without stopping, she stood on the pedals and ran a hand over the back of her skirt, and she was relieved to find that the blocks remained secure. She sat on the seat and bicycled past several vineyards, their vines in desperate need of pruning, and veered onto a dirt road that led to the far east side of Florence.

Several kilometers from the city, she rounded a sharp bend and her eyes widened at the sight of a Wehrmacht Kübelwagen that blocked the road. Gianna's breath stalled in her lungs. She looked for a place to turn off, but it was too late.

A lone soldier, standing on the berm with a rifle slung over his shoulder, raised his hand. "*Halt!*"

Gianna's mouth turned dry. She tightened her grip on the handlebars to keep her arms from shaking. *Keep calm. He'll check my identification papers and I'll be on my way.*

The soldier, adjusting his helmet, stepped into the road.

Gianna coasted to a stop. "*Buongiorno*," she said, pretending to be relieved to take a break from pedaling her bicycle.

The soldier, a tall lantern-jawed young man about nineteen or twenty years of age, given the lack of stubble on his face, clasped his rifle strap. "*Documenti, signorina.*"

Gianna smiled. "Do you speak Italian?"

"*Sì*," he said, abruptly. "*Documenti.*"

Gianna removed papers from her purse, which was stashed in the front basket, and gave them to the soldier.

The soldier examined the papers.

Gianna, her legs straddling the bicycle, slid up her skirt and rubbed a knee.

The soldier's eyes wandered.

She unbuttoned her linen trench coat, pinched the front of her blouse, and puffed it against her breastbone. "It's getting warm. I should have worn a lighter coat."

The soldier handed Gianna her papers. He adjusted his helmet and looked at her bicycle. "What's in the basket?"

Fear flooded Gianna's body. She thought about grabbing her pistol. But her gut told her that she'd never win a gunfight with a soldier, and she'd likely be dead before her weapon was drawn from her girdle.

"A bomb," Gianna said, calmly.

The soldier raised his eyebrows.

"I'm on my way to blow up your headquarters." She leaned forward, closing the space between them. "I'm a saboteur."

His eyes softened. A grin spread over his face.

Gianna chuckled.

The soldier laughed.

Smiling, she removed a jar of seasoned olives from her basket and opened it. "Try one."

The German hesitated.

She plucked out an olive, took a nibble, and held it to him. "Go on."

The soldier took the olive from her fingers, sniffed it, and put it in his mouth and chewed. "It's good."

Gianna got off her bicycle, leaned it on the kickstand, and approached him. "Where are you from?"

He spit out an olive pit and glanced behind him, as if he was concerned that his commander might appear at any moment. "Berlin."

"Maybe you should buy a jar," she said. "You could write to your wife in Berlin and tell her that you've eaten the best olives in all of Tuscany."

"I don't have a wife," the soldier said, appearing amused. He reached into the basket and examined a bottle of wine.

Her heart thudded inside her chest but she held her composure. "The wine is for sale, too—even better than the olives."

He shook his head and pointed at a gourd. "What's that green thing?"

"A warty gourd." Her mind raced. "It's poisonous—Tuscans use it to make rat killer."

He wrinkled his nose.

"What's the matter? Don't they have rodents in Berlin?"

"They do, but they're small. The rats are as big as cats in Firenze."

She inched close, fighting the revulsion that churned in her stomach. Her eyes met his. "What's your name?"

"Lothar," he said, tentatively. "Yours?"

"You read my papers," Gianna said, tucking her hair behind her ear. "Have you forgotten my name already?"

The soldier's face turned flushed.

She smiled. "Gianna."

"Where do you live?" the soldier asked.

"A vineyard near Strada in Chianti. I'm on my way to barter a few things in the city. Where are you stationed?"

"A boardinghouse in Firenze." He adjusted the rifle, slung over his shoulder. "I'm free most evenings. I know of a good café near the Piazza della Signoria."

"Is it the place with dozens of framed Mussolini photographs on the walls?"

He nodded. "Maybe you could find time to join me for a drink."

"That is an intriguing offer." Gianna pretended to ponder the soldier's proposition as she put the lid on her jar of olives. She raised her skirt, being careful not to expose the tape on her legs, and straddled her bicycle.

The soldier placed a hand on the handlebars. "How about meeting me tonight?"

"I wish I could. I need to get back to the vineyard."

He frowned.

"But I'm free on Saturday evenings," she said.

A smile formed on the soldier's lips. The sound of an approaching vehicle filled the air, and he slipped his hand from the bicycle.

"*Arrivederci*, Lothar." Gianna traveled ahead, doing her best to pedal normally with the pistol and packages under her skirt.

"Saturday!" the soldier called. "*Arrivederci*!"

Gianna waved and gained speed, desperately wanting to get as far away from the soldier as possible. Her heart pounded inside her chest, and her blood pumped with a strange meld of disgust and confidence. She recalled her impromptu concoctions to distract the soldier. It wasn't that she had experience flirting with men. Nor did she have voluptuous curves to turn men's heads. It came down to flustering the soldier by any means possible, even if it meant divulging the unfathomable truth.

No real partisan would jest about carrying a bomb. Besides, who would believe a woman with vineyard goods was smuggling explosives? Perhaps the best deceit is created by telling no lie at all. Gianna pumped her bicycle pedals, attempting to dispel her adrenaline. She pushed ahead believing, perhaps for the first time since she joined the partisans, that she was not only capable of being a cunning courier, but that she could also be a skilled saboteur.

Chapter 21

Florence—December 1, 1943

Less than an hour after leaving the vineyard, Gianna arrived at the church of San Pietro a Varlungo. She got off her bicycle, being mindful of the pistol and plastic explosive hidden under her skirt, and scanned the area. The stone courtyard was barren and silent, except for the caws of a hooded crow that was perched on the church's steeple. She pushed her bicycle to the entrance, clasped the handle of the door, and was relieved to find it unlocked as Sister Rosetta had promised.

Gianna wheeled her bicycle inside to find the church empty of people. The only sign of life was a wooden rack with lit votive candles. Her shoulder muscles relaxed and she drew in a deep breath, taking in the smell of ancient wood and incense.

"*Salve*," Gianna called, her voice echoing through the sanctuary.

She paused, waiting for an answer, and then rolled her bicycle through the center aisle. While she made her way past pews, she silently prayed for the safety of Tazio and the partisans, and for the rescue of Lilla and members of DELASEM. The muscles in her arms ached as she lugged her bicycle up two stone steps to the altar and propped it on its kickstand. She located a key that Sister Rosetta had left for her in a compartment inside the altar, and approached an ornate, bronze tabernacle the size of a café's espresso machine.

She inserted the key and froze at the sound of footsteps.

A clack of heels grew from an adjacent corridor.

She stashed the key back into the altar, rolled her bicycle down the steps and stood, peering up at a large wooden crucifix, and pretended to pray.

The footsteps stopped, and a familiar female voice echoed through the church. "Gianna."

Her muscles relaxed, and she turned to see Sister Rosetta standing on the opposite side of the sanctuary. "*Grazie a Dio.* I was hoping it was you." She left her bicycle and walked down the aisle, and as the woman's face came into view, a wave of dread washed over her.

Sister Rosetta, her eyes watery and bloodshot, nervously rubbed a rosary with her age-spotted hands.

Gianna swallowed. "What's wrong?"

"The Germans released Don Casini—" The nun's bottom lip quivered. "He's here, and he's asking for you."

She stepped back. "*Oh, mio Dio!*"

The nun wiped her eyes. "Come with me."

Gianna, shocked and scared, followed Sister Rosetta down a narrow corridor. The nun stopped at an open door and gestured for her to enter.

Gianna stepped inside to what appeared to be an office. On one side of the room was a writing desk with a lamp and stacks of papers, and on the other side was Don Casini, slumped in a leather wingback chair.

The priest, his hair mussed and dirty, raised his head to Gianna. His left eye was swollen shut, and bruises—the color of beetroot—covered both sides of his jaw. The shoulder of his black suit jacket was torn, his clerical collar was missing its white tab, and his fingers were wrapped in handkerchiefs stained with blood.

Her body trembled. "Oh, no."

"Gianna," Don Casini said, his voice raspy.

She approached the priest and kneeled, feeling the weight of the concealed weapon and explosives under her clothing. "What have they done to you?" she cried.

"It doesn't matter." He coughed harshly, covering his mouth with his sleeve.

Sister Rosetta retrieved a glass of water from a side table and held it to the priest's lips.

Don Casini, unable to clasp the glass with his injured hands, took gulps of water, much of which dribbled down his stubble-covered chin. "*Grazie*," he wheezed.

Sister Rosetta nodded and set aside the glass.

"Where are Lilla and Rabbino Nathan?" Gianna asked.

He looked at her with his good eye, filled with sadness. "Deported."

Gianna gasped. "No—they can't be!"

"I'm sorry," he said. "All of the members—Jewish and Catholic—were interrogated by the German SD. Yesterday evening, they were taken to the train station to be sent away to a concentration camp."

No! This can't be happening! Nausea surged through her stomach, and the wall holding back her emotions collapsed. Her vision blurred with tears, and she lowered her head into her hands and sobbed.

Sister Rosetta placed her arm around Gianna.

She wept for several minutes, then raised her head and wiped her eyes.

The nun slipped her arm away but remained at Gianna's side.

"Lilla cares deeply about you," the priest said, breaking the silence. "She thinks of you as a sister."

"Same," Gianna said, her voice quavering. "Did they hurt her?"

"I don't know. She was held in a cell on a different floor, but I suspect that she experienced similar treatment to me and the others." He glanced at a carved wooden cross that was hung on the wall and lowered his chin. "Rabbino Nathan and I pleaded with the interrogators to imprison us and free the others, but it was useless. I hate that I was the only member released from captivity. I was likely let go because I'm a priest, and the Germans want to mitigate acts of reprisal from the Catholic community. They also might want citizens of Firenze to see what they did to me, to serve as an example of what happens to ones who aid Jews."

Gianna drew a jagged breath. "There must be something we can do."

"The train that took them away is long gone." He gingerly placed his bandaged hands together. "We can pray for them. And we will continue to fight to save those who avoided capture."

Gianna dried her eyes with her sleeve.

"The Germans failed to capture all of the Jews," he said. "Some remain hiding in Firenze, and many are out of sight in rural safehouses." He rested his hands on his knees. "Sister Rosetta and I will continue our battle to conceal as many people as we can, but I will understand if you and Beppe wish to step away from hiding refuge seekers."

"Never," Gianna said. "Beppe and I will continue to hide anyone who needs protection."

"*Grazie.*" He leaned back in his chair and winced with pain.

"The doctor will be arriving soon," Sister Rosetta said, "and we'll transport you home to recover."

The priest nodded and looked at Gianna. "It is best that you are not seen with me. Informants are everywhere, and I suspect the Germans will be watching me closely. After you leave here, don't come back. I'll find a way to get messages to you or Beppe."

Gianna got to her feet. "*Va bene.*"

Don Casini raised his bandaged hands. "May the Lord be with you."

"And also with you."

Gianna, devastated and heartbroken, left Don Casini and Sister Rosetta and went to the sanctuary. With no reason to plant the explosives for the partisan operation, she gathered her bicycle and left the church.

She fought back her tears and rode away to inform Tazio to call off the mission. Instead of going home to encrypt a message, she decided to save time by going directly to the dead drop and take the risk of leaving an uncoded note. She traveled backstreets, avoiding the areas which often had checkpoints, to the west side of Florence. Her plan was to leave the city and take one of two routes, depending on sightings of German patrols, that would take her into the Tuscan hills near the abandoned iron mine. But as she passed the Florence train station, images of Lilla, Rabbi Nathan, and the members of DELASEM—loaded into rail cattle cars—ran through her brain. *I need to do something*, she thought, squeezing the handlebars. And with each stroke of the pedals, her heartbreak gradually turned to ire.

As if by reflex, she took a sharp turn, nearly striking an old man who was pulling a hand cart filled with empty glass bottles.

"*Cazzo!*" the man shouted, shaking a fist.

Gianna ignored the man's comment and sped down an alleyway. She made her way around a group of grammar-school-age children who were playing a game of marbles, and turned on to a street that ran parallel to the railroad tracks. *It won't take long.* She pushed harder on the pedals and picked up speed.

Once she was outside the city—with no buildings or people in sight—she veered to the side of the road and stopped. She stashed her bicycle behind an oak tree, hiked up her skirt, and removed layers of tape to access the two blocks of plastic explosive. She gathered her purse and the explosive—including the blocks that were hidden inside the gourds—and threaded her way through a briar patch to reach the rail line.

Using a nail file from her purse, she removed the rubber-coated fabric from the blocks to reveal a gray, clay-like substance that smelled of chemicals. She stuck one block of explosive to each side of the two steel rails, and opened the hidden compartment of her purse to retrieve arm-length fuses, each with an attached detonator that looked like a metal firecracker. She wondered, although briefly, if she was handling the materials properly, but she didn't care. Crouching, she inserted a detonator into each of the explosives and gazed down the railway line. A deep regret tore at her heart. *If I would have acted faster, we might have had a chance to free them.* She blinked back tears and whispered, "I'm sorry, Lilla."

Using a small box of matches, Gianna lit the fuses and smoldering sparks spread toward the detonators. Her heart pounded as she grabbed her purse and ran. But as she crossed the second track, the tip of her left shoe caught the steel rail, and she stumbled and fell, jarring her arms and grinding bits of gravel into her palms.

Pain flared through her hands.

Sparks spattered along the fuses toward the detonators.

Her pulse rate surged. Gripping her purse, she shot up and barreled through the briar patch, its thorns scratching her clothes and exposed skin. As she neared her bicycle, a powerful explosion erupted, knocking her to the ground. She got to her feet, her head buzzing and her legs feeling like twigs about to snap, and peered at the railroad line with two sections of demolished steel rail. She dusted her clothing, got on her bicycle, and—with her ears still ringing from the blast—she pedaled away.

Gianna raced down the road, turned onto a side street, and then abruptly slowed her speed and calmly pedaled her bicycle. Within seconds, a Wehrmacht truck filled with soldiers barreled past her in the opposite direction. A moment later, a fire brigade emerged from an adjacent road and roared toward the railroad tracks. She felt no relief from avoiding detection, nor did the rogue act of sabotage ease the grief that ravaged her heart.

Twenty minutes later, she fled the west side of Florence without encountering a checkpoint. She turned onto a rural road bordered by umbrella pines and pushed hard on the pedals. Her leg muscles smarted as she picked up speed. A kilometer farther, the road descended a steep hill and her bicycle accelerated. The wheels hummed, and her hair fluttered in the wind.

A loud crack, like the sound of a starter pistol, pierced the air. *No!*

She struggled to control the handlebars, shaking violently in her hands, from a blown front tire. She slammed on the brake, locking up the back wheel, and her bicycle skidded out of control into a ditch. Bottles of wine ejected from her basket, and the side of her body struck the ground, sending a pang through her shoulder. She labored to untangle her legs from the bicycle frame, and her hidden handgun came loose from her girdle and fell to the ground. She got to her feet, rubbed the pain in her shoulder, and secured her weapon in the makeshift holster under her skirt.

Gianna glanced at the hole—the size of a grape—in the flat tire, and then looked up at the sun and tried to estimate if she could reach the iron mine on foot before nightfall. A chill drifted down her spine. *I need to stop Tazio from leaving. Oh, God. What have I done?*

With no way to repair the tire, she gathered her purse and ran with her bicycle along the road. Within a few kilometers, her lungs burned and her legs ached, but she trudged ahead. She prayed for a farm truck to appear so she could hitch a ride, but minutes turned to an hour. And she encountered no drivers, except for a Wehrmacht soldier on a motorcycle who veered around her and disappeared down the road.

Chapter 22

Tuscany—December 1, 1943

An hour before Tazio was scheduled to depart for the raid on SD headquarters, he entered a hunting shack in the Tuscan hills and found Carmine sitting alone near an unlit camp stove. He shut the door and approached his friend, who was holding a small unopened cardboard box of US Army field rations that had arrived with the last parachute drop of armament.

"Where have you been?" Carmine asked, setting the box on his lap.

"I went to check the dead drop, and I took a walk to clear my head." Tazio sat down on a wooden crate next to him.

"Any messages?"

"No."

"Is that good or bad?"

"No news is good news." Tazio placed his hands on his knees, and he hoped that Gianna had safely planted the explosives and returned to the vineyard. "She would have informed us of any changes."

Carmine nodded. He lit a cigarette, took a drag, and picked at the corner of the ration box.

"Anxious about the mission?" Tazio asked.

"A little."

"Me too." Tazio turned to him. "We're going to be all right. We have a solid plan and camouflage to enter and exit the city. When we reach Villa Triste, you'll cover me while I scale the wall and plant the explosives. Based on Gianna's surveillance, there is a tree that creates a blind spot for the sentries. I'll be in and out of there before the detonation, and we have a place to hide until the area is clear."

Carmine puffed on his cigarette and placed it on the ground. He opened the side of the ration box and paused. "Do you know what bothers me the most about this raid?"

"That you partnered with me?" Tazio asked, trying to lighten his friend's spirit.

Carmine chuckled. "No. You, I can handle." He glanced at his wristwatch and his levity evaporated. "The worst part is the waiting."

Tazio nodded.

Initially, Carmine had been reluctant to participate in a raid that he deemed to be a suicide mission. However, Gianna's intelligence on Villa Triste had persuaded him that an operation to breach a wall of the building might have a small chance of success. Therefore, Tazio requested Gianna to plant explosives in the vicinity of the SD headquarters, while he and Carmine worked on a scheme for a partisan raid. After a day of analyzing tactical options and a map of the target area, they concocted a simple yet clever plan to smuggle Tazio and another partisan into—and out of—Florence by using a hearse, owned by a friend of Carmine.

Tazio had insisted that Carmine not participate in the raid because he wanted to avoid, if possible, having himself and the partisan leader placed in jeopardy at the same time. But when Tazio presented the plan to Carmine's men and asked for a volunteer to join him, all of them were reluctant to step forward.

"*Merda!*" a gray-haired partisan had shouted. "Only a fool would attack a Nazi lion's den!"

Even Sante, the young partisan who desperately wanted to prove himself as a fighter, wanted no part in a mission to plant explosives at the SD headquarters. Tazio, undeterred by the lack of support, went to work on an alternative plan for him, and him alone, to drive the hearse into the city. It was then that Carmine approached Tazio and gave him an ultimatum—to allow him to be his partner on the mission or he would not arrange to provide the hearse. With time running out for the DELASEM captives and few, if any, other options, Tazio reluctantly agreed.

Over the past few days, Tazio refrained from informing OSS headquarters of the impending raid. It wasn't that Tazio was disobeying orders, considering his role was to train and arm partisans, as well as to conduct raids of sabotage at his discretion. But he knew very well that if he radioed headquarters and informed them that he was planning to blow a hole in the building where the SD was interrogating the Resistance, the OSS would, more than likely, cancel the mission. *I'll inform headquarters after the raid*, he'd thought, examining a map of Florence, *assuming I'm alive to transmit a message.*

Tazio glanced out the window of the shack. "How about we leave?"

"Let's go in thirty minutes," Carmine said. "The hearse will not be dropped off at the abandoned farm until midafternoon. My friend had to use it for a funeral this morning."

Tazio folded his arms. "It won't give us much time to inspect the vehicle and get to Firenze before curfew."

"We'll have enough time. I've known this man for over twenty years, and I trust him. He'll have the hearse fueled, dropped off, and outfitted precisely as we requested." Carmine tamped out his cigarette and opened the cardboard ration box. "You should eat something before we leave."

"No, *grazie*." Tazio's stomach felt queasy, like it did on the eve that he and his OSS partner Frank parachuted into German-occupied Italy.

Carmine examined the labels on the items in the box and furrowed his brow. "I can't read English. Could you tell me what I'm about to eat?"

Tazio peeked into the box and pointed. "A tin of processed American cheese with bacon. A package of dry biscuits. A packet of lemon juice powder. Malted milk-dextrose tablets. Three sugar cubes. Chelsea cigarettes. And one stick of spearmint chewing gum."

Carmine wrinkled his nose. "Maybe I'll have the sugar, cigarettes, and gum."

"I thought you were brave," Tazio said, nudging Carmine with his elbow. "Try it. You might find that American GI food isn't as bad as it sounds."

Thirty minutes later—after Carmine finished off the tin of cheese, half a pack of biscuits, and one sugar cube—they rose from their seats. From a metal parachute container, they filled a large backpack with a case of grenades and boxes of ammunition, including cartridges for the pistols that were stowed in their jackets. Tazio put on the backpack and retrieved two M3 submachine guns, which looked like grease guns used by machinists, and handed one to Carmine.

"Are you ready?" Tazio asked.

Carmine smoothed his beard and nodded.

They left the shack and were greeted by seven partisans who were stationed in the camp. They said their farewells and received wishes of good luck.

Sante, who was holding a shotgun, approached them and lowered eyes. "Would it be all right if I accompanied you out of the forest?"

Carmine glanced at Tazio, who gave a nod. "*Va bene.*"

Tazio, Carmine, and Sante left the camp and made their way through the forest. With their weapons in hand, they trekked without speaking for nearly an hour. The forest gradually thinned and they hiked through an overgrown field to reach a stone barn of an abandoned farm. They opened a weathered double door, its rusted hinges groaning, and slipped inside.

The windowless space was dark, illuminated solely by a bit of sunlight coming from the entrance. A dank smell of earth and old manure pervaded the air, despite the fact that the farm appeared to have been abandoned for many years.

Tazio's eyes locked on the hearse, parked near an empty horse stall, and his jaw dropped open. The vehicle looked like an old black truck that had been modified by a carpenter for funeral use. The rear bed was topped with an egg-shaped compartment that was surrounded in large, curtainless panes of glass, allowing clear visibility to two pine coffins that were covered with red carnations. Ornate brass sconces, each the size of a streetlamp, were affixed to the sides of the tailgate and driver's compartment. Also, much of the vehicle, including the roof, was decorated with black ornamental molding. To Tazio, the hearse looked like a cross between a macabre circus truck and a giant fishbowl.

"Good God," Tazi said, his eyes wide.

"What's wrong?" Carmine asked.

"We need to be inconspicuous."

"What do you mean?" Carmine placed a hand on the hood of the vehicle. "It's a hearse. You wanted one that could hold two caskets, and that's what we got."

Tazio pointed. "But you can see inside."

"Of course," Sante chimed in. "It's to view the dead. Don't *americani* have funeral cars?"

Tazio's skin turned warm. "We do, but the ones we use don't have department store–like windows to display the casket."

"It won't matter," Carmine said. "When you're in the back, you'll be hidden inside a box."

Tazio knew that Carmine was right, but it didn't make him feel any better. Although Tuscans were familiar with this style of hearse, the Germans might not be accustomed to seeing such elaborate funeral cars. *The Wehrmacht will see us coming from a mile away.* He slipped off the backpack and regretted not knowing more about Italian funeral traditions. *I should have asked Carmine to find a bread truck.*

Carmine opened the driver's door to find a black suit, white shirt, necktie, pair of polished shoes, and cap. He held up the jacket. "Looks small."

"Only one way to find out," Tazio said.

While Carmine changed his clothes, Tazio opened the rear of the hearse, pushed aside mounds of carnations, and removed the unsealed lid of each pine coffin. He gathered the backpack and stashed the weapons and ammunition at the foot of each box.

"How do I look?" Carmine asked.

Tazio turned to find him dressed in the driver's uniform. The jacket was a size or two small for his broad chest, and the pant legs were too short, revealing Carmine's worn wool socks. "You look good."

Carmine struggled to button his jacket. "Are you sure?"

Tazio approached him and adjusted his cockeyed necktie. "You have nothing to worry about. You look like a driver."

The lines on Carmine's forehead softened.

Sante cradled his shotgun and rubbed his smooth chin.

"Okay," Tazio said. "Let's get me inside a box and get on the road."

The trio went to the rear of the hearse, where Tazio climbed inside the coffin on the driver's side of the vehicle. He adjusted a crate of grenades behind his knees and slid his submachine gun next to him.

"I wish I was going with you," Sante said, leaning on the tailgate.

Where were you when I asked for volunteers? Tazio thought. He pointed to the coffin next to him. "There is room if you want to join us."

The color drained from Sante's face. "I—I would if—"

"Open the door for us," Carmine said, looking at Sante.

"*Va bene.*" Sante, appearing eager to leave, leaned his weapon on a wall and pushed open the barn's double doors.

Carmine placed the cover on the empty coffin and paused, holding the second lid. "I'll see you in Firenze."

"Godspeed," Tazio said in English.

"What does that mean?"

"I'm wishing you a successful mission."

A smile formed on Carmine's face. "Godspeed."

Tazio's pulse rate quickened as the lid covered his coffin. He expected it to be pitch black inside, but the boards to the lid were slightly warped and did not form a complete seal on the box, leaving a slit-shaped peephole to a view of the side window. A soft patter of carnations being placed on the lid was soon followed by a metal clunk of the rear door closing. His anxiety intensified, and he took in deep breaths, bringing in a scent of pine.

The driver's door opened and shut, and the engine started.

Tazio swallowed. He felt the hearse back out of the barn, turn around, and drive away. The tires of the vehicle rolled over a rutted dirt road, jostling his body, and he pressed his arms and legs against the sides of the coffin to steady himself.

Carmine turned his head to the rear window of the cab that had its glass removed to give open access to the back of the hearse. "How are you doing back there?"

"All right," Tazio called.

Minutes later, Tazio felt the vehicle slow to a near stop, turn on to a main road, and accelerate. Although the ride was much smoother, the roar of the engine and hum of the tires were loud, since the rear compartment of the hearse and pine box had no soundproofing. He thought of the Resistance captives they were trying to save, and he rehearsed the plan for the mission over and over in his head. But as time passed and the vehicle approached Florence, his mind drifted to Gianna and deep regret festered inside him.

If I had known that we would be acquiring a hearse for the raid, I would never have requested her to plant plastic explosives. He felt an area of empty space in the casket with his hand. *I foolishly put her in danger when I could have brought the explosives with me.* He prayed that she was safe, and he'd find a way to complete the mission and see her again.

The vehicle braked and Tazio slid forward, striking his head on the coffin.

"Roadblock ahead," Carmine called out.

Damn it. Tazio's skin turned cold.

The hearse slowed to a stop. Seconds passed and the vehicle moved forward and stopped again. Guttural voices emanated from outside the vehicle, which was followed by the sound of Carmine rolling down his window.

"*Documenti,*" a deep male voice said with a German accent.

Hairs raised on the back of Tazio's neck. *It's going to be okay. Carmine will handle it.*

"*Steigen Sie aus dem Fahrzeug,*" the German voice said.

"*Scusa,*" Carmine said. "I don't understand what you said."

"He wants you to turn off the engine and get out of the vehicle," a young male voice with an Italian dialect said.

Oh, God! Tazio's breath stalled in his lungs.

The engine stopped, the driver's door squeaked open and shut, and footsteps clacked over the pavement.

A cold chill flooded Tazio's veins. He clasped his submachine gun, undid the safety latch, and prepared for a firefight.

Chapter 23

Florence—December 1, 1943

Tazio's pulse pounded inside his eardrums as he peeked through the small gap in the cover of the casket, which provided a view of the large side window of the hearse. An armed German soldier and a mustached member of the Italian Blackshirts, who was wearing a Fascist fez, stepped to the side of the vehicle and peered through the glass at the pine caskets.

A cold sweat dripped down Tazio's forehead. *They can't see me, otherwise the soldier would have raised his weapon.*

The soldier gestured for Carmine, who was standing by the driver's side door, to approach him.

Carmine, his hands clasped in front of him, approached the soldier.

"*Ihn öffnen*," the soldier said, motioning with his rifle.

The Blackshirt looked at Carmine. "He wants you to open the back."

Tazio tightened his grip on the submachine gun, resting on his chest.

"*Va bene*," Carmine said. He removed a white handkerchief from his pocket, cupped it over his nose and mouth, and walked to the rear of the vehicle. With his face turned away from the hearse, he squinted and fumbled as he tried to unlatch the tailgate.

"Is the stench that bad?" the Blackshirt asked.

"No." Carmine eased back, but he continued to cover his face with the handkerchief. "Tuberculosis."

The soldier's eyes widened. "*Tuberkulose*."

"*Sì*," Carmine said.

Tazio placed his finger on the trigger of his weapon.

Carmine snorted and cleared his throat. "The corpses are from the sanatorium in Prato—a husband and wife in their forties who died within hours of each other. I'm taking them to the church of San Pietro a Varlungo, where their funeral will be held." He coughed and spit into his handkerchief. "It's my seventh trip to the sanatorium this week. They're dying like flies."

The Blackshirt turned to the German soldier and interpreted Carmine's words.

Carmine cupped the handkerchief over his nose and mouth, and he clasped the rear latch of the hearse.

"*Halt*," the soldier said.

Carmine froze.

The soldier stepped back from the vehicle and spoke in German to the Blackshirt, who then walked around the perimeter of the vehicle, all the while keeping a distance as he looked through the windows.

The soldier gave a nod.

"You're free to go," the Blackshirt said.

Thank God. Tazio eased his finger away from the trigger.

Carmine stuffed his handkerchief into his pocket, got behind the wheel, and started the engine.

Tazio exhaled as he felt the vehicle pull away. *Well done, Carmine.*

At nightfall, they arrived at the church of San Pietro a Varlungo. Carmine parked behind the building and turned off the engine.

Carmine turned his head to the rear compartment. "We're at the church."

"Nice work," Tazio said.

"I saw a hell of a lot of German vehicles and soldiers on the way here. It looks like everyone is on high alert."

Tazio swallowed. "What do you see now?"

"It's dark. The parking area is empty, and there is no sign of people."

"*Bene.*" Tazio slid the submachine gun from his stomach to a small space on the side of the coffin. "Let me out when you are ready."

Carmine crossed himself and got out of the hearse. He opened the vehicle's rear gate, pushed aside carnations, and removed the lid on the coffin.

Tazio, his adrenaline urging him on, climbed out of the box and scurried around the building to the entrance of the church.

Carmine softly shut the tailgate, returned to the driver's seat, and scrunched down behind the wheel.

Tazio opened a heavy tall door, slipped inside, and was met by the sound of a whimpering baby. Several feet away, a young woman was holding an infant with her left arm while lighting a votive candle.

Tazio calmly made his way along rows of pews and sat near the front of the church. While pretending to pray, he scanned the area behind the altar and his eyes locked on a bronze tabernacle that Gianna had described in her message.

The baby's cries grew louder. Wails echoed through the church.

Tazio glanced at the woman, kneeling in front of the votive candles and pressing her baby to her chest. Tension spread through his shoulders. He turned forward and waited for the woman to leave, but she continued to pray as her baby's cries reverberated through the sanctuary. His mind raced, contemplating whether he should risk going to the tabernacle, but he held his ground.

Minutes later, the baby's cries drifted away as the woman carried her child out of the church.

Tazio sprang from the pew, ran up the steps to the front of the church, and rummaged inside the altar until he located a key. At the tabernacle, he unlocked a small brass door and opened it to find the lockbox empty. A wave of dread washed over him. "Gianna," he breathed.

He locked the box, put back the key where he'd found it, and scoured the areas around the altar but found nothing. With no other choice, he fled the church and sprinted to the hearse.

Carmine jumped out of the vehicle and opened the tailgate.

"The explosives are not there," Tazio whispered.

"*Merda*," Carmine said, his voice low. He crouched next to Tazio. "What should we do?"

"A raid without explosives is out of the question," Tazio said. "Do you think you can drive us out of here without encountering another roadblock?"

"I doubt it. The city is swarming with patrols." Carmine scanned the dark church grounds. "Maybe we should stay here."

"I don't think it's safe. Gianna's attempt to smuggle explosives here was compromised. Let's follow our plan, as if we were fleeing from Villa Triste."

"All right. Get inside." Carmine helped Tazio into his pine coffin, secured the cover, and got behind the wheel and drove away.

Tazio, feeling helpless, braced himself against the sides of the box as the vehicle traveled through the streets of Florence. *God, please let her be okay.*

Minutes later, Carmine veered the hearse to a curb near the city morgue and stopped. He turned off the engine and scanned the area through the windshield and side mirrors.

While planning the mission, Tazio and Carmine had vetted several locations to hide after they performed the raid. They both had agreed that leaving a hearse overnight at a church or cemetery might draw attention. So, they decided to park it by the morgue, where the dead were periodically transported to and from the building at all hours of the day and night.

Carmine locked the doors. "The area is clear. I'm coming to the back."

Tazio pushed off the lid to his coffin, sat up, and lifted the cover on the pine box next to him.

Carmine crawled through the rear missing window of the driver's cab and labored, on his hands and knees, to get into a coffin.

The sound of an approaching engine broke the still air.

Hairs raised on the back of Tazio's neck. "Hurry."

Carmine got onto his back by wedging his broad shoulders against the sides of the coffin, and then folded his arms over his stomach.

The grind of the engine grew closer.

Tazio put on the cover to Carmine's coffin, and then leaned back in his box and slid its lid into place. Within seconds, a vehicle roared past the hearse. He drew in air, laced with a smell of pine, and stared into the stygian blackness.

"I'm sorry I got you into this," Tazio whispered.

"It's not your fault," Carmine said, his voice muted. "I forced you to bring me with you."

Despite his friend's words, guilt needled at his conscience. "Get some rest. We'll get out of here at daybreak."

Tazio's mind toiled over the debacle. He felt awful for the DELASEM captives, who would remain imprisoned by the Nazis, and he agonized over his decision for Gianna to plant supplies in the city. *I should have brought the plastic explosives with me. I would have avoided placing her in danger, and we would have conducted the raid.* He prayed that she was safe, and that she aborted her mission to avoid enemy roadblocks. *But why didn't she get a message to me?* Angst festered inside him. Throughout the night, while German vehicles patrolled the city and he breathed recycled air, his mind and heart remained on Gianna.

At morning twilight, Tazio cracked open the lid of his coffin and scanned the area. The street and sidewalks were empty and quiet, and the windows of nearby buildings were either shuttered or blocked by curtains. He tapped on the side of the pine box next to him.

Carmine stirred and emerged from his hiding place. Without speaking, he crawled into the driver's seat, started the engine, and pulled away from the morgue.

They exited the city without encountering a road block and, as the sun began to rise, Carmine veered the hearse onto an unpaved backroad. Kilometer after kilometer of bone-jarring ruts and holes juddered Tazio inside the dark wooden box, bringing him to the brink of car sickness. Over an hour after leaving Florence, the hearse pulled into the abandoned farm and braked to a stop.

"We're here," Carmine said, turning off the ignition.

Tazio, his stomach nauseous, climbed out of the coffin and squinted at the sunshine beaming through the windows.

Carmine got out of the hearse and lowered the tailgate.

Tazio stepped out of the vehicle and took in deep breaths to quell his queasiness. "I'm going to check the dead drop. Do you mind stashing the hearse in the barn and backpacking the armament to camp?"

"No." Carmine's face turned solemn. "Good luck."

"*Grazie.*"

Tazio grabbed a submachine gun from inside the vehicle and left the abandoned farm. He suppressed his fatigue and made his way through the forest. To ensure that he was taking the shortest path, he relied on the hidden OSS button compass on his jacket to frequently correct his heading.

His anxiousness increased as he climbed the hill to the entrance to the mine. Inside, he made his way through the tunnel and kneeled at the rock that covered the dead drop. He lifted the stone and his hope swelled at the sight of a folded piece of paper. *Thank God.* Although he didn't have his codebook with him, he yearned to see her handwriting, if only for a moment. He unfolded the paper and his eyes widened from the sight of an unencrypted message.

Tazio hurried to the mine's entrance, where the light was better, and sat on the ground. He set aside his weapon, placed the message on his lap, and read her words.

Dear Tazio,

I'm sorry that I didn't reach you in time to inform you about the failed supply drop. While in Firenze, I discovered that all Resis-

A SECRET IN TUSCANY

tance captives, with the exception of Don Casini, who was badly beaten and released, were taken from Villa Triste to the train station and deported to a concentration camp.

"Oh, God," Tazio breathed.

I feel gutted. I wish I could have acted sooner to try to save Lilla and members of DELASEM. Please know that I'm grateful for your endeavors to free them.

My bicycle needs to be repaired, and it might be a day or two before my next communication. Also, please arrange to acquire more explosives. I used it all to blow up a section of rail line. I hope you are not angry with me.

His eyes widened. He swallowed and continued reading.

I pray you are safe, and that my failure to communicate caused you and others no harm. You are in my thoughts, and my memories of our time together give me hope to carry on our fight for freedom.

Gianna

Tazio, feeling stunned and dismayed, folded the message. He knew that he needed to burn the uncoded communication, but he didn't want to leave traces of burned paper near the dead drop and, perhaps even more, he refused to part with her words. He slipped the message into his pocket, picked up his submachine gun, and left the mine. Along his trek through the forest, he made mental notes to draft a communication to Gianna, and to radio headquarters to parachute-drop more plastic explosives.

Chapter 24

Florence—June 14, 2003

Nervousness fluttered in Gianna's stomach as she walked with her daughter Jenn on a sidewalk that led away from the Duomo and its flocks of tourists. Although she had been gone for nearly six decades, she recognized many of the buildings, landmarks, and streets, which resurrected long-suppressed memories of the war. A designer clothing store, that had once been a café that catered to the Wehrmacht, was now home to mannequins wearing pastel-colored hats and minidresses. A remembrance of German soldiers, laughing and drinking wine from bottles, flashed in her brain. She pressed her purse to her belly and made her way onto an adjacent street.

"Where are we going?" Jenn asked, her shoes clicking over cobblestone.

"I'll tell you when we get there," Gianna said. "It's not much farther."

Minutes later, Gianna guided Jenn into an alleyway that looked far different than it did during the German occupation of Florence. The former less traveled pathway had provided access to warehouses and rundown buildings, but now it was a commercialized pedestrian thoroughfare with boutique restaurants, a gelateria, and souvenir shops—including one that sold kitchen aprons with a nude frontal image of Michelangelo's *David*.

"*Mamma mia,*" she said, shaking her head.

They traveled down the alleyway and worked their way around a slow-moving family, all of whom were licking cones of gelato. Gianna glanced over the area, spotted a familiar stone building, and her mouth turned dry. Her pace slowed, and she shuffled to a stop in front of a hostel.

"Is this where you wanted to bring me?" Jenn asked.

"Yes." Gianna gazed through a propped-open door and recognized the wide plank flooring and plaster crown molding. In the hallway, two young women were putting down rucksacks at the same location that Rabbi Nathan had, many years before, disassembled and assembled her bicycle. Her hands trembled.

"Mom, what's wrong?"

"During the war," Gianna said, "this was the underground rendezvous for the members of DELASEM, the Italian and Jewish Resistance network that I told you about."

"Oh my." Jenn glanced inside the building.

"I rode my bicycle here to smuggle fake identification papers for Jews who were hiding on my family's vineyard." She looked up at a third-floor window of the room where Lilla had fabricated documents, and an ache grew inside her chest.

Jenn looked at her mother and swallowed. "Did something bad happen here?"

Gianna nodded and drew a deep breath. "In November of nineteen forty-three—less than a year before the Allied liberation of Florence—the network was infiltrated by the Nazis."

The color drained from Jenn's face.

"All of the network members in the city were arrested and taken to the German intelligence headquarters, a place called Villa Triste, where they were interrogated and tortured." Her eyes welled with tears. "All but one—a priest named Leto Casini who was released from prison—were loaded like cattle into railway cars and sent to a German concentration camp."

"Oh, my God," Jenn said.

"Before they were deported, I worked with Tazio on a plan for partisans to raid Villa Triste. The operation entailed using plastic explosives to breach the wall of the building—a last-ditch effort to give the prisoners a chance of escape. But we were too late." A tear fell down Gianna's cheek, and she made no effort to wipe it away.

Jenn held out her hand but stopped shy of touching her mother.

"I was smuggling plastic explosives into the city when I learned that they had been deported," Gianna said. "I was heartbroken—and enraged at what the Nazis had done. On my way home, I used the explosives to blow up a section of rail line, but the Germans repaired it in less than a day."

Jenn's eyes widened.

"The people of the network sacrificed everything to save Jews." Gianna's bottom lip quivered. "During their interrogation at Villa Triste, they endured beatings and psychological abuse. I'm alive today because none of them disclosed my name."

"Oh, Mom." Jenn blinked her eyes, fending off tears.

"Even after all these years, I can't help wondering—why them and not me?"

"It's not your fault," Jenn said.

Overcome with emotion, Gianna's legs felt weak and unsteady. She pointed to a two-person wooden table with chairs on the sidewalk near the entrance to the hostel. "I think I need to sit."

Jenn helped her mother into a chair. "I'll get you some water."

"There is no need. I'll be fine in a minute."

Jenn ignored her mom's comment and went inside the hostel. A moment later she returned with a bottle of water, untwisted the plastic cap, and handed it to her.

"Thank you." Gianna took a drink of lukewarm water. "I didn't know that hostels sold food and drinks," she said, eager to change the subject.

"This one didn't." Jenn sat across from Gianna. "I bought it from a college student on a backpacking trip through Tuscany."

"In your rush to get here, I'm surprised that you stopped to exchange currency."

"I didn't," Jenn said. "I paid ten US dollars for it."

Gianna took a sip. "You were robbed."

Jenn chuckled. She smoothed her wrinkled dress, and the levity on her face faded away. "What were the DELASEM members like?"

Gianna removed a handkerchief from her purse and wiped her eyes. "Brave, selfless, and willing to do anything to protect those who were persecuted by fascist racial laws."

"Can you tell me more about the people of the Resistance?"

"I will. But right now—right here—it hurts too much to talk about them."

Jenn nodded.

"Instead, how about we talk about something hopeful, like the people we helped to hide and escape to Switzerland?"

A soft smile formed on Jenn's face. "I'd like that."

Gianna raised her chin and searched through her memories. For several minutes, she told her daughter about the Jews who took shelter in the wine cellar of her family's vineyard.

"I was fond of all of our guests," Gianna said. "But one family in particular—a pregnant woman named Aria Cavalieri and her five-year-old son, Eliseo—created a special place in my heart."

Jenn intertwined her fingers and leaned in.

A memory of Beppe, handing Eliseo a farewell gift, flashed in her brain. *"This compass kept me safe during the last war,"* her father's voice echoed inside her head, *"and now it will do the same for you and your mamma."*

"What happened to them?" Jenn asked.

Gianna drew a deep breath and exhaled. "I don't know. Tazio and I took them to partisans, deep in the hills, and they were led away by a guide for the escape line to Switzerland. That was the last time I saw them."

"Did you try to look for them after the war?"

"No."

Jenn furrowed her brow. "Why not?"

"After experiencing so much suffering and death, I couldn't handle any more loss."

The lines on Jenn's face faded.

"I like to believe that they reached freedom when they crossed the border to Switzerland, and that they had a gorgeous life."

Jenn nodded. She clasped her mother's water bottle on the table and picked at its glued paper label. "I feel like I know next to nothing about your family."

Regret pricked Gianna's conscience, and she looked into her daughter's eyes. "I'm sorry. Before we leave Tuscany, I promise to tell you everything, but there are pieces of my story that I need to share with you first."

"Okay." Jenn set aside the water bottle.

"I'm exhausted," Gianna said. "I think I should go back to the hotel and lie down for a while."

Jenn stood and helped her mother to her feet. "While you get some rest, I'll make some calls to see if I can locate that metal detectorist."

Gianna nodded.

Jenn looked into her mother's eyes and confidently said, "We are going to find the man who has Tazio's encrypted message. And some way, somehow, we're going to break that damn code and find out what it says."

Gianna smiled.

She looped her arm around Jenn's elbow and they left the area of the former DELASEM headquarters. As they made their way back to the hotel, Gianna's mind buzzed with thoughts of the past and present. She had little doubt that her assertive, whip-smart daughter would find a way to lead them to the metal detectorist, but she was uncertain that the secret message could be deciphered without the codebook. Most of all, she wondered if she had enough courage left inside her to reveal the rest of her story, and the everlasting repercussions of her decades-old mistakes.

Chapter 25

Strada in Chianti—June 5, 1944

Shortly before sunrise, Gianna lit a lamp in the living room and paused, looking at her golden abstract painting that Tazio had called *Hope*. Memories of him reeled through her mind—the timbre of his voice, his words of comfort, the sensation of his touch. A deep longing rose within her, and she wondered, although briefly, when she would see him again. She unhooked the artwork from the wall, placed it face down on the sofa, and removed the backing to retrieve her Slidex codebook. She gathered a pencil and paper, and while recalling her surveillance of a German stockpile of heavy artillery guns near the town of Impruneta, she encrypted a message.

Over the past six months, Gianna buried herself in her role as a partisan. But her tireless efforts did little to soothe her sadness over the demise of DELASEM and the loss of her friends. Each day, she prayed that Lilla and the imprisoned Resistance members would find a way to survive a German concentration camp. *Hold on, Lilla*, Gianna often thought, lying awake at night. *The Allies are coming—you need to fight to stay alive.* But deep in her gut, she understood that the chances of survival at a Nazi prison camp were bleak. She resolved to hold on to the belief that Lilla and the others would survive, and to carry on her clandestine battle against German occupation while protecting as many Jews as she could.

Don Casini had recovered from the injuries he sustained during his brutal interrogation by the SD, and he'd resumed his work, albeit more cautiously and on a smaller scale, to provide aid to Jews. Months earlier, the priest arranged to smuggle a young Jewish married couple to the Conti family vineyard. But without Lilla as a forger—with her experience of creating counterfeit documents and her ability to acquire special paper, ink, and chemicals—there was no way to create IDs that appeared authentic. Gianna and Beppe encouraged the couple to remain hidden at their vineyard until the war was over. However, the couple feared being discovered because of the immense buildup of German troops in Tuscany, and they insisted on trying to reach the Swiss border. So, after weeks of hiding in the wine cellar, Gianna guided the couple under the cover of darkness to Carmine's camp, where she handed them off to a partisan who led them northward on the first leg of the escape line. And while she was at the camp, she was disappointed not to see Tazio, who had gone on a two-day mission to sabotage an enemy fuel depot.

Gianna had not seen Tazio since she led him to Carmine's group. He went to the iron mine at night, and she traveled there during the day to avoid breaking the German-imposed curfew. Although they kept opposite routines, she'd kept in frequent contact with him through dead drop communications, which included both messages of military intelligence and personal notes of affection. *You are beautiful, selfless, and brave,* he'd written in his last message. *Thoughts of you give me strength and hope.* Despite months of physical separation, Gianna felt close to him, as if their exchange of secret letters had created an unbreakable emotional chain that bound their hearts as one.

Descending footsteps came from the stairs, and Gianna raised her head from her codebook.

"You're up early," Beppe said, entering the living room.

"So are you," she said.

He leaned on his cane. "I couldn't sleep."

"Neither could I, so I thought I would get an early start."

"I'll warm up some leftover barley *caffè*."

"No need," she said.

"I insist. I'll be in the kitchen." He turned and left.

Gianna finished her encrypted message and tucked it away in the hidden compartment of her purse. She placed the codebook inside the painting, affixed the backing, and hung it on the wall.

She entered the kitchen and was met with a comforting smell of burning oak. She sat and crossed her ankles.

Beppe removed a pot from the cast-iron stove, poured the steaming brew into two cups, and gave one to Gianna.

She took a sip, hot and bitter.

Beppe sat across from her and peered out the window at the sunrise casting a reddish-orange glow over the vineyard. His face turned somber. "Someday, we'll wake up to a new and better world."

"We will," she said. "We keep hearing rumors that the Allies are weakening the fortification lines in the south. Eventually, they'll break through and liberate us from the Germans."

"They will." He took a gulp of coffee. "But we still need to remove the cancer that spreads through our country."

She nodded.

"I hate that our people are divided between Fascist collaborators and those who desire democracy. In addition to our fight against Hitler's army, we have our own bloody war to contend with." He leaned forward in his chair and looked at her. "I keep thinking about what happened to the workers in Firenze."

A knot formed in Gianna's stomach.

In the spring, Florentine workers went on strike in a show of solidarity against German authorities and Mussolini's Italian Social Republic, Hitler's puppet state. Hundreds of workers—mostly older men who were employed in textiles, glassworks, and mechanical sectors—were arrested and deported to a Nazi concentration camp called Mauthausen. Unlike other mass arrests, which were led by the German military, this one was conducted by the Italian National Republican Guard.

"It makes me sick to see fellow Italians turned against each other," Beppe said.

"I hate what is happening, too," Gianna said. She clasped her cup but made no effort to drink. "You once told me that things would get worse before they get better. The fact that workers are willing to protest tells me that our people are gaining the confidence to stand against our aggressors. When the Allied forces get to Firenze, our people will find the courage to take up arms and liberate the kingdom from Fascists."

Beppe patted his daughter's hand. "You've got your *madre*'s spirit."

"And yours."

He smiled.

Gianna finished her coffee. "I should go."

"Be careful."

"I will."

Gianna left the kitchen and went to her room. She quietly removed her pistol, given to her by Tazio, from under her mattress and put it in the makeshift holster of her girdle. She left the house, loaded her bicycle basket with items from the wine cellar, and rode down the lane.

Shortly after reaching the main road, Gianna was passed by a Wehrmacht ten-truck convoy, which blasted her body with wind and nearly pushed her and her bicycle into a ditch. She was unnerved by the near crash, but she was far more concerned about where the vehicles were headed. Instead of traveling to the south, the trucks were rumbling northward on a road that led to a German stockpile of artillery near Impruneta, a town less than a twenty-minute bike ride from the Conti vineyard. Hairs rose on the back of Gianna's neck. She gripped her handlebars and pedaled ahead.

Thirty minutes later, Gianna turned onto a dirt road that was partially overgrown with weeds. She traveled for several hundred meters to the ruins of an ancient villa, where there were two parked vehicles—a Wehrmacht half-track tractor and a bulldozer. Over the past few days, she'd observed the motorized machines from a road on an adjacent hill and noticed that they did not move. A section of the hillside was partially excavated, and stacks of concrete blocks and mounds of sand littered the area. To Gianna, it appeared as if the German crew had been temporarily called away from building a lookout bunker.

The air was still, except for a distant bark of a dog. She scanned the area to make certain no one was around and leaned her bicycle against a tree. Her heart rate quickened. From her basket, she removed her purse and two bottles, eyeing them to make sure they were not the ones filled with wine, and scurried to the motorized machines. Using a corkscrew from her purse, she opened the bottles and a whiff of petrol penetrated her nose. She inserted cotton strips into the mouths of each bottle, lit them with a match, and tossed them into the driver's compartment of the tractor and bulldozer, engulfing them in flames. With her veins pumping with adrenaline, she sprinted to her bicycle and pedaled away.

Later that morning, after surveilling several roads and hillsides for military movement, she slowed to a stop and placed her bicycle down in a dense thicket and covered it with foliage. She hiked into the forest, all the while listening and observing her surroundings. She trudged over a section of rugged, hilly terrain, and her leg muscles ached as she ascended the slope to the iron mine. At the entrance, she leaned against an old timber post and took in deep inhales to catch her breath.

I should have brought a canteen of water, she thought, her mouth feeling like cotton.

She rested for a few minutes, until the ache in her legs subsided, and made her way into the tunnel. She paused to allow her eyes to adjust to the darkness, then located the dead drop and kneeled.

Birds fluttered from pines near the opening of the mine.

Gianna straightened her spine and peered at the entrance. She waited, listening intently, and then exhaled. *It's nothing.* She lowered her head and reached for the rock that covered the hole.

A sound of moving stones came from outside.

Her skin turned cold. She stood and lifted the hem of her skirt.

Footsteps grew louder.

She slipped her pistol out, undid the safety, and aimed toward the mouth of the tunnel. Her breath stalled in her lungs. She struggled to steady her trembling hand and placed her finger on the trigger.

Chapter 26

Tuscany—June 5, 1944

Fear flooded Gianna's body as a human shadow appeared at the entrance of the mine. She pressed her back to an earthen wall and loose rock rained onto the ground, echoing through the underground passage. *Oh, Dio!*

The intruder stopped.

With wide eyes, she held her breath and adjusted the aim of her pistol.

A thin shadow, the size and shape of a rifle barrel, rose on the tunnel's entryway.

Every fiber of her body wanted to flee deep into the mine, but she held her ground. Her finger tightened on the trigger.

"Gianna," a male voice said.

She froze. "Tazio?"

"*Sì.*"

She exhaled and lowered her weapon. "*Grazie a Dio!*"

Tazio stepped into the tunnel, placed a submachine gun against a wall, and approached her.

Gianna, relieved and overjoyed, put down her pistol and hugged him. She felt his warm embrace, squeezing her tight, and she nuzzled her head to his chest. "I almost shot you."

"I'm sorry I scared you," he said.

She eased back and looked into his eyes. "I can't believe it's really you."

He smiled. "It's so good to see you."

"What are you doing here during the day?"

"I'm unable to travel here tonight. Carmine and I are leaving for a few days to issue weapons to partisans in Malmantile." He slipped away, took off a backpack, and put it on the ground.

"You could have come to the dead drop after you returned from Malmantile," she said. "Is something wrong?"

"No. I wanted to leave a message with good news." He faced her and smiled. "I received a radio transmission from my headquarters—Rome fell to the United States Fifth Army."

She gasped. "When?"

"Twenty-four hours ago."

"*Madonna mia!*"

He placed a hand on her shoulder. "US forces are less than three hundred kilometers away. A month or two from now, Firenze will be liberated."

Tears of happiness welled up in her eyes. "It's finally going to happen."

"It is." He lowered his hand. "In the meantime, we have much to do to prepare partisans for the fight."

"We do." She wiped her eyes and set aside her elation. "The Germans are stockpiling heavy artillery in Impruneta, and it looks like they are starting to build bunkers on some of the high ground. When the Allies get here, they'll encounter a hell of a firefight. I hope your OSS headquarters has a plan to provide more guns for partisans."

"They do," he said. "Over the next several weeks, Allied planes will parachute-drop large amounts of rifles, submachine guns, and ammunition into the countryside. Soon, we'll have more supplies than partisans, and we need to get weapons into the hands of every able-bodied man and woman who isn't loyal to the Fascists."

"There are few fighting-age men left." She glanced outside. "Don Casini once told me that there are hundreds, maybe even thousands, of women—throughout towns and villages stretching from Firenze to Milano—who are protecting Jews, like me and Beppe. We should use Casini's contacts, as well as people who run safehouses for the escape line to Switzerland, to expedite the issuing of weapons."

"I agree," he said. "Carmine said the same thing, and he's working on it as we speak."

"*Bene.*" Gianna drew a deep breath and looked at his backpack. "I'm thirsty. Do you have any water?"

"I do. Let's go outside."

They sat under a large pine tree that shielded the entrance to mine, and Tazio removed a canteen from his backpack, undid the cap, and gave it to her.

She guzzled water, soothing a dry burn in her throat. "*Grazie.*"

He nodded. "You look great."

"Liar." She smoothed her skirt over her legs. "Pedaling has turned me to skin and bones."

"No," he said. "You look beautiful."

Her face blushed. "So do you."

He picked up a handful of dry, fallen pine needles and sprinkled them onto the ground. "How is Beppe?"

"His spirit is strong," she said. "But with the collapse of DELASEM, he wishes he could be doing more to protect Jews from the Germans. We have room to hide them, but Don Casini is mostly working alone, and he has fewer means to smuggle people to our vineyard."

He turned to her. "I'm sorry about what happened to Lilla and the others."

"Me too." A twinge of remorse needled inside her. "If I had acted sooner, we might have given them a chance to escape."

"You did everything you could to rescue them."

She nodded, reluctantly. "I appreciate what you and Carmine did to try to save them."

"We wanted to help." He peered up at pine branches. "After the Allies liberate Italy, they will carry on the fight until Nazi Germany surrenders. And those in their captivity, including Lilla, will be free."

"*Grazie* for saying that." She swirled water inside the canteen and hoped that she would see her friends again.

"When you get home," Tazio said, changing the subject, "tell Beppe I said hello, and that I intend to fulfill my promise to join him for a grape harvest after the war."

"I will. He'll be happy to hear that you plan to keep your word." *And so am I.* She gulped water and put the cap on the canteen. Her stomach gurgled. "*Scusa*."

"I have some food. Would you like something to eat?"

"Something small would be nice," she said, despite not having eaten all day and her belly aching with hunger.

Tazio grabbed his backpack and placed it between them. He rummaged inside and removed three malted milk-dextrose tablets, a tin of chopped ham and eggs, two fruit bars, and a one-third-full wine bottle that was stopped with a cork.

"Do American soldiers get wine with their field rations?"

He chuckled. "No. It's grappa, given to me by Carmine. He takes all the chewing gum and cigarettes in the ration kits, and he insists that I receive something in exchange for them."

Gianna removed cellophane paper from a fruit bar, took a bite, and chewed, filling her mouth with a sweet figlike flavor. "It's good. Have some with me—it's nice not to eat alone."

Tazio took some of the bar and handed it back to her.

She took a few bites and pointed to the grappa. "Will you have some with me?"

"A little." He picked up the bottle and removed the cork.

Gianna held the tin of chopped ham and eggs. "Do you mind if I take this home to Beppe?"

"No, but are you sure you want to carry something with a label written in English? It would be impossible to explain if you're caught with it at a checkpoint."

She raised her brow. "I've been smuggling forged papers, weapons, and plastic explosives. Also, I carry the pistol you gave me in a makeshift holster attached to my girdle. I think I can handle hiding a tin of meat and egg."

He smiled. "True."

Gianna finished off the fruit bar and felt her energy begin to return.

He handed her the bottle of grappa.

She sniffed the top. "Smells strong."

"It is," he said. "I prefer wine much better."

"Me too." She sipped a bit of the grappa, which tasted more like firewater than a liquor distilled from leftover grape skins, pulp, and seeds from winemaking. A burn drifted down her throat and settled into her stomach. She passed the bottle to Tazio, who took a swig.

For several minutes, they remained silent as they ate the second fruit bar. The sound of birds filled the air, and afternoon sun beamed through a gap in the trees and warmed their faces.

"I've missed you," she said, breaking the silence.

"Me too." He slid his hand next to hers. "It's temporary."

She touched his fingers.

Tazio squeezed her hand. "The war will soon be over. Lilla and the others will be liberated from German camps. You'll resume your studies at the university." He looked into her eyes. "You'll pursue your dreams and will have a long and beautiful life."

Even in the most terrible of times, you give me hope. Anticipation fluttered in her stomach. "Perhaps I want more."

"Like what?"

She swallowed. "You."

He gently caressed her hand with his thumb.

Her skin tingled. "Being surrounded by death and destruction has taught me that there are no guarantees of tomorrow. Even with the war on the brink of coming to an end, I feel like our lives can be taken away at any moment. There might not be a future for us, but I don't want to let another day pass without telling you that you mean everything to me."

"I feel the same way," he said. "I can't imagine my life without you."

A wave of joy washed over her.

He placed his arm around her.

She shifted close and her heartbeat accelerated.

They lowered onto a bed of pine needles and faced each other.

He touched her hand, and their fingers entwined.

As if by reflex, she leaned into him and felt his arms wrap around her back. Her breath quickened. She closed her eyes and sensed his lips approach her own.

Tazio gently kissed her. His lips drifted from her parted mouth to her chin, and then rested against her neck.

Gianna's heart thudded inside her chest. "I want to be with you," she breathed.

He placed a hand to her cheek. "Are you sure?"

"*Sì*," she said, her body molding to his. She returned his kiss, deeper and longer. As their embrace faded, they undressed each other, gliding their fingers to undo buttons. Buckles. Zippers. With her lips, she caressed his palm, and then placed his hand against her bare chest.

"I will never do anything to hurt you," he whispered.

"Nor I," she breathed. Her heart danced, like a bird attempting to free itself from a cage.

They embraced, their hands and lips exploring each other. There were no guarantees for a future together, but she wanted nothing more than to be with him—here and now. As their bodies became one, Gianna's heart soared, and she wished that their time together would never end.

Chapter 27

Tuscany—June 5, 1944

Tazio awakened to the sensation of Gianna's breath, flowing in tranquil waves over his bare chest. She was curled next to him with an arm and leg draped over his body. He peered up inside the branches of the umbrella pine filled with golden rays of afternoon sunlight. For minutes, he remained still, relishing her warmth and listening to the cadence of her breath.

Gianna stirred and opened her eyes.

"*Ciao, bella,*" he said softly.

She smiled. "I fell asleep."

"So did I." He pressed his lips to her hair. A faint scent of olive oil soap filled his nose, resurrecting images of their intimacy.

She glided a finger over his sternum. "This afternoon was wonderful."

His skin tingled. "It was."

"I wish we could stay hidden here, nestled in each other's arms, until the war is over."

"A beautiful thought," he said.

She drew a long breath and exhaled. "It's getting late. I should go."

"Someday," he said, pulling her close, "we won't have to rush off. We'll make love all night and, in the morning, I'll bring you breakfast in bed."

She kissed his shoulder. "Would it be a bed of discarded clothes and pine needles?"

"No. We'll have a real bed with fluffy pillows and fine linen sheets, and food that doesn't come in a field ration kit."

"That's too bad," she said, gently poking his ribs. "This was perfect."

He smiled. "It was."

Tazio stood and helped her to her feet. They collected their clothing and shook them to remove pine needles.

"No peeping at my unmentionables," she said, dusting her girdle.

He chuckled. "A little too late for that, don't you think?"

She turned, covering herself with a bundle of clothes, and smiled.

He held out his hand.

She gingerly stepped to him in her bare feet.

He tossed aside his clothing and wrapped her in his arms.

She laughed.

He squeezed her tight.

She placed a hand to his cheek and kissed him long and soft, and then eased away and whispered, "I want to stay, but we both need to leave."

He nodded.

"When will I see you again?"

"I don't know. I'll communicate through the dead drop as often as I can, but with the Allied invasion drawing near, there is a chance we might not see each other until Firenze is liberated."

"It's temporary," she said, as if reassuring herself.

He looked into her eyes. "It is."

Gianna dressed and raked her fingers through her mussed hair. He put on his clothes and they went inside the mine where they gathered their things and exchanged the coded messages that they'd planned to deposit for each other in the dead drop. They walked outside, kissed goodbye, and departed in separate directions. But several meters into Tazio's trek, he stopped and watched her disappear into the forest.

A deep yearning to be with her grew inside him. He wanted to run after her, hold her in his arms, and never let her go, but they each had a job to do. Since his arrival in German-occupied Italy, he had suffered the loss of his fellow agent Frank, and he had witnessed death, destruction, and suffering bestowed upon innocent civilians. It was heartbreaking for Tazio, given his Jewish heritage, not to be able to do more to shield Jews and their protectors from the Nazis. For months, he'd felt little more than sadness, but Gianna had resurrected his joy and fervor for life. She'd given him friendship, warmth, and—most of all—hope. But regardless of his desire to be with her, he knew that their being together would need to wait. He was committed to his role as an OSS agent, and she was dedicated to fighting as a partisan and aiding Jewish refugees. The only chance for them, he believed, was for the Allies to liberate Italy.

Tazio adjusted the straps on his backpack and hiked through the forest. He gripped his submachine gun and silently prayed for swift progress of the Allied invasion, an end to the Nazis and their evil quest to eradicate Jews, and a chance to see his Gianna again.

Chapter 28

Tuscany—June 5, 1944

Gianna hiked out of the forest and uncovered her bicycle from under the foliage. She placed her purse, which contained Tazio's tin of food under its false bottom, into the front basket and worked to push her bicycle through thigh-high weeds. She stopped near the berm of the road, and she listened and scanned the area for movement. When she was certain no one was around, she rolled the bicycle onto the road, got on her seat, and headed toward home.

Thoughts of Tazio and their intimate interlude played over and over in her mind. She felt a tug at the corners of her mouth and realized that she was smiling. Prior to seeing him, she was mentally spent and her body was riddled with fatigue. But now, her spirit was renewed and her legs felt strong, like steel pistons, as she pumped the pedals of her bicycle. She picked up speed, taking pleasure in the wind blowing her disheveled hair.

An hour or so before sundown, Gianna veered her bicycle onto the dirt lane that led to the vineyard. Eager to see Beppe, she stood up and pedaled hard. Bumps jarred her body and rattled the few remaining bottles of wine in the front basket, but she didn't slow her pace. *He'll be elated that Rome is liberated*, she thought, gripping the handlebars. *And he'll celebrate the victory with an American ration tin of chopped ham and eggs!*

She traveled along a rolling field of grapevines and, as the house came into view, her eyes locked on a Wehrmacht all-terrain staff car that was parked in front of the house. A chill shot down her spine. She braked hard, skidding the bicycle to a stop, and eyed the area but saw no sign of German soldiers or her father. Her heart pounded inside her chest. She considered turning around and pedaling away, but she felt compelled to ensure that Beppe was safe. She gathered her courage, cautiously rode to the house, and propped her bicycle on its kickstand.

A guttural male voice emanated from the home.

Goose bumps cropped up on her arms. She discreetly felt the pistol, hidden under her skirt, to make certain it was secure in its holster. She grabbed her purse and made her way past the German vehicle, its convertible top open, and saw several folded maps on the passenger seat. A sickening ache twisted in her stomach, and she willed herself to approach the front door. *Act calm.* She drew a deep breath and exhaled. *Everything will be okay.*

"*Ciao,*" she said, entering the house.

"In the living room," Beppe called out.

She turned the corner and found her father standing with an SS officer and two Wehrmacht soldiers. Despite her trepidation, she remained poised and stepped forward to the men.

"Gianna," Beppe said, "this is SS-Hauptsturmführer Volker Krahl."

The Nazi officer removed his visor cap and locked eyes with Gianna. "*Buonasera.*"

She swallowed. "*Buonasera.*"

The officer was in his late twenties or early thirties and wore a field-gray uniform with insignia patches on a black collar. His visor cap, tucked under his arm, was emblazoned with a silver skull and eagle, and his polished jackboots shined like volcanic glass. His neatly combed blond hair was long on top but with a crew cut at the back and sides, and his left ear was lumpy and deformed, resembling a cauliflower.

"You may call me Herr Krahl," the officer said in Italian with a German accent.

She held her purse in front of her. "Is there something we may help you with, Herr Krahl?"

He put on his cap. "You must relinquish your home."

Her mouth dropped open. She looked at her father, his eyes filled with angst.

"Herr Krahl is commandeering the house and vineyard," Beppe said.

Her body felt weak. "Why?"

"I deemed it necessary," Krahl said.

"But this is our home," Gianna said, unable to contain her words. "Where will we live?"

Beppe touched his daughter's arm, as if he were trying to temper her emotions. "Herr Krahl has agreed to allow us to stay in the building that contains the wine cellar."

Krahl placed the tips of his fingers together and looked at Gianna. "On the condition that you and your father obey my orders and serve my men. If this is not acceptable, you must go now."

Anger boiled inside Gianna, but she kept her composure and nodded.

"We will follow your rules," Beppe said. "We'll be no trouble to you and your men."

Krahl gave a nod.

One of the soldiers, his face stoic, adjusted the strap of a rifle that was slung over his shoulder.

Gianna's mind toiled, struggling to think of something that she could say or do to convince the officer to find another property in which to billet. But deep in her gut, she knew that if she challenged his authority, it would likely make things worse for her and Beppe. *This can't be happening!*

Krahl clasped his hands behind his back and walked, his jackboots clacking on the wood floor, around the living room. He paused, looking at each of the paintings on the walls.

Gianna's breath stalled in her lungs.

The officer approached Gianna's golden abstract painting and tilted his head.

She imagined him ripping open the painted canvas and discovering her codebook. Fear flooded her body.

Krahl clasped the frame, which was slightly cockeyed, and adjusted it.

She silently exhaled.

Krahl folded his arms and looked at Beppe. "Your collection of modern pieces would be considered degenerate art in Germany."

"*Scusa*," Beppe said. "Most are amateur pieces by my late wife. She did not have formal classical art instruction, and they are hung for sentimental purposes." Beppe shuffled to Gianna's golden painting. "I will remove them for you."

"*Nein*," Krahl said. "Leave them."

Beppe stopped. His eyes met briefly with Gianna's and he leaned on his cane.

"I'd like to see the house and grounds," Krahl said. "With your feebleness, it will be faster if your daughter showed me the property."

"Of course," Beppe said. "I'll follow behind in case you have any questions about—"

"Stay here with my men and get them bottles of your wine to sample."

The soldiers perked up their heads.

Beppe nodded.

Gianna fought back her hatred and looked at the officer. "Follow me."

While Beppe served the soldiers wine, Gianna showed Krahl the washroom and each of the upper-floor bedrooms. The officer asked no questions and appeared satisfied with a quick walk-through of the house. But in the upstairs hallway, Krahl stopped and looked up at the retractable ladder in the ceiling.

"What's in the attic?" he asked.

"Storage boxes, old trunks, and crates with empty bottles," she said.

"Open it."

She pulled down the ladder and stepped aside.

He climbed the ladder, its rungs creaking under his weight, and peered inside.

A memory of Tazio, hiding in the secret space in the attic, flashed in her head. She hugged her arms. "Do you want me to fetch a candle?"

"*Nein.*" He descended the ladder and looked at Gianna. "Show me the rest of the property."

She led him outside to the wine cellar, where Krahl walked along rows of stacked wine barrels and racks of bottled wine. Throughout his inspection, he appeared uninterested, given his brisk pace and silence. After a brief look around the cellar, he ordered her to go outside and show him the grounds.

For nearly an hour, as the sun slowly lowered on the horizon, they walked the rolling hills of the Conti vineyard and olive orchard. Unlike the buildings, he took his time exploring the grounds, and he stopped several times to check a compass and look through a pair of field binoculars.

Krahl, standing a few meters ahead of Gianna, peered southward.

Gianna's mind drifted to her fallen brother Matteo, and then to Lilla and the members of DELASEM, who were likely fighting to survive in a German concentration camp. Anger grew inside her. She placed a hand on her skirt and felt the weapon below the wool material. Her pulse rate quickened. *I can get off a shot before he can turn around*, she thought, biting her bottom lip. *But the soldiers will hear the shot, and Beppe and I will likely be killed.* She folded her arms and resolved to gain as much intelligence about Krahl as she could.

"Your Italian is excellent," Gianna said, breaking the silence between them.

The man ignored her and looked through his binoculars.

"Do you have Italian relatives?"

He wrinkled his forehead. "I studied in Rome for a few years."

"May I ask you a question?"

"*Sì.*"

"What do you plan to accomplish by acquiring our family's land?"

"Defend the Reich."

"With what?"

He lowered his binoculars and looked at her. "With the men and equipment of my Panzergrenadier regiment."

She imagined tanks and armored vehicles rumbling over the vineyard. Her mouth went dry.

"The sun will be down in less than thirty minutes. You have until then for you and your father to collect your things and vacate the house." He turned and raised his field glasses to his eyes.

Gianna, feeling shaken, returned to the house and informed Beppe of Krahl's demand. They scrambled to gather clothes, blankets, and a few personal items, which they tossed into a pair of old suitcases. Also, Gianna inspected her room to make certain there was no evidence that would link her to the Resistance. She desperately wanted to retrieve her codebook, but it was impossible with the soldiers in the living room. *It's safely hidden for now*, she thought, lugging her suitcase and a bundle of blankets. *I'll find a way to get it later.*

As night set in, she and Beppe placed blankets on the ground of the wine cellar to create makeshift beds. She lit a lamp, casting a glow over the dank, cavernous space, and peeked through a crack in the door.

"What are they doing?" Beppe asked

She strained to see through the darkness. "I think the soldiers are removing a few things from their vehicle and placing them into the house. I don't see Krahl, but there is light coming from the living room and your bedroom window."

"*Bastardi.*" Beppe shuffled to her. "I'm sorry you are in this mess."

She hugged him. "There is nothing either of us could have done. We are safe, for now, and that is all that matters."

Beppe nodded.

"Let's sit," she said. "I have some things to tell you."

"Me too." Beppe pulled up the suitcases and sat on one of them. "You go first."

Gianna sat beside him and lowered her voice, even though the Germans were out of earshot. "Krahl commands a regiment of soldiers with armored vehicles. The location and topography of our land caught his attention. He's bringing in his men to set up a defensive line."

Beppe rubbed his bearded chin. "Maybe our vineyard is a temporary place to locate his regiment before moving to the German lines in the south."

"No," Gianna said. "I think he plans to stay."

"What makes you so sure?"

"Because"—she glanced at the door—"Rome has fallen to the Allies."

His eyes turned wide. "Did you hear this from Krahl?"

"No. It came from Tazio."

He clasped his hands. "*Grazie a Dio!*"

"I saw him today at the dead drop," she said. "It's not a rumor. His headquarters sent a radio transmission to inform him that the United States Fifth Army liberated Rome."

"When?"

"Yesterday," she said.

Beppe beamed and raised his cane in the air. "The *americani* finally broke through."

She nodded. "The OSS will be parachute-dropping large amounts of weaponry to Tazio, and we'll be recruiting more men and women to fight the Germans. In a month or two from now, Firenze will be free."

"And so will we," Beppe said.

Gianna retrieved her purse, removed the hidden tin of food, and gave it to Beppe. "A gift from Tazio. He said to tell you that he plans to fulfill his promise to join you for a grape harvest."

"He's a good man," Beppe said.

"He is, Papà."

"How is he?"

"*Bene*," Gianna said.

"I'm glad. It's been far too long since you last saw him. The war will not keep you apart much longer."

"I hope so," she said. "All right. What did you need to tell me?"

Beppe drew a deep breath and exhaled. "This morning—"

A rumble of vehicle engines broke the still night air.

Hairs raised on the back of Gianna's neck.

Beppe stashed the tin of food in his pocket.

Together, they went to the door, cracked it open, and peeked outside. Under the glow of moonlight, two armored vehicles carrying soldiers rumbled up the lane and parked near the house.

"Maybe we should run away tonight," Gianna whispered.

"I can't," he said.

She shut the door and turned to him. "I know that you don't want to abandon our home, and it will be a difficult journey with your leg, but I think we should consider going to Tazio and the partisans."

"That's not it." Beppe placed a hand on his daughter's shoulder. "Soon after you left this morning, Don Casini smuggled two Jewish girls to the vineyard."

"*Oh, Dio*," she breathed. "Where are they?"

He pointed toward the end of the wine cellar. "In the secret chamber."

Her hands trembled.

The voices of soldiers emanated from the house.

"You should go without me," Beppe said. "I'll tell Krahl that you decided to stay with friends in Firenze, and I'll take care of our guests while they remain hidden. In a month or two, this will all be over."

She considered the options, none of which were good, and she looked into his weary eyes and said, "I'm not leaving you. And I cannot and will not abandon Jews in need of protection."

Chapter 29

Tuscany—June 19, 1944

Tazio, accompanied by Carmine and ten partisans, stood on a steep slope of a high-elevation hill that overlooked a barren section of the Pisa–Florence railway. The temperature was warm and the sun was high in a near cloudless sky. Beads of sweat covered the men's faces as they labored to set up M1919 Browning machine guns on tripods.

Tazio grabbed a backpack that contained plastic explosive, detonators, and fuses that he'd recently received in a parachute drop. He approached Carmine and asked, "Would you prefer me to plant the explosives, or do you want to do it?"

"I'll do it," Sante said, leveling a tripod. He adjusted a red bandana on his neck and approached them. "I'm the youngest and fastest of the lot. I can easily get down and up this hill."

Carmine clasped an ammunition belt around his chest and paused, glancing down the sharp incline to the rail line, fifty meters below their position.

"It's not about youth and speed," Tazio said. "It's about timing and precision."

Sante rubbed a bit of stubble on his boyish chin. "You and Carmine taught me how to use explosives. I can do it."

"Give the *bambino* a chance," a mustached partisan said, opening a box of ammunition.

Tazio looked at Carmine. "It's your call."

Carmine wiped sweat from his brow and looked at the young partisan. "*Va bene.*"

Sante smiled. "*Grazie.*"

Tazio handed Sante the backpack. "Plant a block of explosive on each rail and hide in the tall weeds near the tracks. It will take a loaded train a minute or two to stop after applying its brakes. We're using thirty-second fuses, so light them when the locomotive is thirty to forty seconds from reaching you. If you have difficulty estimating the train's speed and distance, look up the hill to me and I will give you a signal."

"All right," Sante said.

"Remember," Tazio said. "We are not here to simply blow up the rail line—the enemy can repair it within a day or two. Our goal is to derail the locomotive, so don't give it time to stop ahead of the destroyed section of rail."

"I got it," Sante said.

"After the fuses are lit," Carmine said, "scramble up the hill. We'll cover you with gunfire, if needed."

Sante nodded.

"Any questions?" Tazio asked.

"No," Sante said.

Tazio glanced at his watch. "The German supply train should be coming through here in about two hours. In the event that it comes early, it's best that you plant the explosives now and remain hidden in the weeds."

"*Va bene.*" Sante put on the backpack and descended the slope.

Carmine turned to the partisans, who were setting up their weapons, and raised a finger to his mouth. "*Silenzio.*"

The men's chatter faded away.

Tazio opened a crate that contained grenades and distributed them among the partisans. He walked over the hillside to make sure the men and their machine gun nests were concealed by either trees, bushes, or piles of foliage, and then climbed to a higher-elevation boulder that provided a bird's-eye view over the railway line.

Carmine scaled the hillside and joined Tazio. "I hate having the men perform a daylight ambush," he said softly.

"Me too," Tazio whispered, "but the German supply trains have been running at midday."

Carmine rubbed the back of his neck.

"It'll be all right," Tazio said. "We'll strike fast and flee the area."

The lines on Carmine's face eased. He sat on the ground and lit a cigarette.

Tazio placed a hand over his eyes to shield the sun, and peered down at the railway that stretched through the base of vast Tuscan hills. He inhaled, bringing in a whiff of tobacco smoke.

"Are you going to the dead drop tonight?" Carmine asked.

"*Sì.*"

"How about I join you?"

"No need."

Carmine took a drag. "In time, you'll hear from her. She probably hasn't had anything out of the ordinary to report, or she's playing it safe by avoiding the dead drop. The number of German transports on the road near the mine has grown tenfold."

Tazio nodded, but an angst stirred inside him.

Since his chance meeting with Gianna two weeks before, he hadn't received a coded message from her at the dead drop. It was unlike her, he believed, to go this long without communicating. Initially, he chalked it up to informing her that he was going away to Malmantile to arm partisans. But days passed with no word from Gianna, and his concern for her well-being weighed heavy on his heart.

Carmine is right, Tazio thought, trying to convince himself that everything was going to be okay. *Eventually, I'll hear from her.*

After nearly two hours of the partisans waiting in silence, thin white plumes appeared in the distance.

Tazio, crouching low to the ground, looked through a pair of binoculars. His pulse rate quickened at the sight of an approaching steam locomotive rolling down the tracks. He nudged Carmine and handed him the binoculars.

Carmine pressed a cigarette butt into the ground and placed the field glasses to his eyes. "There are some passenger carriages, but it's definitely a supply train. I see railcars with artillery guns."

Tazio and Carmine scurried down the slope. Under the cover of shrubs and trees, they made their way from machine gun nest to machine gun nest, placing the partisans on alert.

A rhythmic chug of a fast-moving locomotive, a kilometer or so away, broke the still air.

Partisans got behind their machine guns. A few of them crossed themselves, while others readied their weapons for battle.

Tazio peered down the hill at the railway and his eyes widened. Sante, who had an arm folded over his face, was lying in the weeds with his back against the railway embankment. *What the hell is he doing?* Rather than break silence, he picked up a stone and threw it, like a center fielder throwing a baseball to home plate. The stone sailed through the air and landed near the tracks.

Sante stirred but remained on the ground.

The rumble of the train grew.

Tazio's skin turned hot. With little choice, he placed two fingers to the corners of his mouth and whistled, sending a sharp shrill through the air.

Sante perked up his head.

Carmine peered down at the railway line and a scowl formed on his face.

The young partisan scrambled to his feet and looked up.

Carmine pointed.

Sante peered down the track at the oncoming train.

Tazio grabbed a submachine gun and crouched on the ground.

Be patient, he thought, watching Sante creep up the weed-covered embankment to the railway line.

The chug of the locomotive's pistons filled the air as it barreled toward their location.

Sante ran onto the tracks.

Tazio felt his adrenaline start to flow. *Wait! It's too far away!* He waved an arm, trying to get his attention.

Sante slipped a metal lighter from his pocket and lit a fuse.

Damn it! It's too soon!

Sante darted to the next rail, ignited the second fuse, and sprinted away from the tracks.

"*Merda!*" Carmine hissed.

Tazio, feeling helpless, undid the safety on his weapon and stared at the approaching train.

Seconds passed and, as Sante clambered up the hill, two explosions quaked the ground. A fountain of earth and broken steel rails spewed high into the air, and was followed by a thunderous echo over the valley.

The locomotive braked, its wheels screeching over steel rails.

"Get ready to fire on my command!" Carmine called out to his men.

Partisans swiveled the noses of the machine guns toward the train.

The locomotive slowed. German soldiers, like hornets crawling out of disturbed nests, emerged from passenger carriages, and climbed onto the flatbeds that held artillery guns.

"Fire!" Carmine shouted.

Machine gun fire erupted from the partisans. A barrage of bullets pelted the side of the train. German soldiers scattered, and many of them took cover behind large armored shields of tank artillery guns. Rifles emerged from the windows of the passenger cars and returned fire.

A bullet whizzed over Tazio's head. His pulse pounded in his ears. He fired blasts from his submachine gun, striking the locomotive and spraying sparks over its metal boiler.

A SECRET IN TUSCANY

The train crawled to a stop thirty meters shy of the destroyed rail line. German soldiers, dodging bullets, turned the barrels of the artillery guns to face the flare of gunfire coming from the hillside.

A few of the partisans tossed grenades, but the train was too far away and the bombs exploded short of their target.

Sante, crawling on his belly, reached the partisans and scrambled for cover behind a pine.

German soldiers loaded ammunition into the artillery guns. Barrels were raised and shellfire exploded. High caliber projectiles—which were designed to pierce the armor of Allied tanks—battered the hillside. Explosions erupted near the partisan positions, and pines were splintered like matchwood.

"Fall back!" Carmine shouted.

Tazio shot forward and helped a partisan, lugging a machine gun and tripod, to climb out of his nest.

The Germans adjusted the barrels of their guns.

Artillery shells bombarded the hillside. Shouts and screams pierced the air.

"Retreat!" Carmine shouted.

Tazio dived into bushes as bullets blasted over the ground. He got up, fired rounds from his machine gun, and then ran to a partisan—a forty-year-old man named Alfeo—who was struggling to flee with a wound to his right lower leg. He slung his weapon onto his back, hoisted the man onto his shoulder, and fought to get him up the hill. A shell exploded ten meters away. Pieces of dirt and rock peppered his body. He pushed forward, carrying the injured man away from shellfire.

Tazio—his muscles screaming with fatigue—crested the summit of the hill. The shellfire, coming from the valley, faded to sporadic gunshots. He put Alfeo on the ground, pulled a bandana from his neck, and wrapped it around the man's wound.

"You're going to be all right," Tazio said, struggling to catch his breath. "It looks like a bullet went through your calf without damaging bone or blood vessels." He tightened the bandage.

The man groaned.

Tazio scanned the area and spotted two partisans who were running away through the forest. "We need to keep moving."

"Leave me," Alfeo gasped.

"No. I'm going to get you out of here."

He helped the partisan to stand on his good leg, looped the man's arm around his shoulder, and together they lumbered through the undergrowth. But within minutes, guttural voices shouted in the distance.

"*Beeilung!*"

"*Sehen Sie doch, da drüben!*"

Tazio's heart thudded against his chest. "We're outnumbered and we can't outrun them," he said, his voice low. "We need to hide."

"Go," Alfeo said, struggling to hop on one leg. "Save yourself."

"*Sie sind dort lang!*" a German shouted, closer and louder.

Fear flooded Tazio's veins. He scanned the forest, and his eyes locked on a large uprooted oak tree. They lumbered ahead and Tazio lowered Alfeo into a hole that was partially covered by roots and earth.

"*Schnell!*"

Tazio gathered armfuls of leaf litter and covered Alfeo, who was curled into a fetal position. He placed his weapon to his chest, got in next to him, and pulled in more debris, but it was not enough to conceal him. So, he reached up, grabbed onto the tree roots—which were clumped with soil—and shook as hard as he could. Earthen rain fell onto their bodies. He covered himself and placed his finger on the trigger of his weapon.

Footsteps came closer.

He peeked through a gap in the debris mound. Seven Wehrmacht soldiers—four with submachine guns and three with rifles—sprinted toward his position. He held his breath and silently prayed that they wouldn't see them.

A gunshot echoed over the forest.

A German pointed. "*Schnell!*"

The Wehrmacht soldiers altered their path and disappeared through the pines.

Tazio exhaled and quietly sucked in air.

They remained hidden and silent until they no longer heard voices or gunshots. Tazio emerged from the camouflage, pulled his fellow partisan out of the hole, and helped him to hobble away.

Long after sunset, Tazio and Alfeo arrived at the partisan camp and were met by Carmine and some of the men who conducted the raid.

"*Grazie a Dio!*" Carmine said, greeting them.

Tazio handed Alfeo—his head slumped and standing on one leg—over to a partisan who'd served as a medic in the Great War.

"Wait," Alfeo wheezed. He raised his head to Tazio. "*Grazie.*" He nodded.

The injured partisan was helped away.

Tazio put down his weapon and faced Carmine. "How many did we lose?"

"Two." Carmine blinked his eyes, as if he were fighting back his emotions. "Egidio and Gavino."

An image of the men, playing card games together, flashed in Tazio's head. "Damn it."

Sante emerged from a hunting shack and approached them. "*Mi dispiace*," he said, lowering his head. "I made a mistake."

"You did," Tazio said. "Two men are dead."

Sante slumped his shoulders.

"You're confined to camp duties until further notice," Carmine said, his voice filled with anger. "But tomorrow, you'll be assigned to help recover the bodies, assuming they were not taken by the Germans."

Sante nodded, and he stepped away and sat alone on a fallen log.

"I could have prevented this," Carmine said, looking at Tazio. "I should have never let him handle the detonation."

"Me too." An ache of guilt went through him. "I could have insisted that you or I plant the explosive."

Tazio felt horrible. In his role as an OSS agent, he was responsible to arm and train partisans to combat the enemy. And in doing so, he needed to allow them to take responsibility for guerilla warfare, even at the cost of making mistakes. But nothing in his OSS training prepared him to deal with the death of people whom he cared about. He hoped that this would be the last of the losses inflicted upon Carmine's group, given that the Allied forces were closing in, but deep in his gut he sensed that the worst was yet to come.

Chapter 30

Florence—June 15, 2003

Gianna—wearing a casual blue linen dress, white tennis shoes, and a floppy straw sun hat—left the hotel with her daughter Jenn. On the sidewalk, she spotted a young man in a rental-car uniform who was standing beside a red, compact Fiat hatchback.

"*Buongiorno*," Gianna said.

"*Buongiorno*." The man glanced at papers attached to a clipboard. "Jenn Farro?"

"That's me," Jenn said, approaching him.

While Jenn spoke with the man and signed papers, Gianna got into the passenger seat and was met with a stale smell of cigarette smoke, embedded into the interior of the vehicle. She closed the door and rolled down the window.

Jenn—wearing a white blouse and black wide-leg pants—got behind the wheel and closed her door. She scrunched up her nose and frowned. "It stinks in here."

"It's not so bad," Gianna said. "It's a beautiful day. You'll have your window down most of the time anyway."

Jenn, appearing a bit annoyed, lowered her window.

Gianna glanced at the rental car man on the sidewalk. "If it bothers you, ask him for another car."

"I'll deal with it," Jenn said. "It was difficult getting this one delivered on short notice. With all the narrow roads, I don't want to take a chance of having to get a bigger vehicle."

Gianna removed her hat and tossed it, along with her purse, into the back seat.

Jenn fiddled with the pedals and examined a small diagram on top of the stick shift.

"Are you sure you can drive a manual transmission?" Gianna asked.

"Yes. Dad taught me. My first car in college was that rusty old Volkswagen Beetle with a four-speed manual transmission. Remember?"

"I do, but I thought it was an automatic," Gianna said. "When was the last time you drove a stick?"

Jenn scratched her head. "In college. I sold it when I landed my first job and moved to Manhattan."

Gianna raised her brows. "You haven't driven one since then?"

"No. Only automatics."

"Mamma mia."

"You have nothing to worry about," Jenn said, putting the key in the ignition. "Driving a stick is like riding a bike."

Gianna buckled her safety belt and crossed herself.

Jenn chuckled. She started the engine, adjusted the gear shift, and the car jerked forward as she released the clutch. She drove down a tight one-way street and traveled through the city following a young woman on a Vespa scooter.

The day before, Gianna's daughter tracked down the address and phone number for the metal detectorist, named Aldo Ajello, who'd discovered the encrypted message. Initially, Jenn tried to locate the man by using the hotel's front-desk computer, but it had dreadfully slow internet speed, and she quickly became frustrated with having to discontinue her search each time a guest entered the hotel to check in. So, she contacted an investigative service that sometimes did work for her law firm and faxed them a copy of the newspaper article. Within a few hours, she received the metal detectorist's telephone number and address in the Tuscan town of Lucca.

Gianna, feeling both nervous and excited, had called the metal detectorist a dozen times over the past day. But with each call the phone continued to ring with no answering machine to leave a message. So, Gianna convinced her daughter to make a trip to his home to try to see him and, at the very least, leave a note on his door.

Jenn downshifted, grinding the gears of the rental car, and entered a traffic circle that was congested with cars, trucks, and scooters.

"You need to get over," Gianna said, pointing to an upcoming sign. "Lucca is that way."

"Darn it. Hold on." Jenn glanced at the rearview mirror, stomped on the gas pedal, and veered to the right, cutting off a man driving a tiny three-wheeled truck.

"*Uffa!*" the man shouted, shaking his fist out the window.

Cars honked their horns.

"Sorry!" Jenn said, waving her hand. She exited the traffic circle, upshifted, and accelerated down the road.

Gianna patted her daughter's knee. "Fast and assertive. You almost drive like an Italian."

Jenn smiled. "What do you mean by almost? I thought I handled that blender of a speedway quite well."

"Next time, don't apologize. Cuss back and lay on the horn. Everyone will think you're a local."

Jenn chortled and relaxed her grip on the wheel.

It's good to hear her laugh. Gianna eased back in her seat, and the levity between them faded as they traveled into the countryside. She gazed through the windshield at the road that she'd traveled many years before on her bicycle. She hoped that meeting the metal detectorist could somehow bring closure to her years of heartache and regret. But she knew that holding Tazio's message in her hands, or even cracking the code to read his words, would likely not erase her deep-rooted pain. To forgive herself, she believed, she would need to face the past and divulge everything to Jenn.

Gianna shook away her thoughts and looked at her daughter. "I'm glad you're here."

"Me too," Jenn said, her attention on the road.

Gianna looked at Jenn, her eyes surrounded in dark circles, and she recalled how her daughter tossed and turned in their shared hotel bed. "You were restless last night."

"I hope I didn't keep you awake."

"You didn't," Gianna said, not wanting to make her feel bad. "Were you worrying about me, or missing Bella and Enzo?"

"Both."

"Please don't fret about me."

"It's hard not to," Jenn said. "I'm doing my best to be patient, but I'm still in the dark about much of your life in Italy."

"I know, and I'm sorry." Gianna smoothed her dress over her legs. "After we pay a visit to the metal detectorist, I have some places I'd like to show you, and things to tell you."

She nodded.

"Also, let's make a call on your cell phone to Bella and Enzo when we get back to the hotel. I miss them, too."

"Okay."

Gianna drew a deep breath and exhaled. She gazed at the window and thrummed her fingers against the door.

Jenn glanced at her. "What's on your mind?"

"I was thinking—" Gianna adjusted her safety belt and turned toward her. "Have you given any thought to dating?"

Jenn's eyes widened. "Jesus, Mom. That's the last thing on my mind right now."

"I mean when you get back home," Gianna said. "You're young, smart, and attractive. You've been divorced for quite some time. It wouldn't hurt for you to meet someone."

"I don't have time for a relationship," Jenn said. "I have a career and two children to raise."

"Maybe the best time is now." She leaned against her seat and crossed her ankles. "It's painful for me to be back here. Despite the passing of decades, I lament the consequences of some of the things I've done—and didn't do."

Jenn chewed on her bottom lip.

"I don't want you to wake up one day—many years from now—and wish you had done things differently. I'm not saying that another person will make you happy. I've always believed that true contentment comes within oneself. But sharing your life with someone you adore makes your time on this Earth sweeter."

Jenn blinked her eyes, as if fending off tears.

"You're a great mom, and you've worked your tail off for that law firm to give your kids a wonderful life." Gianna picked at a scratch in the door panel. "Maybe it's time to be good to yourself."

"I'll try," Jenn said.

Gianna looked at her. *"Bene."*

Jenn wiped her eyes. "How about we listen to some music?"

"Sounds good," Gianna said.

Jenn turned on the radio, adjusted a knob, and settled on a station that played classical music. For the rest of the drive they did not speak, with the exception of pointing out road signs.

A few kilometers from Lucca, Jenn stopped at a petrol station and purchased a folded paper map of the city and province. While seated in the parked car, they located the man's street, called Via Romana, on the map, and plotted a course from their current location. They left the gas station and, with Gianna acting as a navigator, they arrived at the address of a large white apartment building. Jenn parallel parked the car between a cluster of scooters and a dust-covered Alfa Romeo convertible, but it took her four tries to get close to the sidewalk.

As they approached the building, butterflies swirled in Gianna's stomach. At the rear of the complex, they located the man's apartment number on a ground-level unit.

"Ready?" Jenn asked.

Gianna nodded.

Jenn knocked on the door. Seconds passed, and she knocked again.

"Are you looking for Aldo?" a woman's voice called out in Italian.

Gianna peered up at a gray-haired woman who was removing laundry from a line outside a second-floor window. "*Sì*. Do you know where he is?"

The woman removed a sock from the line and dropped it into a basket. "He's probably traveling the country and searching for war relics with that radar contraption of his."

"Do you know when he might be home?" Gianna asked.

"No. He often leaves for days, sometimes a week or more at a time."

"*Mamma mia*," Gianna breathed.

"What did she say?" Jenn asked.

"She doesn't know when he'll be back, and that he could be gone for days or a week."

Jenn folded her arms.

Gianna looked up at the woman. "If I give you a message for Aldo, will you deliver it to him when he's home?"

"*Sì*," the woman said, removing a pair of underwear from her line.

"*Grazie*."

Gianna opened her purse and retrieved a small pad of paper and pen that she'd snagged from the hotel room. Using her daughter's back to place the pad, she wrote out a message and gave it to her to deliver to the woman on the second floor. And while Jenn was gone, she scribbled a duplicate message and slipped it into a mailbox with the man's apartment number. *A little insurance can't hurt.*

Gianna, feeling disappointed but not surprised, got in the car with Jenn and left.

"He will call us," Jenn said, shifting gears.

Gianna nodded.

Jenn turned the vehicle onto a main road that led toward Florence. "You said that you wanted to show me something."

"I do." Although she thought she could find her way by memory, she unfolded the map, flipped it over to reveal a larger chart of the roads in Tuscany, and lowered her eyeglasses. "In about four kilometers you're going to make a right."

"Where are you taking me?"

"You'll see when we get there."

Gianna navigated Jenn through several backroads, each traveling deeper into the Tuscan countryside. And thirty minutes after leaving Lucca, she turned to her daughter and said, "Pull over."

Jenn furrowed her brow. "We're in the middle of nowhere."

"Please, pull over."

Jenn veered the vehicle to the berm and turned off the engine.

Gianna got out of the car, scanned over the forest, and her eyes locked on a hill which looked the same as it had during the war. Her heart rate quickened.

Jenn got out of the vehicle and approached her. "What are we doing here?"

"We are going to take a little walk."

"Where?"

Gianna pointed. "An abandoned iron mine. It's where the dead drop was located for messages between me and Tazio."

Jenn's eyes widened. "Mom, we can't go up there."

"Yes, we can. There used to be a trail, and even if it is covered over by undergrowth, I know the way."

"No," Jenn said. "It looks like a dangerous hike. You could fall and break a leg, for God's sake."

Gianna placed her hands on her hips. "I'm in good shape for my age. I take long walks every day."

"Not up wooded hillsides," Jenn said, her voice filled with concern. She looked out over the rolling, treed landscape. "This morning, you insisted that I wear sneakers instead of my dress shoes. You knew we were coming here. Why didn't you tell me?"

Gianna swallowed. "I was scared that you would refuse to drive here, and that you would try to talk me out of it." She glanced at the hill. "I'm going to the mine, with or without your help."

"This is crazy," Jenn said. "What do you expect to accomplish by going up there?"

"It's unlikely that Tazio stashed his codebook in the mine, but I want to search the area of the dead drop to make sure." An ache grew inside Gianna, and tears welled up in her eyes. "Also, I feel that I need to go there—it was the last place Tazio and I were together."

"Oh, Mom."

"Please, I want to go."

"I know you do, but you might not be physically able to reach it."

"I can if you help me." Gianna looked into her eyes. "We can do it together. We've come so far. Why stop now?"

Chapter 31

Strada in Chianti—July 17, 1944

Gianna, carrying a wicker laundry basket, left the house and walked into the yard. She approached a clothesline covered with German military uniforms, underwear, and socks that she'd hand-washed in a tub and hung to dry in the sun. She felt a pair of pants to check that it was no longer damp, and she plucked the garments from the line and tossed them into the basket. She carried the laundry to the house, but stopped at the doorstep and gazed over the Conti vineyard.

In the distance, forty idle Panzer tanks were positioned, with their guns facing south, on the highest ground of the property. Large swaths of grapevines lay in ruins, trampled under steel tank treads. Ten armored vehicles, which were used to transport Wehrmacht troops, were parked among ancient trees in the olive orchard. German dialect filled the air, and scores of military tents dotted her family's land, which had been transformed into a military outpost.

A burning hatred spread through her core. She squeezed the handles of the basket and went inside to the kitchen, where she placed a flat iron on a hot wood stove.

The door opened and closed, and Beppe—who was carrying a burlap sack with clinking bottles of wine—shuffled with his cane into the kitchen.

She set aside the laundry and helped him to remove bottles of wine from the sack and place them on a counter.

"Where's Krahl," he said, his voice low.

Gianna pointed to the ceiling. "Upstairs."

Beppe nodded.

She looked into her father's eyes, surrounded with dark circles. "How are you holding up?"

"*Bene*," he said. "You?"

"I'm all right."

Beppe approached a wall with a framed photograph of his late wife, Luisa, placed his fingers to his lips, and touched the glass.

Gianna clasped her mother's wedding band attached to her necklace. "I miss her, too."

Beppe lowered his hand and turned to her. "We are going to get through this. After the war, we'll fix what they've done to the vineyard."

"We will."

Gianna set up an ironing board, covered it with a Waffen SS tunic, and picked up the hot flat iron from the wood stove.

Beppe looked at the tunic. "Krahl's?"

She nodded.

He glanced over his shoulder and spat on the uniform.

Her brows raised.

"Looks like it could use some starch. What do you think?"

She spat on the tunic and covered it with the hot iron, producing a sharp sizzle.

"*Bravo*." Beppe gave her a pat on the shoulder, picked up the empty sack, and left the house.

Gianna, reinvigorated by her father's unyielding spirit, adjusted the tunic on the board, and pressed it with the iron.

Over the past month, SS-Hauptsturmführer Volker Krahl forbade Gianna to leave the vineyard. He ordered her to perform household chores for him and two of his officers who billeted in the house. She washed and ironed their uniforms, polished their jackboots, made their beds, filled their canteens, and cooked their meals—made from a mix of German officer rations and Italian food that Krahl's soldiers had confiscated from farms and village markets.

Unlike Gianna, who was ordered to perform housework, Beppe was permitted to do chores in the wine cellar and tend to a small sector of grapevines that was far away from the soldiers and their equipment. But at lunchtime, and throughout much of the evening hours, Beppe was commanded by Herr Krahl to act as a wine waiter, serving the best vintages of the Conti vineyard's Chianti to him and his fellow officers.

While Krahl and his soldiers occupied the vineyard, Gianna and Beppe secretly sheltered two Jewish girls—Etta, age fourteen, and Nunzia, age twelve—whose parents were abducted in the German raids to round up Jews in Florence. The two girls remained stowed away in the hidden space of the wine cellar for nearly twenty-four hours a day. For a brief period each night, Beppe stood lookout at the cellar door while Gianna opened the barrel that covered the hidden chamber. She provided them with food and water, and while she disposed of urine and excrement in a slop bucket, Etta and Nunzia stretched their legs by walking along the rows of barrels in the wine cellar. But within minutes, they returned to their hole and the entrance was sealed shut. It broke Gianna's heart to see them hiding like mice. But there was nothing she could do, at least for the moment, while the vineyard was occupied by the enemy.

Beppe had pleaded for Gianna to run away and join the partisans, but she'd refused to abandon him and the refugees in their care. *All of us will be free when the Allied forces liberate Italy,* Gianna had told Beppe. But days turned to weeks, and the tanks and armored vehicles did not move from the property. It became increasingly clear, to Gianna, that Krahl had chosen the ground of her family's vineyard to be a defensive line against the Allies. Eventually, the firefight would arrive, and they needed to find a way to flee with Etta and Nunzia before the cannonade erupted. Beppe felt strongly that they should seek refuge in a nearby church when the

Allies invaded the area. But Gianna—given her months of traveling the Tuscan countryside on her bicycle—believed that the best place to hide Etta and Nunzia would be at a remote mountain village, somewhere northwest of the city of Lucca. She hoped, with time, that she could convince him she was right.

In addition to the refugees being trapped on the property, Gianna failed to recover her codebook and messages because Krahl had transformed the living room into a command center. The sofa and chair were moved aside to make room for a large table with maps and a radio, and throughout the day a steady stream of soldiers entered the house to report to Krahl and his two officers. Also, Krahl often drank himself to sleep on the sofa, a few feet away from her golden abstract painting that concealed her codebook and messages. Eventually, Gianna resigned herself to the fact that it would be too dangerous to attempt to retrieve the codebook, and she told herself that it was in a safe place, where neither Krahl nor his men would find it.

Gianna hated not being able to communicate with Tazio. She hoped that he, or one of the partisans, would eventually learn that the German military had requisitioned the vineyard. It pained her to think that he was worried about her. Even more, she feared for his safety as the fighting drew close. Often at night, she remained awake in her makeshift bed in the wine cellar, reimagining the warmth and passion she'd felt while wrapped in his arms. *Someday, we'll be together, and nothing will ever keep us apart.*

A clack of jackboots emanated from the stairs.

Gianna's skin prickled. She folded the last ironed piece of clothing and added it to a stack on the kitchen counter.

Herr Krahl, wearing his spare uniform, entered the kitchen and eyed the neatly folded laundry. "Before you put the clothes away," he said in Italian, "get me a drink."

A strong-smelling aftershave, reminiscent of bergamot and witch hazel, penetrated Gianna's nose. She lowered her head and picked up a clay pitcher of water.

"*Nein.*" He pointed to the bottles on the counter. "*Vino.*"

Gianna put down the pitcher, retrieved a corkscrew, and opened a bottle. She poured wine into a glass and placed it on the table.

Krahl removed his visor cap, exposing his deformed ear, and placed it on the table. He took a gulp of wine and wiped his lips with the back of his hand.

Gianna scooped up the pressed clothes and placed them into the basket.

He stepped forward, blocking her path out of the kitchen. "I dislike drinking alone. Have *vino* with me."

"No," she said. "Perhaps one of your officers will join you."

"They are busy conducting inspections in the field." He traced her body with his eyes. "They will not be back for a while."

She became anxious.

Krahl took a sip of wine. He moved close and ran his knuckles over her cheek.

Gianna stepped back and looked him directly in the eyes. "Don't touch me," she said firmly.

"It's all right," he said. "I won't bite."

She thought of her pistol, stashed in the wine cellar, and regretted that she hadn't put it in the girdle holster under her skirt. Fear flowed through her but she remained poised. "I need to leave."

"No—you don't."

Her mind raced, and she glanced at a drawer that contained knives.

He drained his wine and refilled his glass, all the while continuing to block her path. "You're always avoiding me and my fellow officers. I know little about you."

She calmly stepped toward the drawer and turned her back to him. "I have no interest in fraternizing with soldiers, especially ones who seize my family's property."

"I'm an officer, and I'm merely following orders."

"It doesn't matter." She discreetly clasped the handle to the drawer, cracked it open, and touched the handle of a blade. Her heart thudded inside her chest.

The sound of an approaching engine emanated from the lane.

Krahl looked out the window. "*Scheiße*," he muttered.

Gianna glanced outside to see a black sedan rumble to the front of the house and stop. She eased her hand from the drawer, as a stout German SS officer stepped out of the vehicle.

A knock came from the door.

"*Komm rein*," Krahl called out.

The door squeaked open, jackboots clacked over the floor, and the officer appeared in the kitchen doorway.

"*Heil Hitler*," the officer said, raising his hand.

Krahl set down his glass. "*Heil Hitler*."

The officer removed an envelope from his pocket and handed it to Krahl.

Gianna contemplated grabbing the laundry basket and squeezing by the men, but feared that it would make things worse with Krahl. With little choice, she stood still and silent.

Krahl, using a flip knife from his pocket, cut open the envelope. He unfolded the message and lines formed on his face. He lowered the paper and conversed, in German, with the officer.

She tried to understand what they were discussing, but recognized few of their words.

The officer gave Krahl a Nazi salute and left the house.

Krahl refilled his wine and guzzled it down. He looked at Gianna and said, "Did you understand what we talked about?"

"No," she said.

"I received a communication from my commanding officer. Partisan raids on German soldiers have escalated, and I have been informed of the consequences that we will enforce for any further attacks by rebels."

She straightened her spine. An image of Tazio and Carmine's partisans, sabotaging a weapons depot, flashed in her head.

"For every German soldier who is killed by a partisan, we will execute ten Italians."

Her blood turned cold.

"My orders are to notify civilians, so they can begin to spread news of our intent." He looked into her eyes. "I am starting with you."

She swallowed.

"Go to the nearby villages of Strada in Chianti, Santa Cristina, and Impruneta. Tell the residents there what I told you."

Her legs felt weak. "Why me?"

"I have other matters that require my attention, and my officers are not fluent in Italian." He refilled his glass, spilling wine on the floor. "Besides, word of our intent will be more effective coming from a native."

"May I take my bicycle?"

He sat in a kitchen chair and nodded. "Before you go, finish the laundry."

Gianna, feeling nauseous, picked up the basket and went upstairs. She quickly put away the uniforms and clothing, then left the house. In the distance, she spotted her father tending to a small sector of grapevines. *I'll tell him later. I barely have enough time to get there and back before curfew.* She dashed to the wine cellar, retrieved her purse, and rode off on her bicycle.

On the main road, she looked over her shoulder to make certain she was not being followed, and sped away. Instead of going directly to nearby villages, she took a detour and pedaled furiously through backroads.

Over an hour later, she reached the entrance to the mine. She sat down and, while struggling to catch her breath, she removed a piece of paper and a pencil from her purse. She scribbled a message, went into the tunnel, and lifted the rock to the dead drop. Inside the hole, she discovered a bullet casing that contained an encrypted message. *God, I wish I could read this,* she thought, staring at his handwritten code. With no hope of deciphering the message, she inserted it back into the bullet casing and returned it to the dead drop. She scribbled more on her message to Tazio, and then deposited it in the hole and covered it with the rock.

For the remainder of the afternoon, Gianna traveled to the villages of Santa Cristina, Impruneta, and Strada in Chianti. She stopped at village halls, churches, and public squares, and she told everyone she could about the German threat to execute citizens. She suspected that the Germans wanted rumors to grow rampant among Italians, who would in turn pressure partisans to cease their attacks. She knew that the news would not deter partisans from fighting back against the German occupiers, nor did she want anyone to cease resisting Fascist rule. But she hoped that spreading the word to civilians about the German threat might keep them safe.

At nightfall, Gianna arrived at the vineyard. The place was quiet, except for the voices of Krahl and his officers coming from the house. She got off her bicycle and walked on shaky legs toward the wine cellar. In the distance, burning cigarettes of German soldiers flickered like fireflies.

She pushed open the cellar door, went inside, and put down her bicycle.

"Gianna!" Beppe shuffled to her and wrapped his arms around her.

She squeezed him.

"I saw you leave on your bicycle," he said. "Are you okay?"

"No." She released him. "Did you speak to Krahl?"

He shook his head.

She told him about the German threat to kill ten Italians for every German soldier who was killed by partisans, and Krahl's orders for her to spread the word to villagers. However, she did not mention Krahl's unwanted advances toward her.

"*Bastardi*," Beppe said. "The Germans are not making threats. They are making promises. Given what they've already done to Jews and anyone who opposes their fascist rule, I have no doubt that the Germans will do what they say."

Gianna—her mind and body drained—sat down on a bed of plywood and wool blankets, and she lowered her head into her hands.

Beppe lit a candle, and then picked up a canteen and placed it next to her. "Drink some water."

"Later," she said, despite her dehydration.

A distant rumble echoed over the vineyard.

Gianna perked up her head.

A faint boom, like faraway thunder, rolled over the countryside.

Beppe's eyes widened. "I know that sound."

Gianna stood and cupped a hand to her mouth.

Beppe beamed. "It's artillery! They're breaking through!"

Gianna's hope surged. Tears of happiness welled up in her eyes. "I can't believe it. The Allies are really coming."

For hours, they listened to the distant sound of exploding artillery, which Beppe estimated to be approximately sixty kilometers away. And when no lights or sound could be detected from the house, Beppe stood lookout at the cracked-open wine cellar door.

Gianna gathered a half loaf of bread and the canteen of water and went to the rear of the cellar. She put down the supplies, gave a soft knock on the wine barrel, and removed its cover.

Etta and Nunzia—their hair oily and tangled and wearing well-worn clothes—crawled out of the hole.

"Come with me," Gianna said. She took the girls by the hand and led them to within a few meters of the entrance and stopped. "Listen."

Etta, pale and thin, tilted her head.

A nearly inaudible rumbling came from outside.

"What is that noise?" Nunzia asked, looking up at the ceiling.

Gianna smiled. "The sound of freedom."

Chapter 32

Strada in Chianti—July 23, 1944

On the eve of the battle for Florence, Gianna and Beppe stood outside the wine cellar and looked out over the rolling Tuscan hills. On the southern horizon, plumes of smoke rose into the midafternoon sky, and a rumble of bombs and guns sounded in the distance. The temperature was hot, and an acrid smell of explosives hung in the air. At the far end of the vineyard, Krahl and his officers were addressing their soldiers, who were lined up in rows of five behind a group of Panzer tanks. And on a neighboring hill, a separate Wehrmacht unit was moving long-range artillery guns into position.

A wave of dread washed over Gianna. "The battle is coming."

"*Sì*," Beppe said. He placed an arm around his daughter. "Hitler's army failed to stop the Allies from capturing Rome and Assisi. They won't be able to stop them here. It's the beginning of the end of Fascist rule."

"I hope so."

Beppe slipped his hand from his daughter's shoulder. "Let's go inside."

She nodded.

Over the past several days, the thunder of Allied artillery had grown closer. Krahl's regiment covered their Panzer tanks and armored vehicles with camouflage nets, and more German soldiers and equipment were brought in and stationed on land that was located to the east of the Conti vineyard. Throughout this time, Gianna kept her distance from Krahl. She timed her work in the house to be when Krahl was away, or when Krahl's fellow officers were present. Also, Beppe accompanied her to and from the house on most of her visits. But as days passed, and the rumble of the conflict drew near, Krahl spent less and less time in the house, with the exception of sleeping or drinking wine with his comrades.

While Krahl and his officers performed their duties in the field, Gianna pilfered German rations, usually field biscuits and tins of meat, to feed Etta and Nunzia. Also, she collected food scraps, which she stored in a coffee tin, when she cooked meals and cleaned dishes for the officers. Bits of cereal. Stems of zucchini. Woody stalks of asparagus. Stone-hard crusts of bread. No morsel, regardless of its size or quality, was wasted. In addition to acquiring daily nourishment for the girls, she needed to collect enough food for four people to take a long and arduous journey away from the oncoming battle.

Gianna followed Beppe into the wine cellar and closed the door behind her. "It's time for us to run away."

Beppe nodded and smoothed his beard. "I've been giving this more thought. With the buildup of troops, it might be best to ride out the invasion by hiding in a church in Impruneta. It's only an hour or so walk from here—much closer than the mountains."

"No," Gianna said. "Impruneta will still be in the path of the oncoming Allied campaign. The American army will likely be battling directly through here, and they'll be fighting the Wehrmacht every step of the way to Firenze. We need to get Etta and Nunzia away from the tanks and into the mountains, far from areas that are a German stronghold."

"It's a long trip on foot to the mountains." He adjusted his grip on the handle of his cane. "I'll slow you down. It will be better if you take the girls and flee without me."

"I'm not leaving without you," Gianna said firmly.

Under normal circumstances, it was a two- to three-day trek to the mountains—northwest of Lucca—from Strada in Chianti. But given Beppe's lack of mobility and that they would need to take detours and hide for much of the time along the route, Gianna estimated that it would take them a week.

She touched her father's arm. "We will make it to the mountains together."

"I don't want to be a burden," he said. "My slow pace could get us captured or killed."

"You won't," Gianna said. "I know the backroads and hiking trails that will keep us away from the Germans. It's going to be a rough trek, but I know that I can get us there safely. You need to trust me."

"I do trust you," he said. "But I don't have confidence that my leg will hold up."

She looked into his eyes. "You can do it, and you're coming with us."

Beppe paused, twisting his wedding band on his finger. "You're strong, like your mother."

"And stubborn, like my *papà*."

He smiled.

A thunderous explosion quaked the ground.

Gianna gasped.

Beppe's eyes widened.

Rounds of German artillery boomed, one after another, from a nearby hill.

"We need to go!" Gianna shouted over the shellfire. "Get the girls and I'll gather our things!"

Beppe nodded and shuffled to the back of the cellar.

Gianna grabbed two empty burlap sacks and filled them with food, canteens, and blankets. She tossed in her purse, and then retrieved her pistol, which was stashed under a plywood cot. She hiked up her skirt and placed the weapon in the homemade holster of her girdle.

Beppe returned with Etta and Nunzia, their hands trembling and their eyes filled with fear.

Gianna stepped to the girls and took them each by a hand. "It's going to be all right," she said calmly. "We are going to the mountains where it will be safe."

A barrage of German artillery fired.

The girls flinched.

"The guns sound scary," Gianna said, "but they are being fired in the opposite direction of where we are going."

Nunzia's bottom lip quivered.

"The soldiers are busy fighting," Gianna said. "This is our chance to run away without being noticed."

Etta, her eyes wide, placed an arm around her sister.

"Gianna's right," Beppe said, as if trying to ease the girls' trepidation. "The soldiers are at the opposite end of the vineyard; they will not see us leave."

Etta nodded and looked at her sister. "Do you think you can run?"

"*Sì*," Nunzia said, her voice frail.

Gianna went to the door and peeked outside. On the south end of the vineyard, Krahl and his officers stood under a tree while some of their men climbed into Panzer tanks. To the east, soldiers fired and rearmed artillery guns from their hilltop position. A deafening barrage of shellfire reverberated over the valley.

She turned to Beppe and the girls. "We have a clear path past the house and to the lane. Once we get to the road, we'll cross over and enter an overgrown field. It will provide us with cover as we leave the area."

"*Va bene*," Beppe said.

Gianna retrieved her bicycle that was propped against a wall. "Get on," she said, rolling it beside Beppe.

"I don't think I can pedal with my bad leg," he said.

"You don't have to. I'll push you to the lane, and you'll coast down the hill to the road. The bicycle will help you to get out of here fast. We can abandon it in the field."

Beppe struggled to straddle the bicycle.

Gianna lifted his left foot up and over the bicycle's center frame. She took his cane and turned to Etta. "Do you think you can run with this?"

"*Sì*," Etta said, taking the cane.

Gianna, her heart thudding inside her chest, placed the sacks of supplies into the basket of the bicycle. She peeked through a crack in the door to make sure that there were no soldiers in the vicinity of the house, then looked at the girls. "Ready?"

The girls nodded.

Artillery guns boomed.

Beppe gripped the handlebars of the bicycle and looked into his daughter's eyes. "Catch the moment."

A swell of courage rose inside her. "Catch the moment."

She opened the door and was met by the shockwaves of artillery fire. Her adrenaline rose. She grabbed the back of the bicycle seat with both hands, lowered her shoulders, and pushed hard.

The handlebars wobbled in Beppe's hands but he kept his balance. He leaned forward and steadied the wheel.

Gianna's calf and thigh muscles flared. Using all her strength, she propelled the bicycle forward and picked up speed.

Etta and Nunzia, their bodies atrophied from weeks of confinement, struggled to keep up.

Artillery guns blared.

Gianna glanced behind her, but didn't see Krahl or his officers. She hoped that they hadn't been spotted and willed her legs to move faster.

At the lane, she gave a hard push, sending her father and the bicycle down the slope.

Beppe, propelled by gravity, picked up speed and stuck out his legs from the pedals. He turned the handlebars, navigating ruts in the path.

Instead of following him, Gianna darted back to Etta and Nunzia, who were slogging toward her and gasping for air. She grabbed them by the hand and helped them to run. Together, they darted down the lane as more German artillery guns opened fire a kilometer or two west of their position. At the road, they paused to catch their breath.

Gianna scanned the area. "Do you see him?"

"No," Etta wheezed. She and her sister lowered their heads and drew in deep breaths.

Gianna's eyes locked on a patch of high weeds, across the road, that were trampled. She sprang forward and worked her way into the thicket, and she found Beppe on the ground with his legs tangled in the bicycle. "*Oh, Dio,*" she breathed.

"I had trouble braking." Beppe raised a badly scraped hand. "Help me up."

Gianna untangled him from the bicycle and got him to his feet. "Can you walk?"

He nodded.

The girls ran to them, and Etta handed Beppe his cane.

He patted her on the head. "*Grazie.*"

Gianna picked up the sacks and slung them over her shoulder. "Follow me."

She trekked through the field, which was overgrown with weeds, brambles, and stinging nettles. With every step, she felt as if Krahl and his men would appear from behind them and gun them down. She glanced behind her to check on Beppe, Etta, and Nunzia, all of whom were slogging several paces behind her. *If we had been spotted by Krahl or his men, we would be captured or dead by now.* She raised her forearm, shielding away branches of thorns, and pushed forward. Artillery guns continued their assault, and she prayed that she had the strength and ingenuity to avoid the Germans and get them to the mountains.

Chapter 33

Larciano — July 27, 1944

Early one morning, Tazio and Carmine, both of whom were carrying long duffel bags filled with weapons, skulked through an orchard of long-abandoned olive trees, their trunks gnarled and twisted with age. In the distance, a rumble of explosions and the sporadic crack of gunfire rolled over the countryside. At the edge of a clearing, they scanned the area to make sure there were no onlookers and sprang from the trees to narrow stone steps that were overgrown with weeds and wildflowers. Tazio, followed by Carmine, scurried up a long terraced incline to an isolated villa that was perched atop a hill with sweeping views of the valley.

Tazio glanced at the villa's closed sun-bleached wooden shutters, which looked like they hadn't been opened in years, given their rusted hinges. "Are you sure this is the right place?"

"*Sì.*" Carmine put down his bag and knocked.

Faintly in the valley below, a goat bleated and a rooster crowed.

Tension spread through Tazio's shoulders, and he wiped beads of sweat from his forehead.

A lock clicked and the door swung open to reveal a petite woman in her early thirties wearing a blue-and-white checked blouse and a black skirt. Her brown shoes were dull and scuffed, and her white socks were rolled down on her ankles.

"Enrica?" Carmine asked.

The woman folded her arms and nodded.

"I'm Carmine." He gestured with his hand. "This is Tazio."

"You must be the *americano*," she said, eyeing Tazio with caution.

"I am." Tazio stepped forward and held out his hand.

She shook it and motioned with her head for them to enter.

They stepped inside the villa to find six women, ranging in age from late teens to their midfifties, in a living room void of furniture. The air was stale and hot, the walls were covered in cracks and flaking plaster, and rays of sunlight beamed through broken pieces of shutters.

The women, standing close together, stared at Tazio and Carmine.

"*Buongiorno*," Tazio said, breaking the silence.

A middle-aged woman in a black dress and headscarf stepped forward. "*Buongiorno*."

Tazio put down his bag and looked at the group of women who were willing to risk their lives to fight for Italy's freedom. A feeling of admiration and respect rose up inside him. He and Carmine went around the room, introduced themselves and greeted each of the women, and stood in front of the group.

"Last week," Tazio said, "the Allies captured Arezzo. The distant explosions you hear are coming from the US Army battling its way toward Firenze."

The women glanced at each other but remained silent.

"We are here to provide you with weapons to fight against German soldiers and members of Mussolini's National Republican Guard. Joining the Resistance is voluntary. If you fight, you might be injured or killed, but you will also aid in the liberation of Italy."

A woman, wearing an apron over a housedress, raised her chin. "I will fight."

"So will I," another woman said.

"If anyone wishes to leave," Carmine said, "please do so now."

The women stood their ground.

"*Bene*," Tazio said. "Let's get to work."

Tazio and Carmine unzipped their duffel bags and removed M3 submachine guns, magazines, and boxes of ammunition. They divided everyone into two groups, and Tazio and Carmine demonstrated how to load and operate the weapons. Each woman was given her own gun, a spare magazine, and a box of ammunition. They did not practice shooting the weapons because of the risk of alerting enemy patrols nearby. Also, with the Allied forces drawing near, there was no time for extensive training or detailed military plans. The message that Tazio and Carmine provided the newly recruited partisans was simple: use the weapons to defend themselves and—when the Allied soldiers reached the area—join them in the fight against the Germans.

Tazio looked at the partisans. "You are strong and brave, and I salute your greatness."

A woman blinked her eyes, as if fending off tears.

"Freedom comes from the sacrifice you make," Tazio said. "Your efforts will liberate Italy, and you will show the rest of the world what can be achieved when you stand up against fascist dictators."

Enrica raised her submachine gun above her head. "*Viva l'Italia!*"

"To freedom!" Another woman shouted.

Carmine lifted his head and clasped his arms behind his back.

Tazio wished Enrica and the group good luck, picked up his duffel bag, which contained one remaining weapon, and left with Carmine.

Outside, they were met by the muted sound of explosions, many kilometers away. Mixed emotions swirled inside him. It was part of his duties to recruit civilians to fight the Germans, but he felt a pang of guilt, given the likelihood that some of the partisans would be killed in their struggle for freedom. He wished that he could give them in-depth training as well as more weapons and ammunition to increase their odds of survival. But time had run out.

Tazio shook away his thoughts and turned to Carmine. "We're

not far from the dead drop. It might be my last chance to check it before the fighting arrives."

"I'll come with you," Carmine said.

"It's not necessary," he said. "I'll meet you back at camp."

"No," Carmine said. "German patrols are everywhere. We've been on the move, dispersing our fighters into small units at separate locations for security. You need someone to have your back—and I need someone to have mine."

Tazio drew a deep breath and nodded. He descended the hillside with Carmine, and they made their way toward the forest.

Weeks earlier, Tazio had learned from a newly recruited partisan whose sister resided near Strada in Chianti that Gianna's family vineyard had been requisitioned by a Wehrmacht Panzergrenadier regiment. Tazio was devastated. He desperately wanted to set aside his duties and go there, but Carmine persuaded him that there was nothing he—or even their collective group of partisans—could do against the firepower of a regiment of Panzer tanks. He felt helpless, and he prayed that Gianna and Beppe would remain safe until Allied troops liberated Florence.

He had not been to the dead drop since he'd learned the news about the Germans commandeering the vineyard. He doubted that he would receive any communication from Gianna, considering her predicament and the fact that they hadn't communicated since their happenstance rendezvous at the dead drop. But he longed to go there, if only to resurrect memories of their time together, and to revive his hope that he would see her again.

Early in the afternoon, Tazio and Carmine ascended the hill to the iron mine. Carmine stood lookout at the entrance, and Tazio entered the tunnel and kneeled at the dead drop. He removed a flashlight received in the last parachute drop from his jacket and turned it on. He lifted the rock and was shocked to find a folded piece of paper, along with the bullet casing that contained the message he'd left during his last visit. His pulse rate quickened as he unfolded the note and shined the light on Gianna's handwriting.

Dear Tazio,
I pray you are safe and that you receive this message. I'm sorry I have been unable to communicate. Our vineyard was requisitioned by a German tank regiment. For now, Beppe and I are unable to leave because we are hiding two Jewish girls from the enemy.

"Oh, God," Tazio breathed. A memory of Aria and her five-year-old son Eliseo hiding in the secret hole behind a wine barrel emerged in his mind.

An SS officer named Volker Krahl received orders to execute ten Italians for each German soldier who is killed by a partisan. I suspect that Krahl is not the only officer with orders to commit war crimes. I'm able to deliver this message because Krahl ordered me to leave the vineyard to inform people in nearby villages of the consequences of partisans killing Germans. Given what the Nazis have done to Jews in Italy, I have little doubt that they will follow through with their threat.

A mix of ire and dread churned inside Tazio. He'd heard rumors about mass killings of civilians in Rome before the city fell to the Allies. But this was the first he'd heard of German orders that established a quota on retribution.

This will likely be my last message to you until after the war. If Beppe and I can escape with the girls, we will flee to the mountains, northwest of Lucca. My brother once told me about a safehouse at the church of San Rocco. I will try to hide them there until Firenze is liberated.
I miss you, my darling. I dream of the day when the world is at peace and we are together.
With all my heart,
Gianna
P.S. This letter is unencrypted because I cannot retrieve the codebook while the Germans occupy the house. I'm sorry that I'm

unable to read your last communication. Perhaps you could keep it and tell me what it says when we see each other again.

Tazio raised his eyes to the ceiling and silently prayed for the safety of Gianna, Beppe, and the children they were protecting. He folded the paper, picked up the bullet casing that contained his unread encrypted message for Gianna, and slipped them into his jacket pocket that contained his codebook. With a heavy heart, he walked out of the mine and told Carmine everything.

"She's going to be all right," Carmine said. "The Germans' aim is to seize land for battle. They are not interested in her and Beppe, otherwise, they would have been harmed by now. When the Allies break through, she'll find a way to flee with Beppe and the children."

Tazio nodded despite his disquietude.

Carmine removed a bandana from his neck and used it to wipe sweat from his brow. "What do you think about the Nazi threat to kill Italians?"

"It's not a bluff. They will do what they say." He looked out over the forest. "But partisans will never give up the fight, no matter how bad things get. They will rebel until Italy is free."

Lines formed on Carmine's face. "We should inform our fighters about this."

"I agree."

Tazio picked up his duffel bag and left the iron mine with Carmine. They traveled through the forest without speaking, and every few minutes they paused to scan the area and listen. They detected no movement and the woodland was silent, except for the piping of birds and the distant rumble of explosions. But several kilometers from camp, everything changed when a barrage of machine gun fire erupted in the forest.

Chapter 34

Tuscany—July 27, 1944

Tazio flinched at the sound of gunshots echoing through the valley. His pulse accelerated as he unzipped his duffel bag and grabbed a submachine gun.

Carmine crouched and slipped a pistol from his jacket.

Tazio checked the magazine of his weapon.

Machine gun and rifle fire reverberated through the woodland.

Tazio listened, attempting to determine the location of the explosions, and his blood turned cold. "It's coming from camp." He sprang forward and ran.

Carmine darted after him, but could not keep up with Tazio's pace.

Tazio, his heart racing, sprinted through the forest. He passed through dense pines for several hundred meters, and then sloshed his way through a shallow stream. With wet, squelching boots, he scrambled up a hillside. Halfway up the slope, the gunfire abruptly stopped but he continued his upward trek, all the while determined to come to the aid of the partisans.

Fifteen minutes after the last shot was fired, Tazio reached a plateau that led to the outer perimeter of camp. He raised his weapon and crept forward through thick foliage. His heartbeat pounded against his eardrums, and a faint smell of burned wood and discharged gunpowder penetrated his nostrils. He emerged from the undergrowth and an overwhelming sense of dread enveloped him as he reached a clearing.

Streams of smoke rose from the smoldering remains of canvas tents. The area was devoid of German soldiers, but the camp was strewn with the bodies of five partisans.

No! Tazio, his hands trembling, lowered his weapon. He ran to the closest partisan—whom he recognized to be a man named Fredo—and immediately realized that there was nothing he could do for him: Fredo's still chest was riddled by bullets.

Carmine, gasping for air, emerged from the trees and froze. "*Mio Dio!*"

Tazio, joined by Carmine, went from partisan to partisan. All were dead, except for Daniele—the bespectacled man who'd repaired Tazio's wireless radio.

"You're going to make it," Tazio said, applying pressure to a bullet wound to Daniele's stomach.

Daniele groaned.

"What happened?" Carmine asked, kneeling beside the maimed partisan.

Daniele gulped air. "A Wehrmacht squad ambushed us."

"Where did they go?" Carmine asked.

"North," Daniele wheezed.

Tazio adjusted his hands and applied more pressure.

Daniele winced. "They took your radio. I—I'm sorry."

"It's all right," Tazio said.

"You were assigned to the camp near Pistoia," Carmine said. "What are you doing here?"

"That camp was ambushed, too," Daniele said.

Carmine lowered his head. "*Bastardi.*"

Daniele swallowed. "We—we fended them off at Pistoia, but two partisans were killed." He drew a labored breath. "I came here to inform you."

Carmine clasped Daniele's hand. "Hang on."

Daniele's eyelids lowered. Blood saturated his shirt.

Tazio pressed harder on the wound. "Stay with me, Daniele."

He drew a raspy breath, and his head tilted to the side. "I miss Francesca."

"You'll be going home to your wife soon," Carmine said.

His body shivered. "I—I'm so cold. Am I dying?"

"No," Tazio said. "You're going to make it."

Minutes passed and Tazio, his hands aching with fatigue, pressed on the wound and fought to control the bleeding. But the plum-size hole in Daniele's abdomen created by a high-caliber German weapon was far too severe. Blood leaked from the man's body, and his face turned pale. Daniele gave a gasp and his lungs deflated, like partially filled balloons snipped with scissors.

Tazio pressed an ear to his chest and blinked back tears. He looked at Carmine and shook his head.

With shaking hands, Carmine brushed over Daniele's face to close his eyes. He stood and turned to the north. "I'm going to track them down and kill them."

"It'll have to wait," Tazio said.

"We can do the burials later."

Tazio, his hands stained with blood, approached Carmine. "We need to relocate each of our partisan cells to new locations."

"Why?"

"Because we've had two ambushes in the same day at separate locations."

"The oncoming invasion is pushing the enemy to expand their patrols deeper into the countryside," Carmine said. "We need to stay put and fight."

"No," Tazio said, firmly. He looked into his friend's eyes, filled with fury and heartbreak. "I think our network has been infiltrated by the Germans."

Chapter 35

Florence—June 15, 2003

Gianna, her legs feeling unsteady, held onto her daughter Jenn's arm as she carefully navigated a trail that led to the iron mine. The path through the forest was littered with rocks and exposed tree roots, many of which were hidden by swaths of weeds. A pungent scent of umbrella pine filled the air, resurrecting Gianna's long-dormant memories of smuggling secret messages to the dead drop. Tension spread through her back and shoulders, and as if by reflex, she squeezed Jenn's elbow.

"Are you okay?" Jenn asked, carrying their purses in her free hand.

"Yes." Gianna eased her grip. "I'll be all right as long as we take it slow."

"We will."

They traveled for several minutes on the rolling and winding trail. To Gianna, the woodland looked much as it did during the war, with the exception of occasional sightings of painted blue lines on trees, which she assumed to be hiking markers. But even after many years of being away, she still felt a strange compulsion to scan the forest and look over her shoulder for the enemy.

"Oh, no," Jenn said, slowing her pace.

Gianna looked up and adjusted her glasses on the bridge of her nose. Twenty meters ahead, the path was blocked by a huge fallen oak tree with a mass of broken limbs. "I don't think I'm capable of crawling through that mess."

Jenn stopped and turned to her mother. "Do you want to turn back?"

"No." Gianna pointed to an area of high weeds and brambles. "Let's go around."

Jenn paused, eyeing the thicket. "Are there ticks in Tuscany?"

"Yes."

Jenn swallowed.

"If ticks get on us, I'll pick them off."

Jenn shifted her weight. "What about disease?"

"*Mamma mia!*"

As a child, Jenn had an innate aversion to arachnids and getting her clothes and shoes dirty. And Gianna wished, although briefly, that she had done more as a young mother to expose her daughter to nature.

"It's not a walk in Central Park," she said, nudging Jenn, "but I'm sure you can get through there without becoming a host for a parasite."

Jenn sighed. "All right."

They left the path and worked their way through thick vegetation and sprawling brambles. They stopped several times to carefully move away thorn-covered branches, but they still received scratches on their arms and legs. Upon reaching the path, Jenn slipped away from her mother and checked her clothing for ticks.

Soon, the path reached an upward slope and Gianna leaned against the base of an umbrella pine to catch her breath.

"It looks too steep," Jenn said, looking at the incline. "I'm not sure it's a good idea for you to continue."

"I'll make it," Gianna said. "You go first. I'll hold your hand."

Jenn gave a reluctant nod. She clasped her mom's hand and helped her up the trail.

With each step, an ache began to grow in Gianna's knees and

hips. Her calf and thigh muscles ached with fatigue, and her breathing turned heavy. *I used to run up this trail. Now, I can barely walk up it. God, I feel old.* She fought back her exhaustion and pushed ahead.

"Mom, we should stop."

Gianna gulped air. "I'll go a little farther and take a break."

She continued upward while holding tightly onto Jenn's hand. But two steps forward, her tennis shoes slipped on loose rocks and she fell on her right knee, sending a sharp pang through her leg. "Ow!"

"Mom!" Jenn, gripping Gianna's hand, helped her to roll onto her back and get to a seated position.

Gianna winced and clasped her knee, throbbing with pain.

"Let me see," Jenn said, kneeling beside her.

She drew deep breaths and moved away her hands.

Jenn lifted Gianna's sundress to reveal a scraped knee. "You're bleeding and it looks like it's starting to swell."

"*Mamma mia*," Gianna said.

"Try bending your knee."

Gianna grimaced as she straightened and bent her leg.

"I don't think anything is broken or torn, but your knee is bruised and is probably going to hurt like hell for a few days. Do you think you can make it back to the car?"

"Yes, but give me a few minutes. If it stops hurting, I want to keep going."

"No."

"I want to give it a try."

"Absolutely not," Jenn said, firmly. She peered up at the tree-covered incline. "The path turns steep and treacherous. You might get seriously injured if you have another fall. We are done."

Gianna lowered her head. She looked at her scraped and bruised knee—radiating with pain—and a wave of disappointment rolled over her. "I'm a fool. I should have known that the climb would be too difficult to make at my age."

"You're not a fool," Jenn said, her tone soft. She retrieved a tissue from her purse and dabbed a bit of blood from her mom's knee.

"Thank you," Gianna said.

"You're welcome." Jenn folded the tissue and handed it to her mom. "You gave it your best try. I'm sorry you can't go up there."

"Me too."

"How close did we get?"

"It's probably a twenty-minute hike from here, but it would have taken me much longer to reach it."

Jenn placed a hand on her mother's shoulder. "If I went up there by myself, do you think you will be okay here for a while?"

Gianna straightened her back. "Of course. But why?"

"I know how much it meant to you for me to see it," Jenn said. "I know it isn't the same, but I'd like to finish what you set out to do."

Tears welled up in Gianna's eyes. "I would love that."

Jenn smiled.

Gianna gave her directions to the mine, as well as the number of paces from the entrance to the location of the dead drop. "Inside my purse, there is a tiny flashlight that is attached to my keychain. It's a bit dark around the area of the dead drop. A light might help."

Jenn got to her feet and retrieved the keychain with the flashlight.

"When you are there," Gianna said, "look around for any crevices or rock-covered holes that could contain Tazio's codebook. I doubt that he would have stored it in the mine, but it's worth a try."

"Okay."

"Also, don't feel bad if you can't locate the entrance to the mine. It was hard to find back then, and now it might be even more concealed by pines."

"I'll find it." Jenn turned and climbed up the slope.

Gianna watched her daughter scale the hill and disappear into the trees. She stretched her knee, sending an ache through her leg, and removed the folded newspaper article from her purse. She held the clipping in her hand, like a good luck charm, and waited for Jenn to return.

An hour later, a rustling came from the trail above her. She looked up and was relieved to see Jenn making her way down the hill.

Jenn, her hair mussed and breathing heavily, sat down next to her.

"Did you locate the mine?"

"Yes."

Gianna beamed with joy.

"I didn't find the codebook, but I think I saw what used to be the dead drop. There was a hole the size of a dinner plate. Nearby, there was a flat rock that was big enough to cover it." Jenn took a few deep breaths. "It looks like hikers or local teenagers have found the mine. There are empty wine bottles, remnants of campfires, and the walls of the tunnel are covered with graffiti."

Gianna put away the newspaper clipping and held her daughter's hand. "I wish I could have been there with you."

"Me too." Jenn squeezed her fingers. "Let's get you back to the hotel and ice down your knee."

Gianna nodded.

Jenn helped her mom to her feet and placed an arm around her to lessen the weight on her sore leg.

Gianna, leaning on her daughter, slowly limped her way back toward the road. Despite the pain in her knee and her failed attempt to see the mine one last time, she was glad she had come. In a strange way, she felt closer to Jenn than she had in years. But as minutes passed, her mind drifted to the things she needed to reveal to her daughter, and she dreaded that the most difficult part of confronting her demons lay ahead.

Chapter 36

Collodi—August 9, 1944

Gianna left the ancient remains of a villa located in the countryside, a few kilometers from the medieval village of Collodi, and scurried into the night rain. She descended a foliage-covered hill to a forest, where she found Beppe, Etta, and Nunzia huddled under a tree.

"There is an abandoned ruin not far from here," Gianna said, wiping rain from her face. "It's isolated, and there is a partial roof in the back of the property that will keep us dry. The sun will be coming up in a few hours. I think we should hide there until it's safe to travel."

"All right," Beppe said.

The girls nodded.

Gianna picked up the two burlap sacks that contained supplies, led them to the rear of the ruin, and entered what looked like a dilapidated stone pigsty. Although one of its walls had collapsed, a section of the tile roof remained intact over sagged wooden beams.

Etta clasped her arms and shivered.

Gianna grabbed blankets from a sack and wrapped them around both girls. Using the end of Nunzia's blanket, she dried the girls' hair.

Tears welled up in Nunzia's eyes, and she drew a jagged breath.

Gianna lowered the end of a blanket. "Did I hurt you?"

"No." Nunzia's bottom lip quivered. "I was thinking of my *mamma*. Sometimes when I washed my hair, she helped me to dry it with a towel."

Gianna's heart ached. She couldn't begin to imagine how hard it was for Nunzia and Etta to be coping with the arrest of their mother and father by the Germans. Like Lilla and the hundreds of Florentine Jews who were captured in raids, the girls' parents were likely imprisoned in a concentration camp.

Etta placed an arm around her younger sister.

Gianna kneeled in front of them. "You are going to see your *mamma* and *papà* again. The Allies will soon free Italy, and you will no longer need to hide. And when the war is over, your parents will come home."

"They will," Etta said, squeezing her sister's shoulder.

Nunzia nodded and wiped her eyes.

Beppe shuffled to the girls. "Your parents would be so proud of you. You're courageous, clever, and kind. If it wasn't for your help, I would not have made it this far."

An image of Etta and Nunzia, assisting Beppe up a hill, flashed in Gianna's mind.

Tension eased on the girls' faces.

Gianna helped the girls to find a dry place to sit, and retrieved a tin of food scraps.

"I'm too tired to eat," Etta said.

"You need food to keep up your strength." Gianna plucked a stale piece of bread from the tin and placed it in Etta's hand. "Eat all of it, then sleep."

Etta nodded.

Gianna gave bread to Nunzia and approached Beppe, who was leaning on his cane. She held out the tin. "Have some."

"In a little while," he said. "I'll drink water first."

Gianna retrieved a canteen, undid the cap, and handed it to him.

He guzzled water and returned the canteen to her.

She took a swig—filling her mouth with a silty, mineral taste of creek water—and helped him to sit on the ground and lean his back against a stone wall. She sat beside him and folded her arms around her knees, covered by her wet wool skirt. A dank smell of mud and rotted wood filled the air. She peered out into the rain-filled night and observed intermittent flashes of light, followed seconds later by the thunder of shellfire, and tried to estimate the distance to the battlefront.

Over the past two weeks, they had trekked their way toward the mountains, all the while trying to avoid the enemy and stay one step ahead of the advancing line of fighting. Gianna often acted as scout, traveling ahead of the group, and returning to let them know that the path was clear. Also, the distance traveled per day was far less than Gianna had originally projected, mainly because Wehrmacht troops and soldiers of Mussolini's National Republican Army had converged on the area to combat the Allied incursion. The enemy was everywhere, and Etta and Nunzia had no forged travel papers to conceal their Jewish identity. Therefore, most of their time was spent hiding in dense woodlands, vacant barns, or abandoned dwellings. She'd expected that Catholic churches would be their primary source of sanctuary, but the sound of shellfire had created an exodus, and masses of Italian citizens were fleeing their homes and seeking refuge with priests and nuns. The hordes of people taking shelter with clergy caught the attention of the German military, and they conducted raids on churches in search of Jews. Two days after fleeing the vineyard, Gianna witnessed soldiers arresting six people at a church, and she and Beppe decided to avoid seeking Catholic shelters until they were far away from the Wehrmacht.

In addition to the presence of enemy troops, Beppe's physical condition slowed their pace of travel. The damage and arthritis to his knee hampered his ability to hike. He often grimaced with pain after several kilometers of trudging over hills. But he never complained, nor did he want to slow down the group by taking breaks. Usually, it was Gianna or the girls who insisted that they stop and rest, sometimes making excuses that they had to go to the bushes to relieve themselves.

Also, Gianna was unable to lead them to areas where she thought Carmine's partisans might be located. She desperately wanted to reach them, especially Tazio, so that they could help her find shelter for Beppe and the girls. But the woodlands, near and beyond the iron mine, were crawling with German patrols. To avoid being detected, Gianna took several long detours on their route toward the mountains.

"Would you like a blanket?" Gianna asked Beppe, breaking the silence between them.

"No, *grazie*. Give mine to Etta and Nunzia. They could use it to keep warm or as a layer to sleep on."

"Are you sure?"

He nodded.

Gianna retrieved his blanket, placed it over the girls who were already asleep, and sat down beside him.

An explosion flashed on the horizon. Seconds passed and a rumble rolled over the area.

"How far away are they?" she asked.

Beppe rubbed his bearded chin. "Twenty, maybe thirty kilometers."

"Do you think the Allied armies have reached Firenze?"

"Most likely," he said. "I pray that the city is liberated."

"Me too." Gianna clasped her arms. "Do you regret that we left the vineyard?"

"No. We couldn't stay there with Krahl and his tank regiment. Eventually, we would have been caught in the middle of a firefight." He peered out into the rain. "But I do think that we should find a safe place to hide and let the Allied troops pass us by."

A knot formed in Gianna's stomach. "We've been through this. There are no safe places for Etta and Nunzia. The Germans are continuing to arrest Jews as they combat the Allies. The best place to take them will be a village in the mountains, where there will be less chance of encountering German patrols because of the remote, rough terrain."

"I don't know," Beppe said. "We can't continue to run away. At some point, we need to stop and let the Allied troops catch up to us."

"We will, once we reach the mountains. We can make it there in a few days, even if we remain hidden most of the time."

"Are you sure about this?"

"Yes—it's a safer bet, even with the risk of more travel." She clasped his hand. "Please, trust me."

He drew a deep breath and gave her fingers a gentle squeeze. "All right."

Gianna slipped her hand away and leaned her back against the stone wall.

"I wish things could have been different for you," Beppe said.

"What do you mean?"

"The Great War was supposed to be the war to end all wars. Your mother and I had thought that you and your brother would not have to experience the death and hardship that our generation faced during the years when millions were killed in the muddy trenches."

She looked at him. A faint flash of faraway shellfire flickered over his face, etched with sadness.

"But the war came back," he said. "Now, the armies of Hitler and Mussolini are battling the Allies, and Italians are fighting Italians. Our once beautiful country is in turmoil, and before complete peace is reached, our people will need to resolve their own civil war." He glanced at Nunzia and Etta, asleep and curled together. "And the good of the world will need to rise up to stop the Nazis and their persecution of Jews."

"It will happen," Gianna said. "I truly believe that."

"So do I." Beppe paused, peering out into the rain, and placed an arm around his daughter. "After this war is over, you'll see Tazio again."

Gianna blinked her eyes, fending back tears. "I worry about him."

"I know," Beppe said softly. "The end of the German reign over Italy is drawing near. Only time and the battle for liberation will keep you and Tazio apart."

A swell of hope rose up inside her. She rested her head on his shoulder, like she did when she was a child. They sat silently and listened to the patter of rain mixed with echoes of gunfire. Exhausted, her eyelids gradually closed and she fell into a deep, dreamless sleep.

Chapter 37

Sant'Anna di Stazzema—August 12, 1944

Gianna's legs ached as she climbed a steep, unpaved mountain road, located approximately thirty-five kilometers northwest of the city of Lucca. An early morning mist filled the valley below, and the sunrise painted the sky in hues of orange and pink. The rumble of explosions had disappeared, and a chorus of whistling sparrows filled the air, then the distant crow of a rooster. She rounded a bend in the road and her eyes widened at the sight of a cluster of stone dwellings perched high on the mountainside.

Her heartbeat quickened. She turned to Beppe, Etta, and Nunzia, who were slogging several paces behind her. "I see it."

Etta perked up her head. "Me too."

Beppe stopped and took in deep breaths.

Gianna approached him. "Do you need a break?"

"No," Beppe said. He extended his elbow and looked at Nunzia. "Do you have the strength to help me climb one last hill?"

Nunzia nodded and clasped his arm.

Forty minutes later, they entered a high-elevation village that was composed of ancient stone homes, many of which had an unobstructed view over the mountains and the valley below. The village was big enough for approximately five hundred or so residents, given the number of homes. Its location was isolated, many kilometers from the coast or nearest city, and it was surrounded by steep tree-covered hills as far as one could see. Unlike the villages that surrounded German-occupied Florence, there were no signs of soldiers or military vehicles. The windows of the homes were not shuttered, nor did they have blackout curtains. In a garden, a young woman was humming a song as she pinned cloth diapers to a laundry line. To Gianna, the village felt like a hidden oasis in a continent at war.

They approached a fenced barn where an elderly woman was milking a goat. The woman, who was sitting on a tiny wooden stool, raised her head from her pail and locked eyes with Gianna.

"*Buongiorno,*" the woman said.

Gianna smiled. "*Buongiorno.*"

Beppe gave a wave.

A sound of bleating goats emanated from the barn.

Gianna pointed. "Is this the way to the church of San Rocco?"

"*Sì.*" The woman lowered her head and resumed milking the goat.

"*Grazie.*" She placed an arm around Etta's shoulders, and the group continued their walk.

At the center of the village, they found a primary school, a shop, and a well-maintained green that was bordered by a knee-high stone wall and contained several sprawling oak trees, one of which was being climbed by two boys. Women in headscarves, seated on wooden benches, were conversing, and a group of primary-school-age girls in well-worn dresses and shoes were playing a game of jump rope. On the opposite end of the green was a cream-colored church with a stone bell tower.

A mix of relief and excitement flowed through Gianna. With renewed energy, she quickened her pace as she led Beppe and the girls to the entrance of the church, its double-hinged wooden doors propped open with bricks. As she was about to go inside, a young priest, wearing a white clerical collar with a black suit and biretta cap, stepped into the doorway.

"*Scusa*," the priest said, almost bumping into Gianna. "I didn't hear you approaching."

"It's my fault," she said. "It's been a long journey for us, and I'm eager to be here."

The priest stopped and extended his hand. "I'm Don Fiore Menguzzo."

"Gianna Conti." She put down her burlap sacks and shook his hand.

Beppe stepped forward and greeted the priest with a handshake. "I'm Beppe, Gianna's *papà*."

"We are from Strada in Chianti," Gianna said. "We fled the fighting and have come here in search of sanctuary for Etta and Nunzia. Their parents were arrested in the mass roundup of Jews in Firenze."

"I'm so sorry," the priest said. "You've come a long way. How did you hear about this place?"

"My brother Matteo," Gianna said. "He was a partisan. Before he was killed by the Germans, he helped to guide refugees on an escape line to Switzerland."

The priest nodded and looked at the girls. "I'm glad you are here. Which one of you is Etta?"

"I am," Etta said, shyly.

He smiled and looked at Nunzia. "Then that would make you Nunzia."

The girl nodded.

"How old are you?"

"I'm twelve," Nunzia said. "Etta is fourteen."

"Those are wonderful ages," the priest said. "While you are here, there are lots of children in the village to make friends with."

The faces of the girls brightened.

The priest turned to Gianna and Beppe. "We've had a huge influx of refugees over the past several weeks. For the moment, the church sanctuary and most of the village homes are beyond capacity, but we will do everything we can to provide food and shelter."

"*Grazie*," Beppe said.

"Give me a moment." The priest turned and entered the church.

Gianna peeked through the open doorway. Inside, the aisle and pews were filled with people resting on blankets. An elderly nun, who was passing out pieces of bread from a basket, paused her work and conversed with Don Menguzzo.

"It looks full," Gianna said.

"It's all right," Beppe said. "We've been sleeping outside for much of the journey. We can do it again until we find shelter."

"We can," Nunzia said, looking up at him.

Beppe patted the girl's head.

A moment later, Don Menguzzo returned with the elderly nun.

"This is Sister Loredana," the priest said. "She will take care of you."

Gianna clasped her hands. *"Grazie mille."*

"Of course," the nun said. "Come with me."

Gianna picked up her sacks of supplies, and she and her group followed Sister Loredana. They crossed the churchyard, which was filled with children who were kicking around a partially deflated leather ball. High-pitched, joyful chatter filled the air.

"It's wonderful to hear children play," Beppe said, shuffling ahead with his cane.

Gianna smiled. "It might be the most beautiful sound I've ever heard."

The nun took them to a small home that was located on the opposite side of the green from the church. They were given a communal sleeping space in the basement, which was shared by several refugees, and then taken to the kitchen, where the nun prepared them a breakfast of bread and fresh goat's milk, lukewarm and rich with butterfat.

After their meal, Gianna and her group took turns washing in a tin tub filled with cold water, and Sister Loredana provided them with old clothing to put on while their dirty clothes were washed and hung on a line in a garden to dry. For the first time in weeks, Gianna's stomach felt full and her mind at ease. But most of all she felt grateful for Beppe, Etta, and Nunzia to have a place to be at peace.

Etta and Nunzia, despite their exhaustion, wanted to forgo resting in the basement and meet some of the children in the village. So, Gianna and Beppe accompanied them to the green. Within a few minutes of their arrival, Etta and Nunzia were talking with a group of children in front of an oak tree.

Gianna bent down and rolled up the legs of Beppe's trousers, which were several sizes too big.

"*Grazie*," he said.

She stood and glanced at Etta and Nunzia. "It's been a long time since they interacted with other children."

"Too long." Beppe leaned on his cane and yawned.

"How about I stay here, and you go back to the house and get some rest?"

"I will in a little while."

The sound of a vehicle engine came from the road.

Hairs raised on the back of Gianna's neck.

A sound of more vehicles, coming from the opposite direction, broke the air.

Several women, who were carrying baskets of folded sheets to the church, stopped and turned toward the approaching noise. The laughter and chatter of children dwindled.

The roar of engines grew. The priest and several people emerged from the church.

"Etta—Nunzia!" Gianna shouted.

The girls turned and ran to her and Beppe.

Fear flooded Gianna's veins as German armored vehicles raced into the village and surrounded the church and green. As if by reflex, she reached a hand to her inner thigh, and she regretted that she'd stashed her weapon in a burlap bag, because she'd washed and hung her girdle with the sewn-in holster on a line to dry.

Women gasped and ran to gather their children. Two gray-haired men, who were repairing a door to a house, put down their tools.

Don Menguzzo raised his arms and walked into the green. "Be calm," he called out to the villagers. "Everything will be all right."

People huddled together.

"Let's go," Beppe whispered.

Gianna clasped hands with Etta and Nunzia and they scurried across the grass, but within seconds their exit was blocked by a dozen German soldiers who rushed into the area and raised their weapons.

Gianna froze and held the girls, their bodies trembling. Beppe wrapped his arms around them.

Throughout the village, German soldiers rounded up large numbers of men, women, and children and forced them to the green near the church. Villagers, their faces filled with fear, huddled together like sheep in a pen.

An SS officer and an Italian member of the Black Brigades got out of a vehicle and walked to the green. While the SS officer approached the priest, the member of the Black Brigades—a tall and skinny young man with peach fuzz on his upper lip—stopped several paces away from Gianna.

She looked at the Italian and her eyes widened with recognition. "Sante."

The young man faced her and his jaw slacked open.

Anger burned inside her. "How could you?"

Sante turned away but held his ground.

"What have you done?" she asked.

"Shut up," he hissed.

Beppe squeezed Gianna's shoulder, as if to warn her to be silent.

The SS officer, his face stoic and devoid of emotion, stepped to Don Menguzzo and spoke softly.

The color drained from the priest's face. Tears welled up in his eyes, and he looked out over the men, women, and children in the crowd. He raised his palms. "Our Father, who art in heaven, hallowed be thy name—"

Gianna's blood turned cold.

People, many of whom were crying or whimpering, got down on their knees and joined in the recital of the Lord's Prayer.

The SS officer barked orders, and soldiers removed wooden crates and machine guns with tripods from vehicles.

Oh, mio Dio! Gianna's legs turned weak. She scanned the area for a path to escape, but the area was surrounded by the soldiers.

Sante, his eyes wide, glanced at Gianna. He rocked back and forth, and then approached the SS Officer.

"I led you here to make arrests," Sante said. "This isn't what we discussed."

The Nazi officer tilted his head.

"You said that—"

The officer slipped a pistol from a holster and fired at point-blank range into Sante's chest.

The young man crumpled to the ground.

Gianna gasped and shielded the girls with her arms.

Screams erupted from the crowd.

The SS officer shouted orders, and the soldiers began to herd people into the church and nearby buildings.

A soldier, brandishing a submachine gun, turned to Gianna's group and he motioned to a stable. "*Schnell!*"

Gianna, the girls clinging to her side, followed Beppe and a group of villagers to the building. *This can't be happening!* Her heartbeat pounded in her ears, and she struggled to control her breathing.

At the entrance to the stable, she turned to the soldier and pleaded, "Please—let the girls go."

The soldier grabbed her by the neck, breaking the necklace that held her mother's wedding band, and pushed her into the stable.

Pain flared through Gianna's neck and spine as she fell hard to the ground.

Beppe and the girls scurried to Gianna's side and helped her to her feet.

The soldier stood, blocking the entrance, and raised his machine gun. He glanced outside, as if he were looking for a signal from his officer.

An elderly couple held each other in their arms, and others huddled on the ground. Cries and words of prayer filled the stable.

Beppe faced Gianna and placed a hand to her cheek.

"I'm sorry, Papà," she whimpered.

"It's not your fault." He motioned with his eyes.

She glanced at an empty horse stall with an open window to a descending hillside. She swallowed and clasped the girls' hands.

"Catch the moment," Beppe whispered.

Tears pooled in her eyes.

Beppe gripped his cane with both hands and rushed at the soldier.

The German's eyebrows raised. He tried to aim his weapon, but Beppe slammed into his body. The nozzle of the submachine gun pointed upward as he fired, spraying bullets over the ceiling.

Screams and shouts pierced the air.

Gianna pulled the girls to the stall and lifted them through the window.

Beppe grappled with the soldier, and the German's weapon discharged again.

Bullets blasted a wall near Gianna's head, and she dived through the opening. She got up from the ground, grabbed Etta and Nunzia by the hand, and they ran down a tree-covered hillside.

A barrage of machine gun fire erupted over the village.

Gianna and the girls fled deep into the woods. Echoes of hundreds, if not thousands, of rounds of gunfire reverberated over the valley. She fought back her heartache and pushed on, determined to save Etta and Nunzia.

At the base of the mountainside, the girls were too exhausted to run. They hid in the bushes and struggled to quietly catch their breath. Soon, two German soldiers rushed by them, coming within meters of their position. When the sound of footsteps could no longer be heard, they rose from their hiding spot and fled in the opposite direction.

An hour later, they stopped at the edge of a shallow stream. Etta and Nunzia slumped to the ground and sucked in air. Gianna, her hands trembling, helped the girls to scoop water to drink, and she looked back at the mountain. Several kilometers away, plumes of smoke rose from Sant'Anna. The wall holding back her emotions collapsed, and she fell to her knees and sobbed.

Chapter 38

Camaiore—August 13, 1944

Tazio entered a safehouse and descended stairs to a windowless basement, where Carmine and five partisans—two women and three men—were conducting an inventory of weapons. Candlelight flickered over the dank space, which contained rifles, submachine guns, a crate of grenades, a few boxes of ammunition, and a sparse supply of plastic explosive.

Carmine looked up from a metal ammunition box and took a drag on a cigarette. "We are running low on forty-five-caliber rounds."

An uneasiness stirred inside Tazio. "We will need to make do with what we have until the Allies reach us."

A woman in her thirties named Bettina, who'd been a school teacher before joining the Resistance, stepped forward. "It might be a week or longer before the Americans get here. How will we fight if we run out of ammunition?"

"I've seen you fire a weapon," Tazio said. "You have excellent aim. I'm sure you'll make every bullet count."

A calm determination filled the woman's eyes. "I will."

Tazio had lost communication with OSS headquarters because the Germans seized his radio, and he'd been unable to coordinate airdrops of armament. The skirmishes with the Germans had grown far more frequent, and he hoped that American forces would arrive before their ammunition was gone. But supplies were not Tazio's only concern. It was his fallen compatriots who weighed heavy on his conscience.

Over the past two weeks, nearly a third of Carmine's partisans, including three women, were killed either in German raids on their hideouts or in clashes in the hills. Even more devastating to Tazio, as well as to Carmine, was that some of the deaths could have been prevented. In hindsight, they should have taken more steps to protect the group against a partisan turned informant for the Germans. Also, they should have configured the network into independent cells that communicated solely with either Tazio or Carmine—not with other cells—which would have reduced the risk of a network collapse, if infiltrated. Two of their locations were raided by the Germans, which accounted for many of the casualties. And Tazio suspected that Sante was the traitor, given that he had abandoned his post and disappeared shortly before the German attacks on their hideouts.

Their group had become depleted by casualties, and they were greatly outnumbered by Wehrmacht squads that patrolled the hills. Therefore, they were forced to move their hideouts deeper into the Tuscan mountains, which put them farther away from the advancing Allied troops. Despite the deteriorating circumstances, he and Carmine refused to lie low until the US troops arrived. They were determined to combat the Wehrmacht, even at the risk of exhausting their supplies and losing more partisans.

Tazio removed a map from his jacket and placed it on an upside-down crate in front of Carmine. "How about we target the location of our next ambush?"

Carmine nodded. He inhaled on his cigarette, flaring its ember, and coughed smoke.

Tazio unfolded the map.

Carmine coughed hard and spat phlegm on the dirt floor.

"Are you all right?"

"*Sì.*" Carmine retrieved a handkerchief and coughed several times while covering his mouth.

Angst rose inside Tazio. His friend had, over the past few months, lost a good deal of weight. His eyes were surrounded in dark circles, and the lines on his face were more pronounced. *The weight of the war and the mounting casualties are taking a toll on him.* He shook away his thoughts and examined the map.

A door opened on the floor above them, and fast-moving footsteps descended the stairs.

Tazio, his adrenaline surging, slipped a pistol from his jacket.

Partisans grabbed rifles.

"It's Gilberto," a familiar voice called out.

The group lowered their weapons, and a short man with a red bandana and a rifle slung over his shoulder entered the basement.

Carmine dropped the butt of his cigarette and ground it with his boot. "We almost shot you. Next time, announce yourself sooner."

"*Va bene.*" Gilberto, appearing winded, took in deep breaths and removed a cap from his head. "My cousin from Valdicastello is hearing rumors that the Germans attacked civilians at a church in Sant'Anna."

Hairs raised on the back of Tazio's neck. "When?"

"Yesterday. Word is spreading about people hearing intense gunfire and seeing smoke coming from the village in the mountains."

A knot formed in Tazio's stomach. "What is the name of the church?"

Gilberto shrugged.

"San Rocco," Carmine said. "It's a safehouse on the escape line to Switzerland."

"Oh, no," Tazio said.

"What is it?" Carmine asked.

"In my last message from Gianna, she mentioned going to the church of San Rocco with Beppe and two girls."

"*Oh, Dio,*" Carmine said.

"I need to leave." Tazio pointed to the map. "Show me the best way to get there."

Carmine shifted his weight. "It's a long grueling hike, and the forest is crawling with German squads."

"I don't care," Tazio said, firmly. "I'm going."

"Then I'm coming with you."

"You are needed here."

"So are you," Carmine said. "If you want to make it there and back, you'll need to take someone along who knows the terrain."

"All right," Tazio said, reluctantly.

They gathered weapons, left the hideout, and traveled through the forest, taking a winding path through valleys and over steep hills. The terrain became more rugged as they traveled to the north, and they were forced to navigate around slopes that were too steep to climb. Their pace was slow, but they continued their slog and did not stop to rest, except for consuming water from their canteen. They did not encounter the enemy, but twice they hunkered in the underbrush at the sound of sporadic gunfire echoing over the valley. Throughout the journey, Tazio's mind remained on Gianna, and he hoped and prayed that she was safe.

Four hours after leaving the hideout, they climbed a steep incline to the village of Sant'Anna and froze. The entire hamlet was destroyed by fire. Buildings were reduced to rubble, and a layer of ash covered much of the ground and the leaves of surrounding trees.

Dread flooded Tazio's chest. "Oh, God," he breathed.

Carmine crossed himself.

They walked along a dirt road, bordered by destroyed homes and a smell of burned wood, to the center of the village. Near a green were the stone remains of a church bell tower, and a handful of old men were shoveling soil onto what appeared to be a mass grave.

No! Tazio's legs turned weak.

Carmine's hands trembled.

Tazio gathered his nerve and approached one of the men. "Can you tell us what happened?"

The man, who appeared to be in his late sixties, nodded and leaned on his shovel. His wrinkled face and clothes were dirtied with soot, and his eyes were watery and bloodshot.

"Yesterday morning," the man said, his voice raw, "I went into the hills in search of one of my goats that got out of its pen. While I was away, I heard machine gun fire and explosions. I felt helpless, and I hid in the forest until the shooting was over." He glanced at the large mound of soil and his jaw quivered. "They killed my wife."

"I'm so sorry," Tazio said.

The old man sniffed back tears.

"I'm looking for someone—her name is Gianna. She might have come to the church of San Rocco with her father and two girls. Do you know if she was here?"

"No."

Tazio glanced at the men shoveling dirt. "Maybe some of the survivors can tell us if they'd seen her."

"The gravediggers are from another village." The old man swallowed. "Everyone is dead."

Tazio's blood went cold.

The old man drew a serrated breath. "The Germans locked everyone in either the church, stables, or houses, and they killed them with machine guns and hand grenades. They set the buildings ablaze to try to erase traces of the massacre."

"*Oh, Dio,*" Carmine said, his voice low. "How many?"

The man wiped his nose with his sleeve. "Over five hundred villagers and refugees. More than a hundred were children."

A wave of nausea rose from Tazio's stomach. He struggled to get his head around the enormity of the murders. "Maybe some of them escaped," he said, refusing to give up hope.

"I don't think so." The man glanced at the earthen mound and his bottom lip quivered. "I helped to recover the remains."

Carmine put a hand on Tazio's shoulder. "We don't know for sure that Gianna was here."

Tazio nodded, despite a foreboding festering inside him.

The old man pointed to a galvanized metal tub. "I collected personal items from the ashes for identification. You are welcome to search through them." He stepped away and resumed shoveling dirt onto the mound.

On shaky legs, Tazio stepped to a tub, which contained over a hundred pieces of charred jewelry and artifacts. Pendants. Earrings. Wedding bands. Necklaces. A tin ear trumpet. Belt buckles. Rings. Bracelets. He gathered his strength and kneeled. He looked through the pieces, all the while silently praying to find nothing he would recognize. But in the back of the tub, he discovered a familiar, matching pair of wedding bands with the engraved words *Amore Mio*. An image of Gianna wearing her mother's ring on a necklace flashed in his mind. His eyes blurred with tears. Devastated, he lowered his head into his hands and wept.

Chapter 39

Tuscany—August 13, 1944

Tazio, gutted and heartbroken, placed the rings into his pocket and wiped tears from his face. Carmine helped him to his feet and embraced him with a hug.

"Are you sure?" Carmine asked.

"*Sì*," he said, his voice quavering.

Without speaking, they joined the group of elderly men. They shoveled soil onto the mass grave, and they collected wildflowers, which they placed at the base of the mound. When nothing more could be done, they gathered their weapons, left the razed village of Sant'Anna, and began their return through the mountains.

"I'm so sorry," Carmine said, his face etched with anguish.

Tazio rubbed his eyes. "How could anyone commit such an atrocity?"

"The Nazis are not human," Carmine said. "They are monsters, and they'll pay for what they did."

Tazio slogged through the forest, and his mind remained on Gianna, Beppe, the girls whom they were protecting, and the hundreds of innocent villagers and refugees who were massacred by the German military. His heart ached, and he wished there was something he could have done to save them. His spirit and body felt ravaged, and he struggled to hike the steep wooded slopes as he thought about Gianna and her long and beautiful life that would never be. He prayed that she and the others did not suffer, and he vowed to fight to the end and not allow their sacrifice to be in vain.

Grief-stricken, he lost sense of time and space, and he relied on Carmine to guide him through the mountains toward Camaiore. To Tazio, the hills felt steeper and more rugged than when he came. His sorrow grew deeper and deeper, and he struggled to lift his feet. Despite his despair, he pushed on, step by step, willing himself to face a future without the woman who had captured his heart.

Carmine, who was walking a few paces ahead of Tazio, paused on a rocky hillside to catch his breath. He placed a hand over his mouth and muffled a cough.

Tazio stopped and raised an arm, shielding his eyes from late afternoon sunshine coming through the trees.

Gunfire exploded.

A sharp pressure pierced Tazio's lower right abdomen. Pain flared from his hip, and he fell to the ground.

Carmine climbed toward Tazio, but a gunshot forced him to dive behind a tree. The discharge echoed through the valley.

Tazio pressed a hand to his wound and crawled over rocks for cover. A bullet ricocheted near his face, sending limestone shrapnel into his cheek.

Carmine raised his submachine gun and fired. He sprang from the tree, grabbed Tazio, and pulled him behind a large boulder. Less than a hundred meters below their position, a Wehrmacht patrol of eight soldiers with rifles clambered up the slope.

Tazio, fighting back the pain in his hip, untangled a submachine gun strap from his shoulder. A bullet whizzed over his head. His pulse pounded. He leaned from the boulder and—using one arm—sprayed bullets and missed.

A German soldier scaled the slope sixty meters below. Carmine aimed and fired. The soldier's back arched, and he collapsed. German helmets turned as their comrade tumbled down the embankment.

Tazio and Carmine fired shots, forcing the soldiers to seek cover behind trees.

"*Bastardi*," Carmine said.

Tazio pressed a hand to his wound. "How many?"

Carmine peeked around the boulder. Shots skipped over stone. He snapped back. "Seven."

Tazio removed his hand, covered with blood, from his wound and checked the magazine of his submachine gun to find it half empty. He winced as he removed a spare magazine from his jacket.

Carmine grabbed his handkerchief and pressed it to Tazio's wound.

A pang shot through his hip.

"How bad is it?" Carmine asked.

"The bullet went through the side of my abdomen." He sucked in air and grimaced. "I think it's lodged in my hip."

"*Da drüben!*" A German soldier called out.

Carmine crawled to the side of the boulder and glanced down the slope. "*Merda*. There are more of them."

"How many?" Tazio pushed himself toward the edge of their rock.

"Five more."

"Damn it." Tazio removed a pistol from his jacket and placed it next to his extra ammunition, and he regretted that he hadn't brought grenades. He pressed hard on his wound, trying to slow the blood loss.

Carmine raised up, fired his submachine gun, and hunkered behind the boulder. "We need to get out of here. Can you walk?"

Tazio tried to move his leg, and a dagger-like pain stabbed through his hip. "No," he groaned.

Carmine stood and fired.

A German soldier yawped. Gunfire battered their rock.

Carmine, squatting on the ground, shoved a spare magazine into his submachine gun. "I'll carry you."

Tazio shook his head. "They'll catch us, and kill us both."

"We need to try."

Tazio gasped for air. Blood, seeping from his wound, saturated his clothing. "I'll cover you while you try to escape."

"No," Carmine said. "We are getting out of here together."

Tazio peeked around the boulder. "They're flanking us, fifty meters away."

Carmine rose up and fired bullets from his submachine gun. He lowered behind the rock and looked at Tazio's shirt and trousers, soaked with blood. "*Oh, Dio.*"

"You need to go." Tazio pressed the handkerchief tight to his abdomen.

"I'll fight."

Bullets battered the boulder, sending bits of rock into Tazio's hair. "You and I both know that I'm not getting out of here."

Carmine's jaw quivered.

"I want you to do something for me." He drew a labored breath, reached into a pocket, and removed the Conti wedding bands. "Take them."

Carmine took the rings.

He looked into Carmine's eyes, filled with sadness. "Promise me that you'll give them a proper funeral."

Carmine placed a hand on Tazio's shoulder. "I will."

Tazio swallowed, his mouth dry. "Liberty is at hand, my friend. It's been an honor fighting alongside you."

Carmine blinked away tears. "The honor is mine."

Using one hand, Tazio raised his submachine gun. "Go on my fire."

Carmine nodded and slipped away his hand.

Pain riddled his hip as he dragged himself to the edge of the boulder. He leaned over, pressed the trigger, and blasted the area below with bullets.

Carmine darted up the hill.

The German soldiers returned gunfire.

Bullets pelted Tazio's boulder, but he continued firing his weapon, forcing the soldiers to duck behind trees.

Tazio fell back behind the rock. He glanced up the hill and was relieved to see Carmine disappear through the trees. *Farewell, my friend.*

He reloaded ammunition into his submachine gun. For fifteen minutes, he kept the enemy soldiers at bay. But his blood loss continued, and his body turned weak and lethargic. Using all his strength, he fired the remaining ammunition from the submachine gun and dropped it on the ground. With his back against the boulder, he grabbed his pistol and reached into an interior jacket pocket with his free hand. He rummaged inside and removed the sealed bullet casing that contained his unread encrypted message for Gianna.

He held the casing in his hand like a worry stone providing him with psychological comfort. The gunfire drew nearer. His breathing slowed and his body turned numb and cold. An image of Gianna flashed in his brain. His arms gradually went limp and the casing fell onto the ground. Amid his pain and regret, one vision held steady. *Gianna.* His eyelids lowered, and everything fell silent.

Chapter 40

Florence—June 16, 2003

Gianna—wearing a robe and resting on a hotel room bed with an ice pack on her knee—perked up her head at the sound of a key being inserted into a lock. The door opened and her daughter Jenn, carrying a cane and a purse, entered and approached the bed.

"You were gone a long time," Gianna said, sitting up.

"I got you the ibuprofen ointment at a pharmacy," Jenn said, "but they only stocked bulky metal quad canes with ugly rubber feet. So, I went to an antique store and bought a less conspicuous one."

"I'm not worried about aesthetics," Gianna said. "I merely need a cane to take weight off of my knee."

"You'd feel differently if you saw the ones at the pharmacy. They looked like stubby intravenous poles." Jenn held up a wooden walking cane with a carved handle in the shape of a rabbit's head. "What do you think?"

"It's lovely. *Grazie*."

Jenn smiled, appearing pleased with herself.

Gianna adjusted her robe and removed the ice pack from her knee—scraped, bruised, and swollen. She slowly bent and straightened her leg, producing an ache. *God, I feel old.*

"How does it feel?"

"Better," Gianna said, not wanting to worry her daughter.

Jenn set aside the cane and removed a tube of ibuprofen ointment from her purse. She undid the cap, squirted a whitish gel onto her hand, and gently applied it to her mom's knee.

A minty smell from the topical medication penetrated Gianna's nose. "I appreciate you taking care of me."

Jenn nodded and rubbed ointment over the bruised area. "It's still swollen. Maybe you should give it another day of rest before we venture out."

"No," Gianna said. "I've waited far too long to face my past. I'm not going to spend my time in Tuscany confined to a hotel room. There are places I need to return to, and being there will help me explain what happened in the war."

"We could talk here."

Gianna shook her head.

"Has anyone ever told you that you can be mulish?"

"Yes," Gianna said. "It runs in the family. And I'm pretty sure I passed the stubborn gene to you."

"Touché," Jenn chuckled. She finished applying ointment, washed her hands in the bathroom, and sat on a padded wooden chair.

"Did you try reaching the metal detectorist?" Gianna asked.

"Yes. I called on my way to the pharmacy. Still no answer."

Gianna adjusted her knee, propped on a pillow. "His neighbor said that he could be gone for days or over a week. He'll eventually call when he gets home and sees my note."

Jenn folded her arms. "I don't understand how anyone could spend that much time scouring hills with a metal detector."

"I'm glad he does," Gianna said. "Otherwise, my message from Tazio would not have been discovered."

"I'm sorry. It came out wrong."

"It's all right." Gianna sat up and carefully placed her feet on the floor. "I want to try walking with the cane."

Jenn rose from the chair, helped her mom to her feet, and handed her the cane.

She gripped the handle and gingerly walked around the hotel room. A dull pain radiated through her knee, but her demeanor remained composed.

"How bad is it?" Jenn asked.

"It's okay if I take it slow and easy."

Gianna shuffled to a full-length mirror near the door and paused, looking at her reflection. She gazed at the cane, then to her gray hair and the wrinkles around her brown eyes. *I look like my father.* An image of Beppe, fending off a German soldier with his cane, flashed in her head. "*Madonna mia,*" she breathed.

"What's wrong?" Jenn asked.

She looked away from her reflection. "I was thinking about my father. He injured his leg in World War One, and he needed a cane to walk."

"I wish I knew more about him," Jenn said. "What was he like?"

Gianna raised her eyes to the ceiling and sifted through memories. "Beppe was sweet, kind, generous, brave, and funny. He always made me feel loved and that I could accomplish anything I put my mind to." She blinked her eyes, holding back tears. "He was the best father anyone could hope for."

"He sounds wonderful."

"He was."

Jenn approached her. "I'd like to know what happened to him—and Tazio."

A surge of guilt and regret rushed through Gianna's veins. She drew in a deep breath, gathering her strength, and said, "Okay."

Jenn touched her mother's arm.

"Call the concierge to have the rental car pulled to the front of the hotel, and I'll get dressed. We are taking a drive and, by the time we return to Florence, you'll know everything."

"Where are we going?"

Gianna shuffled to a desk and unfolded a map that they'd purchased on their trip to Lucca. She scanned the Tuscan province, and her chest filled with dread as she placed her finger on the spot. "Here."

Chapter 41

Lucca—September 5, 1944

Gianna peeked through a gap in a boarded basement window of an abandoned warehouse located outside the city walls of Lucca. The road, lined with dilapidated buildings with shattered windows and doors, was devoid of vehicles and pedestrians. The air was silent and the sun was beginning to rise, painting the sky in tones of fiery orange. A deep disquiet churned inside Gianna, even though the crack of sporadic gunfire—coming from German snipers in bell towers—had stopped hours ago.

Gianna turned to Etta and Nunzia, who were standing behind her, and whispered, "I think the soldiers might be gone, but let's wait to make sure."

The girls nodded.

After their escape from the Germans at Sant'Anna, she and the girls hid in the forest for days. They remained out of sight, hunkered in a dense thicket on a bed of leaf debris, and they survived by foraging for mushrooms, blackberries, dandelion leaves, and wild fennel. But they struggled to find enough food to pacify their pangs of hunger, and it was clear that the mountains remained heavily patrolled by the Wehrmacht, given the sound of gunfire and explosions that echoed through the valleys. An escape attempt to Switzerland was far too long a journey without supplies, and it would be difficult, if not impossible, for them to bypass the buildup of German defensive positions in northern Italy. So, Gianna and the girls—driven by the need for food and shelter—hiked southward under the cover of darkness to the German-occupied city of Lucca, where they eventually found shelter in the basement of an abandoned warehouse.

While Etta and Nunzia remained hidden, Gianna ventured out in search of food. Initially, she attempted to seek help at a convent, but discovered that the nuns had been evicted and the building was occupied by enemy soldiers. After days of foraging, she connected with an elderly woman who provided her with carrots, zucchini, and eggplants from her hidden garden in the woods. Gianna was grateful for the woman's gift of food, and she hoped it would be enough to keep Etta and Nunzia nourished until Allied forces liberated the city.

At night, while huddled in the basement with the girls to keep warm, Gianna's thoughts turned to Beppe. Her heartache remained raw, and she anguished over her insistence to seek sanctuary in the mountains, rather than agree to her father's suggestion to hide in place and wait for Allied troops to reach them. Also, she was plagued with night terrors. In predawn hours, she often awoke gasping for air and filled with the sensation of being chased. Visions of shrieking villagers, locked inside burning buildings, tortured her mind. And the only remedy to keep the nightmares at bay, it seemed, was her fight to keep Etta and Nunzia alive, and her hope of seeing Tazio again.

The distant rumble of shellfire had grown louder by the day as the Allies approached Lucca. Gianna's anxiousness intensified as the fight drew near, but yesterday her spirit rose at the sound of German military vehicles rumbling out of the city. Through the peephole in the basement, she and the girls watched transport trucks filled with Wehrmacht soldiers retreat toward the north. Soon, the roar of engines disappeared. Gianna and the girls crept from the hiding place, and residents of Lucca cautiously emerged from their homes and began to cheer. But their jubilation turned to horror when dozens of Wehrmacht snipers—hidden in bell towers outside the city walls—shot citizens who were celebrating the impending liberation. Gianna fled with the girls into the basement, and she prayed for it all to end.

High-pitched shouts came from outside.

Gianna's skin prickled. She darted to the basement window and peeked through the gap in the boards. Her eyes widened at the sight of a woman, about thirty years of age, running along the road and waving a red headscarf.

"*Americani!*" the woman shouted. "The *americani* are here!"

Gianna gasped.

Etta and Nunzia pressed to her side.

"They're here!" the woman shouted.

"Is it true?" Nunzia asked, clasping Gianna's arm.

"I don't know," Gianna said, "but we need to stay here until we're certain there are no more snipers."

Minutes passed and the road filled with people. Cheers boomed from inside the city walls, but no gunshots erupted over the crowd.

Gianna, her heart pounding inside her chest, gathered the girls and cautiously left the warehouse. Holding hands, they followed a throng of people who were making their way into the city center. The crowd thickened as residents poured into the streets from homes and apartment buildings. At the Piazza Napoleone, the main square of Lucca, jubilant Italians were greeting a large infantry division of black American soldiers, their uniforms emblazoned with a shoulder sleeve insignia of a buffalo.

"*Grazie a Dio!*" an old man shouted, raising his hands toward the sky.

Gray-haired women kissed soldiers on the cheeks, while cheering citizens showered them with flowers.

A woman, raising a shotgun over her head, called out, "*Viva l'Italia!*"

People danced while a gaunt, bearded man played a violin. Church bells rang over the city. Cries of joy filled the air.

"Is it over?" Nunzia asked, her voice quavering.

A wave of emotion crashed over Gianna, and tears welled up her eyes. She kneeled to Nunzia and Etta and squeezed their hands. "We're free."

CHAPTER 42

FLORENCE—SEPTEMBER 7, 1944

Gianna, sitting in the back of a horse-drawn wagon with Etta and Nunzia, looked out over the skyline as they approached the liberated city of Florence. Scores of tile roofs were damaged by shellfire and several buildings were in various states of ruin.

"It must have been a hell of a fight," the elderly man steering the wagon said.

Gianna became more anxious. She placed her arms around the girls, and they sat in silence as the brown swayback horse with protruding ribs pulled the wagon into the city.

They traveled through streets littered with fallen bricks and the remnants of barricades strewn with barbed wire. Broken glass covered sidewalks, and groups of men and women were loading debris into the beds of trucks. Gianna hoped that she'd witnessed the worst of Florence's destruction, but she discovered that was not the case when the driver steered the wagon onto a road that ran parallel to the Arno.

Five of the six bridges that spanned the river were destroyed, leaving the Ponte Vecchio as the sole path over the river. Huge piles of stone from the fallen bridges obstructed the river's flow, like rock dams, and a pair of British soldiers stood on the shoreline surveilling the destruction through binoculars. Many of the buildings lining the waterfront were badly damaged or destroyed by shellfire, and the structures that remained standing were pocked by bullets and shrapnel. Gianna hated seeing the structures in ruins, especially the ancient bridges, some of which had spanned the river since the thirteenth century. But she was grateful that most of the city's iconic structures such as the Duomo and Giotto's Bell Tower remained intact, and most important, that Florentines were no longer under Nazi rule.

"It can be rebuilt," Etta said, looking at the crumbled remains of a bridge.

"It can." Gianna gently squeezed her shoulder. "And it will."

They passed a line of parked British tanks, and Gianna asked the driver to let them out. He tugged on the reins and the horse plodded to a stop. They got out of the wagon, thanked the man for the ride, and made their way on foot.

Minutes later they arrived at the church of San Pietro a Varlungo, and Gianna was relieved to see that it had not suffered damage. She led the girls inside and found Don Leto Casini in the sanctuary.

The priest's face brightened. "Gianna!" He approached her and clasped her hands. "I'm so glad you're safe."

"You too." Gianna released the priest's hands and noticed that his facial wounds from his brutal interrogation had healed, with the exception of a small scar above his right eyebrow.

"*Grazie* for caring for Etta and Nunzia," he said.

Gianna nodded.

The priest looked at the girls. "It's so good to see you again. Are you okay?"

The girls nodded.

"How is Beppe?" the priest asked.

Gianna's eyes blurred with tears. "He's dead."

"Oh, no." The priest's shoulders drooped. "I'm so sorry."

Etta and Nunzia nuzzled next to Gianna, as if to comfort her.

She looked at the girls. "Do you mind having a seat while I speak with Don Casini?"

The girls shook their heads. They walked down an aisle and took a seat in a pew at the front of the church.

Gianna turned to Casini, gathered her courage, and told him about the Wehrmacht requisition of the vineyard, her escape with Beppe and the girls to the mountains, and the massacre at the village of Sant'Anna.

"Hundreds were murdered," Gianna said. "Beppe sacrificed himself by attacking a soldier, which allowed us to get away."

Casini's face went pale. He clasped a wooden cross, attached to a string around his neck.

Gianna wiped tears from her cheeks and glanced at the girls. "Etta and Nunzia need food and shelter, and I don't know if I'm capable of providing for them."

"I will make sure they are cared for," the priest said. "Sister Rosetta and I are working to reunite Florentine Jews with family members, and we will do the same for them. If their parents do not return from German captivity, we'll place them with a relative. I recall that the girls have an aunt in Anzio."

"*Grazie.*"

The priest looked into her eyes. "You saved their lives."

She nodded, but felt like she was abandoning them. "Have you heard from Carmine, or anything about an American agent named Tazio?"

"No. Only rumors that Carmine's partisans were forced to relocate far to the north because of German reinforcements." Casini clasped his hands. "How about I arrange for you to stay with a family in the city?"

"No, *grazie*. I haven't been to the vineyard, and I feel that I need to go there."

"Take my bicycle. It's parked against a tree in the courtyard."

Gianna nodded. She walked alone to the front of the church and sat between Etta and Nunzia.

"Are you leaving us?" Etta asked.

"Yes," Gianna said.

"I—I don't want you to go," Nunzia cried.

"I don't want to go either," Gianna said, her heart aching. "But I don't know the condition of the vineyard, and we need to make certain you have food and a roof over your head. It's best that you stay here."

Etta rubbed her eyes.

"Don Casini and Sister Rosetta will care for you until your parents are free from the Germans and return home."

A tear fell from Nunzia's cheek. "Stay here with us."

"There are things I must do, but I will come here to see you every chance I get." She placed her arms around their shoulders. "Someday, the rest of *Italia* will be free, the war will be over, and you'll see your *mamma* and *papà* again. I believe that with all my heart."

The girls leaned into Gianna.

She gave them long hugs goodbye, rose from the pew, and left the church. Feeling empty and sad, she got on Don Casini's bicycle, its seat several inches too high for her. She made her way through the war-damaged city and her thoughts turned to Tazio. Instead of heading directly to the vineyard, she changed her course and traveled into the countryside.

Because of her weakened state, it took her twice as long as usual to reach the abandoned iron mine. Inside, she kneeled at the dead drop, all the while praying to find a note from Tazio. But her hope sank when she lifted the rock and found the hole to be empty.

"He's going to be all right," she whispered, as if reciting an affirmation. *He got my last message, otherwise it would still be here.* With nothing to write on, she covered the hole with the rock and left the mine.

At sunset, Gianna turned onto the lane that led to the vineyard. Too exhausted to pedal up the hill, she got off the bicycle and labored to push it up the rutted slope. At the summit, the property came into view and she froze. Her hands slipped from the bicycle and it fell to the ground.

The house and its contents were burned to ashes, with the exception of a blackened stone fireplace. The vineyard that Beppe had dedicated his life to cultivating was in ruins. Most of the vine rows were destroyed and appeared to have been crushed under tank treads. The property's rolling hills were marred with deep shell craters, and nearly all the trees in the olive orchard had fallen.

Oh, Dio! Gianna's body trembled.

She walked on shaky legs to the wine cellar, which appeared to be intact because of its mostly subterranean structure. She pried open the door, its hinges broken, and was met by a musty, vinegar-like smell. Her eyes adjusted to the lack of light and she discovered that the cellar was ransacked. Many of the wine barrels were missing or destroyed, and masses of broken bottles covered the ground. With no place to go, she shuffled to the back of the cellar. She removed the head cover of the barrel that accessed the secret chamber, and she crawled inside and cried herself to sleep.

Chapter 43

Strada in Chianti—September 14, 1944

Gianna, using a rake that she'd found in the wine cellar, scraped through ashes and debris that had once been her family's home. For days, she'd searched for possessions that survived the fire but found little of monetary or sentimental value, other than a handful of coins and warped pieces of her mother's old silverware. Although she had never considered herself one to be emotionally attached to objects, it was dispiriting for her to know that she would never again see her mother's paintings, her father's photographs, and Tazio's codebook that contained deciphered messages of heartfelt words.

For the past week, she'd survived on rations that were parachute-dropped from American planes to feed Italians in the wake of the Allied invasion. Boxes of food that contained tinned meat, dry biscuits, malted milk-dextrose tablets, chocolate bars, and powdered milk were distributed to hungry citizens by clergy. Gianna disliked receiving charity, but with barely any money and nothing of value to barter, she gratefully accepted the rations.

The wine cellar had become her living and sleeping quarters, and she used a shallow runoff stream at the far end of the vineyard to bathe and wash her clothes. When she wasn't working to clear away debris, she visited Etta and Nunzia at a temporary shelter in Florence that was set up by Don Casini and Sister Rosetta. She adored seeing the girls and was relieved to see that they were well fed and cared for. For Gianna, time with Etta and Nunzia provided her with a brief respite from her sorrow. But when she returned to the vineyard, her thoughts returned to Beppe and the hundreds of innocent people who were murdered in Sant'Anna, and anguish festered inside her like a wound that refused to heal.

Gianna had gone twice to the dead drop but found no communication. Also, she'd traveled to one of Carmine's former hideouts—the hunting shack where Tazio had taught her to encrypt messages—but she did not find partisans, and it appeared that the camp hadn't been used in quite some time. Rumors had grown rampant amongst Florentines about Allied advances being stalled at the enemy's Gothic Line of defense in northern Italy, and that it might take many months of fighting before the rest of Italy was liberated. *Tazio has gone off to support the US Army's fight in the north*, she often thought, lying awake at night. *He'll return when the war is over.*

Gianna had considered abandoning the vineyard and going off to join partisans in the north, but her mind and body were spent. She'd lost a good deal of weight and strength from her journey to and from the mountains. Her ribs showed, she easily grew fatigued, and she was plagued by muscle cramps. She was in no condition to take up arms and battle the Germans, at least not yet, and she didn't want to leave the area until Don Casini had found Etta and Nunzia a permanent home. To Gianna, it felt like she was caught in a state of purgatory.

Gianna raked over a pile of ash and struck something hard. She kneeled, sifted through the debris with her fingers, and removed a warped tiny spoon. An image of Beppe, stirring his morning *caffè*, flashed in her head. She lowered her chin and tossed the spoon into a metal bucket, which contained an assortment of recovered utensils.

A sound of clopping hooves, coming from the lane, broke the still air.

Gianna set aside the rake and dusted her hands.

A horse-drawn wagon rolled up the lane and stopped. A bearded man, who was wearing a cap and loose-fitting clothes, stepped down from the driver's seat and raised a hand.

She squinted, trying to identify the person in the distance.

The man coughed, then called out, "Gianna."

Her heart leaped at the sound of the voice. "Carmine?"

"*Sì.*"

She ran across the yard and hugged him. His once strong body was now withered and weak.

"I'm so happy you're alive," he said. "I went to see Don Casini, and he told me that you were here."

She slipped away, and her joy vanished. "Where's Tazio?"

Carmine's jaw quivered.

Her blood turned cold. "No, please, no—"

His eyes, dark and sunken, filled with tears. "He's dead."

Her legs buckled, and she collapsed to the ground and sobbed.

Carmine kneeled and held her.

"No, he can't be!" she wailed.

He lowered his chin to her head. "I'm so sorry."

Together, they cried until no tears were left. Gianna wiped her face and looked at him. "Please, tell me what happened."

Carmine coughed and wiped his mouth with a handkerchief. He drew a deep breath and told her about receiving news of a German attack on citizens, about him and Tazio going to Sant'Anna, and about Tazio getting shot when they encountered a German patrol.

"Tazio saved my life," Carmine said. "He held back the enemy with gunfire to allow me to escape."

"Maybe he got out," she said, struggling to come to terms with Tazio's death.

"I'm afraid not," he said, his voice filled with sadness. "He was unable to walk, and there were too many soldiers to fend off for long."

Gianna rubbed her eyes and silently prayed that he didn't suffer.

"Before I left him, he gave these to me." He reached into his pocket and held out his palm.

Her body trembled. With her heart breaking, she gently took her parents' engraved wedding bands and lowered her head to her knees and wept.

Chapter 44

Strada in Chianti—May 15, 1945

Nine months after the massacre, Gianna meandered through the vineyard's war-torn olive grove and picked wildflowers, a mix of field poppies and marigolds. She carried the bunches to the wine cellar and placed them into the front basket of her bicycle, which she had recovered from the thicket where it was abandoned. She got on the seat and pedaled several kilometers to a cemetery. An uneasiness stirred inside her as she leaned her bicycle against an iron gate and carried the flowers past rows of crooked headstones.

About two weeks earlier, news had spread that Hitler was dead, and that Mussolini and his mistress were shot and killed by Italian partisans. Nazi Germany had surrendered to the Allies and Italy was now liberated from the Fascist regime, yet a deep sadness remained within Gianna. Freedom had cost many hundreds of thousands of Italians their lives. And for Gianna, the loss of most of her friends, her father, her only sibling, and the man whom she'd dreamed of spending her life with.

Late the previous autumn, headstones for Beppe and Matteo were placed next to the burial plot of Gianna's mother. Don Casini presided over a private graveside funeral service that was attended by Gianna, Sister Rosetta, and Carmine—whose weight loss and persistent cough the waning months of the war had continued to exacerbate. Etta and Nunzia were not able to attend because they'd gone away to live with their aunt in Anzio. Gianna notified Beppe's brother Uberto of her father's death by sending a message through the International Committee of the Red Cross, but travel between Switzerland and liberated Florence was impossible with the fighting that raged at the German defensive lines in northern Italy.

A box containing Beppe's and Luisa's engraved wedding bands was buried at the site. Although Gianna had always dreamed of wearing her mother's ring on her finger when she got married, her Tazio was gone and she couldn't imagine herself wearing anything that would be a constant reminder of the Nazi massacre at Sant'Anna. *The rings are symbols of Mamma and Papà's undying affection,* Gianna had told herself as the box was buried in the ground. *It's best that the rings are laid to rest with them.*

Gianna, holding her freshly picked wildflowers, approached the Conti family graves and kneeled. She dispersed the flowers over the ground, and rearranged a few of the poppies. As she stared at the engraving on Beppe's headstone, her guilt swelled, crashing like waves in a storm.

"I'm sorry, Papà," she said, her voice quavering. "I should have listened to you. We should never have fled to the mountains." She pressed her fingers to the headstone, cool under her touch. "I miss you all terribly."

She silently prayed for those who were killed in the war, and for her to have the strength to overcome all that she'd lost. With tear-filled eyes, she left the graves, got on her bicycle, and rode away.

She arrived at the vineyard in the late afternoon, and at the top of the lane she paused, staring at the ravaged property. Although much of the debris had been cleared away from the fire-destroyed home, most of the grapevines and the olive orchard remained in ruins. For months, she'd worked to rejuvenate badly damaged vines, but she'd only managed to prune and repair a fraction of the rows. It would take years and a team of laborers, Gianna believed, to undo the damage done by the Panzer tanks. And she pondered whether she had the skills, stamina, and desire to make it happen.

Gianna shook away her thoughts and pedaled to the wine cellar. She propped her bicycle on its kickstand and paused at the sight of the partially open door. Her heart rate quickened. She crept to the entrance and listened.

Maybe I left it open. She set aside her concern and pushed open the door. Sunlight spilled into the cellar, illuminating a blanketed person who was curled asleep on a makeshift bed that Gianna had built from boards and burlap.

Gianna stared with wide eyes. She swallowed and softly said, "*Salve.*"

The person, who appeared to be a woman in ragged clothing, remained motionless.

She cautiously stepped forward. "Are you all right?"

The woman stirred and raised her head, revealing dark sunken eyes and prickly short black hair. Despite the woman's haggard appearance, Gianna immediately recognized her friend.

"*Oh, Dio!*" Gianna gasped. "Lilla!"

"*Ciao*," Lilla wheezed. She struggled to sit up.

Gianna dropped to her knees and hugged the emaciated and fragile Lilla.

"I'm so happy to see you," Lilla cried.

Gianna sobbed, tears of joy streaming down her cheeks.

Lilla's body trembled.

Gianna eased back and wiped tears from Lilla's gaunt face. "What have they done to you?"

"I'm getting better," Lilla said, as if it was too painful to talk about.

"It's over—you're free now." Gianna clasped her friend's hand, which was bony and frail.

A weak smile formed on Lilla's face.

"How did you get here?"

Lilla drew a labored breath. "Trains, wagons, and on foot."

"Did anyone come with you?"

"No."

"*Madonna mia*. You should have gone straight to a hospital."

Lilla looked into Gianna's eyes. "I didn't fulfill my promise to leave the city and stay with you. Is your offer still good?"

A wave of happiness washed over Gianna. "Always."

Chapter 45

Strada in Chianti—June 3, 1945

For weeks, Gianna nursed Lilla back to health. Her friend slept twelve hours per day, not including naps, as if her mind and body craved hibernation. When she awoke, Gianna gave her warm broth, made from boiled cabbage, which she heated on a wood-burning cast-iron stove that she'd salvaged from the house. She fed her mashed zucchini and eggplant from her garden, pecorino cheese and bread that she'd acquired from Sister Rosetta, and leftover US Army rations of dry biscuits and tinned meat. In the afternoon she accompanied Lilla on walks, each a little longer than the one before, for a bit of exercise.

Lilla gradually gained weight and strength, and they confided in each other about the suffering and struggles they'd endured while apart. Gianna revealed everything about the failed attempt to free DELASEM members from Villa Triste, the Wehrmacht takeover of the vineyard, the massacre at Sant'Anna, and the deaths of Beppe and Tazio. And Lilla told her about her brutal interrogation by the SD and her imprisonment at a Nazi concentration camp called Auschwitz.

Gianna was horrified by her friend's accounts of starvation, disease, beatings, and mass murder of prisoners who were mainly Jews. It was a miracle, Gianna believed, that Lilla had survived

Auschwitz, which was partly because she was physically strong and selected for slave labor. After Auschwitz was liberated at the end of January by the Soviet Red Army, Lilla spent a month in a field hospital that was set up by the Soviet military medical service and Polish Red Cross, and it took her several more months to work her way back to Italy.

Of the hundreds of Jews that were rounded up in Florence and sent away to concentration camps, only a handful had returned home. And according to Don Casini, none of the Florentine survivors—other than Lilla—were members of DELASEM or relatives of the refugees who'd hidden on the Conti vineyard. But Gianna continued to hold on to hope that more survivors would return in the coming months.

Gianna entered the wine cellar and approached Lilla, who was resting on a bed of wool blankets. "It's time for your ointment."

"How about we skip a day," Lilla said.

"Not a chance."

Lilla smiled. She slowly got up from the bed, sat on an upside-down crate, and unbuttoned her blouse and lowered it to expose her back.

Gianna retrieved a jar of homemade beeswax and olive oil ointment, and scooped some onto her fingers. She paused, staring at scars from floggings with a bullwhip that Lilla suffered at the hands of a prison guard. The reason for the punishment: helping a feeble Jewish woman to stand for roll call.

Anger burned inside Gianna. "*Bastardi*," she muttered.

"Does it look worse?" Lilla asked.

"No. It's getting better. I hate what they did to you." She gently applied ointment to one of the twenty-four deep, six-inch scars.

"I hate what you've had to go through, too," Lilla said. "I'm so sorry about Beppe, Matteo, and Tazio."

"*Grazie.*"

"I wish I could have met Tazio."

"Me too."

"What was he like?"

"Sweet—kind—brave—selfless. He gave me hope, and made me feel like the world would someday be a better place. You would have liked him."

"I'm sure I would have," Lilla said. "Did you see him often?"

"No. Most of our interaction was through intelligence messages in a dead drop, but we shared personal notes to each other." She drew a deep breath. "Despite the distance between us, I felt connected to him—more so than any man I had ever met."

Lilla turned her head to Gianna. "Were you in love with him?"

She blinked back tears. "Yes."

Lilla reached over her shoulder and clasped her hand.

Gianna squeezed her fingers. "You're wasting ointment."

"Don't care."

Gianna released her hand, wiped her eyes with her sleeve, and applied more ointment to Lilla's back. "Enough about me. Your parents will soon return to Rome from Switzerland. We need to make you well, so you can go there and find them."

Lilla lowered her head. "I feel helpless not knowing how they are doing or when they'll return home."

"They're going to be all right. The Red Cross will eventually track them down, and they'll be overjoyed to see you." Gianna placed a hand on Lilla's bony shoulder. "You are going to be working hard to help your parents rebuild their dry-cleaning business, so we need to fatten you up."

Lilla smiled. "After I'm gone, will you go to Switzerland to live with Beppe's brother?"

Gianna thought of her uncle Uberto's postcard message, delivered by the International Committee of the Red Cross, that urged her to leave Italy to stay with him. "No, but eventually I'll travel to see him."

"There is nothing to keep you here. Why not go?"

"The property is in ruins, and I have things to take care of."

"It can wait." Lilla glanced back at Gianna. "If you won't live with Beppe's brother, you should come with me to Rome."

"I appreciate the offer, but I have the vineyard to restore."

"For you, or for Beppe?"

Gianna straightened her spine. "What do you mean?"

"As long as we've been friends, you've never been passionate about making wine or olive oil. It was Beppe and Matteo who adored the vineyard. What about your studies, painting, and your desire to teach children?"

"Things have changed," Gianna said.

"They have," Lilla said. "But we've already lost so much in this war. Don't allow the past to take away your future."

Gianna took a deep breath and exhaled. As she applied another round of ointment over Lilla's back, she wished for a miracle medicine, one that could—in addition to healing dreadful scars—fade horrid memories and restore broken dreams.

Chapter 46

Florence—June 14, 1945

Gianna and Lilla arrived at the Florence train station in a horse-drawn wagon that was driven by an elderly farmer from Strada in Chianti. Gianna lugged her bicycle out of the back, and Lilla stepped down from the driver's bench with a travel bag that contained clothes, a bit of money, and a train ticket—all of which had been donated by the Red Cross.

Gianna wheeled her bicycle to the front of the wagon and looked up at the gray-haired man with a cigarette in his mouth. "*Grazie* for bringing us here."

Lilla raised her hand. "*Grazie mille.*"

The driver gave a nod. He tugged on the reins of his two horses and drove away.

Gianna, rolling her bicycle, accompanied Lilla into the train station. They worked their way through the crowd to a platform with a train waiting to depart. Lines of people, most of whom were carrying luggage, were making their way through doors and into carriages.

"It was nice of you to come to see me off," Lilla said.

"Of course." Gianna leaned her bicycle on its kickstand.

Lilla put down her bag and looked at an empty platform on a separate railway line. Her face filled with sadness.

"Are you all right?"

Lilla ran a hand over her short hair. "Over there is where the Germans forced us into cattle cars."

"I'm sorry you had to see that."

"I'm okay—it's over now." Lilla drew a deep breath and exhaled. "Are you sure you won't come with me to Rome?"

"I'm sure."

A train whistle blew.

Tears welled up in Gianna's eyes. "I guess this is it."

Lilla's jaw quivered, and she leaned in and hugged her. "I miss you already."

"Me too," Gianna said. "You're going to have a good life."

"So will you. Remember—your future is yours to write."

Gianna held her tight.

Lilla slipped away, gathered her bag, and stepped into the train. She made her way through a carriage and sat at a window seat.

Gianna, remaining on the platform, gave a wave.

A whistle blew and the train jerked forward. Lilla looked through the glass at Gianna and placed a hand over her heart.

A tear fell down Gianna's cheek. The train chugged over the tracks, and she watched her friend disappear.

Gianna, feeling lonely and miserable, pushed her bicycle out of the station, got on the seat, and rode off. The narrow streets were congested with wagons, trucks, and bicyclists, and the air was filled with construction noise from crews who were repairing shellfire-damaged roofs. To avoid the crowds, as well as the war-damaged areas of the city, she took a long route home.

An hour later, she arrived at the vineyard feeling no better than when she'd left the station. She got off her bicycle and paused, looking out over the ruins—the burned down house, ravaged grapevines, mangled fences, cratered fields, and toppled olive trees. As she stood there alone, an avalanche of heartbreak came crashing down upon her. She sat on the ground and lowered her head into her hands.

Conflicting emotions surged through her. She was overjoyed

that Lilla was alive and would soon reunite with her parents, yet she felt sad that her friend had to leave. Also, she felt torn between remaining at home and moving away. *I need to honor my family by restoring the vineyard. But I can't do it alone, nor do I have the skills and enthusiasm to keep it going.* Her family, especially Beppe, had always encouraged her to forge her own path in the world, but it didn't make her dilemma easier to resolve.

She raised her head and peered at the rolling Tuscan hills, and Beppe's voice echoed in her head. *Catch the moment.*

A decision clicked inside her. Before she changed her mind, she went to the wine cellar and packed a bag, including the postcard with her uncle Uberto's address. Not knowing when she would be back, she gathered wildflowers to take to the cemetery for her goodbyes. She loaded her things into the bicycle's basket and got on the seat. She took one last look at her family's vineyard and pedaled away, unaware that she would not return for over half a century.

Chapter 47

Sant'Anna di Stazzema—June 16, 2003

Gianna peered through the windshield at a forested mountainside as Jenn steered the rental car over a steep, winding road. Anxiousness stirred inside her, and a dull ache, compounded by the compact car's lack of legroom, filled her bruised knee. She drew a deep breath, taking in a fragrant scent of flowers—a blend of lilies, carnations, and chrysanthemums that they'd purchased in Florence.

"We haven't seen a vehicle for miles," Jenn said. "Are you sure this is the right route?"

"I think so." Gianna lowered her glasses and looked at an open map on her lap. "We should be there soon."

Jenn steered around a sharp bend and downshifted, grinding the gears. She pressed the accelerator and drove up a steep road, bordered by dense pines.

Minutes later, they entered the village of Sant'Anna. Only a handful of buildings remained in the area. Scores of dwellings, which had once been homes for hundreds of people, were missing from both sides of the road and a nearby hillside.

They never rebuilt, Gianna thought. *But how could anyone live here after what happened?* She pointed to a small, unpaved parking lot with a couple of cars. "Pull over."

Jenn turned into the lot, braked to a stop, and turned off the ignition.

Gianna clasped her cane. "Let's take a walk. Could you get the flowers?"

"Of course." She exited the car, helped her mother out of the passenger seat, and retrieved the bouquet of flowers from the back of the car.

Gianna walked to the edge of the road and her eyes locked on the rebuilt church, which looked much like it did during the war. An image of German soldiers, aiming machine guns at helpless people huddled together on the ground, flashed in her head. She gripped her cane to keep her hand from trembling.

Jenn stepped to Gianna and offered her elbow. "Ready?"

Gianna nodded, despite a feeling of dread rising within her. She clasped her daughter's arm and, together, they walked to the churchyard that had, long ago, been filled with joyful children playing games. The place was empty, except for a sightseeing couple with a camera and a groundskeeper who was trimming bushes. Instead of going into the church, they traveled down an earthen path that led to a tall stone tower with four arches. Gianna's body felt weak, but she pressed on, taking slow steps, to the monument.

Under the arches, they reached a marble sculpture that depicted a bare-chested woman and her baby who were killed by Nazi-Fascist gunfire.

"Oh, my," Jenn breathed. She stared at the Italian engraving on the base of the sculpture, as if she were having trouble translating the words.

Gianna swallowed. "It's a commemoration to the five hundred and sixty innocent people who were massacred here by the Nazis." Tears welled up in her eyes.

Jenn turned to her mom. "Did you know people who died here?"

"Yes." Gianna drew a jagged breath. "I was here when it happened."

Jenn's face went pale. "Oh, God. I'm so sorry." She clasped her mom's hand.

A tear fell down Gianna's cheek but she made no effort to wipe it away. "Shall we place the flowers?"

Jenn nodded.

They dispersed the flowers at the base of the monument, and Gianna led her daughter to a nearby bench where they sat, staring at the sculpture in silence. Memories of gunfire and screams echoed inside her brain. Her blood went cold and a shiver traveled down her spine.

"All those poor people," Gianna said, her voice quavering.

Jenn removed a tissue from her purse and gave it to her.

Gianna dabbed her eyes. She took in several deep breaths, gathering her courage, and said, "I'm ready to tell you."

"Okay."

Gianna looked at Jenn, her eyes filled with worry. "In the summer of nineteen forty-four, the Germans seized our family's vineyard." She looked up at the cloud-covered sky and sifted through her memories. "At the time, Beppe and I were hiding two Jewish girls—Etta and Nunzia—in our wine cellar. Our property was in the path of the oncoming Allied invasion, and we needed to find someplace out of harm's way to ride out the battle. Beppe thought we should seek shelter at a village close to the vineyard, but I convinced him that the mountains were the safest place to hide until Florence and the surrounding areas were liberated."

"So, you came here."

Gianna nodded. "The church in Sant'Anna had been used to harbor Jews on the escape line to Switzerland, so I thought it would be secure. But soon after we arrived, an armored regiment of SS soldiers, along with Italian members of the Black Brigades, swarmed the village." She closed her eyes, and her jaw quivered.

Jenn placed a hand on her mom's leg.

"The Germans unloaded machine guns from their vehicles. They rounded up the villagers and Jewish refugees—men, women, and children—and they forced them into the church and surrounding buildings." Gianna paused, wiping a hand over her face. "It's been nearly sixty years and I can still hear their cries for mercy in my head."

"Oh, Mom."

Gianna swallowed. "Beppe, the girls, and I were forced into a stable. Before the order was given for the mass execution, Beppe sacrificed his life by attacking a soldier, which allowed me and the girls to escape through a window."

Jenn cupped a hand to her mouth.

"We fled into the woods and hid. The sound of machine gun fire felt like it would never end, and when the shooting stopped, it was followed by explosions of grenades and a smell of smoke drifting through the valley." She clasped her cane. "The Germans killed everyone, and they burned the buildings and bodies to hide evidence of what they'd done."

Jenn lowered her hand. "Oh, my God."

Gianna looked at the sculpture and deep sorrow roiled inside her. "Eventually, the Allies liberated the area. I placed Etta and Nunzia in the care of Don Casini, a Florentine priest who was a member of the Resistance, and I returned to the vineyard and found it in ruins. A month after the massacre, a partisan leader named Carmine came to see me, and he told me that Tazio was dead."

Jenn placed an arm over her mom's shoulder.

"Tazio had heard the news of the mass murder," Gianna said. "I'd previously informed him in a dead drop communication that we planned to seek refuge in the mountains, and I provided him with the name of the church. He came here looking for us with Carmine. He discovered Beppe's engraved wedding band, along with my mother's ring that had fallen off my necklace, in the ashes and presumed we were dead." She drew a serrated breath. "Tazio was killed in a German ambush on his return from Sant'Anna."

Tears welled up in Jenn's eyes. "I'm so sorry."

A pang of guilt pricked at Gianna's heart. "I should have listened to my father. My insistence to come here got him and Tazio killed."

"No," Jenn said. "You're not responsible for what happened to them, or any of the innocent victims at Sant'Anna. The acts of evil men did this."

"I still feel culpable—they would have survived if I had chosen someplace else to go."

"There was no way you could have known what was going to happen here."

Gianna lowered her chin.

"It's not your fault." Jenn kneeled in front of her mother and held her hands.

Gianna's eyes met hers.

"It's not your fault," Jenn said softly.

Gianna's body trembled. She felt Jenn wrap her arms around her and hold her tight. The dam that contained her guilt and torment slowly began to crack. Her emotions spilled over, and she pressed her head to her daughter's shoulder and wept.

Chapter 48

Strada in Chianti—June 18, 2003

A mix of anticipation and nervousness stirred inside Gianna as her daughter pulled the rental car to the side of the road and stopped. She got out of the vehicle and stood with her cane at the edge of the overgrown lane that led to the vineyard. Although her bruised knee was feeling much better, she'd brought the cane with her in the event her leg got sore on the walk.

Jenn stepped out of the vehicle and looked at the upward-sloping path, covered with high weeds and bordered by brambles.

"Don't worry," Gianna said. "I'll check you for ticks."

Jenn smiled.

Gianna approached her daughter and hooked an arm around her elbow. Together, they made their way up the lane.

Over the past days, Gianna had confided in Jenn. She told her everything about the DELASEM resistance organization, the Italian partisans, and her and Beppe's efforts to hide Jews on the vineyard. Also, she revealed her feelings for Tazio, and her losses and regrets that she'd kept from her family for decades. They visited the Conti family gravesite. And they talked over cappuccinos, during meals, and on walks around the medieval sites of Florence. She told stories about Beppe, Luisa, Matteo, Tazio, Lilla, Rabbi Nathan, Don Casini, Sister Rosetta, Carmine, and each of the Jewish refugees who'd made an indelible mark on her heart.

Jenn was a good listener, and without her empathy and encouragement, Gianna doubted that she would have been able to divulge her past. Also, Jenn disclosed her struggles as a divorced single mother, the difficulties she faced as one of the few female attorneys in a male-dominated law firm, and her interest in dating again. Their conversations were effortless, and Gianna felt closer to Jenn than she had in years, perhaps ever, and she was determined to maintain their bond when they returned to New York.

"We're almost there," Gianna said, working her way up the path.

Jenn maneuvered around overgrown bushes, and her eyes widened as she reached the summit.

Gianna stood beside her, leaned on her cane, and looked out over the vineyard and the surrounding Tuscan hills. The property was badly overgrown, and the entrance to the wine cellar was barely visible through thick vegetation, yet she could still feel the warm aura of her family's land. A childhood memory of having a picnic with Matteo and her parents emerged in her mind, and a wistful smile formed on her face.

"It's beautiful," Jenn said.

"I'm glad you like it." Gianna gazed at the lush, raw landscape. "Someday, it will be yours."

Jenn's jaw slacked open. "You still own it?"

Gianna nodded. "If you ever get tired of that corporate job of yours, you can fly away and restore a vineyard."

"Sounds enticing, even though I'm a city girl at heart."

"You can pass it on to Bella and Enzo. Maybe when they are all grown up, they'll return to their Italian roots."

"That would be wonderful." Jenn looked at her mom. "Is it hard for you to be here?"

"Not anymore."

"I'm glad," Jenn said. "I wish you had some of your friends and family here to share this with. I'm sorry they're all gone."

"Me too," she said, "but for many years, I did have Lilla."

Jenn turned to her. "You did?"

She nodded. "I think you knew her as Mrs. Lafleur."

Jenn's eyes widened. "Your friend from Montreal?"

"Yes," Gianna said. "Not long after the war, Lilla met a Canadian and left Rome. She got married, had three children and five grandchildren, and a rewarding career as an archivist at McGill University." Gianna fiddled with the carved handle of her cane. "Like me, she didn't talk with her family about what she'd endured in the war. But we did have each other. We kept in contact through letters, phone calls, and occasional visits until she passed away—the year before your father died."

"It makes me happy to know that you had her as a friend." Jenn hooked her arm around her mom's elbow. "Are there any other secrets you haven't told me about?"

Gianna chuckled. "No. That's it. I promise."

Jenn peered at the rolling hills. "I'm sure that the metal detectorist will eventually get the message and call, but I thought we might try stopping by his apartment again."

"Okay," Gianna said. "You probably need to get home soon."

"I'm in no hurry. The kids are in good hands with Theresa, and I want to see this thing through with you."

Gianna patted her hand. "Thank you."

She nodded. "With your knee feeling better, how about we go out for dinner tonight?"

"I'd like that. We've had far too many takeout meals in the hotel room with my leg elevated on pillows."

Gianna walked with her daughter around the property as the sun slowly set over the Tuscan hills, brushing the sky in hues of orange and pink. Even if her message from Tazio might never be solved, she was grateful to have rekindled her relationship with her daughter. And for the first time in decades, she felt at peace with her past.

Gianna, wearing a white cardigan over a navy sundress, entered a Florentine restaurant and was met with bustling chatter and an aroma of sauteed garlic and baked bread. The place was packed with customers, and several people appeared to be waiting for a table.

Gianna turned to Jenn. "It smells wonderful, but it's busy. Do you want to wait or try someplace else?"

"We're good. I called for a reservation."

That's my Jenn. Always prepared and thinking ahead.

Jenn left Gianna near the entrance, walked by the people who were waiting for a table, and approached a host with a black bow tie. Seconds later, Jenn turned and waved for her mom.

Gianna, lightly using her cane, made her way to Jenn. They followed the host through the restaurant and down a stone stairway to a lower level with an arched brick ceiling and shelves of bottled wine along the walls.

"Fancy," Gianna said.

Jenn nodded.

The host stopped and gestured to a doorway.

Gianna followed Jenn into a large private room and froze.

Over a dozen people—ranging from children to adults in their early seventies—looked at Gianna and rose from their chairs at a large wooden table.

Gianna turned to Jenn. "What's this?"

"A surprise." Jenn placed a hand on her back. "I enlisted help from my firm's investigative service."

Gianna's breath stalled in her chest.

Two smiling attractive gray-haired women—who appeared to be sisters—approached Gianna.

"Do you remember us?" one of the women said in Italian.

Gianna's eyes widened. "*Oh, Dio*! Etta! Nunzia!" She dropped her cane and wrapped her arms around them.

"It's so good to see you," Nunzia said.

Tears of joy filled Gianna's eyes. "I can't believe it," she cried.

"I'm so happy to see you," Etta said.

The women released her, and a handsome gray-haired man and woman stepped forward.

Gianna studied the man's face and gasped, "Eliseo!"

The man grinned, gave her a warm hug, and turned to the woman next him. "Gianna, this is my sister Filippa."

"*Oh, Madonna!*" Gianna clasped the woman's hands. "Aria was pregnant when she and Eliseo stayed with us. Was she carrying you?"

"*Sì.*" Filippa embraced her and kissed her on both cheeks. "*Grazie* for saving us."

Tears fell from Gianna's cheeks.

Jenn smiled and wiped her eyes.

"My *mamma* is in a nursing home in Siena and was not able to make the trip," Eliseo said. "But she wanted me to pass along her gratitude for what you and your father did for us."

"Of course," Gianna said, her voice quavering. "Would it be okay if I go and see her while I'm here?"

"She'd love it," Eliseo said.

People—who appeared to be relatives of Eliseo, Filippa, Etta, and Nunzia—began to form a receiving line to meet Gianna.

"I have something I want to give you," Eliseo said, smiling. He reached into his pocket and held out a tarnished metal object.

Waves of emotion washed over Gianna, and her eyes blurred with tears at the sight of Beppe's compass.

Chapter 49

Lucca—June 21, 2003

Gianna came out of the hotel lobby and spotted Jenn at the wheel of the rental car that was idling at the curb. She walked—without a cane and no longer feeling pain in her knee—over the tourist-congested sidewalk and got into the vehicle.

"Do you remember the way to the metal detectorist's apartment?" Gianna asked, buckling her seatbelt.

"I think so," Jenn said, "but it will help if you navigate."

Gianna retrieved the map from her purse and unfolded it. She lowered her glasses on the bridge of her nose and searched for the route.

"How are you feeling about this?" Jenn asked.

"Nervous." Gianna lowered the map. "When he called last night, he was skeptical about my story. It wasn't easy to persuade him to allow us to examine the message. I doubt that he'd be willing to part with it."

"He'll warm up to you when he meets you."

"I hope so." Gianna looked at Jenn. "Even if I never get to keep or decipher Tazio's message, I want you to know that this trip has given me far more peace and joy than I could ever have imagined. It was wonderful to see Etta, Nunzia, Eliseo, and Filippa—and to meet their families. I feel like I have put the ghosts of my past behind me, and I couldn't have done it without you."

"I'm glad I could help," Jenn said. "This time with you has meant the world to me."

Gianna blinked back tears and patted Jenn's hand, resting on the gearshift.

A smile spread over Jenn's face. "Let's not forget that the investigative service is working to locate others who took shelter with you and Beppe. Maybe we'll need to make another trip with Bella and Enzo."

"That would be lovely." Gianna lowered her eyes to the map. She ran her finger over the route and said, "Pull out and take the second right."

Jenn put the car in gear and drove away.

Gianna had relished her reunion with her long-lost friends. Their dinner and conversation lasted long into the night before they said their farewells with promises to keep in touch. Also, Gianna made a visit to see Eliseo's mother Aria at a nursing home in Siena. Despite Aria's frailty, her mind was sharp and she recalled her time with Gianna and Beppe with great clarity and fondness. Gianna was sad to learn that Aria's husband, as well as Etta and Nunzia's parents, did not return from the concentration camps. But she gained immense comfort from Aria's heartfelt stories of raising her children, whom Aria believed would have perished if it hadn't been for Gianna's help.

While waiting for the metal detectorist to contact them, Gianna and Jenn took walks through the city and along the Arno. They chatted at cafés and restaurants, and they visited the Uffizi Gallery, where they marveled at some of the world's most well-known and priceless works of art. And each evening they called Bella and Enzo to talk about their day. As time passed, Gianna began to think that the metal detectorist might never call, but things changed one evening when Jenn's cell phone rang while they were preparing to go to bed.

An hour after leaving Florence, they arrived in Lucca. Jenn parallel parked the car and they got out and walked to the apartment complex. A mix of hope and apprehension swirled within Gianna as she stepped to the door and knocked.

Footsteps approached from inside the apartment and the door opened to reveal a short, jowly man in his late fifties with mussed gray hair and an unshaven face.

"*Buongiorno*," Gianna said. "Aldo?"

"*Sì*—you must be Gianna," he said in Italian.

She nodded and gestured with her hand. "This is my daughter, Jenn."

"*Buongiorno*," Jenn said.

"Come in," Aldo said, stepping aside.

They entered a small apartment that opened directly into a living room with a worn leather sofa and two blue upholstered chairs. The air was stale, as if the apartment had been left vacant for weeks. A metal detector—which resembled an electric weed trimmer with a metal plate on the bottom—was propped in a corner with a set of headphones, and the walls were covered with shelves that displayed war relics. Bullet casings. Shell casings. Rusty rifle barrels. A broken pair of field binoculars. Metal cigarette lighters. Allied and Axis helmets. Food tins. Belt buckles. And dozens of metal military badges.

Aldo sat on the sofa and pointed to the chairs. "Please sit."

Gianna sat in a chair next to Jenn. She felt uncomfortable being surrounded by military relics, many of which had likely been carried by men who were killed in battle, but she buried her discomfort and calmly removed the newspaper clipping from her purse.

"*Grazie* for taking time for us to visit." Gianna handed the man the clipping. "That's the article that led me here. Like I mentioned on the phone, I was a partisan who provided encrypted intelligence messages to an American agent."

The man glanced at the article with a photograph of his discovery and handed it back to her.

A knot formed in Gianna's stomach. "May I see the bullet casing and the enclosed message that you found?"

Aldo nodded. He stood and retrieved a brass casing with an inverted bullet from a display shelf.

Gianna swallowed.

He removed the bullet, carefully slipped out the message and unfolded it, and then handed it to her.

She gazed at the encrypted message, the paper brittle and aged the color of light coffee. Her hands trembled. "It's definitely Tazio's handwriting and the codes that we used." She returned the message to him.

Jenn furrowed her brow and leaned forward, as if she were trying to interpret what was being discussed.

Aldo carefully folded and tucked the paper back into the bullet casing.

"The message means a lot to me," Gianna said. "I'd like to purchase it."

"It's not for sale," Aldo said, "but I'd gladly give it to you if you can provide proof that the message was intended for you."

"Like I said on the phone," Gianna said. "The codebooks were destroyed in the war."

Aldo frowned.

"Mom," Jenn said, "is everything okay?"

She nodded and looked at Aldo. "Name your price."

"It's not for sale."

A knock came from the door and a gray-haired woman stuck her head inside the apartment. "Aldo."

He turned his head. "*Sì*."

The woman, whom Gianna recognized as the upstairs tenant from her first visit, stepped into the doorway. "There is a man outside looking for you."

"What does he want?" Aldo asked.

The woman folded her arms. "He wants to talk to you about that secret message that you found."

Gianna perked up her head.

"*Mamma mia*," Aldo grumbled.

The woman glanced at Gianna. "This one is an *americano*, too."

Hairs rose on the back of Gianna's neck.

The woman stepped aside and a tall white-haired man with a walking cane appeared in the doorway.

"*Buongiorno*," the man said.

The timbre of the voice sent shivers down Gianna's spine. Her heart thudded against her rib cage. *It can't be—*

"I'm looking for Signor Ajello," the man said, peering into the apartment.

"That's me," Aldo said.

Gianna stared at the man. Although his cheeks and forehead were heavily wrinkled, she recognized his jawline, cheekbones, and the curvature of his nose. His caramel-colored eyes were dulled from age, and his once thick brown hair was now white and wispy. She rose from her seat but her legs remained planted, as if her feet had suddenly sprouted roots. "Tazio?"

"*Sì.*" He looked at her, and his eyes widened. "Oh, my God. Gianna?"

She nodded. Tears flooded her eyes.

"I—I can't believe it," Tazio said, his voice quavering. He dropped his walking cane, shuffled to Gianna, and wrapped his arms around her.

"You're alive!" she cried.

He lowered his cheek to her hair and sobbed.

Jenn cupped a hand to her mouth.

Aldo and the woman, their mouths agape, stared at the couple. They stepped aside, giving them space.

Tazio gently placed his hands to her cheeks and looked into her tear-filled eyes. "I thought you were dead. I found your ring at Sant'Anna."

"I lost it during my escape," she cried. Tears streamed down her face. Waves of emotion flooded her body.

Together, they wept, oblivious to the others in the room.

He gently wiped away her tears.

"Carmine told me you were killed," she said. "What happened?"

He drew a deep breath and peered at the ceiling, as if he were sifting through his memories. "Carmine and I were ambushed by a German patrol in the mountains. I was badly injured and unable to walk, and I convinced Carmine to save himself and leave me."

"Oh, God." She placed a hand to his cheek.

"I held off the enemy for a while, but I eventually ran out of ammunition and I became weak from blood loss. As I was losing consciousness, a scout unit with the US Ninety-Second Infantry division arrived and fended off the German soldiers. An American medic was carrying dried blood plasma—he saved my life."

Gianna drew a jagged breath.

"I was transported to a field hospital, and then to a hospital in the US for months of recovery. After the war, I wrote letters to find Carmine, and I was informed by the mayor of his town that he'd become sick and died of cancer." He lowered his head. "If only I had come back to Tuscany, I might have found you."

"We can't blame ourselves," Gianna said. "It was the war that drove us apart."

He gently held her hand.

She squeezed his fingers, sensing the time between them begin to melt away.

He looked into her eyes. "I never stopped thinking of you."

A secret chamber of her heart, which she'd kept closed for over half a century, began to open. "Nor I," she whispered.

Tears fell from Jenn's cheeks. Aldo and his neighbor wiped their eyes.

Gianna felt Tazio wrap her in his arms. Together, they wept. And the years of separation vanished.

Chapter 50

Florence—June 21, 2003

Gianna and Tazio sat on a stone bench in the Piazzale Michelangelo, an elevated square with a panoramic view of the city and surrounding hills. The sun was setting on the horizon, casting a warm golden glow over the Arno River. In a nearby garden, Jenn was standing near a row of woody bushes while talking to Bella and Enzo on her cell phone.

Jenn glanced at them, gave a small wave, and continued talking to her children.

Gianna smiled.

"You have a wonderful daughter," Tazio said. "I'm glad I got the chance to meet her."

"Me too."

They'd spent the day catching up on lost time. Gianna told him about her life and family, and he did the same. Tazio—like Gianna—was a widower. His wife, Alice, had passed away six years earlier from leukemia. He had one child, a son named William, who'd taken over Tazio's boutique vineyard and winery in California after his retirement, and he had three grandchildren. They'd talked for hours, telling one story after another. To Gianna, she felt that the time between them had been erased, and her warm connection with him was the same as it was when she was a young woman.

"I'd like to read what you wrote," Gianna said, touching his hand.

Tazio nodded. He reached into his pocket and removed the bullet casing with the encrypted message that they'd convinced the metal detectorist to give them. He handed it to her, and he slipped his old, leatherbound codebook from his jacket.

Gianna opened her purse and removed a pad of paper and pen that she'd taken from her hotel room. She placed the codebook and paper on her lap and—using the corresponding letters and phrases in the cells—she deciphered the message.

Gianna,

I can't imagine my life without you in it. I want to be with you forever and grow old with you. Will you do me the honor of becoming my wife?

Tears of happiness welled up in Gianna's eyes.
Tazio wrapped an arm around her.
"Did you really feel that way about me?"
He nodded and looked into her eyes. "Still do."
She nuzzled into him. "Then my answer is yes."

AUTHOR'S NOTE

While developing the plot for *A Secret in Tuscany*, I became intrigued by a 2015 news report about an Italian metal detectorist who discovered an encrypted message inside a World War II bullet casing in Tuscany. Expert code-breakers think that the communication was encrypted with a British or American field cipher, but the content of the message remains an enigma. The communication was written on August 13, 1944, the day after the Sant'Anna di Stazzema massacre, and the mystery of this secret message served as inspiration for writing the story.

During my research for the book, I was engrossed by the massacre. On the morning of August 12, 1944, German troops of the 2nd Battalion of SS Panzergrenadier Regiment 35—who were accompanied by Fascist members of Benito Mussolini's Black Brigades—entered the mountain village of Sant'Anna di Stazzema. The soldiers rounded up hundreds of villagers and refugees, and they locked them in a church and several barns and dwellings before executing them. The murders were committed by shooting groups of people with machine guns or by herding them into basements and tossing in hand grenades. Afterward, the German soldiers burned the bodies and the buildings to hide evidence of their crimes. A total of five hundred and sixty people were killed,

Author's Note

including one hundred and thirty children. Other than a divisional commander, named Max Simon, no one was prosecuted for the massacre until 2004, when a trial of ten former Waffen-SS soldiers living in Germany was held by a military court in Italy. The court found the accused guilty of participation in the murders and sentenced them in absentia to life imprisonment. However, Italian extradition requests were rejected by Germany. The war crime that occurred at Sant'Anna di Stazzema served as inspiration for writing the story, and it is my hope that this book will commemorate the hundreds of civilians and refugees who perished in the massacre.

During my research, I also became increasingly captivated by the brave women who served in the Italian Resistance in World War II. In the summer of 1944, there were approximately two hundred thousand partisans, including thirty-five thousand women. Many of the female partisans harbored Jews and acted as couriers to deliver supplies and weapons to men in the mountains. Most of the Resistance women served in noncombat roles, but many took up arms to fight for freedom, including some three hundred women partisans who fought alongside men in the streets to liberate Florence from German occupation. It is hard to imagine how dangerous and difficult it was for partisans, who used hunting rifles and a smorgasbord of weapons from different countries, to combat the heavily armed German military. Several real Resistance members—including a woman named Anna Maria Enriques Agnoletti, who was honored postmortem with Italy's Gold Medal of Military Valor—provided inspiration for the creation of Gianna Conti's character.

In addition to the women who served in the Italian Resistance, I was intrigued to learn about the American secret agents of the Office of Strategic Services (OSS) who were parachuted into German-occupied Italy to aid the Resistance and prepare for the Allied invasion. These courageous men were often selected because of their Italian roots and knowledge of the language, and they were trained at the Congressional Country Club, where they

Author's Note

were given instruction in guerilla warfare and the art of sabotage. Based on my research, many of the OSS agents assigned to the Italian campaign were parachuted into areas near Siena, Ravenna, or Turin. In the book, I imagine that OSS agent Tazio Napoli, who is the son of Jewish Italian immigrants, misses his landing zone so as to place him near Florence and the Conti family vineyard. Several real OSS agents—most notably Peter Tompkins and Morris "Moe" Berg—inspired Tazio's character.

Prior to doing research for the book, I knew nothing about DELASEM, the Italian and Jewish resistance organization that operated in Italy during World War II. Despite operating underground for much of the war, DELASEM was incredibly successful at providing food, money, shelter, and fake identification cards, and managed the illegal emigration to Switzerland of some thirty-five thousand Italian and foreign Jews. Rabbi Nathan Cassuto and Don Leto Casini—both of whom make appearances in the book—were real leaders of the DELASEM network in Florence. In November of 1943, the network was infiltrated by the Nazis and the entire DELASEM committee was arrested. Most of the members were deported to concentration camps, including Rabbi Nathan Cassuto, who perished in February of 1945 at the Gross-Rosen concentration camp. After a brutal interrogation and short period of imprisonment, Don Leto Casini carried on his clandestine activity to protect Jews and, decades after the war, he received a medal from Yad Vashem, the World Holocaust Remembrance Center, as one of the Righteous Among the Nations, in recognition of his efforts to save Jews during the Holocaust. This novel pays tribute to the brave and selfless members of DELASEM.

I discovered many intriguing historical events in the course of my research, and I endeavored to accurately weave them into the timeline of the book. For example, on September 25, 1943, Allied bombers attempted to strike the railway in Florence but missed their target, destroying many buildings and killing two hundred and fifteen civilians. In November of 1943, the German military conducted a mass arrest of hundreds of Florentine Jews and deported them to Auschwitz and other concentration camps. The story accurately reflects the timeline and locations of the advancing Allied invasion of Italy, specifically the liberation of Rome, Florence, and Lucca. Additionally, I believe I have precisely depicted the types of Allied aircraft, OSS weaponry, and German military equipment used during the battle for Italy. Any historical inaccuracies in this book are mine and mine alone. While a number of historical figures make appearances in this book, including Rabbi Cassuto, Don Casini, and Don Fiore Menguzzo of the San Rocco church in Sant'Anna, it is important to emphasize that *A Secret in Tuscany* is fiction, and that I took creative liberties in writing this tale.

Numerous books, documentaries, and historical archives were crucial for my research. I found *A House in the Mountains: The Women Who Liberated Italy from Fascism* by Caroline Moorehead and *Partisan Diary: A Woman's Life in the Italian Resistance* by Ada Gobetti incredibly helpful for gaining an understanding of the roles, sacrifices, and struggles of female partisans. *A Civil War: A History of the Italian Resistance* by Claudio Pavone was an exceptional resource in learning about Italy's complex political environment and the fight against Mussolini's Fascist regime. *Operatives, Spies, and Saboteurs: The Unknown Story of the Men and Women of World War II's OSS* by Patrick K. O'Donnell provided great insight into the role of an OSS operative. Also, *Miracle at St. Anna* by James McBride and its film adaptation by Spike Lee were tremendous resources.

It was a privilege to write this book. I will forever be inspired by the courageous Italian women who fought to liberate Italy from fascism and the OSS agents who were parachuted into German-occupied territory to aid the Resistance. I will never forget the thousands of Italian Jews who were killed in the Holocaust and the courageous members of DELASEM who risked everything to protect people who were persecuted under Italian racial laws and Nazi rule.

A Secret in Tuscany would not have been possible without the

Author's Note

support of many people. I'm eternally thankful to the following gifted individuals:

I am deeply grateful to my brilliant editor, John Scognamiglio. John's guidance, encouragement, and enthusiasm were immensely helpful with the writing of this book.

Many thanks to my fabulous agent, Mark Gottlieb, for his support and counsel with my journey as an author. I feel extremely fortunate to have Mark as my agent.

My deepest appreciation to my publicist, Vida Engstrand. I am profoundly grateful for Vida's tireless efforts to promote my stories to readers.

It takes a team effort to publish a book, and I am forever grateful to everyone at Kensington Publishing for bringing this story to life.

I'm thankful to have Kim Taylor Blakemore, Pamela K. Johnson, Tonya Mitchell, and Jacqueline Vick as my accountability partners. Our weekly video conferences helped us to finish our manuscripts on time.

My sincere thanks to Akron Writers' Group: Betty Woodlee, Ken Waters, Dave Rais, John Stein, Rachel Freggiaro, Marcie Blandford, and Cheri Passell. And a special heartfelt thanks to Betty Woodlee, who critiqued an early draft of the manuscript.

This story would not have been possible without the love and support of my wife, Laurie, and our children, Catherine, Philip, Lizzy, Lauren, and Rachel. Laurie, you are—and always will be—*meu céu*.

A READING GROUP GUIDE

A SECRET IN TUSCANY

ABOUT THIS GUIDE

The suggested questions are included to enhance your group's reading of Alan Hlad's *A Secret in Tuscany*.

Discussion Questions

1. Before reading *A Secret in Tuscany*, what did you know about the German occupation of Italy in World War II? Were you aware of the Racial Laws and the Italian and Jewish resistance organization called DELASEM? What did you know about the women who served in the Italian Resistance?

2. Why is Gianna willing to risk her life by hiding Jews on her family's vineyard? How does the death of Gianna's brother influence her service in the Resistance?

3. Why do you think Tazio volunteered to join the OSS? How does his Jewish ethnicity shape his actions in German-occupied Italy?

4. Describe Gianna. What kind of woman is she? What attributes did Gianna possess that made her well suited for the Italian Resistance? What is meant by the affirmation *Catch the moment*? Describe her relationship with her father, Beppe. What role does Beppe play in shaping Gianna's values and beliefs?

5. While fighting in the Italian Resistance, Gianna and Tazio fall in love. What brings them together? Why does their relationship develop so quickly? At what point do you think Gianna realized she loved Tazio? How is the war a catalyst for their affection? What are Gianna and Tazio's hopes and dreams?

6. Describe Lilla. Why do you think Gianna and Lilla formed a strong friendship?

7. Prior to reading the book, what did you know about the Sant'Anna di Stazzema massacre? What did you know about the Allied bombing raid on Florence in September of 1943?

Discussion Questions

8. What are the major themes of *A Secret in Tuscany*?

9. Why do many readers enjoy historical fiction, in particular, novels set in World War II? To what degree do you think Hlad took creative liberties with this story?

10. How do you envision what happens after the end of the book? What do you think Gianna and Tazio's lives will be like?

Visit our website at
KensingtonBooks.com
to sign up for our newsletters, read more from your favorite authors, see books by series, view reading group guides, and more!

BOOK CLUB
BETWEEN THE CHAPTERS

Become a Part of Our
Between the Chapters Book Club
Community and Join the Conversation

Betweenthechapters.net

Submit your book review for a chance to win exclusive Between the Chapters swag you can't get anywhere else!
https://www.kensingtonbooks.com/pages/review/